Praise for *The Trespassers*:

'An irresistible read . . . This is trusty Joanna Trollope turf; the very centre of Middle England'

Independent

'A thoughtful, sensitively-written novel about a very topical issue: relationships and dilemmas in the 1990s'

Birmingham Post

'A delightful, ripping tale, an intriguing story: just the sort of book I'd like to read on holiday'

Fiona Castle

Praise for Pam Rhodes' first novel, *With Hearts and Hymns and Voices*:

'Warm and witty . . . a very readable story of village life'

Woman's Weekly

'A light-hearted and enjoyable read'

Home & Family

'A delightful story with fascinating characters and a very realistic portrayal of village life'

Church of England Newspaper

Also by Pam Rhodes

With Hearts and Hymns and Voices

The Trespassers

Pam Rhodes

CORONET BOOKS
Hodder and Stoughton

A CIP catalogue record for this title is available
from the British Library

ISBN 0 340 71236 8

Typeset by
Phoenix Typesetting, Ilkley, West Yorkshire
Printed and bound in Great Britain by
Mackays of Chatham plc, Chatham, Kent

Hodder and Stoughton
A division of Hodder Headline PLC
338 Euston Road
London NW1 3BH

Forgive us our trespasses . . .

Chapter One

'Not that way, Chas! Round to the right. Follow Graham. And try to swing your opposite arm to leg as you walk, or you'll look like a gorilla!'

Sue Golding's shrill voice rang out across the barn of a hall, cutting through the plodding, out-of-tune piano. Bill Spellman was a wonderful church organist. On an organ, his 'Te Deum' could bring tears to the eyes. On this ancient old piano, 'Zipadee Doo Dah' was enough to make anyone cry.

Not that the group in the hall with him minded much. Their concentration was intense as they struggled to coordinate legs, arms and voices too.

'Pauline – stop looking at your feet! You're doing fine. That's right, Jean, head over to the front corner.'

Sue's smile never slipped as she encouraged and cajoled her latest choreography into life. But when Philip, waiting beside the piano for his cue, caught her glance he chuckled to see her eyes roll heavenwards in mock despair.

'"Zipadee doo dah! Zipadee-ay!"'

The group came to a triumphant, relieved finish, not quite as Sue had planned, but with gusto and panache.

'You should finish in two straight lines at the front of the stage, men standing at the back, feet apart, arms up, and ladies on their left knee – *left* knee, Debbie – at the front, with arms stretched out and down, like this. Okay?'

'Where do I go then?' asked Barbara, the fifty-something deputy head teacher, who with her short cropped hair and sensible shoes could quell a class of fifteen years olds with just a look. 'I'm a man in this number, aren't I? Even though I'm a Village Maid in "O What a Beautiful Morning"?'

'Might as well sit down, I reckon,' said Barbara's husband, Brian Gilpin, at Philip's elbow. 'This is going to take ages. Do you want a coffee? Barbara made up a flask.'

Philip grinned. 'We Ugly Sisters need to put our feet up whenever we can.' He looked towards the piano. 'What about you, Bill? Coffee?'

Bill peered over his glasses, pencil in hand, as he wrote a note to himself on the sheet music. 'Love to, but it's strictly forbidden, I'm afraid. Doctor's orders. Gives me palpitations, so he says – and now Myra won't keep any coffee in the house, because she knows I'll drink it.'

'Heavens!' said Brian, thinking that life without coffee would be no life at all.

'And she keeps trying to slip me those herbal teas,' moaned Bill. 'Have you ever tasted that camomile stuff? It's like cabbage water.'

Laughing, Brian and Philip made their way over to the side of the hall, where Brian delved into his holdall to draw out the flask. Philip sat back and gazed absently at the scene in front of him. They were a great lot, his congregation, enthusiastic, good-hearted, and there for each other - well, on the whole, anyway. From the moment the decision had been taken to raise money for the new church centre, they had rallied round with their time, their donations, and a wealth of fundraising ideas – from the practical to the downright foolhardy. They'd organised coffee mornings, tea afternoons, craft fayres and fairy grottos, teddybears' picnics and beetle drives, sponsored silences and pay-as-you-sing hymn evenings. They'd baked and hammered and painted and knitted. They'd pasted and iced and rattled collecting tins. And penny by penny, pound by hard-earned pound, the money came in. They'd placed a huge 'thermometer' at the front of the church, on which they proudly marked every two hundred and fifty pounds they raised. It was a slow, frustrating, painstaking business, and so far they'd enjoyed every minute of it. Certainly, the fundraising committee seemed to live, breathe and dream about the centre. For each of them – from Margie who could organise a jumble sale at a day's notice, to Brian Gilpin, the retired accountant, whose Business Plan for the centre had worked wonders with the bank manager – raising funds had become an obsession.

Not that they had to do it all themselves. The need for a community centre in their West Country town was obvious, whether you were a part of the church community or not. The Local Council seemed relieved that someone, not them, was doing something, and their unofficial encouragement had brought in various grants from different council committees without too much of a fight. Several significant pledges had been forthcoming from within the church community itself. Charitable trusts came up trumps for them too – and when the frozen food packing factory, which was the main employer in the town, got a picture in the paper as the Managing Director handed over a cheque for £20,000, the committee knew they were really on their way. At the end of the Thanksgiving Service they'd organised then, the first foundation had been dug by Philip, as Vicar of St John's – and now, in just over three months time, on Good Friday, the Bishop was booked to perform the grand opening ceremony.

Of course, building the hall was one thing. Keeping it going once it was open was quite another. And so the fundraising continued, with the panto looming all too quickly as their next money-making venture. Brian had come up with the idea of a Christmas show. Barbara had adapted an old script she'd used at school for *Cinderella and the Seven Dwarfs*. Sue, an

3

ex-professional dancer (well, rumour had it she'd once done a summer season in Torquay), was the obvious choice as producer and choreographer – and the result was the happy chaos in front of them now. Three and a half weeks to go, and one of those was Christmas week. Never mind, thought Philip, whoever wants to see a local panto where everything goes according to plan?

'Dad, I'm going back now. Homework.'

Philip smiled as Rachel leaned over to hug him, her auburn hair falling across his face. At fourteen, his daughter was an endearing mix of a young woman and small girl. Too fast, he thought. Children grow up much too fast.

'Okay, love. Is that all right with Sue? Has she finished with you?'

'Yep. You're next!'

Philip looked up to see Sue beckoning to him and Brian. 'Can we try the Sisters' routine, please? And would you try it in those high heels? You'll need a bit of practice in them!'

Rachel giggled at the look of apprehension on Philip's face. 'Someone asked me the other day if it was boring having a dad who's a vicar. They should see you now!'

'Listen,' interrupted Brian, as he tried to squeeze his foot, woolly sock and all, into a high-heeled shoe the size of a saucepan, 'the Ugly Sisters are going to steal this show. You'll be proud of him then!' Rachel laughed out loud as she watched him struggle - her Uncle Brian, whose figure owed a great deal to years of business lunches, and very little to anything remotely resembling physical exercise. He was cuddly and smiley, just the way they all liked him.

'Rachel, tell Mum I'm popping into Brian's after the rehearsal, would you, to go over some accounts? I'll be back by eleven, tell her.'

'Okay. 'Bye!' And she was gone.

★

In fact, it was much later than that when Philip finally locked their front door and switched off the porch light. He was surprised to hear movement in the living room, and opened the door to find his wife, Ruth, deep in concentration at the sewing machine, amid a pool of brightly coloured material. She looked up and tried to smile in his direction, but her lips were clenched around a couple of pins she'd just removed from her sewing.

'Tea?' he asked, dropping a kiss on her dark red, thick, curly hair. He turned towards the kitchen without waiting for her answer, which was always yes.

'Sue says she'll pop in tomorrow morning, if that's all right with you, to talk about Cinderella's ballgown. She's dug up an evening dress from Margie's last jumble sale that might do the job.'

Ruth stopped the machine, removed the pins from her teeth and sat back, rubbing her neck. In spite of being tired, there was still a prettiness about her, with her nose that turned defiantly up at the end and the suggestion of freckles scattered across her cheeks. She gazed wearily around the mountain of material lying in what was supposed to be an organised heap on the floor. 'Why did I ever let myself in for this? Haven't we got enough to do, with Christmas in little more than a week's time? And why were we daft enough to agree to *seven* dwarfs in a story about Cinderella, who shouldn't have dwarfs anyway! Wouldn't just *one* dwarf do?'

Philip came over to stand behind her, rubbing her shoulders gently.

'Come on. We'll take our tea up to bed.'

'It wouldn't be so bad if those flipping dwarfs didn't keep growing an inch every week! That's the trouble with kids – not professional at all!'

Philip leant over to silence her with a kiss. She sighed and relaxed against him.

'How was the rehearsal?' she asked at last. 'And how was your number? Did you remember the words?'

'Don't ask!' He grinned. 'I just wonder how I, a Doctor of Theology, a sober man of the cloth, ended up in three-inch stilettos in front of a crowd who are supposed to look to me for moral guidance. Where did I go wrong?'

'You volunteered,' laughed Ruth. 'Come on, bed!'

'You're not worried about sleeping with a cross-dresser?' asked Philip, his face suddenly serious.

'Can't think of anything nicer,' smiled Ruth, as she stood to switch off the machine and the lights, and took his hand to head for the stairs.

Ruth was never quite sure whether the phone always started ringing early in their house because her husband was the vicar, or because two of their children were teenagers. That morning, the first call came before eight o'clock, just two minutes before Number One Son, Steven, was due to leave for school.

'It's Jamie, Mum,' Steven yelled out to the kitchen. 'He wants to know if I'd like to stay over tonight, seeing it's Friday. I would, and I will, so I'll see you in the morning, all right?'

'Hang on!' said Ruth, drying her hands as she went to join him in the hall. 'Haven't you got to get your Art Project finished this weekend. You know, for your "A" Level?'

'It's all under control, Mum. It's sorted.' Steven smiled, stooping his six-foot frame to give her a quick hug.

'Steven, are you sure? Have a word with Dad first . . .' But, with bag slung over his shoulder, he was through the door and halfway down the path before she'd finished her sentence.

'Steven, ring me tonight, from Jamie's house. Don't forget!' Showing no sign of having heard, he gave a cheery wave over his shoulder as he strolled down the road.

'There's a party tonight. That's why he wants to stay with Jamie,' said Rachel, her mouth bulging with cereal as she spoke.

'It's at Natalie's house, and her mum and dad are out for the night. Everyone's going.'

'You too?' asked Mark, who was almost as tall as Rachel, even though he was two years younger, the baby of the family at only twelve. Disappointment shot across Rachel's face for just a moment before she adopted a suitably disinterested expression. 'Wouldn't want to. Sounds pretty boring, really.'

'Not invited, eh?' teased Mark, stretching over for another bit of toast.

'If Steven's going, I'm definitely not. It's such a pain having a brother who wants to act like a parent all the time.'

'Well, I'm glad he does,' commented Ruth, popping foil-wrapped packages into Mark's lunchbox. 'Not every brother would care so much.'

'Not every brother has to stick his nose in where he's not wanted,' muttered Rachel under her breath, pushing back her chair and heading through to the living room for ten minutes' practice on her beloved piano before leaving for school.

The phone rang again. This time Ruth got to it first. It was Brian Gilpin.

'I'm going off to the coast early in the morning for a spot of bird watching,' he began.

'Don't tell me,' laughed Ruth. 'Barbara's threatening to take you Christmas shopping, am I right?'

'Bang on!' he chuckled. 'The Saturday before Christmas? She's got to be joking! But I did wonder what that young godson of mine's up to. Do you think he'd like to join me?'

'Brian, Mark would love to. He was only saying the other night he wondered when he'd get a chance to go bird watching again. I think he was scared you'd go without him.'

'You tell him I need him. His eyesight's better than mine. Nowadays, unless a bird is the size a heron, I'd probably not see it until it was close enough to pinch my sandwiches!'

'Well, he's upstairs at the moment, hopefully cleaning his

teeth. Assume the answer's yes. What time do you need him ready in the morning?'

'Six o'clock too early?'

Ruth groaned.

'Yes, but we'll see you then!'

Brian replaced the phone just as Barbara came downstairs, pulling on her sensible much-worn jacket, and a woollen version of a hat that would have looked at home on the head of a jungle explorer. She was a tall woman, thin rather than slender, handsome rather than attractive.

'Right!' she said, in exactly the tone that turned the knees of her third-year maths class to jelly. 'The casserole's in. You need to switch the oven on at 150 degrees at three o'clock precisely. I've left a note on the kitchen table, so don't forget. The budgie's cage needs cleaning. The milkman will call for his cheque – it's on the mantelpiece. I've signed it, you've just got to fill in the amount. And if you don't take that library book in today, it'll be overdue and there may not be another chance to get it back till after Christmas. Can you ring Addison's and tell them I'll pick up the turkey and hock on Thursday? And you need to ring Sally. Ask her what time she thinks they'll arrive on Christmas Eve. I must know who I'm catering for, and when. And don't forget she goes to collect Daniel from playgroup at quarter to twelve, so ring her before then. I'll be back at four-thirty, and out again at seven for the School Carol Concert.' She paused to draw breath and zip up her boots. 'Goodbye, dear.' And planting a kiss on Brian's cheek, she picked up her bulging briefcase and walked through the front door he held open for her.

"Bye,' said Brian.

At the gate she stopped, hand on the latch, then turned.

'The hamper! The prize for the Christmas Raffle! I said we'd do it! There's a basket in the shed, crêpe paper in the bottom dresser drawer under the teatowels. Raid the larder for what to put in it – and you'll have to part with a decent bottle of wine from your collection.'

And as he watched her striding purposefully in the direction of the local comprehensive school, Brian mused that women never seem able to understand the tender relationship between a man and his wine cellar.

Philip enjoyed Fridays, which surprised him. For most people four hours spent wandering the wards of the local hospital would be depressing, but for him they never were. He'd become a priest to serve God through serving others. In his parish he often felt like an optional facility – nice that the vicar's there, but it wouldn't matter much if he wasn't. Here, illness was a great leveller. The affluent, the influential, the believer, the non-believer, all were brought suddenly face to face with inevitable human frailty. And as thoughts turned to the dreadful possibility of death, so the same man they might never have chosen to listen to as a vicar in his church was welcomed warmly as chaplain in the hospital.

Not that many conversations mentioned death at all, or faith for that matter. Mostly he chatted about the state of the food, the weather and the country, providing five minutes of company for the lonely, a listening ear for the worried, and a calming hand for the frightened. And he gave communion to those who were too frail to join him at eleven for the Eucharist Service he held in the small hospital chapel.

That morning, he'd already worked his way through Men's General before he arrived in Bunyan, the Women's Orthopaedic ward. Jill, the Sister on duty that morning, was a regular at St John's and gave a quick wave in his direction as she hurried back to the nurses' station.

The ward was divided into a series of smaller rooms, some with just one patient, some with as many as six. Because orthopaedic injuries often took weeks to heal, Philip's arrival was greeted by friendly smiles from ladies he'd come to recognise and chat to over a period of weeks. They didn't seem to mind that they only wore frilly nighties or fluffy dressing gowns. He was the vicar, after all!

He took his time moving along from bed to bed, until at last he got as far as Mrs Roper, a well-upholstered, jolly grandmother, whose corner of the ward seemed to be a permanent campsite for one or more of her diverse, rambling family. She was in with knee trouble, she told Philip, offering him a chocolate from the pile of boxes that perched between cards and flowers on her crowded bedside cabinet. 'If they'd left my op even an hour later,' she said dramatically, unwrapping a coffee cream, 'I might have lost feeling in my leg for ever, the nurse said!'

'So, the operation was a success, was it?' asked Philip.

'Who can tell? Too early to know,' she shrugged as her fingers ranged over the chocolates, hovering at last above an almond cluster. 'I'll be glad to get out of here, mind. The company's not much fun at the moment.'

There were three beds in her small ward. One was empty but Philip glanced across at the bed just opposite, where a small figure lay huddled and motionless. Mrs Roper followed his glance.

'Cries all the time. Or sleeps. Broken hip, I think, but she doesn't talk, so I can't ask.'

At that moment, one of Mrs Roper's sons appeared with his wife and two huge sons, who were exact younger versions of himself, with the addition of puppy fat. When more boxes of chocolates appeared, and another large display of flowers, Mrs Roper grabbed Philip's arm as he turned to move away. 'Here!' she said, handing him a bunch of dripping chrysanths plucked from a vase on her locker. 'I'm running out of space.' She nodded her head in the direction of the opposite bed. 'See if she'd like them.'

He took the flowers and tiptoed quietly across the room.

MINNIE BARTON, MISS, read the label above the bed. Beside it the locker was bare except for an old china vase. No cards. No flowers. No chocolates. No sign at all that this small, sleeping woman mattered to anyone. He dropped the chrysanths into the vase and walked over to fill it with water. He came back to the locker and tried clumsily to arrange the blooms so that they didn't look too straggly. He looked down at the silent figure in the bed, then gently stretched out his hand to stroke aside a wispy strand of hair that had fallen over the lined forehead.

'The Lord be with you,' he whispered, almost to himself.

'And also with you . . .'

She spoke without moving, eyes tightly shut. Two bright, sad tears seeped under the closed lids and slid down her cheek. He pulled up a chair and lowered himself into it until his face was almost level with hers, his hand gently covering the thin fingers that lay by her side.

'Sometimes,' she said, so quietly he had to put his ear closer to hear her, 'I talk to God and he's not there. He's not there now. Not for me. Perhaps he never was.'

'I know that feeling,' said Philip softly. 'As if my prayers are going nowhere. But he does hear, you know. Prayers are answered, but not always when, or how, we hope they will be.'

Her eyes opened suddenly, blue and piercing.

'You would believe that, wouldn't you? It's your job.'

'It's my job, *because* I believe it, with all my heart.'

The blue eyes closed again. Philip watched, wondering if he'd imagined the faint flicker of a smile on her thin, dry lips.

'You'd better pray for me then, seeing as you've got a hot line.'

'A party line!' he laughed, as her hand tightened on his. 'Come and join me. We'll pray together.' Closing his eyes, he began to speak. 'Lord Jesus, you lived on earth and knew our pain, our frailty, our human weakness. You knew fear too, when you faced the certainty of your own death, giving your life for our sake. Be with us now, when we're frightened and hurting and tired. Be with Minnie. Comfort her in her pain. Help her to get well again. Be near her. Stay with her. Love and protect her. And grant her the sure knowledge of your presence and your strength.' He laid his hand gently on her head. 'And may the blessing of the Father, the Son, and the Holy Ghost remain with you always. Amen.'

But Minnie didn't answer. With the smallest of sighs, she was asleep.

As Philip made to leave the ward, Jill held up a cup and beckoned him towards her office. 'Just a quick one, then,' he said, taking the coffee gratefully, 'I've got to get down to the chapel.'

'Well, you brought about a minor miracle this morning,' replied Jill, perching on the side of her desk. 'Minnie Barton. You got her talking.'

'Why's that a miracle?'

'We've hardly had a peep out of her since she got here.'

'What's her problem?'

'Medically, a broken hip. Quite a messy break, and the operation she had at the beginning of the week will only make the best of a bad job. She's not going to find walking easy from now on – although from the little I do know, I don't think she got about much before her fall.'

'Where does she live?'

'On the Stonegate Estate, so her notes say. One of the other nurses thinks Minnie was the lady who ran a little wool shop there for years, although that shut down ages ago. No one seems to have seen much of her since. I suppose they all thought she'd died, or moved away, or something.'

'No family then?'

'No one's been in, and we've had no calls.'

'Does she need anything? Clothes? Toilet things?'

'Well, we can provide most bits and pieces.' They both looked out towards Minnie's bed. 'She's a poor little mite, though. She could do with a bit of love, if you've got any of that to spare.'

Philip gulped down the last mouthful of coffee. 'Plenty. I'll try and pop in to see her again in the week.'

'The thing is,' said Sue, helping herself to a Hobnob from Ruth's biscuit tin, 'they completely panic when they see their fortieth birthday looming. All women need to know about the mid-life crisis, is that their husbands are bound to suffer from it!'

'Martin was forty then, was he, when he left?' Ruth asked, wondering at the injustice that allowed Sue to eat Hobnobs to her heart's content, when just one scrummy mouthful seemed to add two inches to Ruth's own waistline. It hardly seemed fair when Sue was also blessed with a delightful personality, golden hair, and a figure where everything went in and out in all the right places. And to top it all, she was tall. Willowy, with legs up to her armpits. I hate being only five foot two, thought Ruth, deliberately dunking another Hobnob in her coffee.

'He left me a Dear John letter, two kids and a mortgage, and walked off with his secretary, all in the week of his birthday! She was a lot younger than me, of course, ten years or so. After thirteen years of marriage, it's humiliating to be traded in for a newer model.'

'Did it last?' asked Ruth, settling down on the other side of the kitchen table. 'How long did he stay with her?'

'How long did she stay with him, you mean? Three months. No longer than that before she decided that Mr Whizzkid at work was Mr Couch Potato at home.'

Sue picked up her coffee and drank thoughtfully. 'The grass never is greener, is it? They think it will be, but it never is.'

'And how do you feel about him now?'

'Hurt. Insulted. Offended. Angry. Furious. Sad. Hurt, and more hurt.'

'Still, after all this time?'

'Nearly two years now, and there's been a lot of water under the bridge since then, for both of us. He wanted to come back, of course.'

'Did you think about letting him?'

'Yes, I did. Well, for the children really. They need a dad, and I felt they'd been damaged enough by everything that had happened. We invited him to come and spend the weekend with us, and it was pretty difficult all round. But then he walloped Davey. He was only eight, for heaven's sake, and just being a kid – you know, mucking about a bit – and Martin walloped him! That was it for me. I had him out of the house before he knew what hit him. I'll teach him to wallop my kids!'

'His kids, too,' Ruth pointed out gently.

'A fat lot that meant to him when he walked out on them, and didn't bother to speak to them for six weeks!'

Ruth's mind wandered for a moment, as she thought with relief about how dotty Philip was their children. He would never be able to turn his back on his family. She wondered how any man ever could. She looked across at Sue, who was tracing an angry pattern on the table cloth with her finger.

'So, how are things now?'

'Well, he does see them. He's pretty good about coming most Saturdays, and Davey and Polly really love seeing him. But I make it quite clear that I'm not part of the deal. The less I have to do with him, the more I like it.'

'Do you have any feelings for him at all? Thirteen years together is a long time.'

Sue picked up her cup and looked levelly at Ruth over the rim.

'No, I suppose not. I can't agree with anything he's done. I don't like him at all.' She paused for a moment as her expression softened. She said nothing more, and when she finally caught Ruth's questioning gaze, merely shrugged with a small smile that didn't quite reach her eyes.

'Don't you get lonely, Sue? Bringing up a couple of kids on your own?'

'Well, I work, of course, although to be frank I'm hardly likely to meet the next man of my dreams working four days a week in a beauty salon! But, yes, I do get lonely. And that's probably why I enjoy doing things like producing the pantomime. It's just good to get out and be with people, all sorts of people.'

Ruth laughed. 'There's certainly all sorts in our panto – and sizes too! Have you any idea how much material I need to fit round Brian Gilpin's waist?'

The two women stood up and walked towards the lounge, which was brim full with material of every colour and texture.

'Ruth!' exclaimed Sue. 'You need help. You can't do all this on your own.'

'I know,' she said wearily, 'but I don't feel it's organised enough to share with anyone else. And in any case, who could do it? Dot, perhaps, but her eyesight's so bad. And Eileen said she'd help, but I know she's up to her neck with the Drama Club's Old Tyme Music Hall. Who else is there?'

'My mum!' announced Sue firmly. 'She's been running up costumes for me since I was a baby ballerina. If she can make tutus for three year olds, she can certainly cope with a dwarf or two.'

'Won't she mind? She deserves to put her feet up, after all those years of sewing.'

'Once a dressmaker, always a costume designer.' Sue grinned. 'Leave her to me. We'll go through the usual ritual – I'll grovel a lot, she'll hesitate a bit, I'll cajole and bribe, she'll give in gracefully. And we both know she'll love every minute of being busy and indispensable.'

'Well, if you're sure . . .' Ruth started, doubtfully.

'Ruth,' said Sue, placing a comforting arm around her shoulder, 'consider it sorted.'

It was gone nine o'clock by the time Steven and Jamie arrived at Natalie's house, and the party was obviously already in full swing. The front door was open with the hallway packed full of bodies, so it took them some time to make their way through to the kitchen, deposit the two cans of cheap French lager they'd brought with them, and help themselves to the last couple of cans of Stella in the fridge, opening one, and storing the other in their pocket for later. Against the blare of music, talking was out of the question, so they edged themselves slowly through the crowd towards the lounge, which was a mass of tangled bodies standing around, moving vaguely in time with the rhythm. It took a while to accustom their eyes to the dark smoke-filled room, but gradually they began to make out faces, some they knew, many they didn't.

It was a face they didn't know that drew the eyes of both boys. Silhouetted against the window stood a girl, her long hair falling in a silver curtain around her face. There was a heart-stopping moment when she looked up, straight across at Steven as he and Jamie stood wedged in the doorway. The welcome in her slow smile was unmistakable.

'Hey, she's looking at me!' whispered Jamie in his ear, 'She smiled. I'm in there. See you, Steve!'

'Hang on!' yelled Steven, trying to keep up with him as he disappeared into the crowd. 'It's me she smiled at.'

But Jamie didn't hear. He was already pinning on his best Brad Pitt smile as he headed for the window, ready for the kill. Steven hesitated. Jamie was a good bloke, and a great friend, but where girls were concerned he had no conscience at all. Friendship meant nothing. And girls seemed to go for his blond hair and grey eyes that were a little too large, Steven sometimes thought, for a man's face. He sighed as the old feeling of shyness and inadequacy crept over him. It wasn't that he was bad-looking himself. Six foot, good body from all the sport he played, only a few spots now and then – but not everyone liked thick dark red hair that seemed to curl with a mind of its own – and glasses like his were definitely out. Lenses would be cool, but that was another problem about Dad being a vicar. Never any money to spare for anything.

Steven glanced ahead, to where Miss Silverhair was leaning nonchalantly against the window frame, watching Jamie as he approached. Steven thought he'd never seen anyone so beautiful.

Right, he decided, running his fingers nervously through his hair as he tried to flatten the wayward curls. At the very least, he'd give Jamie a run for his money. He pushed his way through to join them, in time to hear the angel with the long hair tell Jamie her name was Debbie.

'Hi, Debbie,' interrupted Steven, before Jamie had a chance to answer. 'I'm Steve, his *best* mate.'

'And this is my best friend, Liz,' replied Debbie, her eyes moving tantalisingly down the length of Steven and back up to his face again. She pulled a reluctant figure into their circle – a smaller, darker girl, who peered up at them through very serious glasses.

'Hello,' she said shyly. It might have been the loud music drowning her out that made both boys ignore her. Or it might have been that for Steven and Jamie there was no-one in the room worth listening to except the exquisite Debbie.

Mark loved bird watching. Or perhaps it was just that he loved his Uncle Brian, and it didn't really matter what they did together, he loved it. He didn't even mind getting up while it was still dark, although it wasn't even a school day. He'd hardly slept a wink all night, thinking he might miss the alarm clock. In the end, it wasn't the clock that woke him but his mum who came in to tousle his hair and tell him the kettle and toaster were on downstairs.

Uncle Brian was really old, of course, but he was still quite good fun. Often they did the kind of things Mark would have liked to have shared with his dad, but he was always busy. Whatever Mark ended up doing when he grew up, he knew he definitely would not become a vicar. Too much work.

Armed with a pack of sandwiches and a flask of hot black-currant, Mark couldn't wait to jump into Uncle Brian's car.

'Where are we going?' he asked as he fastened his seatbelt over his thick anorak.

'Out to the flats, I thought, down by the coast. I heard on the radio that the White-fronted Geese have arrived, and there might be one or two smaller birds to watch out for too.'

'Want a bit of chocolate?' asked Mark, pulling a dog-eared, misshapen bar of something from his pocket.

Brian glanced at the packet doubtfully. 'Ask me later,' he said. 'I may be desperate then.'

And desperately cold it definitely was when, an hour and a half later, the two of them lay crouched in the dunes, in a dip that barely gave them shelter from the biting wind. Brian drew the zip of his anorak up to his chin and looked enviously across at Mark, who hadn't even bothered to do up his coat as he lay stretched out, peering through binoculars towards the seashore, deep in concentration. He doesn't feel the cold at all, thought Brian. Was I ever that young?

'Look, Uncle Brian! Isn't that a peregrine? Over there!'

Brian rolled over to look through this own binoculars, focusing in the right direction just in time to catch sight of the peregrine before it disappeared from view.

'You're right! Well, he's early, isn't he? When was it we saw one last year? After Christmas, wasn't it?'

Mark nodded in agreement, then sat up to dig into his ruck-sack for breakfast. Chocolate spread sandwiches, his favourite.

'It'll be Christmas next week,' he said, taking a mouthful. 'I can't wait! I'm getting a bike, a mountain bike.'

'You've got a bike, haven't you? The one you come round to us on?'

'That's my old one, but it's too small for me now. It's really ancient, and the gears stick all the time. And I've seen the bike I want – a Muddy Fox. It's in The Bike Shop in Princes Street, in the window. It's really chunky, and it's got all sorts of extras and fifteen gears! And it's a really cool shiny black colour with a sort of fluorescent pattern all over it. Ben – you know, my friend from school – he reckons he's going to get one too. We've both asked for the same model so it'll be fair when we do our time trials over on the rec. We thought we might join the Nomads – you know, the bike club in town? They do proper time trials. It's really cool.' Mark stopped, not to draw breath but to sink his teeth into his chocolate sandwich.

'Sounds great – and expensive,' said Brian gently.

'Yeah, well, I'm not asking for anything else, just that bike. I don't want any other presents. I've told Mum.'

'Are you sure about that? No stocking? No bits and pieces under the tree?'

Mark looked at him levelly. 'Just the bike. That's all I want.'

'Well, I hope you get it.'

'And I'm not going to church all the time either. I'm fed up with church. It's boring.'

'Boring?'

'Very boring. Full of old people.'

'Oh,' said Brian, with a private smile. 'I see.'

'Oh, not you! You're not boring. But you know what I mean. They're all over twenty, really old.'

Brian struggled to hide a grin as he stared down at the binoculars in his hand.

'Anyway, I don't believe in all that stuff any more.'

'Uh-huh.'

'I've told Dad, and he said it was all right to have my own

opinion. For heaven's sake, I'm nearly a teenager! I know what I think – and I don't think there's any such thing as God. That's it!'

'And your dad didn't mind?'

'Well, he probably did but he was okay about it. He's pretty cool, really.'

'Cool, eh?'

'Well, he must be a bit disappointed because he believes in all that stuff. But I just told him, I don't any more. Besides, I hate getting up early on Sundays, just to go to church. None of my friends goes to church. Why should I, just 'cos my dad's the vicar?'

'You got up early this morning without any trouble.'

'That's different. I like doing this.'

Mark stuffed the silver foil, now containing only the crusts of his sandwiches, back into the rucksack, and was just about to reach for the flask when he stopped.

'Hey! What's that?'

By the time Brian got the binoculars to his eyes, whatever it was that Mark had spotted in the sky had disappeared.

'I'm not concentrating, am I?' He put the binoculars down. 'Tell you what. Let's stay for half an hour more, then call in at that cafe on the way home for tea and a bacon roll?'

'You bet!' agreed Mark, chocolate sandwiches already forgotten.

'Are you all right, Bill? You look a bit peaky.'

Bill Spellman had been making his way up the aisle towards the organ, to play as usual for the Sunday morning service when Ruth caught up with him. As he turned to answer her, the pallor of his skin took her by surprise.

'Just a bit puffed out, that's all. Always gets me in the winter.'

'Look, the service doesn't start for ten minutes or so. Sit

down a bit and get your breath back. Can I get you a drink of water or something?'

'Ruth, I'm fine. Stop fussing. You're as bad as Myra. I'm just taking my time but I'm fine, really.' As he set off again, she watched him make slow, careful progress through the choir stalls towards the organ.

'Ruth, it's all sorted with my mum!'

Sue Golding hailed her from the church door. 'She's delighted to help with the costumes. Can I bring her over this evening to decide who'll do what?'

'Great! Tonight? After the Youth Club, about eight-thirty, okay?'

'Fine. And I need to talk to you about – hang on, there's Brian! I must catch him. See you later.' And Sue was gone.

A few minutes before the Family Eucharist Service began at nine-thirty, Ruth thought of an excuse to pop up to the organ to check on Bill. The colour seemed to have returned to his cheeks as he quietly played some mood-setting music. He didn't stop to speak but she was relieved to see him wink at her, the normal twinkle in his eye.

Thank goodness, thought Ruth, as she made her way to the vestry to take up her position in the choir. We'd never manage without Bill. He's been playing at services here for so long, the whole place would collapse without him.

With only a minute to spare, Rachel slipped into place beside her.

'Mark won't come, Mum. He says he told Dad he doesn't want to come to church any more, and Dad said it was all right.'

'Did he now?' said Ruth. 'That's news to me. And Steven? Any sign of him?'

'I took him up a cup of tea about half an hour ago, and he was dead to the world.'

'I give up. I'm a failure as a mother. I've lost my grip.'

'You?' chuckled Rachel. 'Never! Come on, here's Dad – we're off!'

And as Bill struck up 'Away in a Manger' with a flourish on the organ, the small procession began its stately journey towards the front of the church.

Steven lay in bed, eyes closed, his Walkman plugged into his ears. He wasn't quite awake, yet not sleepy enough to stop his mind from wandering back to the unexpected events of Friday night. He could still picture Debbie's lovely face as he first caught sight of her at the party – the slow smile she'd given him as he'd said hello, the way her hand brushed his as she'd made her way, with Jamie, into the dancing crowd. He remembered standing awkwardly, watching the two of them as they swayed close together in time with the music. And then he remembered becoming aware that Debbie's friend was still beside him, looking up at him with a shy, nervous smile.

'She's great, isn't she? Everyone likes her. She has that effect on every fella she meets.'

Steven peered through the dim light at her. Linda, wasn't it? He couldn't recall her name. One thing was for sure: he didn't intend to get stuck with her. And he wasn't going to let Jamie get away with monopolising Debbie, not when he knew, *knew*, from the look she'd given him that he was definitely in with a chance there.

'I'm going to get a drink,' he yelled casually in the direction of Debbie's friend, as he turned away towards the kitchen.

'Good idea. I'd love one.'

And before he knew it, she'd slipped her hand into his, to make sure he didn't lose her. He was about to pull away, when in the light from the hall he caught the expression of despair in her eyes, fear of being left alone in that crowd. I'm lumbered, he thought. How am I going to get rid of her now? He looked down at the small, round face, eyes enormous behind her glasses, and decided: I'll get her a drink, then go to the bog and not bother to join her again.

'Come on then,' he said, giving her hand a squeeze. 'Follow me.'

Lying in bed, the tape in his Walkman came to an abrupt end. Steven roused himself enough to turn it over then lay back against the pillow, his eyes closed.

Funny how things turned out, really. The route back to the kitchen, where the drink was, turned out to be packed full of people who didn't feel like moving. Eventually, Steven and Liz (that was her name, he discovered some time later) found themselves jammed together at the side of the stairs, unable to move forward, unwilling to move back. He'd glanced up, to see if he could make his escape by heading that way towards the bathroom, but the stairs had disappeared beneath a sea of bodies. He was trapped.

'Do you find,' asked Liz suddenly in his ear, 'that people expect too much of you, because of who your father is?'

He stared down at her in amazement, wondering if he'd heard her right.

'I mean, with your dad being a vicar and everything, do people expect you to be something you aren't, just because of him?'

For the first time, he looked properly at her earnest upturned face. 'Yeah, I suppose they do,' he replied carefully. 'Teachers always used to come out with "Whatever would your father say?" As if he'd say anything different from any other parent!'

'Do you get on with him?'

'Yeah, I do. He's great.'

Liz was silent for a while, when more people arrived at the front door, pushing Steven close against her as they edged their way towards the kitchen.

She looked up at him, eyes huge through her thick glasses. 'That must be nice,' she said at last, 'to have a dad you can talk to.'

'Can't you? Talk to your dad, I mean?'

'Don't see him much really. He works in the city, so he goes

23

off before I'm up in the morning and often doesn't come home at all during the week. He travels a lot, sometimes abroad. He's been in America this week.'

'What does he do?'

'He's the Financial Director of a big electronics company. He's always busy. Doesn't seem to have a lot of time for us these days. I miss him.'

'And your mum? What's she like?'

'Oh, she's okay. Quite busy too, teaching all the time, but she's okay. Nice, really.'

'How did you know my dad is a vicar?'

'I don't know how I know. Just noticed you around, I suppose. Someone must have told me.'

'You noticed me?'

'Yes.' That shy smile crept across her face again as she held his gaze. Suddenly, she giggled. 'I remember someone saying vicars' sons are always the worst, and I wondered if that was true . . .'

'Oh, it's true all right!' grinned Steven, thinking that if he could, he'd willingly prove that fact to the Sublime Debbie. So what was he doing out here, when she was in the front room, doing heaven knows what with Jamie? At least if he took Liz back to where the dancing was going on, he could muscle in on his friend and let *him* look after Liz for a bit.

'Come on!' he said suddenly, and grabbing her hand, he propelled her back to where they'd started.

It was some minutes later, having looked around the dingy room with growing despair, he realised that Jamie and Debbie had disappeared – and he was cornered, in the middle of a moving sea of dancing couples, with Liz looking hopefully up at him. What could he do? Nothing, except start to sway unenthusiastically in time with the music and hope that she would get the clear message that she was to stay at arm's length.

He hadn't planned to stay long. He hadn't expected the

music to be just the sort he enjoyed most, so that the two of them got drawn into the crowd around them, all singing and dancing together. He hadn't meant to down the couple of pints that were handed through to him, until before long he felt high, carefree and mellow. And he hadn't given a thought to the consequences when the tempo slowed, the room plunged into darkness, and Liz was suddenly warm and comforting in his arms. As his lips found hers, he closed his eyes and his mind to who, or what, she was. She was there. She was willing. She would do.

Steven rolled over in bed and drew his knees up towards his body with a sigh. Well, he should have thought! He should have been more prepared for the moment when the two of them emerged into the brightness of the hall and he looked down to see the unmistakable glow of expectation and pleasure in Liz's face. There was a sweetness about her that made it impossible for him to abandon her, even though his instinct at that moment was to run, and run fast.

In the end, he walked, and she walked with him. She clasped his hand tightly, as the two of them made their way along the empty streets towards her home. He didn't say much. He didn't need to, because she hardly drew breath as she chatted all the way about her family, her studies, her music, her girl friends. Steven barely listened to a word. He just wanted to deliver her safely, and escape.

At her gate, he kissed her. He didn't feel he could avoid it.

''Bye then,' he said, turning to go.

'Will I see you again?'

The small, pale face. That plaintive, hopeful expression.

'Yeah, sure. I'll give you a ring.'

'You don't know my number.'

'I know where you live.'

He started to stride away.

'You will call, won't you? Please.'

He couldn't bear to look back. With a wave over his

shoulder, he kept his gaze steadfastly forward as he headed for the end of the road.

Philip didn't wait until Friday morning, his usual time for visiting the hospital, to pop in and see Minnie again. There was something about her dignity, her vulnerability, the lack of friendship and love around her, that touched him deeply.

He wondered whether she'd remember him. As time went on, he would learn that Minnie never forgot a thing.

'Come back to save my lost soul?'

'And see if you're feeling better,' he smiled in reply, as he drew up a seat to the side of her bed. 'And bring you these.' He held out a bunch of brightly coloured chrysanths.

'Pinch from them the church displays, did you?' She grinned, reaching out to smell them.

'From my wife's favourite flower bed – and don't you dare tell her!'

'Is she pretty, your wife?'

Philip's eyebrows rose in surprise. 'Yes,' he said, after a moment's thought. 'Yes, she's pretty and clever and tremendously kind. You'd like her, Minnie.'

'Better bring her in to see me, then, hadn't you? Introduce her to your other woman – the one you pinch her flowers for!' Her eyes shone with laughter, until her expression changed to one of sudden pain. Philip touched her thin, frail hand until at last her face became calmer.

'Your hip giving you trouble?'

'I can't seem to get comfy, and every now and then my leg goes into a kind of spasm. It's nature's way of telling me I need a cup of tea. Any sign of that trolley yet?'

'If it doesn't arrive in the next five minutes, I'll go and put the kettle on for us both in Sister's office.'

'Didn't expect to see you, really, not this week.'

'Well, it is a bit manic. Christmas always is. But I needed a breather, so if I come and sit beside you for half an hour, everyone will think I'm working. Don't you let on I enjoy it, or I won't come again.'

Minnie chuckled loudly, then fell silent for while.

'Not keen on Christmas. Never liked it much.'

'Why not?'

'No one to share it with.'

'No family?'

'Not any more. I used to have a brother, but he moved away when I was still a young woman, and we lost touch in the end. I heard he died. I tried to feel sad about losing him, but in the end I realised I just felt sad for myself, that I'd never really known my only relative.'

'And you never married?'

'Well, I wasn't without suitors, you know.' The familiar twinkle was back in her eye. 'There was a time when I'd be showing one out the back door, while the next was knocking at the front.' She smiled to herself at the memory.

'But . . .' prompted Philip gently.

'But the one I really wanted, never wanted me. Oh, he said he did, and I believed him for a long time, even waited for him when he went off with the army. But he came back with a bride on his arm, and a baby on the way – and that was that.'

'I can't believe those other suitors weren't still knocking at the door.'

'No, not really. While I'd been waiting for him, they'd given up waiting for me. I wasn't interested in anyone else anyway.'

'So, what did you do?'

'I had a shop. It used to be my mother's, a haberdashery business in the old days, although I made it more of a wool shop later because I always liked knitting. And in the end, that was enough for me. The children used to come and see me with their mums. Somehow that became enough, watching other people's children grow up, instead of having my own.'

'Is the shop still going?'

'No, I sold it years ago. It's a turf accountant's now.'

'Well, you must have got to know so many people over the years, all those families you saw grow up.'

'It's different when you're not really "family" though, isn't it? And people stopped knitting – or, at least, those little ones grew up into teenagers who wouldn't be seen dead in a home-knitted pullover. So they grew up and away, and I grew old and grouchy.'

'Not you, Minnie. I don't believe it.'

'Ah, you lose the art of small talk when you've no one to talk to. And then you get nervous about meeting people at all, because you're so out of practice. In the end, if I didn't have to go out, I'd just stay in and be happy that way.'

'What about church? You never thought of going there?'

'I used to. It used to be important to me, when I was a girl. But I drifted away, as you do. I've thought about it a lot lately.' She smiled to herself. 'Those pearly gates seem awfully close these days. Time to put my house in order, I reckon.'

'Would you like me to help you?'

'I can't go to church. I'd feel dreadful in a crowd of people I don't know.'

'Then I'll come to you. It'll be just the two of us.'

'And you'll bring me the odd bunch of flowers – and organise a cup of tea or two?'

'How many sugars do you like?'

'None!' She giggled. 'Can't you see, I'm sweet enough?'

★

It was Friday, the day before Christmas Eve, when disaster struck. The call came just before two o'clock that afternoon, and Ruth picked up the hall phone on her way out of the house. The woman's voice was soft and muffled. It wasn't one Ruth recognised immediately.

'Ruth? It's Jane here, Bill and Myra's daughter.'

'Jane! My goodness, it's ages since I saw you. How are you?
Are you home for Christmas?'

'Well, yes, it seems that way, although that wasn't what I'd
planned. I've just come down from London this afternoon,
because of Dad . . .'

'Bill? Why? What's happened?'

The image of his pale face, just before the Eucharist Service
the previous Sunday morning, swam into Ruth's mind.

'He's in hospital. He had a really bad turn in the night. They
called it crescendo angina which means there was barely enough
blood and oxygen getting to his heart. They're talking about a
by-pass operation, Ruth. They're going to decide tomorrow
whether to send him on to a specialist centre.'

'Oh!' said Ruth inadequately, while her thoughts raced
between sympathy for her old friend, and panic that they were
suddenly without their dependable, popular organist, with
Christmas Eve looming in just a few hours.

'How's your mum?' she asked at last.

'Not good. You know, he's her life. She's very scared.'

'Is there anything we can do? Do you need anything?'

'There's not much anyone can do at the moment. We're just
camped out at the hospital, waiting for news.'

'Are you all right for transport? Do you need things from the
house? You will ring me if you need something, anything at all?'

'Just your prayers, Ruth.' Jane's voice broke. 'He looks so
small and frail. They've taken his teeth out. . .'

'Oh, Jane! Would you like me to come, and be at the hospital
for a while so you and your mum can get a bit of sleep?'

'No. No, we'll stay, but I'll ring you if there's any news.'

'We're thinking of you. Tell your mum, and Bill too, if you
can. Tell him we're all thinking of him, and praying with all our
hearts. Give him our love . . .'

'Thanks, Ruth. 'Bye.'

Her eyes clouded with tears as she replaced the receiver and sat down heavily on the chair at the side of the hall stand. Over the few years they'd been at St John's, Bill had become a very special friend to them all. Dear God, let him be okay. Be with him, God, and Myra too. Pull him through, please!

At last, when she felt calmer, she picked up the phone again. Philip was probably at the hospital. Perhaps she could catch him there.

In the end, it was their daughter, Rachel, who came up with the most practical suggestion about who could step into the breach to play for the Christmas services at such short notice.

By teatime that night the news about Bill was no more detailed or hopeful than it had been when Jane first rang. Ruth did manage to catch Philip at the hospital, and he went immediately to the ward to visit Bill himself. He was sleeping, a restless, pain-filled sleep, his drawn face barely recognisable. Myra was beside him, staring blankly down his hand, as if by clutching that, she held on to his life too.

Somehow words were not needed. Philip simply pulled up a chair beside her and bowed his head in prayer. Together, drawing strength and comfort from each other, they remained by the bedside until some time later a nurse asked them to leave so that the doctor could examine Bill. Philip was with Myra and Jane when at last the doctor came to speak to them.

'The results of the angiogram show that he needs a bypass operation as soon as possible, and my instinct is that we should get him to the specialist cardiac unit in Bristol whenever they can take him. But,' he continued, looking directly at Philip, 'I don't need to tell you that the whole thing is complicated by the fact it's Christmas. Staff just aren't around to perform operations like that as they would be at any other time of year.'

Myra's clasp on Philip's hand tightened. She said nothing.

'So I suggest we keep him here for a day or two, so we can monitor his condition and he can get some proper rest. In the meantime, I'll get him booked into Bristol for the middle of next week.'

It was Jane who asked the question to which they all dreaded the answer.

'This operation . . . How dangerous is it? What are the chances of Dad pulling through, given his age and illness?'

The doctor seemed to weigh his words before answering. 'The procedure itself is fairly commonplace nowadays – almost a bit of basic plumbing, really. But, of course, any major surgery has an element of risk attached to it, especially when the age and condition of the patient are contributory factors. All I can say is that he will be in very experienced hands.'

Jane and Myra's eyes met.

'Look,' the doctor went on. 'he's resting and stable now, and that's what he needs most of all. The operation is the best possible option for him, and there is every reason to think the quality of his life will be greatly enhanced as a result of it. In many ways, it will be a very positive step.'

'Is he likely to wake up this afternoon?' asked Philip.

'Well, he's sedated, because we are anxious to let him have as much rest as possible. I hope he'll feel like having something light to eat this evening, and he'll need you around then.' He looked directly at Myra, taking in her pale, tired face. 'Why don't you go home for a few hours and get some sleep, then pop back about six? He should be awake then.'

'Will you ring me if he wakes before that? Will you promise to ring me?'

'I'll make sure they do,' smiled the doctor, as he glanced quickly at his watch. 'Must go. Do ask the Sister to contact me if you have any more questions.' And he was gone.

By the time Philip and his family assembled round the tea table later that evening, he'd already made several calls to colleagues at other churches in the area, to see if anyone could possibly help out with the music for the crucial Christmas services. Obviously it wasn't only hospital theatre staff who disappeared at this time of year. He'd drawn a complete blank.

'Perhaps we could tell everyone we're going all atmospheric for the services this year – you know, candle light and unaccompanied singing?' suggested Ruth.

'But it's not just this weekend we've got to sort out, is it?' said Philip, running his fingers through his short dark hair. 'Where are we going to find someone to fill in for Bill for what might be months, while he recuperates from such major surgery?'

'He may not come back at all. He might die. Simon's granddad died when he had one of those operations,' commented Mark helpfully, between bites of jam sandwich.

Philip and Ruth both looked at him in appalled silence.

'You could try asking Mrs Kenton.'

It was Rachel who spoke. All eyes turned towards her.

'Mrs Kenton. You know, my piano teacher. She plays the organ, I think.'

Philip turned to Ruth. 'Do you know her? What's she like? Is it worth asking?'

'Well,' said Ruth thoughtfully, 'she's certainly been good with Rachel, but I can't say I know her very well. She's not a churchgoer, as far as I know, so whether she'd be interested in something like this, I'm not sure. Hang on, I've got her number somewhere . . .'

'She's nice, Dad. You'll like her. Give her a ring and ask her.'

Chapter Two

Louise Kenton stared in surprise as the small gold watch tumbled down on to the bedroom carpet and settled at her feet. Slowly, with shaking hands, she bent to pick it up. 'Gucci' she read, in fine letters across the top of its face. She ran the heavy, elegant bracelet through her fingers. It was refined and beautiful. And it was definitely not hers.

So what was it doing in her husband's back pocket?

Richard had been in the States for most of the week and had arrived back, via London, late that afternoon. After barely an hour in the house he'd left again with their son, Matthew, for a Rotary Christmas 'do'. At nineteen, with the first term of an Economics degree course under his belt, Matthew was already a chip off the old block, a future Financial Director in the making.

The house seemed empty when they'd gone. With her piano students now on their Christmas break, Louise felt at a loose end. It wasn't as if she hadn't a lot to do, quite the opposite, but there was a restlessness about her. The thought that, whatever she did, it would matter to no one.

And then she found the watch. Out of habit born of many years of marriage, she'd opened Richard's case to collect his dirty washing and shake the creases out of whatever could be hung up in the wardrobe. As she unfolded his favourite dark grey suit, the watch dropped to the floor.

Still staring at it, she sat down heavily on the bed, to steady the shaking that seemed to be taking over her body. Perhaps there was a logical explanation. Perhaps the watch was the innocent possession of Mrs Carter, Richard's middle-aged and very married secretary, which he'd found, meaning to return it to her.

Or perhaps it belonged to whoever it was he was currently having an affair with – taken off in a moment of passion, and overlooked when the moment was past.

He was having an affair, she knew that. She'd known about most of his affairs from the very start. She'd always been able to pinpoint when they started and sense when they were over. Occasionally she even challenged him. Richard would look down at her with mocking innocence and tell her she was imagining things. She wasn't – but because she dreaded the consequences, because her greatest fear was that he'd leave her, she let the subject drop.

'Louise? Can you hear me, Louise? I'm thirsty! Louise?'

The sound of her mother-in-law's voice made her start. Guiltily, she pushed the watch back into Richard's suit pocket.

'Coming, Eileen. Won't be a minute.'

'And I'm cold! I shouldn't be cold, should I?'

Louise hurried downstairs to the lounge where Eileen was sitting in a chair, looking out through the french doors on to the garden. She'd taken off the jumper that Louise had painstakingly helped her into earlier that day and was sitting there in just her petticoat.

'Oh, for heaven's sake, you'll catch your death. Let me get you back into that.'

'Isn't it bedtime then?'

'We haven't had tea yet. What would you like for tea?'

'I'm thirsty.'

'A cup of tea, then – and would you like some casserole? It's chicken, your favourite.'

'I like Horlicks at bedtime.'

'It's not bedtime yet. Have some tea first.'

'Horlicks. I like Horlicks.'

Eileen turned her vacant stare back to the garden. Louise sighed as she made her way through to the kitchen. Richard's mother was a hard woman to love, and Louise wondered now if she had ever really *liked* her, even in the early days. Richard was an only child and still a small boy when Eileen was widowed, leaving him as the centre of her life. That soon wore thin for the ambitious, good-looking young man he became. By the time Louise met him, Richard's attitude towards his mother fluctuated between complete indifference and guilt-filled over-indulgence. With the benefit of hindsight, Louise now realised that in accepting his proposal of marriage, she also took over his responsibility for Eileen. When his mother suggested she should move into a house two doors down from them, Richard thought it was a wonderful idea – great company for his new young wife. When their children came along, and Eileen lost no opportunity to criticise Louise for her inadequacy as a mother, Richard's mind was too full of work to notice his mother's insensitivity or his wife's unhappiness. And when, five years ago, Eileen started to slip into the early stages of dementia, he didn't even bother to discuss with the family his decision to move his mother into their home. There was no question that Louise would look after her. She always had. For nigh on twenty years, Louise's life had been dominated by her mother-in-law's wishes and needs. As far as Eileen was concerned, no one could care for her son as well as she had. For twenty years, she had niggled and criticised and undermined the confidence of her daughter-in-law with relish. For every minute of every day during that time, Louise had resented her interference and rudeness, and yet she'd kept her mouth shut and accepted the inevitability of her situation. And now, as Eileen's dementia increased, her logic and ability were slipping away, and she was more cantankerous than ever. Louise wished she had the generosity of spirit to pity the tired old woman – but she hadn't.

Louise glanced at the clock. It was half-past five. Lizzie was late. She'd never be on time for tonight's concert if she didn't come back from her last-minute Christmas shopping trip soon. Her daughter had inherited Louise's own talent for music, except that instead of playing the piano like her mum, Lizzie, at sixteen, was already an accomplished cellist. Her plan was to go on to study for a music degree once she'd finished her 'A' Levels; in the meantime playing in the County Youth Orchestra was a great thrill for her. The orchestra's traditional Carol Concert at the Town Hall was always a local highlight – but Lizzie was cutting it a bit fine if she meant to be there by half-past six.

As she put the kettle on for Eileen's tea, Louise heard a key in the door. It was Matthew, first into the house as his father put away and locked up the car. At nineteen, Matthew was tall and solid, the image of Richard with his stylish, fair hair and striking blue eyes. And like his dad, he had inherited a love of working, and playing, hard. Ever since he'd been a small boy, he'd loved figures, and that love had allowed him to sail through school, exams, and now his degree course. There was no doubt that Matthew would excel. He expected nothing less.

And as if academic achievements weren't enough, he had a quick wit and confident manner that made him a natural leader. Did anyone ever seriously doubt he'd be chosen as Head Boy in his last year at school? For a lad who was already Captain of the Rugby Team, and President of the Debating Club, he was the obvious choice. And it was no surprise to hear that it was the girls of the sixth form who'd voted overwhelmingly for him to become Head Boy, although their votes probably had less to do with his leadership skills and more with his broad shoulders, easy smile, and the striking figure he presented when he strode out on to the rugby field in shorts and striped jersey.

Matthew didn't come into the kitchen.

'When's dinner? I'm going out in an hour. Were there any calls for me?' He threw a barrage of questions over his shoulder as he headed upstairs to his room.

'Sara rang, not urgent – and Michelle, can you give her a call back? And Rob dropped some Rugby Club papers in for you – they're on the hall table!' Louise called up the stairs after him as Matthew's door slammed shut.

When Richard finally came in, he had his arm around their daughter's shoulders. Apparently, Lizzie had spotted his car and cadged a lift for the last uphill stretch towards home. She was loaded with carrier bags of intriguing shapes and sizes. 'Don't you dare peep!' she laughed at her dad. 'Promise you'll stay here while I go and put these away?' She turned to hold out a long, thin package towards Louise. 'Oh, and Mum, these are for you! I couldn't believe they're in the shops so early. I know you like them.'

Louise carefully unwrapped the paper to find a bunch of daffodils. They'd always been her favourite – so bright, brave and brittle in the face of winter weather.

'Lizzie, they're lovely . . .' But she was gone, disappearing into her room to hide her treasures.

Richard took off his coat, checking his reflection in the hall stand mirror as he reached into the pocket to retrieve his phone. He's a handsome man, thought Louise, clutching the daffodils as she watched from the kitchen doorway. And he's charming too. No wonder we're all drawn to him. Good-looking people never have to work as hard for love and friendship as those of us who sparkle less, who find the shadows more comfortable than the spotlight. No wonder women love him. After all, I do.

As she poured milk into mugs, and lifted the lid of the casserole in the oven, Louise watched quietly as Richard checked his mobile phone for messages.

Do I love him? Of course I do, he's my husband.

Do I like him?

'Louise, did Doug ring? He said he'd send a fax. Did he?' His blue eyes turned towards her, distant and impersonal.

'Upstairs on your desk. It came about an hour ago.'

Without a word, he climbed the stairs two at a time.

No, she thought. I don't like him much at all.

'Louise!' Eileen's voice rang through from the lounge. 'I'm thirsty, Louise!'

Minutes later, Lizzie joined Louise to help set the table. She was like her mother in more ways than just the bob of dark, straight hair they shared, and the small elfin face. She was artistic and self-contained. Unlike her gregarious, confident brother, Lizzie blushed scarlet among people she didn't know. She was content to take a back seat, and happiest of all in her own room, with just her cello for company.

'I don't suppose anyone called for me, did they?' Her voice was carefully casual as she laid out the knives and forks.

'Sorry, Lizzie, no.'

Louise wondered again who it was that she was hoping to hear from. She didn't ask, though. Her daughter guarded her privacy, and would talk when she wanted to – if she wanted to.

'This isn't Horlicks!' spluttered Eileen, taking a sip of tea. 'I want Horlicks or I'll never sleep.'

The phone rang. In seconds Lizzie had grabbed the receiver in the hall. 'Hello?' she said. 'This is 435450.'

There was a silence while she listened to whoever was at the other end. 'Hold on a minute,' she said then, 'I'll get her.'

Louise looked up as her daughter came back into the kitchen, noticing the slight flush on her usually pale cheeks.

'It's for you, Mum. It's the vicar from St John's. You know, Philip Barnes.'

Louise didn't know. At least, she knew the Barnes family, because Rachel Barnes had been a piano pupil of hers for several years now, but she'd never met Rachel's father. How odd. Whatever could he want?

She listened in surprise to the voice at the other end of the line as Philip explained the sad circumstances of Bill Spellman's illness.

'And I'm so sorry to be ringing you like this, out of the blue, but quite frankly we're . . .'

'Desperate?' she finished with a smile.

Philip laughed, a warm friendly sound. 'I stopped myself from saying that just in time because I suddenly thought how awful that must sound! But, yes, I suppose we are.'

'Well, I haven't played the organ for a good few years – and I'm not much of a churchgoer . . .'

'But can you imagine,' interrupted Philip, 'how disappointing it would be for people to come along to the Christmas Eve service, perhaps the only time some of them go to church all year, and find there's no music? No booming organ for "Hark The Herald Angels Sing . . ."'

'No twiddly bits to keep the "Glorias" together in "Angels From The Realms of Glory"!' added Louise.

'It would be tragic!' said Philip.

'Desperate!' she agreed – and they both burst out laughing.

'Will you help? Could you?' he asked at last.

'Would it be just for Christmas Eve?'

'And Christmas Day – if you could?'

'I'll have to ask my husband, check if it will work out with the family . . .'

'Oh, of course. Naturally. And then will you ring me and let me know?' There was just enough despair in Philip's voice to persuade Louise to make the decision herself.

'Look, I'd love to help but I do need to see the organ, perhaps have a bit of practice in the morning. And you need to tell me exactly what I have to play, and when. I haven't been to a church service for so long.'

'Mrs Kenton, you're an angel! And don't worry about a thing. I'll make sure there's someone at your elbow all the time. Now, a practice . . . What time would you like to pop in?'

Louise glanced at the calendar on the hall stand. It was Christmas Eve tomorrow. There was always so much to do that day, presents to wrap and deliver, meals to prepare, and they usually popped round to the neighbours in the afternoon. And what about Eileen? It was more difficult than ever to leave her nowadays.

And then it hit her – that old, now unfamiliar thrill at the thought of such a musical challenge. It would be nerve-wracking, she'd be thrown in at the deep end – but she could do it. She knew she could, and probably love every minute of it. For once the family would have to fit in with her.

'Is ten o'clock too early? I reckon the sooner I get down to practice, the better.'

'I'll see you then, in the church.' The delight and relief in Philip's voice was plain. 'And, thanks. Thanks again.'

The news that Louise was planning to help out with the music for the Christmas services at St John's was met with delight from Lizzie, disbelief from Matthew and impatience from Richard.

'Louise, how can you possibly think of such a thing? What about Mother? What about the cooking and our own family arrangements? They've got to come first.'

'Why should the fact that I'm playing for the service interfere with our arrangements at all? I'll just have to be better organised, make sure I get things ready in advance.'

'But if you're going to be out all Christmas morning,' interrupted Matthew, 'we'll end up having lunch about four o'clock in the afternoon. It's just not on. You'll spoil the day for all of us!'

'Why don't we all go to church with Mum and join in?' suggested Lizzie, looking hopefully at her brother.

'No way!' retorted Matthew. 'No!'

'Louise, you've got to be reasonable about this.' Richard's fingers drummed emphatically on the table as he spoke. 'It just won't work.'

'It will, because you'll all have to help me make it work,' she replied, carefully avoiding her husband's stare. 'It will only take a few hours. Anyway, if I can help, I should. They need me.'

'They need someone, anyone,' retorted Richard, his eyes steely. 'You are needed here.'

Louise looked at her husband – and the image of that small gold watch in his suit pocket shot into her mind.

'Too late now,' she said firmly, 'I've promised. And I'm not going to let them down. More tea, anyone?'

The next morning, Christmas Eve, Louise walked the last few yards along the road towards the church gate with her stomach knotted in trepidation. She stopped for a moment, to fumble in her handbag for a hankie, buying herself a few precious seconds to control her thumping heart.

What a fool I am, she thought to herself. I can do this. I've trained for this. I've been teaching the piano for years. I can do it.

She dabbed the cool, clean hankie across her dry lips.

But I've not played in public for so long now. Suppose I muck it all up, lose my place, get the notes wrong? Suppose I spoil it for everyone?

'You're not Mrs Kenton by any chance, are you?'

The man striding down the path to meet her was smiling broadly, a warm, welcoming smile in a square, open face that probably smiled often. He was casually dressed in corduroy trousers, his wiry dark hair curling with a will of its own over the collar of his jacket. There was an air of solidness about him, with his broad shoulders and confident stride. In fact, if it weren't for the dog collar that was just visible at the neck of his comfortable woollen jersey, she wouldn't have thought him a vicar at all. He was nice. Very nice.

Her nerves disappeared. He took her arm to guide her

towards the church, and she thought as she watched him speak that his daughter, Rachel, looked very like him. She was fairer, her build slighter, but the square face and ready smile were just the same.

'I can't tell you how grateful I am that you're here. Bill Spellman's illness has been a terrible blow for us in every way.'

'How is he? Any news?'

'I spoke to his wife this morning. They've decided a bypass operation is needed urgently. They're going to try and fit it in between Christmas and the New Year.'

'It's always worse somehow, isn't it, when bad news like this comes just before Christmas?'

Philip turned to look at her then, his hand poised on the handle of the church door.

'It's hit his family very hard – well, it's been a shock for all of us, really . . .'

For a fleeting moment his expression was so bleak that Louise almost stretched out to touch him. Then the moment was gone. Briskly, Philip opened the door and led her inside.

'This way, Mrs Kenton.'

'Louise – please call me Louise.'

Philip's expression lightened. 'Louise it is then. Over here, Louise – the organ awaits you!'

Much later, she realised with relief that playing the organ was a bit like riding a bike. She hadn't done either for years, but once in the seat, with the organ in front of her, the years slipped away. Her feet instinctively found the bass pedals, her hands took to playing on two different keyboards as if that was always the way, and gradually the layout of the buttons and stops that surrounded her began to make sense.

And then it came – the almost forgotten thrill that had always engulfed her as the rich sound of the organ filled the church – notes that responded to her touch, chords that echoed and resounded around her head and her heart, familiar cherished melodies that lifted the soul. She forgot the technicalities of the instrument. She forgot Philip. Every fibre of her being was lost in playing, as if her thirst was quenched, her hunger fed. She played carols. She played hymns. And then she played not just the notes that were before her eyes, but the music in her head. Fingers that could strike the keys with passion one moment, gently stroked life into tender harmonies the next. She opened her heart and played. She played until she realised her eyes were pricking with tears. Then she stopped suddenly, embarrassment engulfing her as she remembered she was not alone.

Philip was leaning against the choir stall, just a few yards from her, unable to draw his gaze away from the bright dark cap of hair that fell across her face as her body swayed in time to the movement of her hands. He knew as he watched her that his presence was irrelevant. He'd meant to leave, get on with other work so that she could practise at leisure – but there was something about this quiet, self-contained woman that made him stay. At first she'd seemed unsure, vulnerable, even shy – but once he'd talked through the services with her, and her hands had run over the keys, her growing confidence transformed her. Gradually, she peered less and less at the notes on the page before her. She didn't need music as she remembered her past pleasure in playing these pieces. Her expression changed from anxiety to fulfilment, from concentration to inspiration. And at last, as the music moved on from familiar carols to gentle cherished favourites she knew and loved, Philip watched in fascination as her face softened, her slight, rigid body relaxed. There was an intimacy between this woman and the music she played, a relationship Philip could not intrude upon. He simply watched, deeply moved by the sight of her.

Suddenly she stopped. Her eyes held his for a moment before she looked away in confusion.

'I'm sorry, I'd forgotten . . .'

'It was a privilege,' he said quietly. 'I've never heard our organ played so lovingly.'

She looked at him, grateful for his understanding. And then she laughed.

'I promise not to get so carried away tomorrow!'

'I think it might be rather nice for us all if you did.'

'Do you think someone could be spared to sit at my elbow, and dig me in the ribs to make sure I come in with the right thing at the right time?'

'I have the perfect volunteer lined up. You'll be in good hands.'

Louise stood up and gathered her things together.

'What time should I be here?'

'The service begins at eleven tonight, and finishes about quarter past midnight. Could you be here about half-past ten, so you can meet everyone you need to know?'

'Fine.'

They walked together towards the church door where Louise waited while he locked up.

Philip turned to her. 'Louise, thank you for this.'

'Do you know,' she replied. 'I'm surprised to say that I think I'm going to enjoy every moment of it.'

'So, are you seeing her again?'

Steven was stretched out across the bed as he asked, music blaring so loudly from Jamie's sound system his voice could barely be heard.

'Dunno, really,' replied Jamie casually. 'I might.'

'You mean, you don't think she'd go out with you if you asked her?'

'She might. I'm just not sure I want to . . .'

'Rejection!' Steven chanted, as the pillow he aimed hit the bed head Jamie was leaning on.

'Shut up,' Jamie grinned. 'I'm just not sure *I'm* interested really. She's a great looker and all that – but I'm not sure we have anything to talk about.'

'What would you need to *talk* to her for? Just go for it!'

'I just mean Debbie seems to be into different things from me . . .'

'She's already got a fella!'

'She might have . . .'

'More than one! You mean, you'd have to join a queue?'

'No, it's not that. It's just . . .'

'She doesn't fancy you?'

Jamie nodded. 'Probably not.'

'How can you tell?'

'Well, she seemed keen enough to leave with me – something about going on to another party she knew about. It was over in Barton Road somewhere, and she didn't want to walk there on her own, so I said I'd take her.'

'Did you hold her hand?'

'Nearly.'

'*Nearly*! Did you, or didn't you?'

'Well, I sort of had my arm round her a bit . . .'

'Did you get off with her?'

'Not much chance while we were walking.'

'What happened when you got there?'

'Well, you know that bloke, Trevor Palmer, the one who's got all those brothers – one of them is Robbie who's the year above Mark, I think . . . you know, he's a bit of a gangster, hangs round with that mob who meet in the town square? Well, he opened the door, snogged Debbie right in front of me then practically slammed the door in my face!'

'So what? Did you sort him out?'

'I never saw him again. Or Debbie. They just kind of disappeared, and I didn't know anyone else there. I wandered about a bit – but I don't like Trev Palmer's lot much, there wasn't any booze left, and everyone was stoned. In the end, I got bored and went home.'

Steven threw his head back and laughed out loud as he asked. 'So are you going to ring her?'

'Don't know her number.'

'She lives in Moreton Lane. Her friend told me.'

'Yeah, what happened to her friend? Did you manage to lose her?'

'No chance! She stuck like glue. I ended up taking her home.'

'What was she like?'

Steven pictured Liz's small round face, the huge eyes behind her glasses.

'OK. Quite sweet really. Just OK.'

'And?' prompted Jamie.

'And nothing! I took her home. End of story.'

'Did you say you'd ring her?'

'Can't remember.'

'Well, look, if you ring her, then she could get me back in touch with Debbie. She's probably wondering why I never rang her after that night.'

'No!' said Steven emphatically. 'Liz might get the wrong idea. Think I'm interested or something.'

'Come on, Steve. What are best mates for?'

'For setting up, I reckon! No, Jamie, you're on your own with this one.'

The pillow came winging back, a direct hit on Steven's head, knocking over Jamie's alarm clock as it fell to the floor.

Steven bent to pick it up, grimacing as he saw the time.

'I've got to get going. I said I'd be home an hour ago.'

And as Jamie aimed the pillow again, Steven slammed the door shut behind him.

'I told you you'd like her, Dad. She's great! And she plays really well, doesn't she?'

It was six o'clock. All the Barnes family were gathered around the tea table, with the exception of Steven who was late as usual.

'Is she happy about being called in at such short notice?' asked Ruth, as she offered a piece of cake to Philip.

'Well, she was a bit worried at first, about fitting in with the family and everything,' he replied, 'but when she turned up this morning, she seemed quite happy.'

'And she's going to play tonight, and for the morning service tomorrow too?'

'She says she will.'

'Honestly, Mum,' enthused Rachel, a slice of chocolate cake hovering halfway between her plate and her mouth. 'Mrs Kenton's really nice. She can play all sorts of music!' The cake disappeared while Rachel munched thoughtfully. 'I wasn't sure if she played the organ, though.'

'She certainly can,' said Philip, and was about to say more, but didn't. He thought again, as he had so often since, of the way Louise had played that morning, the expression on her face as her fingers moved across the keys. It had been a deeply private experience for her, one he'd felt privileged to share. Yes, it had been private. It was not his place to talk about it.

The front door banged. Steven was home. His coat was off and he was seated at the table, gathering food on to his plate, within seconds.

'You're late,' said his mother.

He shrugged. 'Got held up.'

'Are you coming to the Midnight Service tonight?' asked Rachel.

He shrugged again. 'Maybe.'

'Go on! It'll be good. You always like the Christmas Service.'

'But there's a good film on telly. A ghost thing.'

'Well, there's a Holy Ghost thing at the church tonight,' said Philip, 'and we'd like you to be there. Please.'

Steven knew that tonight of all nights his father's request should be taken as an order. And he knew when he was beaten.

'Have we got a tape for me to record that film on then – or has *he* used them all up?'

He looked pointedly at Mark.

'You can over-record *Batman*, if you like. I hate that film now.' Mark's face was serious, in spite of the dollop of red jam smeared across his chin.

'I hope you're going to wash your face before you come to church,' said his mum sternly. 'And you're not to wear jeans! That goes for you too, Steven.'

'I'm not coming at all if I've got to dress up!' he retorted.

'And you told me, Dad, that I don't have to go to church if I don't want to. That's what you said!' Mark's face was flushed with indignation.

'There are exceptions, and Christmas Eve is one of them. So is Christmas morning. It's a family affair. No argument. No discussion. Just do it!' Philip's voice was quiet and dangerously final. Neither of his sons felt it worth a reply. Tea continued in silence.

'What time have we got to leave then?' asked Steven moodily.

'I could do with some help with the music stands. Could you come across about half-ten?'

His silence was taken as agreement.

Philip turned towards his daughter. 'And you're coming to help me with the candles, aren't you, Rachel? Shall we go over in an hour or so, to get them sorted?'

'Can I come too?' asked Mark. 'I'm good at lighting things. Rachel can put the ribbons and stuff on them, then I'll be in charge of lighting.'

'Well,' said Ruth slowly, 'I could do with the whole lot of you being out of the house for a while tonight . . .'

All eyes turned towards her.

'I have a thing or two to arrange with Father Christmas.'

Mark's eyes shone. She's going to get my bike, he thought. I wonder where she's been keeping it?

He pushed back his chair with a scraping sound and stood up. 'I'll go and get changed.'

'And washed!' yelled his mum after him. And as she caught Philip's eye, the look they exchanged was of love and pride, and the shared accomplishment of parents who knew without a doubt they had the best kids in the world.

Tea that night in the Kenton household was a rushed affair. From the time Louise had finished her visit to St John's that morning, worked her way home via the butcher's, the supermarket and the off licence, she was flustered, bedraggled and already running late. But the euphoria of her time playing the organ never left her. It warmed and comforted her, a blanket of secret pleasure that shielded her from Matthew's pointed criticism and Richard's cold disapproval.

As if sensing the atmosphere, Eileen was more demanding than ever. Louise answered her umpteenth call while trying simultaneously to sort out the meal for that evening, peel vegetables and stuff the turkey for the following day. Why, she wondered, does Richard seem unable to hear his own mother's voice? Her husband and her son were closeted together in the office upstairs, absorbed and busy on the computer.

Busy, she thought bitterly. Busy, my foot! *I'm* busy! They're on Christmas holiday.

In the end, it was Lizzie who saved the day, sitting with Eileen and listening patiently to her grandmother's confused ramblings with affectionate good humour.

And it was Lizzie who kept a bright babble of chatter going at the dinner table, as the two men made their disapproval of Louise's decision to 'desert the family' brutally clear.

Stuff them, thought Louise. I won't back down. I won't give in to their pettiness. I'm alway on call for them. If they can't support me now, stuff them!

The clock was ticking round to nine o'clock as she thankfully lowered her aching shoulders into the bath water and closed her eyes in blissful relief. She'd done everything possible to get things ready for the next day. It would be different, leaving the family to it as she went off to play for the Christmas morning service. And she'd be tired out from the late night this evening. But the rising excitement that bubbled inside her made the tiredness, the work, even their disapproval, more than worthwhile.

'Mum?'

It was Lizzie, banging on the bathroom door.

What now? thought Louise wearily.

'Leave the bath water for me, will you? I'm coming to the service with you!'

'Lizzie, that's great! Give me a minute to wash my hair and the bathroom's yours.'

Barbara Gilpin was in head teacher mode as she ordered extra seating to be laid out, moved the flowers to yet another position, and ticked off her husband, Brian, for not slipping the church notices into the hymn books earlier.

Philip, who was talking to his lay reader by the pulpit, caught Brian's eye and grinned. Both men knew Barbara was in her element: harassed, put upon – and loving every minute of it.

By half-past ten people began to wander in, anxious to claim the best seats. And among them came Louise, her confidence boosted by Lizzie's presence at her side.

At first she was unsure where to go, until she spotted Philip striding down the aisle to meet her, arms outstretched in welcome.

'Louise, you made it! Come along, let me introduce you to a few people you ought to meet.'

'By the way,' she managed to say before he marched her off, 'this is my daughter Elizabeth. Can she grab a seat somewhere?'

'I've just the place. You can sit with my boys, if you'd like to?' Philip drew her over to the front side pew. 'I'll introduce you to Mark, our youngest, if I ever find him – but this is Steven.'

Lizzie's courage nearly failed her as she looked up into Steven's eyes. His expression was difficult to read. Was he pleased to see her again after that wonderful night at the party? After all, he hadn't rung her. He'd said he would, but he hadn't.

In fact, Steven didn't recognise her at first. He didn't connect the smartly dressed young woman, without glasses, who was smiling up at him now, with the bespectacled, clinging violet he'd seen only in semi-darkness at the party.

It was her voice that made the penny drop.

'We've met,' said Lizzie. 'Hello, Steven.'

He looked down into warm brown eyes and a determined little face framed by soft dark hair.

'Liz?'

'Liz Kenton,' she replied. 'It's my mum who's playing the organ tonight.'

'The one who's been teaching Rachel the piano?'

'Small world!'

'It sure is,' muttered Steven.

'Great!' beamed Philip. 'We'll leave you two to keep each other company then. Louise, come over and meet one of our church wardens, Brian Gilpin. It's his wife Barbara who's going to be at your side tonight.'

Steven and Lizzie watched in awkward silence as their parents disappeared, neither quite sure what to say.

Then they both began to speak at the same time – and when Lizzie giggled, Steven found himself laughing too.

'I didn't really think you'd come along to something like this,' she said at last.

'I didn't want to! But I'm the vicar's son and . . .'

'. . . we all know what they're like!' finished Lizzie, face alight with amusement.

Louise glanced back towards the pews to see her daughter and Philip's son laughing together. Good, she thought. At least I haven't got to worry about Liz tonight. She's obviously in safe hands.

Philip led the way over to the organ where he introduced Louise to a tall, no-nonsense woman with short-cropped hair and an air of permanent exasperation about her. Barbara Gilpin's welcome was businesslike but pleasant enough, and once Philip had left them to it, she went through the service with military efficiency.

'Is that clear?' she asked, when she came to the end of her list of directions.

'Perfectly,' smiled Louise in return.

Barbara eyed the slightly built, elfin-faced woman sitting on the organ stool beside her. She was attractively but plainly dressed in muted autumn colours. The whole impression was mouselike, of someone playing safe, careful, conservative, merging into the background as if to protect herself. A bit pale, Barbara thought, and in need of some fresh air and exercise, but pleasant in an unassuming sort of way.

By the time the service was over, though, her opinion of Louise had risen considerably. As a regular at St John's for years, she'd become used to the plodding security of Bill Spellman's playing. This younger woman brought new life to the familiar melodies of Christmas. Of course, occasionally Louise had been a bit free with the tempos, and rather flowery with the Voluntary at the end of the service, but Barbara had to admit that her music contributed a special sweetness and atmosphere to what was already a moving occasion. Not bad, thought Barbara. Not bad at all.

Naturally she said none of this to Louise. There was no need to, as within minutes of the service finishing, the organ was surrounded by people congratulating her, even before she'd gathered together her music. Ruth was there, of course. Well, she would be. Ruth was always generous with her praise, especially to newcomers. Steven was there too – quite a surprise, Barbara mused, because he was definitely in the awkward, not-interested-in-anyone-but-himself-stage of his teenage life. A young girl hovered nearby – Louise's daughter, perhaps? There was a certain likeness in the small, dainty features. And Barbara looked on as her own husband, Brian, approached to shake Louise's hand, watched by Philip, who stood to one side with an interesting expression on his face. Pride? Yes, that was almost it. But admiration too, and relief that his protégée had passed the test with flying colours. Men! Barbara observed the gaggle of admirers with cold detachment. It took just one little mouse of a woman, looking as if she needed their encouragement and protection, and they were buzzing round like flies! Barbara watched for what she considered to be long enough before marching over and saying briskly. 'Now, you're all right for tomorrow morning, aren't you? You know when we start, and what we need?'

When Louise turned to reply, her face was animated with the warmth of the congratulations around her. 'I wouldn't have managed anything at all without you at my elbow, Barbara. Thank you so much. You gave me the confidence I needed.'

Barbara almost smiled, but hid the inclination with her usual efficiency. 'The service starts at ten in the morning. Can you be here about nine-thirty, to give us time to run through the programme first?'

'Of course.' Louise smiled. 'I'm looking forward to it.'

'So are we,' said Philip warmly. 'You've been wonderful. Absolutely wonderful!'

The group began to make their slow way out of the church, some breaking off to finish a few essential jobs on the way. Dawdling behind at the back of the crowd came Liz and Steven.

'I'm not sure whether to come in the morning or not,' mused Liz casually. 'I don't know if I can be bothered to get up.'

'Lucky you don't live in our house, then. We've got no choice on Christmas Day. It's a three-line whip!'

'Well, I wouldn't like being in the crowd here if I didn't know anyone,' she continued. 'But if you're going to be here . . .'

'. . . perhaps you'll come?' finished Steven.

'Perhaps I will.'

And, to his surprise, for the rest of the night, Steven was unable to get the memory of those warm brown eyes out of his mind.

Chapter Three

Louise felt as if she didn't sleep a wink that night. Probably she did doze off between her moments of reliving the service, the feeling of playing the organ again, the sound of so many people singing along with enthusiasm to her music. Perhaps her mind did relax into sleep, even though it was teeming with faces – Richard, clutching a gold watch, floating into view, unsmiling and disapproving; Lizzie, with that secret, knowing expression Louise had noticed her wearing at the end of the service; Matthew – his face fading away, with no time to hear or talk to her; Barbara Gilpin, with her matter-of-fact welcome. And then Philip. She could only think of Philip with a smile on his face and that warmth in his eyes she'd noticed both times she'd met him at St John's – Philip listening to her play; Philip, who had drawn her into the welcoming embrace of his church and his world.

Beside her, Richard breathed heavily as he slept. He had his back turned to her, an instinctive dismissal, even when asleep. His fair hair – once golden, now elegantly streaked with silver – gleamed eerily in the light that filtered through the curtains. She loved his hair. She always had. It was one of the first things that attracted her to him. She remembered him all those years ago, in the days when he was less sure of himself, more careful about the feelings of others, more anxious that people should think well of him. She remembered the tall, uncertain young man, with his lop-sided grin and pale blue eyes that lit up with enthusiasm whenever he spoke of his work and his future. And she remembered her surprise that he'd noticed her at all.

They'd met in London, in a small, cheap cafe that was always filled with starving, penny-pinching students. He was in his final year of an Economics degree. She was shortly to emerge from the Guildhall School with a qualification to teach music. There had been a time when she'd pictured herself as an international concert pianist. Shyness and the overwhelming talent of her contemporaries had changed all that. Those who can, do. Those who can't, teach. Louise knew her place. She would become a teacher.

Richard had been in a noisy, confident group of students when she'd first caught his eye. Or rather, his foot. Somehow, as she'd been manoeuvring her rucksack and laden tray towards a window seat, she'd collided with his foot as it protruded from underneath the table. If he hadn't been quickwitted enough to steady the tray, her roll and tomato soup would have landed in his lap. Instead, he'd risen from his seat, taken her tray, and somehow not gone back to his friends again once they'd started talking. Friendship between them was easy and immediate. Love grew more slowly. For her, the quickness of his mind, his clarity of vision, his determination to achieve so much, balanced compellingly with the funny, slightly unsure, endearing lover he became. She never quite understood what he saw in her, but she felt safe and comfortable in his presence, and he seemed to draw strength from her confidence and belief in him.

When their courses finished, they both got jobs in London. A year later, when Richard was offered a promising position with an international company based in the West Country, he made sure Louise would accept him, before telling the company he would accept them. Even then, he was a businessman. It was his business to make deals that would bring him maximum return for minimum outlay. It wasn't until after they'd married that Louise realised he stopped talking about love altogether.

She reached out her hand in the darkness to touch his pale hair. She loved the feel of it, the smell of him. He still had that effect on her, after all these years. How she longed for him to turn round, to hold her in the darkness.

She sighed, and drew back her hand. She was dreaming of something that would never happen. If he held anyone in the dark these days, it wasn't her. He slept beside her, not with her. She was his wife. She was not his love.

A simple business deal – maximum return for minimum outlay – that was what their marriage had become.

But before the threatened tears could reach her eyes, she delved again into the reservoir of happiness the evening before had given her. It was hard to put into words the depth of achievement and fulfilment she felt. It had been such a long time since anyone had really *looked* at her, wanted to listen to her, felt that she was actually worth something. She had felt mundane and worthless and middle-aged for so long she'd forgotten what heady stuff it was to be praised. Just for tonight, and perhaps again tomorrow morning, she was *somebody*. Not just Richard's wife, not Matthew's mum – but somebody special. Louise Kenton – organist.

And warmed by that thought, she drifted gently off to sleep.

Along the corridor, her rarely worn contact lenses in their box next to her glasses, Lizzie slept with a smile on her face, as if she were hugging a treasure to herself.

In the Barnes household, Philip and Ruth flopped together in exhaustion on their comfy old settee. They held hands and sipped a late-night sherry while they waited for Mark, Rachel and Steven to go to bed – finally! Once silence had fallen on the old house, and they felt the coast was clear, Ruth dug out the Christmas stockings from a black plastic bag she'd hidden carefully under the stairs.

'I buried them behind the vacuum cleaner,' she told Philip with a giggle. 'I knew there was no chance they'd ever look for them there!'

Together, as they had on so many Christmas Eves over the years, they crept into each of their children's rooms, to drop stockings on the end of their beds. The last stocking went to Mark, whose face in slumber reminded Ruth so much of the baby he'd been. Although it was a closely guarded family secret, when he fell asleep Mark would often revert to his babyhood habit of sucking his thumb, as he was now.

Ruth and Philip stood wordlessly looking down at their youngest son.

'You know,' said Ruth quietly, 'they say you never experience an emotion as deep as the love you feel for your own child.'

'Except for your husband, of course,' whispered Philip, drawing her close. In the darkness, their lips met in a kiss that lingered and tantalised.

Ruth drew back at last and laid her head on his shoulder with a sigh.

'Except for my husband, of course. I don't just love him. He's my whole life . . .'

And, as his arms tightened around her, they stood as one in the soft darkness of the room.

'Oh, Mum!' begged Mark. 'Go on. Just one present – please!'

'Mark, it's nine o'clock already. We'll never make the service at all if you don't get a move on. Anyway, you know how we always do things. Stockings before church, proper presents after.'

'Just one, Mum, please! It *is* Christmas.'

'And it'll be next Christmas before we get out of the house, if you don't get cracking. Go and put some clothes on – *smart* trousers, mind, not jeans. And wash your face. I'll be checking!'

Mark's face was a picture of exasperation and resignation as he stomped upstairs, crossing paths with a barely-awake Steven on the way. Steven headed for the kettle, and reached up to get the coffee jar out of the cupboard. Ruth watched him in amusement.

'Merry Christmas, Steven.'

'What?' His expression was vacant. 'Oh, Merry Christmas, Mum.'

'Did you open your stocking? What did you get?' Rachel's questions came out in an excited rush.

'Oh, no. I forgot. I'll have a look when I go upstairs.'

'You forgot?' she asked incredulously.

He grinned at her. 'Don't bug me, little sis, or I'll squash you.'

'You're not allowed. It's Christmas . . .'

'It's Christmas,' interrupted Ruth, 'and your dad's already over at the church. The service starts in . . .' she glanced at the kitchen clock, '. . . exactly fifty-five minutes. You've got half an hour to get yourself in gear and out of the door. Right?'

Steven groaned. 'Am I allowed to have breakfast?'

'You can have anything you like for breakfast. It's Christmas.'

'Am I allowed anything I like too?' asked Rachel innocently. 'Even chocolate? Can I eat the Mars bar out of my stocking?' And before Ruth could answer, Rachel was off, pounding up the stairs. 'And my gobstoppers!' she shouted back as she reached the landing. 'They're the sort that turn your tongue black.'

'Yuk!' said Steven, laying his head on his arms across the kitchen table.

Later, over in the church, Philip looked up as Louise and Lizzie made their way down the aisle towards him, smiling and acknowledging new friends. 'My!' he commented, taking in Louise's cheerful red scarf and cosy woollen hat. 'You look bright and Christmassy, in spite of your late night.'

Her eyes sparkled as she walked towards him. 'I'm looking forward to this, I really am.'

Just for a second, into Philip's mind flashed a vision of Louise as he'd first seen her that morning at the church gate – apprehensive and timid. Quite a transformation, he thought, a revelation to see how, in just a matter of hours, this lovely, talented woman had changed. A revelation – and a pleasure.

Just then Barbara Gilpin swept across the church to whisk Louise away to the organ, as if she were a dawdling pupil. For some time Lizzie watched her mum with indulgent pride, when she felt a hand on her shoulder. Without even turning, she knew it was Steven.

'Bit early for you, isn't it?' she asked, her voice carefully casual.

'Yep. I need to find a dark corner and hide in it until this whole thing is over. I'm going to sit over at the back there, in the side block. Coming?'

I won't be able to see the organ from there, thought Liz. Mum might think I'm not supporting her at all. That would be a bit unfair really.

'Okay!' she said without further thought. 'And this time if you don't sing, I won't either.'

Ruth and Rachel were just heading for the vestry to climb into their choir robes when Sue Golding caught Ruth's attention from the other side of the church. She waved dramatically and wove her way through the gathering crowd until she reached Ruth's side, where she clasped her in an affectionate bearhug.

'Happy Christmas, Ruth! Are things as manic at your house as they are at mine?'

Ruth grimaced. 'I thought we'd never make it – not with Steven *and* Mark anyway. Which reminds me, I haven't seen Steven lately. He is here, isn't he?'

'Sitting over in that back corner with a sweet little brunette,' whispered Sue conspiratorially. 'I don't know her, do you? Is she good enough for him?'

Ruth peered across the church, where she could just make

out her eldest son deep in conversation with an attentive young girl. Recognition dawned slowly.

'Well, I never! That's Louise's daughter, I think. What was her name? I can't remember now . . .'

'Ah, Louise!' interrupted Sue, grabbing her friend's arm. 'That's who I want to speak to you about. I've just been talking to Myra Spellman. Did you see her? I'm quite surprised she managed to come along this morning really, what with Bill being so ill.'

Ruth nodded. 'Apparently they're going to move him to a specialist hospital after Christmas, if they can get a bed. They're talking about a by-pass operation.'

'So Myra was telling me. Poor woman. It's really hit her hard. Anyway, he's going to be away for months. In fact, Myra says he may never come back at all.'

'I know,' replied Ruth quietly, 'We've been thinking about that. He's been with St John's for so many years, I wonder how we'll ever get by without him.'

'Exactly! And that's why I want to talk to you about Louise. What's she like? Any good?'

'Oh, she's fine. She did a brilliant job last night, considering she was thrown in at the deep end. In fact, several people said they enjoyed the service more than usual because of her music.'

'But is she just an organist? Does she only play hymns and classical stuff?'

'I'm not sure. She teaches Rachel the piano, so I suppose she plays most things.'

'"Zipadee Doo Dah"? "Oh, What a Beautiful Morning"? What do you think?'

'The pantomime! Of course, you need a pianist for that.' Ruth looked thoughtfully in Louise's direction. 'Well, why don't you ask her after the service? She can only say no.'

'That's what I'm afraid of!' groaned Sue. 'If we don't find a really good pianist soon, we may have to call the whole thing off.'

'After I've made all those dwarf costumes? Not likely! Look, we'll buttonhole her as soon as we've finished today. She's nice, I like her. I'm sure she'll help if she possibly can.'

As if on cue, organ music began to fill the church, playing the congregation in as they made their way to the pews. Sue disappeared over to the other side of the church to separate her two youngsters, Davey and Polly, who were pricking each other with holly leaves they'd prised off the displays on the windowsills. Ruth went to join Rachel in the vestry, glancing with a smile over in Steven's direction as she went.

'What have you got for Christmas?' he was asking Lizzie. 'Do you know yet?'

'No. Mum and I are going to open our presents when we get home. Dad was pretty mad about her coming here, especially on Christmas morning, because it means he and Matthew will have to open their presents on their own, or wait for us to get back.'

'But you won't be that long, will you? What's his problem?'

Lizzie shrugged, unwilling to be disloyal.

'Well, he's a bit impatient, I suppose, especially where Mum's concerned. He likes her to be at home when he is. He's away a lot, you know, and I suppose he just thinks she should be there for him.'

'And isn't she usually?'

Lizzie turned to look at him thoughtfully. 'Yes, she always is. It's so unusual for her to make a stand like this.'

'Why do you think she's doing it now?'

'Because she was asked to, I think. Because she was flattered, and glad to help out in an emergency. Because she's always loved playing the piano, but my guess is there was a time she loved playing the organ too. She gets no chance to do that these days. And now this opportunity's come up, she's loving it, really loving it.'

'Are you pretty close to your mum?'

Lizzie thought about that for a moment. 'I suppose I am –

closer than I am to Dad, because he's away so much. But I do get on with him when he's around. There's something about dads and daughters, isn't there? Well, there is for us, anyway.'

She looked round at Steven. 'How about you? Your parents OK?'

'Yeah, not bad.' He smiled to himself. 'I suppose we all have our moments, but on the whole they're all right.'

'Are you closer to one of them than the other?'

'Maybe to Mum. She's the one I see most. But she can be a bit strict about things I don't think matter much . . .'

'. . . like washing, hanging up your clothes, not using the phone too much, and coming in on time?'

'Exactly!' agreed Steven. 'But Dad – well, I like my dad a lot, but there's quite a lot of stuff he believes in, that he expects me to accept just because I'm his son.'

'Like being a Christian?'

'Yes, but more than that. He thinks I should go to university. It doesn't matter to him that I've no idea what I want to do as a job yet, and perhaps university might not be the best route for me. He just thinks I should go anyway, end of story.'

'Because he did?' asked Lizzie.

'Because he *didn't*, or not when he was my age anyway, and he wants me to have the chance he didn't have himself.'

'You might enjoy it.'

'I might. And I might choose to go. In fact, I went for an interview up in London a couple of weeks ago. I'm thinking of studying Sociology and Political Science.'

'Did you like what you saw?'

'Yeah, I did, but I don't know if they're going to offer me a place yet. Anyway, I just want the choice to be mine, because I feel it's right for me, not because I want to please my dad.'

'Apart from that, he's OK, is he?'

'Most of the time – but it gets up my nose sometimes that he always seems to take the moral high ground.'

'Well, he's a Christian minister. I suppose he has to.'

'No, it's more than that. He didn't decide to become a minister until quite late in life. He'd been working for an engineering firm first of all, which never really suited him. In fact, when he talks about being a teenager himself, he always says he was agnostic, and that was at the heart of his problems. He got into quite a bit of trouble then – you know, in with a bad crowd? He was actually arrested for unruly behaviour on one occasion! Can you believe it? He was hardly a saint, was he?'

'And you think he expects you to be one now?'

'I think he's forgotten what it's like to be young.' Steven grinned. 'Well, it's a long time since he was. He's forty-one now, poor old fella.'

'Past it!' agreed Lizzie, matching his grin. 'And I know parents think that just because they were our age once, they know exactly how we feel, but they don't. Life is completely different for us. Times have changed. We've got more pressures on us, and they're different from the ones they knew. They don't understand us at all . . .'

'. . . and you can never make them see that,' finished Steven. 'Never!'

And their eyes met in mutual understanding and total agreement.

The service, once it began, was joyful and stirring. There was familiar comfort for each member of the congregation as they joined in with the much-loved carols, sung on countless Christmas Days before this one. As he sang, Philip's eyes wandered over his congregation with affection: faces that had grown dear to him, friends who formed a larger family around his own. It was on days like today that his heart filled with thanks for his vocation, his position of trust in this community. God had touched his life and called him to the priesthood – his wasn't a job but a reason for being. He was needed, and ready to give in Christian love anything to anyone. The pay was lousy, the hours endless, and he couldn't be happier.

His eyes strayed to Ruth, standing beside their daughter as they sang in the choir. Rachel, at fourteen, was growing more and more like her mum, although her hair was longer and several shades lighter than Ruth's dark red curls. Philip had always loved his wife's eyes, which he remembered noticing on the first day he met her: warm and hazel-coloured. Rachel's eyes were more green, with pale golden lashes that on very special occasions she was allowed to coat with mascara. With make-up on, he could see the woman she would become. She was growing up too fast, his Rachel, far too fast.

He smiled to himself. Sentimental old fool, he thought. That's what Christmas does to you. Memories of years gone by, apprehension about the years ahead. Dear Lord, he had so much to be thankful for!

And then it was over. The grand finale – 'Hark The Herald Angels Sing' – followed by the blessing, and Philip followed at the end of the procession as the choir filed out towards the vestry. Nodding in greeting to familiar faces in his congregation, he found himself listening to the organ music ringing around the old church. Louise's playing was simply inspired. What a talent she had! What a blessing she'd been for St John's, stepping in in an emergency and excelling at the task. The thing was, would she stay? Could she?

By the time he had said goodbye to people as they made their way out of the church, Louise had already been buttonholed by Ruth and Sue.

'You see,' Sue was saying, as Philip approached, 'he didn't write down any of the panto music. Bill just busked his way through it, and I know that's really hard to do.'

'But would I know all the songs?' Louise asked. 'Do you think I'd be able to find music for them?'

Ruth and Sue looked at each other, not really knowing the answer. 'Yes! Absolutely! Of course, we could!' answered Sue emphatically. 'Just say you'll help, please! Come along to the next rehearsal at least, and see what you think.'

Richard will be furious if I take on any more, thought Louise. I really shouldn't. I know I shouldn't.

'Of course she will!' she heard Lizzie say, from somewhere behind her shoulder. 'She'd love to – and she'd be marvellous at it.'

'Lizzie,' interrupted Louise doubtfully, 'I need to chat it over with Dad first . . .'

Her daughter's chin went up stubbornly. 'Tell him you're doing it. Just *tell* him! Or I will, if you like?' She bent so that her face was closer to her mother's. 'You do want to play for the panto, don't you?'

Louise smiled at her determined expression. 'Yes, of course, but . . .'

'But nothing! Do it.'

Ruth watched the interchange between the two of them with fascination. They were obviously very close, Louise and Lizzie. Ruth wondered what Louise's husband was like. Richard sounded a bit of an ogre. He probably wasn't at all, but she could never imagine being nervous about asking Philip anything. He could never frighten anybody. Too much of a softie, thank goodness.

'Mum!' It was Mark calling her, his face full of exasperation that his parents were taking so long about leaving the church when there were presents waiting to be opened at home. A bike, perhaps? A Muddy Fox? He wondered where they'd kept it. It wasn't in the garage or the garden shed. Perhaps they'd kept it at Brian's? They couldn't think him babyish enough to search for presents before Christmas? Parents could be such an embarrassment at times.

The last choir members gathered together their belongings, and amid hugs and wishes for the best Christmas ever, slowly the church cleared. Steven and Lizzie made their way to the porch, to wait for their respective parents to join them.

'What are you doing over the holiday then?' he asked casually.

'Not a lot. I didn't fancy planning much.' Lizzie paused for a while until at last she asked, 'And you?'

'Depends a bit what I get for Christmas, really. If I get that new game for my Megadrive, I'll probably be on that quite a bit.'

'That's not Mortal Kombat, is it?'

'Yes. Do you know it?'

'Matthew, my brother, has it. He's brilliant, knows all the cheats. I'm catching up with him though!'

Steven looked at her and grinned. 'You know the cheats, eh? They'd be useful . . .'

'. . . if you get the game, of course.'

He paused, studying his shoes with careful concentration.

'If I do – would you come over and take a look at it?'

A slow smile spread over Lizzie's face. 'Perhaps,' she replied softly. 'Give me a ring and I'll see.'

They both looked up as the final group to leave the church made their way towards the porch.

'So you'll come along to the next rehearsal then, and see what you think . . .' Sue Golding's voice could be heard above the rest.

'I'd love to – and if you could let me have a list of the numbers you need, I'll dig through my sheet music and see what I've already got.'

Louise suddenly found herself enveloped in a bearhug, a theatrical gesture that was typical of Sue. 'You're an angel! An absolute angel!'

Philip, a few paces ahead of them, caught the expression of surprise on Louise's face and smiled at her when she glanced in his direction. She disentangled herself and moved towards him, stretching out her hand.

'What have you got me into, Philip? What have you done?'

Instead of releasing her hand, he covered her fingers with his own, smiling down at her.

'Nothing you won't enjoy, I hope. You've brought us so

much, more than you know. I just hope you don't feel we're taking advantage of you.

'It's been so unexpected,' she answered quietly, 'an unexpected pleasure. Thank you all for asking me. Thank *you*, Philip, for making me so welcome.'

And as much to her surprise as his, she swiftly reached up to brush her lips across his cheek in the lightest of kisses. And then, as her natural shyness returned, she grabbed Lizzie's arm and scurried away to her car.

Mark's excitement was at fever-pitch half an hour later as present-opening was at its height. There had been squeals of delight from Rachel as she'd unwrapped the tape she'd been angling for, followed by the jersey she'd had her eye on for weeks. Steven didn't bother to open the presents that remained for him under the tree once the CD of Mortal Kombat had been unwrapped. Ruth wondered if they'd see him again for the rest of the day as he disappeared two at a time up the stairs to his room.

For Mark, the youngest, there were the most parcels to unwrap, which he tackled with enthusiasm. It was when he opened the large square box labelled with love from his godparents, Brian and Barbara, that he discovered the brand new cycling helmet. Yes! It was going to be all right. A Muddy Fox was his, he knew it.

Finally, right at the very bottom of the pile of presents, was an envelope on which was written his name. He tore it open to reveal a rhyme, obviously composed by his father, who was standing to one side with Mum, smiling with indulgent affection.

> *Follow fast this simple clue*
> *And a treat you'll find for you*
> *By this letter you'll be led*

> *Far beyond the garden shed,*
> *Round the corner, down the path,*
> *Your Christmas present to unearth!*

He was off! Out the back door with Mum, Dad and Rachel hard on his heels. He pounded past the shed and on down the path to the very bottom of the garden. He looked around frantically until his eyes settled on a bulky-looking something propped up against the back fence. That's it, he thought. I've found it.

He tore away at the black plastic wrapping – and then he stopped. His face fell.

It was a bike, and a mountain bike too – but it wasn't a Muddy Fox. And what's more, it obviously wasn't new. The paintwork had been repainted, but he could still see where it had been chipped in places and patches of rust stood out on the silver spokes of the wheels.

'Do you like it, Mark?' Ruth asked him anxiously. 'We know it's not exactly the model you wanted, but the people we bought it from said this one is very similar. And it's only a couple of years old. Their son has just grown out of it . . .'

Tears pricked Mark's eyes as he struggled to hide his disappointment. Of course he wouldn't get a new bike. No one in their family ever had a new bike. He looked up into Ruth's worried eyes, and bit his lip to stop it trembling.

'It's great, Mum,' he said at last. 'Thanks.'

Philip reached out to squeeze Ruth's hand as they watched him finish unwrapping the bike and begin to wheel it towards the house.

'Is the seat the right height?' asked Philip. 'I can adjust it.'

'It's fine, Dad. Really great. Thanks.' Mark spoke without turning, and carried on pushing the bike away. Ruth looked at Philip forlornly as, hand in hand, they too made their way back into the house.

★

It was almost three o'clock in the Kenton household before Christmas dinner was over. Louise had put the turkey on a low heat in the oven before she'd gone to church, but by the time she'd finished all the rest of the preparation, lunch was much later than the family were used to having it.

Surprisingly, Richard was in good spirits. He didn't mention her visit to church, and as he already had a glass of whisky in his hand by the time she and Lizzie arrived home, he was plainly in holiday mood. Matthew joined them to sit around the tree and open presents. Louise loved the whole idea of Christmas presents. She loved thinking of gifts for people she cared about. She loved the searching, the wrapping and the hiding. Most of all, she loved to watch their faces as they unwrapped each parcel to discover its contents.

On the whole, she mused later as she spooned honey over the carrots and popped them into the oven, her presents had been well received. Matthew seemed to be genuinely delighted with his new jacket, and there was no doubting Lizzie's enthusiastic reaction to the gold earrings Louise had bought her. Eileen was confused by the strangeness of the day, and seemed ill at ease with the break in her usual routine but she'd obviously loved her new slippers, even though she clutched them to her like a hotwater bottle rather than putting them on her feet.

As Louise basted the roast potatoes and took the silver foil off the breast of the turkey, she thought of the presents Richard had given her. There had been two large, impressive-looking parcels under the tree. When she peeled the paper off the first, she discovered a dressing gown. It was plum-coloured, in an unexciting, warm brushed material. It was the sort of thing you'd buy your granny, she thought wryly: functional, unflattering and homely. It wasn't that she didn't need a dressing gown, it was simply boringly practical – boring and practical, to match the way in which Richard viewed her.

The second parcel was more intriguing. It was large and rectangular and heavy. She opened it to discover a new microwave cooker, one of the new whizzbang versions that grilled and cooked conventionally as well as by microwave. She didn't need a new microwave oven. The one she had was perfectly adequate. And once again Louise felt a pang of disappointment that Richard could only view her as needing useful, practical presents.

What happened to the silky nighties and the bottle of something alluring to dab behind her ears? Beautifully wrapped up for Miss Gold Watch, probably! She'd hardly need a microwave, would she, for the kind of treats she cooked up for him?

Louise slammed the oven shut and laid her hot forehead against the cool door of the fridge. In a crowd, amidst her own family, she was lonely. Lonely and tired and bitter. There was no one to tell. No one who cared. And the fridge door felt hard and cold against her skin as hot tears rolled down her cheek.

As Philip turned into Bunyan Ward later that afternoon, he was struck by the false gaiety of hospital wards on Christmas Day. Minnie's room was garlanded with glittering decorations and looked festive enough – and yet there was an air of loneliness and desolation about the few patients who had to be there, either because they were too ill to move, or because they simply had nowhere else to go.

At first he thought she was asleep, but as he drew up a chair to sit down beside her, Minnie's bright blue, bird-like eyes opened immediately.

'I was thinking,' she said, as if he'd been there all the time, 'of my mother. She loved Christmas. She made it so special for us. When she died, the specialness went out of it, somehow.'

'When did you lose her?' asked Philip softly.

She closed her eyes again.

'I don't remember now. Quite a long time ago, I think.'

He sat beside her in silence, uncertain what to say, unsure if she'd welcome him saying anything.

Her eyes were on him again. 'Do you miss your mother?'

'Yes.' He smiled. 'But not in the way you mean. She's alive and mostly well, living down in Dorset.'

'Did you always get on with her?'

'Honestly?'

'Of course!'

'Well, honestly, she doesn't think much of me being a vicar. She'd have liked me to go into business and make a bob or two. I think she hoped I'd be able to keep her in the manner to which she'd like to become accustomed!'

Minnie chuckled, her eyes twinkling with amusement.

'And your father?'

'Keeping your mother company, I'm afraid. He died some years ago.'

'And you do miss him.' It was a statement, not a question.

'I do. I think of him often. He was a gentle, caring man. His work was pretty ordinary really. He was an administrative assistant at the local town hall for years, but he escaped in his thoughts. He was a deep thinker, always looking for answers.'

'Did he need to escape from your mum sometimes too?'

Philip looked down at Minnie's guileless expression and thought what a canny, intuitive little bird she was.

'Theirs wasn't a marriage made in heaven. Not towards the end anyway. She thought she was marrying a man with prospects and ambition. Perhaps he seemed ambitious when she first met him, but he lost all that along the way. He was just happy to plod on, with his work, his home, his family, his fishing . . .'

'Fishing?'

'He loved it. He'd get up in the wee small hours and sit in the dark beside the river bank. He liked his solitude.'

Minnie closed her eyes with a sigh. There was silence for a while, before she spoke.

'You cared a lot about him then, did you?'

Philip smiled at the memory. 'I did. He was a wonderful man. Always had time for us. I remember him being great company – warm, funny, the one I'd want to tell first if I was upset or hurt. And I sometimes think even now, how sad it was that I was still quite young when he died. I never really got the chance to know him as an adult, as an equal, a friend.'

'And he believed in God? He had a faith?'

'He did. A very deep belief. He didn't talk about it much, but it meant a lot to him. It seemed to give him contentment. He was at peace with the world. That was one of the things I loved most about him.'

'You loved him, and when you lost him, you took up his faith. It worked for him so you thought it would work for you . . .'

Minnie's eyes were still closed, as if she wasn't giving much attention to the conversation. Philip was not deceived. She missed nothing.

'You wanted to find the same peace and contentment in your life as you saw in his – to believe in a divine being who sees all, understands all, and deals with all the problems, like a kind of security blanket. It's comforting to believe in a God like that. It was a comfort to your dad – and now it comforts you. A comfy faith. That's what you have. That's what we all want.'

Philip was stunned into silence until at last he said quietly, 'There's nothing easy about dedicating your whole life to God, Minnie. It's a constant struggle, but one that, for me, makes sense of everything I do.'

Her blue eyes shot open, to stare into his. 'But your faith has never really been challenged, has it? You've never faced a time of such despair you've had to put that God of yours to the test. And if you did, would he be there? Would he? Or is it all just a comfort blanket? Not real at all.'

Philip laid his hand over hers as he replied. 'Minnie, you

mustn't doubt for one moment that he would be there for me – and he'll be there for you too.'

She turned her hand upwards, to return his clasp. 'Goodbye, Vicar. Thank you for coming.' And as he sat with his hand in hers, watching her gentle breathing as she slept, he thought that for a woman who played the role of devil's advocate so well, she had the face of an angel.

Chapter Four

Sue Golding didn't really expect many pantomime performers to turn up at the rehearsal between Christmas and New Year, but in the end, she was pleasantly surprised. It seemed that after several days of enforced family get-togethers, and an overdose of old film favourites on the TV, she wasn't the only one relieved to get out of the house and back to something approaching normal life. Philip and Brian had been two of the first to arrive, and to make the most of rehearsal time she decided to go through their big number first. As in all the best pantomimes, they were singing 'Sisters', a number they attacked with gusto and improvisation. Rachel recognised her dad didn't feel it was entirely appropriate for a member of the clergy to dress up in fancy frocks and stiletto heels, so made it her mission to cajole him into the spirit of the thing.

'Honestly, Dad,' she enthused, as she drew an exaggerated scarlet bow around his mouth. 'A touch of lipstick and your stilettos, and you'll get into the part right away!'

One of the qualities that had always endeared Philip to his congregation was his infectious sense of humour and ability to laugh at himself. Having been roped in to be an Ugly Sister, he decided to give it his all.

With a tape recording of the Beverley Sisters belting out the number, the two men wiggled their way on to the stage, to the delight of everyone in the room. Philip cut a particularly dashing figure. Because he'd come straight from a diocesan meeting to the rehearsal, he was still dressed in clerical gear and dog collar – which was greatly enhanced by his painted lips, a babydoll wig balanced on top of his thick dark hair, two different-sized balloons stuck up his jumper, and his trouser legs rolled to his knees so that the full glory of his shiny black patent leather high heels could be appreciated! With his hands clasped under his bulging bosom, his eyes flirting and flashing towards the audience, he was enjoying himself!

When a certain gentleman arrived from Rome
She wore the dress, and I stayed at home!

It was at just that moment that Louise slipped quietly into the hall, to be met with a vision of the vicar that made her jaw drop. There was Philip – the man who took his work and responsibilities as a minister so seriously – as she'd never seen him before! She laughed out loud with the rest of the cast when a bright green balloon fell out of his jumper as he took a bow to acknowledge their applause. She watched as Rachel ran over to clasp him in a bear hug, which toppled him off his high heels so that the pair of them almost ended up in a heap on the floor. And she kept on watching as he smiled with delight at his daughter, and the friends who surrounded and congratulated both Ugly Sisters.

A sudden image of Richard came to mind. Could she ever imagine her own husband having the sense of fun to do something like this? Could she picture him hugging her or their children with the unselfconscious affection that poured out of Philip as his arm circled Rachel's shoulders? The affectionate love between father and daughter touched her as she looked on quietly from a corner of the hall. And, to her surprise, she recognised a pang of jealousy. How wonderful it must be to have the love of such a man!

Barbara Gilpin spotted her first. Looking every inch the

teacher in her twin set and no-nonsense lace-ups, she strode across to Louise and steered her towards the piano. Sue waved enthusiastically from the centre of the rehearsal floor. 'Barbara will show you what's needed. I've just got to sort out a few things here.'

Louise was relieved to see they'd gathered together sheet music for quite a few of the numbers they hoped to use. Under Barbara's precise instruction, she soon got the hang of what was needed. By the time they got round to rehearsing the grand finale (a reprise of 'Zipadee Doo Dah', leading into 'There's No Business Like Show Business'), Louise was really enjoying herself.

At the end, when most people had drifted away, Philip and a few pressganged 'volunteers' stayed behind to rearrange the seating for the Senior Citizens' Club meeting in the hall the following morning. Everyone who used the draughty, dusty old Legion Hall for meetings at present was longing for the time when the new church centre, with its smart new facilities, would be opened by the Bishop on Good Friday – not a day too soon!

It took a good twenty minutes at the end of the rehearsal for Louise to go through all the extra music Sue needed. Finally, exhilarated and with her mind buzzing, she pulled on her coat and headed for the door. Philip reached for the handle at the same time as her, and together they stepped out into a sudden downpour of rain.

'Have you got your car nearby?' he asked as Louise tucked the pantomime music inside her coat.

'No, I walked. It seemed like a good idea at the time.'

'Come on, I'll drive you. I wouldn't normally have my car here either but I've just come back from a diocesan meeting. I'm parked outside the gate.'

By the time they'd splashed down the path, and Philip had fumbled in the dark for the key, they were both soaked. Finally, they collapsed thankfully into their seats, and Louise started giggling as she looked down to see that Philip was still clutching his curly blonde wig and high heels. The absurdity of it struck him too, as he threw back his head and laughed out loud.

I haven't laughed like this for so long, she thought. How good it feels!

The drive to her house was over in no time, and as Philip pulled up at the kerb and switched off the engine, he turned to face Louise.

'I can't thank you enough, you know, for all you're doing for us.'

In the darkness, she felt herself redden with pleasure.

'Oh, please, it's no trouble at all. I'm loving every minute of it.'

'And your family? They don't feel it's taking up too much of your time?'

Her lips tightened. 'They might, but they shouldn't. I've always put them first. I never let them down.'

There was an awkward silence while he chose his words carefully.

'Your husband – Richard, isn't it? He's quite happy about all this, is he?'

Louise looked him directly in the eye. 'Probably not, but that's his problem. I so rarely ask for time to do things I want to do. I've always been at the beck and call of Richard, and the family. But the children are almost grown up now. They don't need me babysitting them all the time. And now, at last, I'd like time for myself. Time to do things I enjoy, things like this.'

Philip was taken back by the intensity of her outburst and the flush of defensive determination that coloured her face. Sudden embarrassment overcame her as she sank back into the seat, her hands clasped in her lap.

'I'm sorry. You must think me very odd.'

'What I think is that you're talented. And generous. And unhappy.'

She didn't answer. She couldn't. She was looking down at

her tightly locked hands so it seemed as if her eyes were closed. And then Philip saw that slow, shiny tears were slipping down her cheeks.

'Oh, Louise, I'm sorry. That was insensitive of me . . .'

She shook her head sadly. 'No, you could never be that.'

She groped for a hankie in her sleeve to wipe her eyes and face. He watched her in silence, unwilling to intrude. It was some time before he spoke again.

'Would it help to talk about it? I'm a good listener.'

She smiled weakly at him. 'I'm sure you are. I'm sure anyone would find it easy to pour their heart out to you.'

Philip realised she was trembling. With great care, he prised apart her clasped fingers and took her small hand in his. Gently stroking it with his thumb, it was several minutes before he saw her body relax, her shoulders lower, and her features soften. With a small sigh, she finally leant her head back against the seat, eyes closed.

'I'm always here, Louise. Any time. If you want to talk. Even if you don't, but need a friend, I'm still here.'

She looked down at his hand wrapped around hers. 'There's nothing to say. Not yet. Not that I could put into words anyway. But I promise you, if I ever need a shoulder, it'll be yours.'

Suddenly the car was bathed in a shaft of light as Matthew flung open the front door.

'Mum, what are you doing? Are you coming in?'

Louise snapped into action, guiltily gathering together her music and bag. With her hand on the door handle, she turned towards Philip.

'I'll see you on Sunday, then. For the church service. And, Philip – thank you.'

Then she was gone, and Philip felt moved and helpless as she scurried anxiously through the gate and disappeared inside the house.

*

Lizzie had almost given up hope of hearing from Steven over the holiday, in spite of their rapport at the Christmas Morning service. For several days she jumped every time the phone rang. By the end of the week she'd written him off as a bad job. Typical male. Not worth it.

But all that was forgotten on the morning of New Year's Eve when she absent-mindedly picked up the phone to discover that it wasn't someone for Matthew, as usual. It was Steven. For her.

'Hi! Get any good computer games for Christmas?'

'No, but I hope you did!'

'Were you serious about knowing all the cheats for Mortal Kombat?'

'Some of them. Not all.'

'What are you doing today?'

Homework, she thought. Cello practice. Clearing out my room . . .

'Not sure yet. Why?'

'Do you fancy popping round?'

'When?'

'Whenever you like.'

Fortunately, Steven couldn't see the broad smile on Lizzie's face as she paused for dramatic effect before answering.

'We-ll, I'm a bit busy this morning . . . (washing my hair, and ironing my new trousers before I go over there, she thought to herself) . . . but this afternoon should be OK. About three suit you?'

'Great! Shall I come round and pick you up?'

'No need. I know the way.'

'Right. Well, see you then.'

''Bye.'

'Yes!' Lizzie whooped with triumph! So he was keen after all!

*

Not many people knew about the loft in the Gilpin house. Not many people looking at Brian – solid, sensible, retired accountant Brian – would guess his secret passion. And he didn't want them to know. It was his secret, one he guarded carefully. A secret hideaway he shared with only one other person – his godson, Mark.

Mark loved model railways too. Brian had made sure of that by buying him a train set for his christening, when he was only a few weeks old. Barbara thought it was a daft idea, but then, she would never understand. In time, Mark's few trains and tracks were amalgamated into the complex, true-to-life layout Brian had painstakingly created in his loft over the years. That loft was a no-go area except for Mark and Brian. Even Barbara knew that however much she might rule the roost in every other part of the house, for her the loft was out of bounds.

The layout was at waist level for Brian, and he had to take into account the generous proportions of his waistline when he cut out an access hole in the middle of the spread, so he could survey the whole scene from the best vantage point. That morning it was Mark's turn to be Controller, directing loco-motives and changing tracks from the centre of the whole operation.

Mark had been unusually quiet since Christmas. Brian hadn't mentioned it. When the lad wanted to talk, he would.

Funnily enough, it was the train set itself that finally got the conversation going. Mark especially loved the little lifelike figures Brian had dotted about on station platforms and in the streets. He'd made it Mark's special responsibility to paint and maintain the figures, and that morning the miniature model of a paperboy on his bike was absorbing Mark's attention.

'Doesn't look much like your bike, that one,' commented Brian. 'More like the old banger of a bike I remember having as a boy!'

Mark said nothing as he moved the model around the layout, trying to decide on the best place to put it.

'Your new bike looks really flashy. How many gears did you say it has?'

'Eight,' replied Mark bluntly.

'Wow! I don't remember having more than two. One to go forward and one to go back.'

Mark concentrated on the little figure, tongue between his teeth.

'Have you managed to get out for a really good spin yet?'

'Not really.'

'Shall we pop your bike in the back of the van tomorrow and go up to Sharpen Hill? You could really put a mountain bike through its paces there.'

'If you like,' replied Mark, without enthusiasm.

Brian eyed the boy thoughtfully as he took off his glasses and cleaned them absentmindedly on his much loved and worn old jersey. He crossed to the side of the loft where he'd left the Coke bottle. Pouring a glass for each of them, he fumbled in his pocket to fish out a couple of wrapped chocolate biscuits.

'Elevenses,' he said. 'Come and sit down for a bit.'

Reluctantly, Mark extricated himself from the train layout, and taking the Coke and biscuit, wedged himself against the wall next to Brian.

'What's up, son?'

'Nothing.'

'Come on . . . it's me you're talking to here. This is just between us. What's up?'

'It's nothing, really.'

'Is it your bike?'

Mark turned to Brian, his face indignant.

'I didn't want *that* bike! I'd rather not have had a bike at all than get the wrong one!'

'But you'd grown too big for your old one. You did need something new . . .'

'Something *new*, yes! I wanted a Muddy Fox. And who wants a bike that someone else has thrown away? They've painted it, you know – and it's the worst colour in the world. I hate it! I hate that bike! I'd like to crash it and smash it up so they really see I meant what I said about knowing *exactly* what bike I wanted.'

'I've been doing a bit of checking on the price of Muddy Fox bikes. Do you know how expensive they are?'

Mark stopped then and looked down at the chocolate from his biscuit which was now smeared all over his fingers.

'I know they're a lot. But I'd get a paper round – I told Mum I would. I'll save up if they'll help me. Only now they've bought that awful bike, they'll never take me seriously if I ask for what I really want. Dad will talk about all the children who have nothing in Africa. But I'm not there! And the boys in Africa probably wouldn't want a Muddy Fox anyway.'

'Have you tried talking to your dad?'

'He wouldn't listen. And Mum would just say I'm spoilt and ungrateful . . .'

'Are you?'

'I don't think so. I'm not spoilt! If I was, they would have got me the bike I wanted, wouldn't they?'

Brian thought for a moment.

'How about if I have a word with them? Would that help?'

Mark turned huge green eyes in his godfather's direction.

'Would you? Really? What would you say?'

'Oh, I think I'd sugar the pill a bit. You know, tell them that you do really appreciate the bike they gave you, but you'd still love to have the model you've really got your eye on. And I could say that if you try and save up some of the money yourself, then I'll match you pound for pound. And what's more, I might be able to find a few jobs here you could give me a hand with – you know, in the garden, washing the car. Things like that. You do jobs for me, and I'll pay you fairly. How's that?'

'Really, Uncle Brian? You'd do that?

'Of course.'

'And you don't think Mum and Dad would mind?'

'Let's ask them, shall we?'

'Today?'

'Why not? When I take you home this afternoon.'

'Great! That would be great!'

'Come on then, let's get that other engine working. Then we'll have a spot of lunch, and call it a day.'

Beaming from ear to ear, Mark worked in silence for a whole minute. Brian watched out of the corner of his eye as the boy was obviously deep in thought. At last he asked, 'So how much will you pay me if I wash your car?'

'A couple of quid?'

'And if I wax the outside, and polish and vacuum the inside too – how much then?'

'Oh, that should be worth a fiver, I think.'

Mark paused, his mind working overtime.

'And how often do you think you'll need it cleaned?'

Brian laughed out loud. He ruffled his godson's mop of hair affectionately. 'That's my boy! A future accountant in the making!'

It was more than a week later, and Sue Golding had been on the phone to Louise for almost half an hour, talking in circles about the panto – what music was needed here, what suggestions she had for there, and who was doing what wrong. She was just in the middle of a long saga about how haphazardly the ticket sales were being organised (and couldn't anyone organise *anything* without her having to step in to sort out the mess?) when the doorbell rang.

'Louise!' Eileen's thin voice floated through from the living room. 'Louise, I think I hear someone.'

Sue was in full flow, not even drawing breath at the other end of the line.

With her hair still pinned up in the curlers she slept in, Eileen shuffled into the doorway, dressed in a soft pink dressing gown and clutching her new Christmas slippers.

'Louise, I can hear someone. Who's here? Is it Richard? Is Richard here?'

Louise finally managed to break into Sue's monologue. 'Hang on, Sue. There's someone at the door. Can I ring you back?'

'Don't worry. Give me a call later!' said Sue's cheery voice, and she hung up.

'Richard shouldn't be here now, should he?' Eileen's face was furrowed with worry. 'Why would Richard be here now?'

The doorbell rang again. Louise turned to propel her mother-in-law back towards the living room.

'I'll go. Don't you worry. I'll let you know who it is.'

It was the milkman, calling for payment of the weekly bill. It took just a minute for Louise to sort out the right money when, as the milkman was about to leave, she suddenly remembered she needed cream for the dish she was cooking that evening.

'I've got some on the van,' he said.' Won't be a jiffy.'

At that moment, the phone rang again.

'Louise, have you got a moment?'

She smiled at the sound of Philip's voice.

'Here's your carton!' yelled the milkman from the doorstep.

'Great, thank you!'

'Sorry,' Philip said, 'I've obviously caught you at an awkward moment.'

'No, it's all under control now.'

'Well, I just wanted to have a word with you about something the Youth Club youngsters are planning for a couple of weeks' time. Have you ever heard the music from Taize?'

'Can't say I have.'

'Well, there's a monastic community in France that young people travel from all round the world to visit. Over the years, the monks have created a very distinctive style of worship that centres around music. They sing quite simple chants, just one line sometimes, repeated over and over again in a variety of languages – but the harmonies are beautiful. And because anyone can sing them, they've really become popular, especially with the younger generation.'

'And your Youth Club is thinking of using some of those chants?'

'They'd like to, but they don't know much about it. They asked me to send off for a book of the music, which I did. It arrived this morning.'

'Would you like me to take a look at it?'

'Would you? They're obviously going to need a bit of help going through the songs and choosing which ones they'd like to use. You know they're running the Sunday morning service themselves in a fortnight's time, and I think they'd like to be able to sing them from memory by then.'

'Of course I'll help. I'd love to!'

'That's another thing we're asking you to do. Are you sure this won't be too much?'

Louise laughed. 'I'm already up to my ears in this panto. A little bit more won't make much difference one way or the other.'

'Oh, talking of the panto,' he said, 'you didn't by any chance pick up a brown envelope addressed to Brian Gilpin at the rehearsal the other night, did you? He thought he'd left it on top of the piano, so you might have scooped it up with your music.'

'Give me a minute. I'll just go and have a quick look.'

Louise walked down the hall into the study where her piano stood in one corner. Quickly, she sifted through her music, to find Brian's envelope right at the very bottom.

'I've got it,' she told Philip when she returned to the phone. 'I'm so sorry about picking it up when it wasn't for me.'

'Look, I'll be heading over to the hospital in a few minutes. Would you mind if I called in on the way round, to pick up the envelope and drop off this Taize book for you to have a look at?'

'Fine. I'll be here.'

Louise was smiling as she replaced the receiver. Philip coming here! Heavens, the living room would need a vacuum.

She was surprised to find Eileen wasn't in there. She was probably in the loo.

Minutes later, when Louise had tidied up the newspapers and cleared away some coffee cups, Eileen had still not returned. Curious now, Louise called her mother-in-law's name. There was no reply.

She must be upstairs. Strange, because the elderly woman had difficulty managing the stairs on her own.

But Eileen was not upstairs. She was nowhere to be found. And it was when Louise came back downstairs, to see the front door standing slightly ajar, she felt the blood run cold in her veins.

Throwing open the door, she rushed outside, down the garden path to the gate where she scanned the quiet road urgently.

'Eileen!' she called out. 'Eileen, where are you?'

Perhaps she'd gone round the back. That's it! She must be in the back garden!'

But she wasn't.

What to do? What should she do?

Louise started running along the road in the direction of the small parade of shops that Eileen loved to visit. How far could an old lady possibly get when she was so slow and uncertain on her legs nowadays?

At the point where the road straightened out before her, so that she could see quite a distance ahead, Louise realised that Eileen could not have come this way. Panicking now, she turned and started to run in the other direction.

'Eileen! Eileen! Where are you? Where've you gone?'

A car slowed down as it passed her. The driver looked at her curiously and then drove on. I must look hysterical, Louise thought, running down the street shouting my head off.

Looking into each garden as she ran by, Louise covered the distance to the far end of the road in a few minutes. She felt cold fear building inside her. Eileen was so frail and unworldly. She knew nothing about crossing roads. She was in her dressing gown and curlers, for heaven's sake! And no shoes on her feet!

'Eileen! Oh, Eileen, where on earth are you?'

Another car drew up alongside her. This time it stopped and she became dimly aware that someone was calling her name.

'Louise! Is something wrong?'

Philip grabbed her arm to stop her running. Thank God he was here. He'd know what to do.

'My mother-in-law! She's disappeared! She must have let herself out the front door when I went to look for Brian's letter . . .' Louise couldn't see him properly. Tears brought on by fear, and the relief that he was with her, misted her vision. 'I don't know where she is! She can't have got far, but I just can't find her!'

'Are you sure she's not gone back into the house?' His voice was calm and reassuring.

Louise looked up at him then, grasping at the possibility.

'She might! Yes, she might!' And, turning on her heel, Louise started running again, with Philip following closely behind her.

But the house was empty.

'She's losing her memory, you see. She suffers from senile dementia, and it's got quite bad recently. She doesn't know what she's doing really . . .'

'Come on,' said Philip, taking command of the situation. 'Hop in my car and we'll drive around the block. We're sure to come across her. She hasn't had long enough to get far.'

They drove up and down the local roads. They stopped and asked everyone they passed. They called into the post office.

They got out and searched the small park at the crossroads. But Eileen had disappeared.

Philip glanced at Louise's pale face. 'She'll be all right, believe me.'

She looked at him, eyes enormous with worry.

'Look, let's go back to the house, just to check she's not there by now. And then I think we should call the police.'

'Oh, Philip, this is awful! How could I let this happen? How could I have done this?'

'Louise, you've done nothing. You're not to blame. Things like this happen. Come on, we'll find her. We will.'

'Richard will be furious . . .'

'He may not need to know, if she turns up fairly quickly. Has she got any friends? Anyone she might have felt like popping in to see?'

Louise's expression changed. 'Of course! Her friend Connie. Eileen may have been trying to find her. She's always talking about her, although neither of them is well enough these days to get out and see each other much.'

'Where does Connie live?'

'A couple of streets away, but I don't think Eileen would remember how to get there.'

'Is she on the phone?'

Louise nodded.

'Then let's go home in case your mother-in-law's got herself back to the house. We can ring Connie and anyone else you can think of from there.'

Louise didn't answer as she allowed him to propel her back to the car.

But Eileen was not at home. And Connie hadn't seen her.

Louise sat down heavily on the edge of the settee, her face pale, hands knotted together.

Philip knelt down in front of her and took her shaking hands in his.

'I'll ring the police. They may have had a report in already.'

'Whatever will they think of me? They'll think I've been so irresponsible. How could I have done this?'

He reached up to cup her face in his hands so that she had no choice but to look directly at him.

'Louise, this is not your fault. You have nothing at all to blame yourself for. You must believe that.'

Her face was etched with misery and fear, and when the tears came she tilted her head so that it rested in the circle of his hand. Her eyes closed as she stayed there for a moment, comforted by the solid reassurance of him. It was a gesture of childlike trust – and the feeling of compassion and care that swept through Philip as he held her face took him by surprise.

Her eyes opened, huge and dark with tears. He watched her silently, stroking her cheek, touched by the depth of sadness in her. She was not crying for her mother-in-law. She was crying for herself.

'When this is over,' he said quietly, 'if you're ready – will you talk to me, really talk to me? Only if you'd like to . . .'

With the faintest nod of her head, she almost smiled through her tears. Gently, she covered his hand with her own, as it circled her face.

'What a very special man you are, Philip Barnes. Or do women blub over you all the time?'

He chuckled. 'Oh, all the time. Occupational hazard . . .'

She moved away and fumbled for her handkerchief.

'What a mess of a woman you must think me. Always bawling my eyes out!'

'I'm glad you feel you can. It's a great compliment.'

'I don't usually fall to pieces like this.'

'I know that.'

'Do you?'

'Come on,' he said, standing up. 'Let's make this phone call, and get a bit of help finding Eileen.'

Louise couldn't bear to listen. Instead she disappeared into the bathroom, coming out minutes later, her face shiny from being rinsed in cold water, her lipstick freshly applied.

He stood up as she came into the lounge. 'They're sending someone round.'

'They've not heard from anyone who's seen her then?'

'Apparently not. Look,' he said, taking her by the shoulders, 'I'm going to drive around a bit more, just in case I spot her. You stay here, in case the police arrive.'

'Should I ring Richard? Let him know what's happened.'

Fear crept back into her expression.

'Only you can answer that. But she's been gone for such a short time – and she may be back at any moment. There's probably nothing to worry about. Why not give it a little longer, before worrying him unnecessarily?'

'Yes,' she whispered gratefully. 'That's the best idea.'

With Philip gone, Louise paced the house, going over the possibilities in her head. The hands of the clock moved slowly, so slowly – and still there was no news. No Philip. No police. No Eileen.

She jumped as the clock chimed once. Quarter past eleven.

At twenty-five past, she went out to fill the kettle. She'd make a cup of tea. Philip might like that when he got back. Where was he? How far away was he looking? Had he found her? Was she ill or hurt? Why was he taking so long?

She walked out of the kitchen without switching the kettle on.

By twenty to, she was staring out of the french doors, her thumb nail between her teeth in a childlike gesture of nervousness.

She glanced at the clock. Quarter to twelve. Where on earth were the police? Where was Philip? And where, oh, where, was Eileen?

She jumped at the shrill ringing of the telephone, and seized the receiver with a mixture of dread and relief.

'Hello!'

'Is that Mrs Kenton?'

'Yes.'

'The Desk Sergeant here, from Walsworth Road police station. I believe you're missing an elderly lady?'

'Yes! Are you sending an officer round?'

'Better than that. We think we've found her.'

Louise's knees buckled with relief. 'Where? Is she OK? What happened?'

'As far as I know, she's fine. She's at Dacre Road Junior School. Apparently, she wandered in to join the children at play time. One of the teachers eventually found her walking along a corridor in her dressing gown.'

'Thank God! Oh, thank God she's OK! Where is she now? Should I come and collect her?'

'Not to worry, madam. One of our officers is at the scene. They should be bringing her home any minute. I just thought you'd like to hear the good news as soon as possible.'

'Yes. Oh, yes!'

'Can I leave it to you to let her doctor know? He should call round and see her once she's back, just to make sure no harm's been done. She's obviously got some sort of a problem?'

'Dementia. It's been getting much worse lately.'

'She lives with you, does she?'

'Yes.'

'Had to go out, did you?'

'No, nothing like that. I was just paying the milkman when the phone rang. I must have left the door open. A minute later, when I got off the phone, she'd gone.'

'Well, madam, my officer, and probably the doctor too, will want to talk to you and the family, to make sure the lady is quite safe in future. It seems to have ended well this time – but who knows, if it should happen again?'

Louise's mouth went dry.

'Right, madam. They should be with you shortly.'

'Thank you. Thank you so much. Goodbye.'

The doorbell rang. She scooted to the door to find Philip there. Her expression alone told him the good news.

An untouched cup of tea, and fifteen minutes later, a police car drew up outside. Louise flung open the front door long before Eileen, supported by a young policewoman, made her slow way up the garden path. She was wearing her pink fluffy dressing gown, curlers still in one side of her hair, and for once her new Christmas slippers were on her feet rather than clutched in her arms. Her eyes opened wide as she spotted Louise.

'I couldn't find him. I was sure I heard Richard. I wonder where he's got to?'

Louise said nothing. She couldn't. She simply clasped Eileen to her in relief and exasperation.

The policewoman gently led the two of them inside, where Eileen quickly settled into her favourite chair and switched on the television.

'Looks like there's no damage done,' commented the police-woman. 'She just appeared in Dacre Road School playground. The children thought it was a hoot. When they went in for classes, she went in too. It was the headmaster who rang us, because he didn't recognise her at all. Apparently, though, one of the girls there did – a pupil of yours. You teach the piano, don't you?'

As Louise nodded the doorbell rang again. Philip let in the local GP, Dr Bevan. A quick check and a chat to Eileen, in between scenes on the TV soap she refused to stop watching, soon convinced him her adventure had done her no harm.

'So, Doctor, are you concerned that arrangements should be made to prevent this happening again?' It was the policewoman who spoke. 'The outcome this morning could have been very different, you know.'

Dr Bevan sat himself down at one end of the settee. 'Well, she's suffering from dementia. Her mind wanders. She is unaware of the consequences of her actions. She has little sense of time or place. She forgets who people are, even those closest to her. It's a fairly typical case, really.' He turned to Louise. 'Do you feel she's getting worse? Becoming a danger to herself and others?'

Louise glanced in Philip's direction before she spoke. 'No, this morning was just a silly error on my part. I left the door open for the milkman and got distracted. It was unforgivable of me. My fault entirely.'

'Perhaps not, Louise,' said the doctor gently. 'Dementia patients are extremely trying and time-consuming for the carers in the household. Perhaps Eileen is getting to the stage where she needs more professional help. A residential home, maybe?'

Louise flushed red as she answered, 'Absolutely not. Richard would never hear of it.'

'But he's seldom here, is he?' persisted the doctor. 'It's you who's bearing the brunt of this.'

'I'm fine. I'm coping just fine. Things are OK, really.'

'Are you sure, Louise? With your history, it's every bit as important to take care of you as it is of Eileen.'

Louise shot an embarrassed glance in Philip's direction.

'Please, I'm doing fine, just fine!' Louise's face was pale, as she picked furiously at the skin on the side of her thumb.

'How are you doing these days?' Dr Bevan continued quietly. 'You haven't been to see me lately.'

She shook her head.

'Are you keeping on top of things? Feeling OK?'

Another nod.

'You haven't been in for your prescription for some time. I checked before I came out.'

'I don't feel I need them any more,' replied Louise, looking directly at him.

'Well, that's great!' the doctor replied, returning her gaze. 'But just remember that I'm here any time you'd like a chat –

not about you, necessarily, but about Eileen too. In fact, when Richard's back, how about me popping round then? We could talk over what you both feel is best as far as Eileen's care is concerned.'

'No!' Louise's answer was abrupt and definite. 'No, please, we're fine. This morning was just an accident, a silly accident. Over now. No harm done . . .'

The doctor eyed her for several seconds before he got to his feet.

'Right, I must go. But I'd like you to make an appointment to see me in the surgery, Louise, within the next couple of weeks. Bring Eileen with you. I want to check you both over.'

She made no reply.

Philip watched Louise from the corner of the room, as the doctor and policewoman said their goodbyes, and left. She felt his gaze on her. He was wondering about her, she knew. Curious to know what her 'history' was. Questions hung in the air. She said nothing, and to her relief neither did he.

'Oh, the Taize music!' he said at last. 'I left it in the car in all the excitement. Are you still willing . . . ?'

'Yes, of course.' Her relief at the change of subject was plain. 'I'll come out and get it.' She hurried towards the front door, chuckling as she grabbed the house keys from the hall stand on the way.

'I'll shut the door this time. She's not going to escape again.'

The music book safely in Louise's hands, she stood beside Philip as he opened the driver's door.

'Philip, thank you for this morning. Thank you for just being here. For being you.'

'I'm always here, Louise. Any time. If you need a hand with Eileen – talk to me. We may be able to organise help for you through the church. After all, you're doing so much for us. We're your friends. Call on us.'

Louise returned the warmth of his smile. 'You're my friend, I know that. And I'm grateful, more than you know.'

Philip was thoughtful as he drove away. What an enigma Louise was turning out to be. She fascinated him in so many ways – this woman who could look so desolate one moment, and quite radiant the next on the rare occasions when a smile lit up her face.

Chapter Five

Months after the St John's pantomime had come, been and gone, people talked about it. Everyone who was anyone in the area was there. Tickets were like gold dust. Two members of the Over-60s Club stood for three hours at the door to be sure of front-row seats on the first night, and they'd sold out of icecreams before the end of the interval during the Friday performance. Those who couldn't get a seat had to wait for the report in Saturday's local paper, which was topped with a particularly fetching picture of the vicar as an Ugly Sister, complete with bulging bodice, painted lips, and a Kiss Me Quick hat balanced on top of his curly blonde wig.

'A triumph of imagination, enthusiasm and slapstick!' read the report. 'Producer Sue Golding allows for the spontaneity and comic talents of her cast, creating a performance which often has the audience weeping in the aisles – for one reason or another.'

'What does that mean?' demanded Sue, as she joined Philip and Ruth at their kitchen table that morning, reading the first copy of the paper they'd been able to lay hands on. 'Were they crying with laughter because they liked us, or because they couldn't believe how bad it was?'

'Sue, it was brilliant, just brilliant,' said Ruth. 'I went out into the audience last night and they loved every minute. It couldn't matter less that things didn't always go precisely as planned . . .'

'Look, I just didn't see that wet patch on the stage,' said Philip, helping himself to a biscuit. 'Those dwarfs had left flour and water everywhere after their kitchen scene. I was flat on my back before I knew it!'

Ruth was almost tearful with laughter. 'At least you had your bloomers on! If the Bishop had only seen you then . . .'

'The Bishop! I must remember to ring him back today. He wants to talk about the arrangements for the church centre opening – as if I've had time to give it any thought at all over the last few weeks.'

'Do you still want the choir to do something special for that service?' asked Ruth. 'Only we were talking about that the other day – and what with Bill being ill, we wondered how much we could manage without him.'

'Won't Louise help?' asked Sue, dunking her biscuit into her coffee cup.

Philip looked thoughtful for a moment. 'I'm sure she would, and she'd do a marvellous job. But I feel we're asking a lot of her already . . .'

'But she seems to be enjoying it.' replied Sue. 'Loving it, even.'

'Well, she does have her own family to consider.'

'Do they mind, then?'

Philip took a gulp of coffee.

'I think her husband might. I've not met him, but I get the impression he's not very supportive about this.'

'Yet her daughter couldn't be nicer,' said Ruth, grinning in Sue's direction. 'You know she's been here a few times, with Steven. He's playing it very cool if any of us mention her, but they do seem to be getting along quite well.'

'Love's young dream!' Sue downed the last gulp of coffee. 'I could do with a bit of that.'

Ruth covered her friend's hand as she spoke. 'It'll come, Sue.

Probably some big impresario from the city will hear of your success as a producer and . . .'

'. . . whisk me away from all this? Some hope! Anyway, I'd rather have no man around at all, than one who stops me doing what I really want to do, like Louise's husband.'

'I can't say I know her very well, even after all these weeks,' said Ruth. 'She's so busy during rehearsals and services – and, of course, always scurries off really quickly at the end.'

'She's a bit of a mouse, isn't she? Hardly says a word, and I can never fathom anyone like that. She's nice-looking though, in a funny sort of way. Don't you think so, Philip? Give us a man's opinion?'

He grimaced. 'Oh, that's a minefield. I'm not getting into this conversation. Strictly girls' talk!'

'Oh, go on, Philip.' Sue was unstoppable. 'Do you think she's attractive? Don't men always fall over themselves for delicate little ladies who seem in need of their manly protection? You know, women who actually *are* very capable, but *look* helpless? And don't men go for women like her, who seem reserved and mysterious, because they don't say a lot – when the truth is they really haven't got a lot to say? Do you think that's where I'm going wrong?'

'Look, I haven't even thought about the way Louise looks. I just think she's an extremely nice person – talented, and very generous with her time, especially when she's got so much on her plate at the moment.'

'Like what?' demanded Sue. 'Come on, Philip. Tell us all. Has she got a dark secret we should all know about?'

He pushed his chair back abruptly and stood up. 'Got to go. I'll be down at the hospital if anyone needs me.' He dropped a kiss on his wife's head. ''Bye, love. See you later.'

The two women watched as he left the kitchen without a backward glance.

'Well!' said Sue dramatically. 'Hit a raw nerve there, didn't we? You'll have to watch him, Ruth. He's obviously fallen under the Louise Spell, just like every other man in the church!'

And as the thought of her husband even looking in the direction of another woman was so unlikely, Ruth joined her in delighted laughter.

'Please, Richard, it would mean so much to me if you'd come.'

'Louise, it's really not my scene.'

'But I've met some lovely people through this pantomime, *local* people, our neighbours. You're away so much, people must think we're a single-parent family!'

'Don't be ridiculous, Louise. Does it matter what people think? I've got a lot of work on my mind at the moment, and really don't want to take on more commitment right now.'

'How can going to an end-of-show party be a commitment? You might even enjoy it!'

'Look, it's just not me. Let's leave it, shall we?'

Louise bit her lower lip to stop it trembling. As he turned back to his computer screen, she watched him for a few seconds, then moved over absent-mindedly to tidy a few tapes and books on his shelf.

'Richard, please. This is important to me.'

With an exaggerated sigh, he stopped writing and sat back in his chair. Louise moved across to him, and put her hands on his shoulders.

'We do so little together nowadays. I sometimes feel I haven't got a husband at all.'

'Louise, you're being melodramatic, and I've got to get this report done. Can't this wait till later?'

'But the party's tonight. And Lizzie will be coming with me. Couldn't we all go together? Please, Richard?'

Slowly, he turned round to face her.

'And who will look after Mother?'

'How about Mrs Betts? She'd come and stay overnight, if I asked her. I'm sure she would.'

His eyes were cold as he replied. 'After that episode the other week, I'm not prepared to leave Mother with just anyone. She could have been killed.'

Two hot patches of fury coloured Louise's cheeks. 'Now you're the one who's being melodramatic. There was never any danger. She was only gone a few minutes before I started the search for her . . .'

'She was out on the road in her dressing gown and curlers. It was the busiest time of the morning, cars everywhere. We're lucky it was a police car and not an ambulance that brought her home.'

'Look, her mind's going! She's always wandering off, although admittedly usually round the house. But I can't keep her under lock and key!'

'Then clearly the front door should be kept closed.'

'Oh, for heaven's sake, Richard, I've explained all that . . .'

'Louise, if I can't trust my own wife, why should I trust anyone else? A dotty old neighbour like Mrs Betts? I really don't think so.'

To her horror, Louise felt her eyes prick with tears. She wouldn't cry. She must never let him see how much he hurt her. She stood in awkward silence as he turned back to the computer screen, his attention apparently absorbed. She was dismissed.

Louise stood rooted to the spot, unsure what to do next. It was some minutes before she spoke.

'Why are you always so angry, Richard? Is it me? Is it us, the family? Is it work? Are you unhappy there?'

He said nothing, eyes fixed on the screen before him.

'Can I help? Can we talk about what's happening to us?'

'Is there an *us*?'

The shrill ringing of the telephone startled them both.

Richard reached out for the receiver, his face stony, but as soon as he heard what was obviously a woman's voice at the end of the line, his expression changed to a warm smile.

'Oh, hi! Hold on just one minute.'

He put his hand over the mouthpiece and turned to glare at Louise. 'This is important,' he said coldly, 'and it's business.'

Humiliated, she turned on her heel, and although she closed the door with a bang behind her, she stopped immediately to lean against the door frame, her heart racing.

She shouldn't have done. If she'd moved on, she wouldn't have overheard the start of his conversation.

'Darling, how did it go last night? Did you miss me . . . ?'

Louise's hand tightened into a fist and she dug her nails into her palm as she slipped downstairs. Then at last, behind the shelter of the kitchen door, she covered her face with her hands, overwhelmed with despair and cold anger.

The last night performance was a triumph. For the first time during the run, no one needed prompting, probably because, by then, most of the lines were ad libs and much more entertaining than the script had ever been! The smallest, and most precocious, of the Seven Dwarfs burst into tears when Sue made her go on stage just as she announced dramatically that she needed the loo – now! And when, during the 'Two Ballerinas, One Large Balloon' routine, to the accompanying music of the Sugar Plum Fairy, the vicar nearly lost his tights as he caught them on the other Ugly Sister's tiara, it brought the house down!

But for Lizzie, watching with Steven from their seats towards the back of the hall, the most heart-warming moment came during the last curtain call when Philip brought everyone to silence.

'Ladies and gentlemen, I'd like you to give a special round of applause to someone who's worked extremely hard to make this whole event possible. When Bill Spellman was taken ill, we thought the pantomime would have to be abandoned – that is, until a wonderful lady stepped in, bringing her own brand of magic and inspiration to our show. She's had practically no time to rehearse, and we've worked her fingers to the bone – yet not once has she complained or told us what she *really* thinks of us! As a token of our appreciation and heartfelt thanks, we'd like to present her with a little gift from us all. Ladies and gentlemen, Louise Kenton!'

Pink with happy embarrassment, Louise made her way on to the stage, to be presented with a huge bouquet from the smallest dwarf, who hadn't lost the scowl from her face since the loo incident. Then Philip handed her a card, whispering, 'That's your contract for next year's panto!' before clasping her in a bearhug and planting a kiss on both her cheeks. He looked down into her sparkling eyes and wondered how anyone could ever think her plain. She looked lovely, blushing, radiant, and obviously overwhelmed.

It was well over an hour later before he spotted her again. By that time, the party was in full swing. Sausage rolls, cheese, French bread and bottles had appeared from every lady performer's shopping bag, and the sixties tape that someone had dug out had got most of the cast on the floor, dancing and singing their heads off. Louise was standing alone in the corner of the room, watching fondly as Lizzie and Steven stamped and clapped with the best of them in the middle of the crowd. Philip quietly made his way around the dancers and stood at her side for some time before he spoke.

'They look good together, don't they? Should we be talking terms?'

She giggled. 'Oh, you know what we mums are like. No one will ever be good enough for our daughters! Mind you, your Steven certainly has pedigree. He comes from good stock.'

'Well, I must say he's got impeccable taste. He gets it from his father, you know.'

Louise turned her laughing face towards his then looked at him more closely, stretching out to rub her finger across the lid of his right eye. 'Should I worry about my daughter getting involved with a family of men who wear eye make-up?'

'Oh, I'm not, am I? I thought I'd got it all off.' He groped in his pocket for a hankie, and, when none was forthcoming, Louise reached out to turn his face towards her. Gently, so it was almost a caress, she began to wipe away the remains of make-up with her finger. Her expression was oddly tender and intimate, and Philip felt her breath warm on his face as he gazed down into the soft darkness of her eyes. How easy it would be to kiss her . . . so easy . . .

Startled by the unexpected turn of his thoughts, he pulled back, smiling as he reached up to the side of his face to take her hand. 'Come on, you! Time we had a dance!'

Across the room, the whole interchange caught the eye of Sue, who'd been listening half-heartedly to Barbara in the semi-darkness. As her gaze rested on Philip and Louise, now dancing with their arms around each other in the middle of a sea of people dancing on their own, Barbara's eyes followed.

And when Ruth, who was making her way over to Sue with two drinks in her hand, wondered what they were looking at, she stopped in her tracks as she followed their gaze. She watched as Louise looked up into Philip's eyes. She saw the expression on her husband's face as he held her, swaying closely with Louise on the dance floor. And as Ruth looked, a tiny shudder of premonition drained like icy water down her spine.

It was a rather bleary-eyed Philip who opened the church early next morning to prepare for the family service at nine-thirty. With some satisfaction he realised he wasn't the only one suffering from the after-effects of the night before. Brian, as church warden, was usually in the building some time before him. Not today, though. That'll teach him to stay up all hours of the night, Philip thought wryly to himself. It was a lesson he could do with remembering too!

Brian, when he arrived, was irritatingly cheerful. Eyeing Philip's pale face with interest, he put a companionable arm round his friend's shoulders.

'Never mind, Phil. I reckon a lot of the regulars will be catching up on their beauty sleep this morning.'

He was right. Most of the choir, who had formed the backbone of the chorus for the panto, were missing. The congregation, on the other hand, were out in numbers, brimming over with enthusiasm about the wonderful pantomime; saying, far too loudly for Philip's delicate state, that it was the best production the church had ever mustered.

'And here's the little lady who made it all happen!' gushed Bert Hillyer who, with his wife Margie, was among the most regular members of the congregation. 'Well done, my dear! A splendid performance.'

Catching Philip's eye across the small group of people as she made her way towards the front of the church, Louise smiled. 'Well, this morning won't be much of a performance, Bert, unless I go and sort the music out. Excuse me.'

Brian was still at Philip's side as the two of them watched her move away and up to the organ.

'Funny her husband didn't come along last night. I rather thought he would.'

Philip turned abruptly from watching Louise's progress. 'Busy, I expect,' he replied non-committally. 'He's often away from home.'

'Have you met him?'

'No.'

'Things all right there, do you think?'

Philip stared at Brian for a second. 'I've really no idea. Why would I? I don't know the man – and I hardly know her.'

'It didn't look that way last night.'

'What?'

'When the two of you were huddled in that corner, doing whatever it was she was doing to your face, and then going off to smooch together on the dance floor – there was quite a lot of interest in that elsewhere in the room.'

Philip ran his fingers through his thick dark hair. 'Oh, for heaven's sake, haven't people got anything better to think about?'

'They were just teasing, Nothing serious.' Brian paused, choosing his words carefully. 'But you know what they're like . . .'

Philip simply glared at him in disbelief, unable to reply.

'Philip!' It was Louise, calling to him urgently from her seat at the organ. 'Can I just check a couple of things with you before we start?'

With one last glance in Brian's direction, Philip headed over to where Louise was waiting for him.

In the doorway of the vestry, Rachel watched her dad with affection. She was standing with her mother and the few members of the choir who had turned up. She glanced up at Ruth, noticing with satisfaction that her mum didn't seem able to take her eyes off Dad either. They might be old, she thought, but how reassuring it was to see they were still so soppy about each other. Quaint, really – but good to know.

'The trouble is,' said Louise to Philip, as she walked towards the door of the church on their way out after the service, 'I don't really understand the significance of what I'm playing during the Eucharist. I was a kid when I last went to church regularly, and I've forgotten so much – if I ever understood it at all. I have a feeling I could do a much better job, perhaps even make a few suggestions about how small changes in the music could add to the atmosphere of worship, if I were more familiar with the meaning of it all.'

'Louise, that's an excellent idea, and of course, I'd love to talk it through with you. Do you want to pop over to the Vicarage some time this week, and we can chat over a cup of tea?'

'Well', she said doubtfully, 'it's a bit difficult with my mum-in-law, you know, since the other day!'

He touched her arm gently. 'I quite understand. I'll come to you then. How about Tuesday? That's officially my day off so I won't be watching the clock all the time. We can talk at leisure.'

'Thank you, Philip. I'll see you then.'

'I'll look forward to it!' And as he turned to join Ruth, who was talking to Barbara just outside the church door, warmth flooded through him as he realised he was looking forward to spending time with Louise rather more than he probably should.

Sunday lunch at the Kenton house was a quiet affair. Matthew had gone back to university, so just Louise, Lizzie and Richard sat down to the leg of roast lamb that was always a family favourite. Eileen was asleep. She'd taken to nodding off at peculiar times of day, as a result of which she'd become a very light sleeper at other times. Rarely a night went by nowadays, without Louise finding a disorientated Eileen wandering about the house, in need of a guiding hand to take her back to bed.

But between Richard and Louise, this lunch was not simply quiet, it was painfully silent. He hadn't said a word to her all morning. Was he annoyed that she'd stayed so long at the end-of-show party the night before? Was he just annoyed anyway, at some work problem she knew nothing about? Or were impatience and disinterest so much a part of his attitude to home life nowadays that he simply had nothing to say to his wife and daughter?

In fairness, Lizzie didn't seem to notice. The sparkle that had appeared in her eye the minute Steven Barnes had come on the scene had seen her blossom from a gauche, introverted sixteen year old to a confident, pretty young woman. Louise watched with affection as she chatted on about how great the party had been, how nice the Barnes family were, and how entertaining and wonderful Steven was – yes, plenty about how entertaining and wonderful Steven was! Every word he'd uttered, every joke they'd shared, were faithfully relayed, as if they were sure to be of as much significance to her parents as they were to her. Louise smiled to herself. Had she ever been that young and excited? She glanced at her husband, engrossed in his meal. Yes, she thought, I remember feeling just like that about you. Did I ever fill your thoughts in the same way? And because she knew in her heart the answer to that question, her smile dropped away.

'Mum, will it be all right if I do down to the Wimpy now?'

'But you've only just had lunch!'

'We're not eating. It's only for coffee.'

'What about your homework?'

'Done it. Well, most of it.'

'How long will the rest take you?'

'Mum, I'll get it done. I always do.'

'Look, get it done first, then I'll drive you down to the Wimpy.'

'No, thanks.'

'But it'll be much quicker for you . . .'

'Mum, we're walking. Steven and I. We want to walk.'

'Oh,' replied Louise lamely.

Suddenly, Richard pushed back his chair and stood up. 'I'm off too. You know I'm driving to London this afternoon.'

'Are you? You didn't say . . .'

'I did, Louise. You just didn't hear.'

'When are you back?'

'Wednesday – probably.'

'You're disappearing for three days, and you're only just mentioning it?'

'I mentioned it, Louise. You didn't listen.'

She stood up, following him towards the door. 'But what

about your mum's visit to Dr Bevan on Tuesday morning? Didn't you mean to be here for that?'

'Well, I can't now. You'll have to take her.'

'But you said you wanted to be there. You said you couldn't trust anyone else to ask the right questions, let alone understand the answers. You said . . .'

'Have you been to see Dr Bevan yet, Louise?' His question was direct, his face hard.

'No, there hasn't been much time, what with the show . . .'

'He said he wanted to see you. Why haven't you made time?'

'Because there's no need. I'm fine.'

'Dr Bevan plainly didn't think so, or he wouldn't have insisted on your making an appointment to see him.'

'Richard, that was just a precaution. He was being thorough and thoughtful. There's nothing wrong with me. I'd know if there was.'

'You *never* know. That's the problem. You're the last person to know what's happening to you.'

'Richard, that's not fair!'

'Louise, in the past you've repeatedly become so morose and incompetent that the real responsibilities of life are lost to you.'

'Hardly *repeatedly*. A few times. Twice mainly – and both times there was a reason for that. I'd just had a baby . . .'

'Precisely! And the responsibilities of motherhood eluded you so much, you just let everything slip. All you could think of was yourself – you, and what you needed!'

'It was post–natal depression. It's quite common, not unusual at all . . .'

'How usual is it for a mother to care so little about her children that she tries to take her own life?'

For a moment Louise stared at him in stunned silence. Then her body seemed to crumple, her knees buckled, and she sank down heavily on the chair behind her.

'You're behaving very strangely these days, Louise, taking on too much, and these attacks of depression always happen when you try to overdo things. I worry about Mum's welfare when you're like this. And Dr Bevan is plainly worried too.'

Louise started picking nervously at the skin at the side of her thumb. She said nothing.

'Make an appointment. Go and see him. And I'll ring him later this week to ask what he thinks. Do you understand?' Richard spoke deliberately, as if she were an uncomprehending child.

'Do you understand?' he repeated.

She nodded dumbly. If she'd been looking at him, she might have seen his face soften a little.

'You must go, Louise. Please. Don't let me down.'

She looked up at him then, small and forlorn, sitting beside the debris of the meal she'd just cooked for them.

And by the time a single tear ran its glistening path down her cheek, he was already on his way upstairs, his mind full of what he needed to pack.

Later that week, when Philip popped into Bunyan Ward, Jill beckoned to him as he walked past the Sister's Office.

'Bad news about your girlfriend, I'm afraid. Minnie's not doing so well. I don't know quite what the trouble is. Nothing particularly medical, I reckon. She just seems worn out, as if she can't be bothered to make the effort to get better.'

'Has she had any visitors?'

Jill shook her head. 'Poor old dear. No one seems to love her.'

'Is she in pain?'

'Her hip must be sore, but she's not moving it much. She can't be persuaded out of bed, to get it going and build up her strength again. She's just lying there, fading away.'

'I'll go and see her.'

'Thanks, Philip, I'll organise a cuppa in a quarter of an hour or so. Come back and let me know if you get any life out of her.'

His progress to Minnie was slow as on the way he stopped to chat to several other patients, some familiar, some new. Finally, he approached the small, huddled figure, almost invisible under the neat covers of her bed.

An odd tenderness touched him as he looked down at her pale little face. Even in sleep, she seemed ill at ease, uncomfortable, breathing in shallow, irregular gasps. So frail, so vulnerable, so very much alone.

He reached out to pull in the chair that stood a few feet from the bed, and sat down so that his face was just a few inches from hers. Without thinking, he began to stroke the soft hair on her forehead, as he would to comfort Rachel or Mark. At first she didn't stir, and then, as if she had to drag herself back from somewhere far away, slowly, hesitantly, she opened her eyes. He knew she saw him. He could tell from the smile that flickered across her lips, only to disappear again as pain engulfed her. Wearily, her eyes closed, and he thought she'd fallen back to sleep.

For minutes he sat beside her in silence, still stroking her head, lost in his own thoughts. And then, with her eyes still closed, her voice barely more than a whisper, she said, 'I want to go now. I want to die.'

He took her hand then. 'In God's good time, Minnie, you will. And he'll be there to receive you. But Sister tells me that you've got plenty of living to do first. There's no reason why you shouldn't make a good recovery.'

'She's wrong. And so are you. I won't get better.'

'You won't if you don't put your heart into it! Where's your fighting spirit, Minnie? Where's that determination that kept the shop going all those years? You *can* get better – and I promise I'll do all I can to make life more comfortable for you when you get out.'

She sighed. 'When I go out of here, it will be in a box.'

'Minnie . . .'

'I thought you'd understand. I don't want to get better. I want to go. Help me.' She clenched and released her hands in anguish and frustration.

'Minnie, don't say that. Let me get a nurse . . .'

'You know I've got nothing to live for. You tell me there are better things ahead. If you really believe that, help me!'

As Philip looked around helplessly, she clung to his hand, her expression urgent and tortured.

'Please, you mustn't talk like this. It's not right!'

'How can it be wrong to want to meet my Maker?'

'Only when the time is right – his time, not yours.'

The fight went out of her then. Her hunched shoulders fell, and she sank back again into her pillow.

'It's time for me to go. God knows that. Why don't you?'

'Everything all right here?'

Jill appeared at Philip's shoulder. 'OK, Minnie? Shall I plump up your pillow a bit, make you more comfy?'

The old lady said nothing, but as Sister fussed around her, her unblinking gaze was fixed on Philip, challenging and condemning.

Minutes later he was in Jill's office, still shaken from the encounter.

'Does that happen often?' he asked. 'Patients asking for help to die?'

She looked thoughtfully down into her tea. 'More than you probably think. And can you really blame them? It's not much of a life for someone like Minnie, is it?'

'What do you do? How do you react?'

'Professionally, we ignore it. Privately, I am more moved than I can say. Quite frankly, sometimes it would be the kindest thing to do. But I can't, I just can't. Life's too precious for that. I'm a Christian too, Philip, so you understand. I have no right to take a God-given life. No one has – not even if that life's their own.'

'Will she get better, do you think? Is this just a bad patch?'

Jill shrugged her shoulders, glancing through the glass towards Minnie's bed. 'Difficult to say. She's no spring chicken.'

'Can't you give her something to help her out of this depression?'

'Maybe. I'll have a word with the doctor. He'll probably come up with something stronger for the pain. It might knock her out for a bit, but that's probably not a bad thing for the time being. She may feel more confident and positive once she's rested.'

Philip followed her gaze towards Minnie's slight figure.

'Poor old thing,' he said, almost under his breath. 'Fancy being so low you'd actually prefer to stop living.'

'It happens' said Jill, 'and not just with elderly people either. It's harder to accept when someone comes in after a suicide attempt. I've seen how much it hurts the people who love them. I can't understand how they can squander something as precious as their own lives.'

'I suppose they're just running away, without thinking what they're running to,' replied Philip thoughtfully, perching on the desk as he spoke. 'Perhaps they think it will just be oblivion, but we Christians know that death is not the end. And just as God will be there for them then, he's here for them now, when they need it. All they have to do is trust in him and they'll find the strength to cope, however dreadful things may seem.'

Jill smiled wryly. 'As a member of your congregation, I can't dispute that. But as a nurse – well, I've seen such despair. It seems to me that anyone, absolutely anyone, can be brought to a point where death may seem more appealing than carrying on with life. It doesn't have to be something you plan, or even think about in any rational way. It can be an instant reaction to the deepest, blackest despair, where there's no hope, no help, and no conscience. No thought of anyone else. No thought at all. Just run away. A few Paracetamols, and sink into nothing. No pain. No fear. No failure. No guilt. Just the comforting possibility of nothing at all.'

The door to the office opened abruptly as a young nurse popped her head in to tell Jill some relatives were asking to speak to her.

Philip looked at this watch. 'Five o'clock. I've got to go too. Do you mind if I ring Ruth from your office, just to let her know I've one more call to make before I get back?'

'Help yourself. See you on Sunday.'

The phone rang for some time before Ruth picked it up. 'Sorry, love,' she said breathlessly. 'I was just outside talking to Ken, the decorator. He says he and his team are ready to start on the new centre next week, if that's all right with us? He'd like to have a proper chat to you about it.'

'Is he still there?'

'No, he had to leave, but he'd like you to phone him this evening. Before seven, if possible.'

'That should be fine. I promised I'd pop over to see Louise this evening so I'm going straight there now. I should only be an hour or so.'

There was the briefest of hesitations before Ruth replied, 'Something about music, is it?'

'In a way. She feels she doesn't understand enough about the Eucharist Service, and it would help her to make the music more relevant if she appreciated the meaning more.'

'Wouldn't it be easier to have discussions like that here, at the Vicarage?'

'Probably, but that's not really an option. She has her mother-in-law at home who needs constant care. Anyway, it's no trouble for me to pop in on my way back from the hospital. Jill sends her love, by the way.'

'Don't be long, Philip. We miss you.'

He chuckled. 'That's nice! And very unlike you to say so.'

'I don't need to say it, do I? You know how much we love you.'

'I love you too, And I'll be back before you know it.'

He replaced the receiver, smiling for a moment at the thought of Ruth's affection. Of all the blessings in his life, she was the dearest.

Digging into his pocket for the car keys, there was a spring in his step as he headed for the hospital exit, and Louise.

Slowly, Ruth replaced the receiver, gazing at the phone for some moments before she moved away. At the sink, she ran hot water, squeezed in washing-up liquid, automatically washing the dishes she'd used to prepare that night's supper. As she worked, she tried to analyse her thoughts about Philip's phone call. He was going to see Louise, a parishioner, a friend, an enthusiastic helper in their church. What was wrong with that?

Nothing at all – except it bothered her. Louise bothered her. Ruth couldn't put her finger on exactly what it was about that quiet, apparently unassuming woman that disturbed her so – but the very thought of Louise, and Philip's reaction to her, set tiny, cold alarm bells ringing.

What was it? She wasn't particularly pretty. Ordinary-looking really, but smart and neat. She didn't have much of a personality, at least not amongst the large circle of people at church where Ruth usually saw her. Mostly, she kept herself to herself. She wasn't a flirt. She was willing, anxious to please, but not in a pushy way.

What was it then that had men smiling fondly at her? What did Philip see in her?

An image of Louise's face swam into Ruth's mind, her face guileless, eyes large and brown.

Vulnerability. That was it. In her eyes there was old hurt – and the expectation of more to come.

And Ruth recalled the picture, etched into her memory, of Louise reaching out to touch Philip's face during the after-show party. What she had glimpsed in Louise at that moment was more than just friendship or even attraction. Deep in her eyes was need. A need to understand and be understood. A hunger for comfort and tenderness. Desire. Damage. Danger.

Ruth stopped washing up, hands still submerged in the soapy water.

Well, what better for someone who was damaged and unhappy than to seek the help and guidance of their local minister? And Louise couldn't possibly have found a better one than Philip. He was totally professional and experienced, a sympathetic listener, constructive with advice and support. That would be a great comfort to her. And it was a comfort to Ruth too. Philip was used to dealing with hurt and need. He was a trained minister. A professional.

So why was she so on edge about what was, after all, just part of a minister's job?

Because Philip was a man. And men could be very blind in the face of a vulnerable, admiring woman. And every instinct in Ruth's body told her that where Louise was concerned, Philip was out of his depth in the pools of need in her eyes.

Chapter Six

The end of February blew in with a flurry of snow and bitter north-east winds that froze the breath and chilled the bones. Brian puffed into his gloves to warm his fingers then turned the handle on the door to the new church centre. The sound of Radio 1 hit his cold ears as it blared around the building. Ken and his team were already at work although it was barely nine in the morning. Brian squeezed his comfortable waistline around a stepladder then picked his way through the decorating materials, planks of wood and dust sheets, to find three painters tackling what they hoped would be the final coat on the walls of the main hall.

'Everything going OK?' he yelled over the radio. 'Is there anything I can help with?'

Ken peered down from the top of the ladder. He was a cheerful hard worker, with a mop of fair hair that usually took on the hue of whatever colour he was painting that day.

'Well, I was thinking of going down to the wholesaler later, to get the other paint and the exterior coating we need for that side wall. Do you want me to organise the strip lights while I'm there?'

'That would be great!' shouted Brian in reply, taking off his glasses to clean away the sudden layer of dust that coated them.

'What time are you thinking of going? Shall I come with you, to pay the bill?'

'Do you know, mate, I could do with one of you at home!' chuckled Ken, turning back to his painting.

Brian took his time wandering around the building, relishing that now-familiar bubble of excitement he always felt as more and more areas of the new centre neared completion. In the six weeks since the decorating had begun, the place had been transformed from the building site it had been in the New Year. It was still cold, dusty and bare, of course, but already it was possible to picture the hall, kitchen, coffee shop area and the two small meeting rooms, full of life and people. This centre would put the church back where it belonged, right at the heart of community life, exactly where those long-ago builders who'd originally built St John's intended it to be.

Brian sighed, and looked at his watch. He had an appointment with the Archdeacon, Timothy Fulford, in an hour's time, to talk over finances, plans for the running of the centre, and the arrangements for Bishop David's opening ceremony on Good Friday. The meeting was set for three o'clock at the Vicarage, which would mean Mark would be home from school very shortly after they started. If Brian took his car over, Mark could earn himself a couple of pounds washing and polishing it. The boy couldn't be faulted on his determination to raise money for the bike he really wanted. Even his dad was impressed.

And perhaps, thought Brian, as he made his way out of the building, he could persuade Mark over for an hour or two on the train set in the loft before bed time. And with that possibility in mind, he smiled in spite of the cold wind that almost knocked him off his feet as he pulled the door shut behind him.

As Lizzie turned the corner halfway through her walk home from school, her delight at seeing Steven leaning against the wall was carefully concealed behind an expression she hoped was friendly but cool. He didn't wait every day, and she had learned never to expect him, but their meetings had gradually become more regular.

They never spoke about the fact they were spending an increasing amount of time in each other's company. They simply hung around together, sometimes deep in conversation, sometimes happy to be quiet together. They never talked about 'going-out', nor plans for the future. And they never mentioned that night at the 'Debbie' party either.

Lizzie thought a lot about why Steven didn't allow the subject to be mentioned. For her, it had been the most wonderful evening of her life. She couldn't forget a moment of it – the way they'd talked, danced, and held hands on the walk back to her house. And the way he'd kissed her . . .

But in the weeks since Christmas that kiss had never been repeated. Oh, he'd put a casual arm around her shoulders every now and then. He'd even held her hand a couple of times. But he'd never kissed her. And rarely did they share their time together with other friends. They were nearly always on their own, sometimes at her house but usually at the Vicarage. And if his friend Jamie was due to come around, then Lizzie was not invited.

Was he ashamed of her? Was he uncertain that someone like Jamie would approve of his choice? Was she his choice – or simply a convenience – fine for filling time when no one more interesting was available?

For Lizzie, who had never been the most confident or girls, Steven's behaviour was confusing. She had no doubt he liked her. When they were on their own, they never seemed to stop talking and laughing together. And once, when they were in her room and he'd begged her to play something on the cello, she'd caught an expression of real admiration in his eyes as he listened to her. But although she longed to speak of her feelings, to ask him about his, she said nothing and neither did he.

As she approached him now, school bag hanging heavily

from her shoulder, she noticed with pleasure how his face lit up the moment he saw her, only to be quickly hidden by a show of indifference as he fell into step beside her.

She sighed to herself. Perhaps this was enough for now, their secret to share, a delicate bud of feeling that needed nurturing so privately they couldn't even speak of it to each other. She watched his face, already so familiar to her, as he told her about the trouble he'd had with one of the teachers that afternoon – but her thoughts were her own, savouring the warmth that coursed through her body at the thought that one day, that dear face might be near enough to her own to kiss her again.

Philip sat in the semi-darkness of the church, letting the music flow through his mind and body. He closed his eyes, surrendering his senses to the emotion, in all its beauty and power. He could picture the scene so graphically – three crosses high on the hill as the sunlight fell behind them, the resignation, the suffering, the dignity of the Passion. No words were needed. All the pathos, all the pain, all the wonder were there in the music. It was quite simply the most breathtakingly beautiful piece he'd ever heard.

Slowly, he opened his eyes to gaze at the woman who'd created a work of such perfection. Louise had her back to him, stroking the keys of the organ with exquisite tenderness. She played with her heart. She played with love.

And as Philip watched, he thought that a creation of such perception and beauty could only come from someone who was herself truly beautiful. He had seen the beauty in her on that very first occasion on Christmas Eve when he'd heard her play. In the couple of months since then, over countless hours of searching discussion, she'd very gradually allowed him the privilege of glimpsing fascinating depths within her. This shy, diffident woman had opened her soul to him, and he recognised the treasure there. He saw that the faith he rationalised with his mind, she was discovering in her heart. His belief was based on logic, learning and consideration. Hers was growing from instinct. Without churchgoing, without the complexities of theology, instinctively she knew God. Although she'd only recently come to recognise it, he had always been there, part of her very being.

Since the pantomime, Philip and Louise had been meeting almost daily. It had begun because she wanted to understand the real meaning of the service, to help her appreciate more about the role music could play within worship. But that was just the start. Philip had been a minister for years, trained to answer all the usual questions that were asked. But Louise didn't stop at the usual questions. She wanted to explore everything he said. She scrutinised each small detail. She demanded explanations, and the moment he slipped into jargon or complacency, she challenged him.

'But *how* can you say that this is a loving God, if he allows babies to be born who are suffering and in pain? Where's the love in that?'

'How do you know that Jesus was the Son of God? The Moslems and the Jews think that he was just a great prophet. How do you know they aren't right and you're the one who's wrong?'

'Do you really believe that life is planned and ordained for us, that nothing is left to chance? If I step out in front of a bus, and it kills me, surely that's my doing, not God's? My decision, my fault. What's God got to do with it?'

'If God's the guiding hand behind the whole of creation in all its complexity, how can I possibly believe that he can take a personal interest in insignificant little me? Why should he?'

'What is prayer? How should it feel? Why do I find it so difficult? How will I know when it's working?'

'How can I believe in something I can't see or prove? *Why* should I believe?'

Philip found himself exhilarated and absorbed by their discussions. Her hunger for answers was matched by a desire in him to share his own passionate belief in a way that would prove to her that it was true. He drew on all his knowledge and experience to answer and satisfy her questions – and slowly, like a flower unfolding, he watched as faith began to grow in her. In the end, she didn't need to analyse every little detail. It simply began to make sense to her. Instinctively, she believed, revealing a need and a depth within herself that she had never truly known was there.

And then, one afternoon, at the end of a long and oddly intimate discussion, Louise turned to him, 'Will you pray with me? Will you help me to reach out to God and invite him in? My prayers won't be worth much on their own. Help me. Please?'

As she held out her hand to clasp his, her eyes huge and bright, he gently drew them both down to their knees. Neither of them knew how long they stayed there. Neither remembered the words they used. But much later, when dusk had drawn long shadows around them, they were still kneeling together, hands tightly clasped, heads touching, locked in the shared belief that the Holy Spirit was at the heart of the small loving circle they created.

Love. That was what he saw in her eyes when she looked at him. And with a realisation which somehow didn't surprise him, he knew that same love was reflected in his own. A love that was above worldly dimension. The love of God.

Now, as he sat in the church listening to the music she'd written in preparation for the Good Friday service, when Bishop David would be with them to open the new centre, his emotions soared with the sound around him.

Finally, she drew to an end, and as the last notes echoed across the empty church, turned to face him, her expression anxious.

'Well? What do you think?'

He didn't answer immediately but stood to walk across the

church towards the organ stool. Slowly, he drew her to her feet, until their faces were almost touching.

'It's wonderful . . . the most beautiful thing I've ever heard.'

Because she closed her eyes with relief, then leant forward to rest her head upon his shoulder, neither of them noticed the door at the other end of the church swing shut as whoever had been standing there quietly left the building.

It was just on half-past three when Ruth drew her old green Metro to a standstill just down from the school gates. Perhaps she'd be too late to catch them, especially as they had no idea she'd be there. When the heavens opened just as she left the Tradecraft volunteers meeting that afternoon, she realised she might be in time to offer her youngsters a lift home. But had she missed them?

She switched off the engine and peered through the windscreen for as long as she could before the steady drizzle of rain blocked out everything around her. And even then she continued to stare at the window, the relentless tumble of raindrops seeming to echo the uncharacteristic melancholy that filled her.

Whatever was the matter with her? Was she sickening for something? Was that it? Could it be some bug that was dragging down her spirits? Did she need antibiotics? A tonic? A week in the sun?

But in her heart she knew it was none of these. She just wanted her husband back.

Philip. Her own dear Philip. Philip, her best friend, her confidant, her lover – at least until the past few weeks when loving her seemed to be the last thing on his mind. He was fading away, slipping from her grasp – and she didn't know how to stop it.

He wouldn't recognise it, of course. He probably didn't even know it was happening. That was clear whenever she tried to talk to him. Taking care to keep the conversation light, she'd asked him if he preferred his dinners dried up and re-heated, because that was how he usually ate them, at whatever late hour he eventually came in. She teased him about how their kids were saying they only remembered what he looked like when he came into their school once a fortnight, to take morning assembly. She told him she thought he was working too hard, and that he needed to take care of himself, as well as everyone else. He'd replied with long explanations about how much of his time and energy it took to keep the church centre on course, how many meetings he had to attend, how much financial planning there was, how many visits he had to make either to say 'thank you' for donations or to beg for more. And there was all the planning for the grand opening on Good Friday: invitations to send out, VIPs to involve, press releases to write, speeches to prepare . . .

And then there was Louise. She seemed to creep into their conversations more and more these days.

Louise. From the moment at the pantomime party when Ruth had seen the way she looked at Philip, she knew Louise would become part of their lives – welcome in his, a growing threat in hers. It was an odd thing that Ruth had never before worried about the many women who, over the years, had turned to Philip for support, guidance and comfort. He was their priest, a warm, friendly man who combined the ability to listen with an intuitive sense of what to say and how to help. It wasn't at all surprising that Louise should turn to him in the same way. What was surprising was his reaction to her.

Ruth rubbed her fist against the steamy window, peering out to see if the schoolboy, huddled into his anorak, head down as he made his way towards the car, was Mark. Wrong anorak, she thought. Wrong age too. Far too old to be Mark. She leant forward, folding her arms over the steering wheel, straining her eyes in search of faces she recognised.

Philip was far too honest to think of hiding his deepening friendship with Louise. He didn't think twice about telling Ruth where he was going. And it didn't occur to him that she might not be as excited as he evidently was at Louise's steady path to faith. He talked about her openly. In fact nowadays, it seemed to Ruth, he talked of little else. Louise's name would be mentioned in every context – about services, about the centre opening, about the youth club, about Steven.

Sometimes, it's as though the Kenton family's taking over my own, thought Ruth bitterly. If it's not Philip telling me how talented, sensitive and under-rated Louise is, then it's Steven talking about Lizzie all the time!

That was unfair, she told herself sternly. She was beginning to sound neurotic. Unfair – and unChristian.

She sighed. It was clear she had to talk to Philip about this. Other people took their problems to him and he sorted them out. She must talk to him too, pour out all her jumbled thoughts and let him reassure her, hold her, comfort her, as he always could. After all, they'd been married for twenty odd years. They had never kept anything from each other – at least, she didn't think so. They loved and trusted each other. They always had.

'And I always will.' To her surprise, Ruth spoke the words out loud, her head still buried in her arms.

She jumped at a sudden thumping on the window. She leant over to unlock the passenger door, and a wet, grinning Mark sank unceremoniously into the seat beside her.

'Brill, Mum! I wondered if you might come, with all this rain.' He opened the glove compartment. 'Got anything to eat?'

'At home I have. Did you see Rachel? Is she coming?'

'Yes, I did – and no, she's not. Drama practice.'

'And Steven?'

'Gone already. With Lizzie. Her mum took them both back to her house in the car.'

She would, thought Ruth.

With a determined smile, she ruffled Mark's unruly hair then turned back to get the car going.

'More fool him! We've got hot dogs for tea, his favourite – and I bet he'll be home late, and miss them.'

'I'll have his!'

She laughed as she glanced in the side mirror, putting on the indicator as she slowly eased the car out of its parking place.

'Sounds fair enough to me!'

'Just one more box, then that's it.'

Sue leant into the back of her car to draw out the last of the leaflets and followed Barbara, already laden with boxes herself, through the front door.

'We'll put them over there, under the stairs. Brian can take them down to the church office later.'

Barbara straightened up carefully, and with obvious discomfort. Sue eyed her thoughtfully.

'You know, you ought to come along to my keep fit class. It's for all ages and would really help to keep you supple.'

'Not my scene at all,' replied Barbara briskly, turning towards the kitchen. 'Now, coffee. I can fit in ten minutes before I have to leave.'

Sue smiled to herself. Barbara always managed to make an invitation sound like a huge favour. The worst thing was that her schoolma'am attitude had even grown women, like Sue herself, reacting like anxious schoolgirls. She was pretty short of time too but to turn down coffee now would be unthinkable. She followed the older woman into the kitchen, noting with surprise that two cups and a plate of biscuits were already waiting on the work surface.

'Where's Brian this morning? Up at the centre?'

'Not on a Saturday,' replied Barbara. 'He's never around on a Saturday morning in the winter months. Football.'

'Brian plays football?'

Kettle in hand, Barbara turned round to look at Sue as if she were a deliberately simple-minded child.

'Of course not. At his age?' She turned back to continue pouring. 'No, he's always been in the habit of going along to watch Mark play on Saturday mornings. He's done that ever since Mark got into the Fearnhill Junior Team. Sugar?'

Sue shook her head and reached out to take the steaming cup. 'I wish my kids had a godfather like Brian. He really takes his responsibilities seriously.' She took a small sip then smiled wryly to herself. 'Mind you, I wish they had a *father* who had any idea of responsibility at all.'

Barbara's expression softened. 'How much do they see him?'

'Oh, now and then. Most weekends. Not often enough.'

'Do they mind him not being around all the time?'

'I'm not sure they mind very much at all – and that's the saddest thing really. They've grown apart from him. To them he's a bit like an uncle who comes every once in a while, bearing gifts and telling them off, but he's just not a part of their everyday lives any more. And he should be! That's the awful thing, he should be.'

'You still love him.' A statement, not a question.

Sue thought for a while before answering.

'I wouldn't want to live with him any more. I can't even be sure I like him. I'd love to have seen how he'd have managed if I'd been the one to walk out with someone else, leaving him with two kids to bring up on his own! He's selfish, immature, inadequate . . .' She lifted her cup, holding it in mid-air without drinking from it.

'And you love him.'

'Old habits die hard, don't they? I suppose I probably do, Pathetic, aren't I?'

'Well, you embarked on marriage and parenthood as a couple. You made a promise to stay together, and you expected him to keep it. It's unfair of him to walk away and leave you to cope on your own, just because some floozy threw herself at him.'

'She didn't even stay with him, that's the bit that really gets me! She broke up our marriage, our home, our family – and then she waltzed off and left him!'

Barbara placed her coffee cup precisely in the middle of her place mat. 'Ah, but then, men can be particularly stupid where other women are concerned. Even those you'd expect better of . . .'

Sue eyed her with curiosity. 'Who? Who might you expect better of ?'

Carefully, Barbara ran a finger round the rim of her cup, as if checking that it was scrupulously clean.

'Well, I just think it would be a nice idea if young Mark's father could get along to his football matches once in a while, rather than being too busy with other things – and people – to make time for his own son.'

'Philip? *Philip* should know better? About a woman?' Sue's eyes were alight with interest now. 'Do I gather we're talking about the ever fragrant, ever so wonderful Louise?'

'I'm not one to spread gossip . . .'

'Absolutely not, though I have noticed, of course . . .'

'She does seem to monopolise his time . . .'

'It is very hard to get hold of him these days . . .'

'Well, if you want to find him, the chances are he'll be over at Wycombe Avenue, at her house . . .'

'Why? Whatever do they do there?'

Barbara pursed her lips as she picked up her cup.

'That's exactly what we'd all like to know!'

'You're not saying he's doing something he shouldn't with her? Not Philip! I mean, I've known him and Ruth for years, and I've never seen such a loving couple.'

'Even the most devoted husband can have his head turned by a determined woman.'

'Determined? Do you think she's after him then? She's married . . .'

'Have you ever seen her husband with her? Not much of a marriage there, if you ask me!'

'And Philip is a priest. A very good one.'

'Exactly! But he's a man too. Gullible and open to flattery, like all men.'

Sue leant forward on her stool in her eagerness to reply. 'But Philip takes his role as a priest very seriously. He's not an insincere man. He's caring and warm-hearted. He's like that with everyone. I'm sure he's just being friendly with Louise. That's all it is.'

Barbara folded her arms. 'I saw them embracing.'

'What! Where? When was this?'

'A couple of days ago, in the church. She was playing the organ, some piece she's supposed to have written for the opening. I walked into the back of the church while he was listening to her – and just as I was about to go up and speak to them both, he went over and embraced her!'

'What do you mean – embraced? Kissed, you mean?'

'No, I didn't see them kiss . . .'

'So he was just hugging her? Look, you know Philip. He's always hugging people. Heavens, he hugged me enough when Martin left. I blubbed all over him for weeks! There was nothing in it then, and I bet there's nothing now, not so far as Philip's concerned.'

Barbara said nothing, with a look that said it all.

'But Ruth and Philip are madly in love with each other. Anyone can see that.'

'I'm not saying he doesn't love Ruth. I'm simply saying he's being less than wise where this Louise is concerned.'

Both women fell silent for a while, unsure that to say next. Finally, it was Sue who spoke.

'Do you think Ruth knows?'

'She's the trusting sort. Perhaps not.'

'Better that she doesn't.'

'Then someone must speak to him.'

'I'm sure this is all a big misunderstanding. He probably has no idea people are talking.'

'Well, I don't think there's much talk yet – but there will be, unless we nip this in the bud.'

'Brian? Could he have a word? He's always got on so well with Philip.'

'You're right. I'll discuss it with him today. He's the best person to handle this.' Barbara rose abruptly, looking at her watch. 'Quarter past eleven and I have an appointment at half-past.'

Suitably dismissed, Sue gathered up her keys and handbag. As the two women reached the front door, Barbara turned back towards her. 'Now, mum's the word. We must keep this strictly confidential. Not just for Ruth's sake, but for the whole parish. Agreed.'

'Certainly,' nodded Sue.

But for the rest of the day, she found she could think of little else. It became a hard nugget of worry that nagged away at her. Ruth was probably her best friend. And what are best friends for, if not to tell you what you probably ought to know?

That afternoon, Minnie looked better than Philip had ever seen her. There was a pale splash of colour in her cheeks, and she was even smiling as she watched him make his way over to her bed.

'Flowers again! You spoil me. Does your wife know you pinched them this time?'

'She was the one who cut them for you. She said she'd like to pop in and see you herself some time, if you fancy visitors?'

Minnie looked doubtful. 'Well, I know you. You're a minister. But she's a stranger. I'm not sure I want to meet anyone new, looking like this.'

'Oh, she won't mind. She's used to seeing me in the mornings. You can't get worse than that!'

'Poor woman. Got her work cut out with you, I reckon.'

'She certainly has. I'm always late for everything. I'm disorganised and untidy. I hang all my clothes on the floor each night, which drives her mad. I'm always saying yes, when I ought to say no more often. I'm over-enthusiastic, impatient, intolerant, and very grumpy for the first hour of every morning. Apart from that, I'm perfect in every way!'

'And you're a flirt. That must drive her mad too.'

Philip laughed. 'She'd never think anyone else would have me, and she's probably right!'

'Just as long as you don't find someone *you'd* like to have.'

There was the slightest hesitation before he answered. 'I'm a priest, Minnie.'

'And you're a lovely man too. You make everyone you meet feel special. Even me, and I'm nobody.'

He covered her hand with his. 'Minnie, you are very special indeed.'

'See what I mean? You don't even know you're doing it! You're a dear, warm-hearted person, and I bet all the ladies fall for you.'

The smile in his voice didn't quite reach his eyes. 'Not that I've noticed, Minnie, and not that I'd want it anyway. You see before you a very happily married family man. Nothing on earth would make me want to change that.'

She peered at him for several seconds before her expression changed. Pain flashed across her face as she shifted in the bed, trying to find a more comfortable position. Philip watched her anxiously.

'Is it feeling any easier?'

'A bit. It's difficult to tell. They keep trying to get me to sit on that chair, and even walk a bit, but I just think, what for? I've got nothing to get out of bed for. I feel so tired all the time. I just wish they'd stop fussing, and let me rest.'

'But if you get more mobile, perhaps you'd be able to go home?'

'I like it better here.'

'But you'll have to leave some time, and I wonder if you could manage alone? Have you thought about perhaps spending some time in a convalescent home when you leave here, just to make sure you really are better?'

'You're trying to ship me off to an old folks' home, aren't you?'

'Well, would it be such a bad idea to let someone else do the cooking and housework, while you get the rest you need?'

'I'll never go into a place like that. That's for old people.'

'It's for people who aren't able to look after themselves for a while. You've worked hard all your life, Minnie. Why not let other people take the strain now?'

'Because the way I appear to you, and the way I feel inside, are two quite different things. My body may be battered and worn out, but I refuse to accept I'm an old person. I'm the same person I've always been. And I'd hate being locked up with a lot of old fogeys who've got shrivelled minds to match their shrivelled bodies. That would be no life at all. I'd rather die.'

'But we've got to work out what's best for you in the immediate future. Hospital isn't the right place, now you're feeling better. Sister and I were having a word with the Social Services people about you this morning, and they think that . . .'

'I won't go into a home. I won't need to.'

'Why not? Where else could you go?'

'I've been doing a lot of praying while I've been lying here. Don't smile like that because you may not approve of what I've been praying for. I've made a bargain with God. He'll forgive me for wanting to take my own life that time, and he'll make sure I join him before they try and throw me out of here.'

'Minnie . . .'

'Don't "oh Minnie" me! I'm not an idiot. I know what I'm

saying, and I understand exactly what the arrangement is between God and me. I had a conversation with him that was as clear and normal as the one we're having now.'

'You were praying – and he spoke to you?'

'I don't know if I was praying at that precise moment. I might have been dozing, or even asleep, I'm not sure. All I do know is that I remember every word of the conversation as if it happened just seconds ago.'

'And you were talking to some*body*?'

'If you're asking me what he looked like, I can't tell you. I was just aware of a presence, and I understood the meaning without words being spoken. The message was that I wasn't to worry about dying, and I should never, ever try to make it happen myself. When I asked you to help me that other time, I was very wrong. I know that now. But I won't need to worry about that again, because any day now I'll be on my way.'

'Minnie, I . . .'

'And I'm not afraid. There is no fear in me for what lies ahead. Because of that conversation, I know there's a better life beyond this, because God told me so. And, frankly, I can't wait to get there.'

Philip looked down at her determined face and felt there was little he could say.

'You don't believe me, do you? You think I'm a batty old woman. Well, you should know better. You're a man who's devoted his life to God. Don't you believe he's a real presence in your life? Why shouldn't he be in mine?'

'I think, Minnie, you believe what you think you experienced, and if that brings you comfort, I'm glad for you. I just wonder if medical science might confound his plans, and make you better more quickly than you think. In which case, it might be wise to think through what to do in the immediate future, if things don't work out as you expect.'

'No need. They will.'

'Don't wish your life away, Minnie.'

'Why not? Who'd miss me?'

'I would.'

She chuckled. 'Listen, I'm a small insignificant cog in the circle of admiring women around you. Of course you won't miss me. Nobody will. And what I want is to move on from here. So be happy for me. Don't come up with trite platitudes you don't really believe and I don't want to hear. I want to die, Philip. As my minister, I would like you to share that with me, help me prepare for it. If you don't want to, then push off! I don't need you.'

He sat back in his chair, a slow affectionate smile creeping across his face.

'A very special woman,' he said softly. 'Of course I'll help you, Minnie. Shall we pray together now?'

Some time later, he was heading out of the main hospital doors towards the place where he'd left his car. He jangled the coins in his pocket and thought about Minnie as he walked. What a complex, challenging little soul she was! Canny too. Her incisive mind, that disarming intuition.

'. . . *as long as you don't find someone you'd like to have.*'

Philip turned the key in the lock, and opened the door to drop his briefcase on the back seat. Then he lowered himself behind the wheel, slamming the door behind him.

Of course he'd never want another woman! What a ridiculous thought! That could never happen to him. He was a trained minister. Over the years, he'd always recognised if anyone was becoming too dependent on him, and that included women who may have confused professional compassion with personal affection. There had never been anything like that he couldn't deal with. Besides, with a noisy, happy family like his and Ruth's, right at the heart of his church community, there was no doubt that theirs was a successful and contented marriage.

He turned the ignition key and moved off, slowly edging his way out of the car park and on to the dual carriageway towards the centre of town. The spire of St John's loomed before him, towering over the grey rooftops, stiff, uncompromising, above temptation.

Well, he smiled to himself, on this occasion Minnie couldn't be further off course. He could never be tempted, not with a wonderful wife and family like his.

And so, as he indicated right to turn up the hill towards the church, it was with some surprise that he realised an image of Louise's face had drifted unbidden into his mind. And with that thought came a longing that gnawed at his heart and tore at his conscience.

Chapter Seven

'So it'll be Friday then, before we see you?'

There was resignation in Louise's voice as she listened to Richard's voice on the phone and his curt explanation about the sales trip and conference he had to plan, and the VIP clients from Europe only he could entertain. She'd heard it all before. She wasn't worried about his work commitments or the fact that he had to entertain clients. Her only concern was how he'd entertain himself once the work was over.

'Louise, are you listening?'

'Sorry?' She dragged her mind back to the conversation.

'I asked you what the doctor said. He was coming to see Mum this morning, wasn't he?'

'Oh, yes. He's not been yet.'

'You will remember to tell him how she keeps wandering around at night? She needs some sleeping pills.'

'She takes so many pills already . . .'

'Louise, she needs pills to help her sleep at night, so that we can all get some rest. Tell him she needs sleeping pills.'

'I'll discuss it with him, of course I will.'

Perhaps the telephone disguised the hard edge that had crept into her voice. If he noticed, Richard chose to ignore it.

'And you took my grey suit to the cleaner's?'

'Yes.'

'Did the tiler come?'

'On Wednesday. It's all in hand.'

'You gave him the message about me deciding on the other tiles? You know, the ones with the smaller pattern?'

'I did.'

'And Lizzie's OK?'

'Well, her head's permanently in the clouds since she met Steven, but yes, she's fine.'

'Is she seeing too much of this boy? Is it interfering with her studies?'

'He's delightful, Richard. They're a nice family.'

'You should know. You see enough of them.'

'Not really. I see Philip because of the church.'

'Can't imagine what you find to do down there all the time. Ever since this "finding God" business, you seem to have become obsessed.'

Louise was silent.

'Still, whatever helps you, Louise. I'm all in favour if it means you cope. But just remember every time you're gallivanting off to church, you have Mother to look after too.'

'I've organised all that – or, at least, Dr Bevan has. He's arranged for her to go along to a day care centre for a few hours every now and then, to give me a break.'

'Where? Who runs it? Do they have qualified medical staff there?'

'It's in Parr Street. It's run by the local Health Authority. And, yes, everyone there has suitable qualifications.'

'I think I'd better talk to Dr Bevan about this.'

'There's no need.'

'Of course there is! I'm very surprised he organised something like this without discussing it first.'

'He did. With me.'

'Well, she's my mother, and I should have been consulted.'

'You weren't here. I was. You're making a fuss over something that's already working very well.'

'But you never mentioned this arrangement to me. Why not?'

'Because you're never here, and you never asked.'

There was a pause before he said, 'Just ask Dr Bevan to call me immediately. Do you understand?'

'You know his number. Perhaps you should call him yourself.'

She heard, or perhaps sensed, his sharp intake of breath.

'Have you been taking your pills, Louise?'

'I'm fine, thank you.'

'Your pills. Have you been taking them?'

'How nice of you to ask. Yes, Richard, I always take my pills, and I'm fine – thank you.'

'There's no need to be sarcastic. If I didn't care, I wouldn't ask.'

'Wouldn't you?'

'Louise, when you're in this sort of mood, there is very little point in talking to you. I'll ring again when you're feeling better. Say hello to Lizzie for me.' And with that he slammed down the phone.

She stood with the receiver to her ear for several seconds before she finally replaced it. *'If I didn't care, I wouldn't ask.'* Of course he didn't care! At least, not for her. For his precious mother, perhaps, if it didn't involve any inconvenience to himself – but for her? Of course not.

Had she taken her pills? As if that mattered to him, except insofar as he wanted to be sure she was able to look after Eileen. Where was the 'care' in that? Did he even know what 'caring' was, what it could be? Did he have any idea that one person could feel and show for another the kind of care that was infinite – practically, emotionally and spiritually? Was he capable of understanding that through care exactly like that, she had found God? Because of a man who really did care, about everyone in general, and her in particular. A man who was sensitive, educated and patient. A man who had answers to questions she had never really thought of until she met him. A man who laughed often, but whose eyes filled with tears when emotion moved him. A man who was warm and responsive and infinitely caring. Philip. Dear Philip.

She glanced at her watch. It was nearly twelve. She'd arranged to meet him at the church at half-past for Bible Study. She wanted to ask him about the passage from St John, Chapter 6 to which she found herself going back time and time again, the passage about Jesus being 'the bread of life.' It was how it went on from there that intrigued her. 'Everyone who sees the Son and believes in him shall have eternal life.' What sort of life would that be? A life of exquisite peace, in the presence of God? She looked around her – at the pile of ironing waiting accusingly for her in the basket, the oven that needed cleaning, the seat Eileen sat on that looked suspiciously damp again. And she thought of Richard, distant, patronising, uncaring Richard. An eternal life of peace and understanding. How wonderful that sounded!

She turned away from the ironing, closed the kitchen door with a bang, and grabbing her Bible from the hall table, slammed the garden gate shut behind her.

'What? You mean, he's got one? A Muddy Fox! The lucky beggar.'

Mark's eyes were out on stalks as he looked at his friend. Ben was four months younger but a whole two inches taller than him, an irritating fact Mark disliked but never mentioned. The other thing that really got up his nose was that Ben liked to give the impression of being much more streetwise than someone who was, after all, a vicar's son. It was probably true, but Mark hated to be reminded of it.

'And Robbie's allowed to ride it?'

'Sometimes, if Trev's in a good mood. Course, you don't

know him, do you? He's really cool. I know him quite well because me and Robbie are such good mates.'

'Wow!' said Mark, suitably impressed. He knew Robbie Palmer's older brother by sight, but had never dared to speak to him. Trev hung around with a gang of teenagers who were to be seen at all hours of the day on the seats in the town square. A lot of them smoked whilst casually downing cans of lager. Like most of the kids his age, Mark would walk round the corners of the square to avoid their attention, but stay near enough to admire them from afar.

'Yeah, I've seen the bike,' continued Ben, relishing the way in which Mark was hanging on his every word. 'He got it last week. It's brill.'

'But they cost hundreds! Where did he buy it? That place in Princes Street?'

Ben hesitated for just a moment before shrugging his shoulders nonchalantly. 'Dunno. Probably.'

'Wow!' said Mark again. 'He must have been saving for months. I have, and I've hardly got anywhere near it yet. It'll take me years before I get mine, I reckon.'

'Yeah, well, Trev's a man of means. I don't think money's much of a problem for him.'

'Does he work then? He must have a good job.'

There was the merest hint of condescension in Ben's voice as he replied, 'Trev doesn't need to work. I told you, he's a man of means.'

'Oh,' replied Mark, as he pictured Robbie, who normally had holes in his elbow sleeves, and hand-me-down jeans that had plainly belonged to older members of the family before they reached him.

The two boys were sitting on the railway bridge, a place totally forbidden by most parents, but very popular with all the local youngsters whenever they thought the coast was clear. They sat without speaking for a while as they helped themselves to another piece of gum from the packet Ben had found in his pocket. At last he said, 'Do you want to see it?'

Mark's eyes became enormous. 'What, the bike? Would Trev let me?'

'Sure he would, if I asked him.'

'But he doesn't know me. Do you really think he wouldn't mind?'

'Look, it'll be all right, as long as I'm with you. Trev knows me.'

'When?'

Ben gave the question due consideration. 'Well, I *might* be able to see him tonight – if he's in, and he isn't always. But I might. And if he says OK, then I could take you round tomorrow after school.'

'Wow!' was all Mark could think of to say. He was speechless with anticipation.

'No promises, mind, but I'll ask him. That's all I can do.'

'Right,' said Mark, unable to hide his excitement. 'When will you let me know?'

'I'll ring you tonight if I've got anything to tell you.'

'Great! Thanks, Ben.'

'And, just remember – if you do get to meet Trev, he needs to be treated with respect. Everyone sort of looks up to him – so don't forget. He's all right with me, of course, 'cos he knows me. But he can be really funny with strangers.'

Mark nodded earnestly in agreement. 'Speak to you tonight, then.'

'Maybe,' replied Ben, standing up to tower over him. 'I only said *maybe*.'

Mark watched him for a while as he meandered off. Once he was out of sight, Mark leapt off the bridge, punching the air with his fist and whooping with childish delight.

★

'You know, Sue, you've worn me out!' complained Ruth. 'I know keep fit is meant to be good for me, but I'm too exhausted to be sure I believe that at the moment.'

Sue eyed her friend thoughtfully. 'Been a busy week, has it?'

Ruth grimaced. 'Something like that.'

'What you need is a cup of coffee and a cream cake. Come on.'

Ruth smiled wearily. 'Are you sure my keep fit teacher is supposed to say things like that?'

'Certainly not. This is your friend talking. The cream cakes are on me!'

Ten minutes later the two women had settled themselves into a quiet alcove in Crispin's Teashop, with a large cafetière in front of them and two eclairs on the way.

'Right!' started Sue. 'Out with it. What's up with you?'

'Nothing,' replied Ruth too quickly. 'I'm fine.'

'Fine, my foot. Ruth, how long have we known each other? You've got something on your mind. What is it? The kids?'

Ruth smiled in spite of herself. 'The kids are great. Messy, unreliable, infuriating – and, in Steven's case, very secretive – but great.'

'Then it must be Philip.'

A tell-tale flush of colour appeared on Ruth's cheeks. 'No, he's fine too. Busy, of course, with the opening of the church centre coming up, but he's OK.'

Sue said nothing as her expression changed to one of friendly disbelief. 'So,' she said at last, 'it's Philip, is it? Anything in particular, or everything in general?'

'No, Philip's fine. We're fine. Honestly!'

Sue reached out to cover Ruth's hand with her own. 'Now,' she said quietly, 'why don't you tell me the truth?'

A sudden glassiness appeared in Ruth's eyes and she dropped her head immediately. Sue held her hand a few moments longer, then reached out to the cafetière to pour Ruth a cup of coffee, which she pushed towards her.

'I'm only guessing, of course, and tell me to mind my own business if I'm way out of line – but could this have anything to do with a certain musical godsend who's been making herself pretty indispensable at St John's recently?'

Without lifting her head, Ruth nodded slowly.

'Thought so,' sighed Sue as she sat back in her seat.

Ruth reached into the sleeve of her jersey to fish out a paper hankie with which she wiped her eyes and blew her nose as inconspicuously as possible. Slowly, she took a sip of the coffee, then, resting her head on her hand so her face was hidden from everyone except Sue, said, 'I'm probably being completely neurotic. Heavens, I know Philip well enough, and I know he'd never do anything at all improper. But there's something about her that really unnerves me.'

'Oh?'

'It's nothing I can put my finger on exactly. It's not as if she's on the phone all the time, or is harassing him, or anything like that. As far as I can see, she's behaving perfectly reasonably – but he just seems to be spending so much time with her, *on* her, if you know what I mean?'

'Hmm,' said Sue, who knew exactly what she meant.

'She's come to faith recently, and that's all thanks to him. He says she's full of questions and he's found her very challenging, I know. But usually, at this stage with anyone else, he'd just suggest she come along to the confirmation classes and he'd step back a bit.'

'And he hasn't?'

'Well, I must be fair. There's no-one in the confirmation class this time who's over the age of fifteen, and she'd probably feel quite out of it there. It's not surprising he's carrying on with her tuition on a private basis. Not surprising at all.'

'But. . .' prompted Sue.

Ruth looked directly at her. 'But I feel it's Philip himself who's enjoying their get-togethers. I think it's he who suggests they need to meet every day. He tells me the two of them have detailed discussions about the Bible, all the ethics and implications of various passages she needs to study, and I know how much he loves the challenge of discussions like that.' She smiled. 'I remember we used to do just the same for hours on end when I first met him.'

'What? You met the man of your dreams and in the first heady days of your romance, the two of you spent hours talking about the Bible?'

Ruth grinned. 'Amongst other things.'

'And you think he may have "other things" on his mind now, with Louise?'

She nodded.

'Why? Have you talked to him?'

'I don't need to. He talks about her all the time. It's "Louise thinks this" and "Louise said that". I could quite cheerfully throttle him, if he mentions Louise much more!'

'Wouldn't it be more worrying if he didn't talk about her? If he was secretive?'

'Philip isn't the secretive sort. He shows everything in his face. I don't believe he could ever tell a lie, not to me anyway.'

'So, have you tackled him about extra-curricular activities with the fair Louise? What did he say?'

'Well, I'm very careful how I put it. I've never been a nag, and I never will be. I have to handle it all carefully, in case I'm completely wrong about this. But whenever I ask if he needs to see Louise quite so often, or whether it needs to be at *her* house rather than at home at the Vicarage where he'd normally have meetings like that, he always has very plausible and practical answers – mostly the fact she's got to look after her mother-in-law, of course.'

'Perhaps he's so open about her because he's got nothing to hide?'

'He may not have. I'm just not so sure about her . . .'

Sue dropped a sweetener into her coffee and stirred it thoughtfully. 'Neither am I.'

'Really? Why not?'

'Oh, the way she never seems to take her eyes off him, the way they go into a huddle before every service to talk over the music, the way she makes a beeline for him once it's finished, always seems to be standing next to him at coffee – that sort of thing. And the way she laughs . . .'

'I've noticed that! As if everything he says is either very profound or hilariously entertaining. That irritates me beyond belief.'

The eclairs arrived. Sue took a couple of cream-laden bites then sat back in her seat thoughtfully.

'How are you and Philip getting along? Any changes there?'

'Oh, he's affectionate in an off-hand, familiar sort of way.'

'Is that different from normal?'

Ruth thought for a moment. 'Probably not. Probably that's what it's like when you've been married for a long time. You stop seeing each other, don't you? I've become as much a part of the background to him as the sofa and the washing machine.'

'And sex?'

'Well, that's always been quite important to both of us. You know, when things were really difficult, like when Rachel was so ill a few years back, and when his dad died, we sort of clung together and sex was always a central part of that. It's something we both enjoy.'

'So? Has that changed?'

'I put it down to tiredness, really. He's always late home, always got so much on his mind. There are some days when we hardly seem to see each other awake.'

'And how long has that been going on?'

'Since Christmas, I suppose. It's got worse lately.'

'And have you talked about it?'

'I mention it. You know, in a jokey sort of way. He just gives me a great big hug, tells me I'm on a promise for later that night – then completely forgets about it!'

Sue snorted. 'And what do you put that down to? Is it just because he's tired and overworked? Or more than that?'

The question hung in the air while Ruth considered her answer.

'He's not the disloyal sort. No-one could know him better than I do, and I'm sure he'd never do anything to damage me or the family, or compromise his faith.'

'Do you suspect something is actually going on with Louise at the moment?'

Ruth looked directly at her. 'I don't know. Perhaps not. Philip is too sensible to allow that. But actions and thoughts can be quite at odds with each other, can't they? I've seen the way his face lights up when she walks into the church. I've heard his end of their conversations on the phone, the interest and excitement in his voice. I've noticed the way he says he's off to see her for an hour, and it's three hours before we see him again. No, I don't necessarily think he's doing anything about it. But I think he'd like to.' Her eyes were suspiciously bright again. 'I really do. And I don't know what to do about it.'

'Right! Well, I'll tell you what you'll do. You'll pin him down a bit. Make sure he's tied up with firm commitments at home – for the children, for the family, for church work – but create something every day that means he has to be home on time. Then, you make sure that family life is just as wonderful as it can be. Enlist the help of the children if you can, without saying too much to them, of course. Just tell them that Dad's a bit under the weather and has too much on his plate. Tell them he needs spoiling, and that they need to help make him feel very welcome and relaxed at home.'

Ruth nodded doubtfully.

'Then,' continued Sue, 'you get out the sexy underwear.'

Ruth nearly choked on her coffee. 'What sexy underwear?' She giggled. 'I'm an impoverished vicar's wife, you know. Whatever it is, if it's not on special offer at Sainsbury's, I don't get it!'

'Well, you should. It might be the best investment you ever make. Make Philip see you again. Better than that, make him see you with new eyes.'

'He'd laugh. We both would.' Ruth chuckled before her face became serious. 'And if he didn't laugh with me, but at me, I'd be destroyed.'

'Why should he laugh at you? He loves you, you know that. Perhaps he just needs to be reminded – and the way to do that is to make sure he realises you still find him attractive and sexy.'

Ruth looked unconvinced.

'You *do* find him attractive and sexy, don't you?'

'More than ever.'

'Then show him! Fight for him, Ruth. Get out your suspenders, cook him his favourite meals, comfort and cherish him. Fight for him!'

Ruth smiled with affection at her friend. 'You sound like an agony aunt. How do you know all this, Sue?'

'I learnt the hard way. And perhaps if a good friend had told me what I'm telling you now, Martin would never have left me.'

Steven was just about to pick up the receiver to call Lizzie when the phone rang.

'Is Mark there?' It was a young voice, one of his brother's friends.

'Not sure. Hang on!' Steven moved over to the foot of the stairs and bellowed out Mark's name. There was no reply.

'Sorry,' he said when he returned to the phone. 'I don't know where he is, but he doesn't seem to be here. Can I give him a message?'

'Yeah. Tell him Ben called, and it's all on for tomorrow night.'

'What is?'

'What's what?'

'What's on for tomorrow night?'

'He'll know,' replied Ben mysteriously.

'Oh. OK, I'll tell him. Does he need to ring you back?'

'Nope. I'll see him at school tomorrow. 'Bye.'

When the phone went dead, Steven rang Lizzie's number. Her mum answered.

'Oh, hello, Steven,' said Louise. 'Lizzie isn't here at the moment, I'm afraid. She's out with her cello. She's got that recital coming up, and she's gone round to practise with Graham. You know, the one who's playing the piano with her.'

How come she didn't tell me that? thought Steven.

'Can I give her a message?'

'No, thanks. It's fine.'

He heard a rumble of conversation and laughter from someone in the room with Louise.

'And your dad says, shouldn't you be doing your homework first?'

'Is he there?'

'Yes, but he says to tell you he'll be home soon.'

'Oh,' replied Steven, unsure how to respond. ' 'Bye then.'

Louise went back to the kitchen to collect the two cups of tea she'd made before the phone rang. Philip was looking very much at home in the corner of her comfy settee.

'So,' he said, picking up the conversation they had previously been having, 'I'm quite pleased really that the youngsters feel so enthusiastic about this. That Taize service you helped me organise really made a tremendous impact on them, but I hadn't thought it would lead to so many of them wanting to go off to France for a week and camp there in May. It's a good time to go though, before it gets too busy with thousands of other young people from all over the world. I'm told they sometimes have ten thousand there during the summer weeks.'

'What is it, then? A church? asked Louise.

'Yes, but much more than that. It's a monastic community with about seventy brothers resident there, and many more scattered throughout the world. They run all sorts of classes and discussion groups in different languages each day, and then there's the worship – thousands of people all kneeling and singing together three times a day. It's very moving.'

'The music's quite hypnotic,' agreed Louise. 'Repetitive and simple, but in the way of most chants, it creates just the right atmosphere for worship.'

'Hmm, it does,' agreed Philip, taking a sip of tea.

'From the little I've heard of it, I'd love to go there myself.'

'Come with us then. That would be terrific. Come with me when I take the youth group in May.'

'Could I?'

'I can't think of anyone in our church community who would have more to offer the group on an occasion like that.'

'Well, I'd certainly like . . .'

'Louise!'

Eileen's voice echoed from the top of the stairs.

'Yes, Eileen, do you need some help?' Louise didn't move, and her eyes remained on Philip as she spoke.

'My hair needs washing.'

'We washed it this morning, when you had your bath.'

'This morning? Did we?'

'Yes, we did, and I put it in rollers for you.'

'Rollers?'

'Are you hungry?' Louise called, still not leaving her seat. 'Would you like me to make you a sandwich?'

'Am I tired?'

'I shouldn't think so. You had a nap this morning. Perhaps you're hungry?'

'Hungry?'

'Are you hungry?'

'Perhaps I'm hungry,' intoned Eileen, her voice fading as she turned away and headed back to her room.

'Excuse me,' apologised Louise, rising. 'I'd better go and check on her.'

'No day care club today?'

'They don't have a place for her on Mondays. I don't mind, though, because the relief they give me with those few hours on all the other weekdays really makes a difference.'

She disappeared upstairs then, and Philip overheard snatches of her conversation with her mother-in-law. Several minutes later she returned to the lounge.

'OK?'

'Yes, she's sitting in her comfy chair, cuddling her slippers and watching an Australian soap on TV. Her favourite pastime!'

Philip eyed her carefully. 'Does it get a bit much for you, constantly having to be on hand for her?'

Louise studied the cup clasped in both her hands. 'Sometimes. Sometimes I think that while I'm making life easier for Eileen, life is passing me by.'

'I've heard so many carers say that. She's a huge responsibility for you.'

'I don't mind, really. I think I've got used to it.'

'What about Richard? Is he supportive? He must know how frustrating she can be.'

Louise smiled wryly. 'I suppose he might, when he's here – which he isn't a great deal these days.'

'Do you mind that?' asked Philip gently.

Louise looked at him directly, pondering her answer. Finally, her eyes fell once again to her cup.

'No,' she replied softly. 'I don't think I do mind very much any more. I don't think I care at all.'

He reached out to touch her hand. 'Do you really mean that? Aren't you just going through a bad patch?'

Louise gave a short, bitter laugh. 'A bad patch that's lasted for about nineteen years!'

'How long have you been married?'

'Nearly twenty-one years. That doesn't leave much time when Richard and I were truly happy with each other, does it? And even then, I think I was just kidding myself that things were all right between us. I'm not sure, looking back, he was ever really happy with me.'

'Why did you marry then?'

'Why did *I* marry? Because I loved him very much indeed, or thought I did. Why did *he* marry me? Because I fitted the bill, I was convenient and available when he needed a wife, and prepared to take his mother on board as part of our family from the very start. Because I was compliant, and overwhelmed, and I adored him. Who knows? He may even have cared a little for me too.'

Philip squeezed her hand. 'Of course he did. He probably still does, in his own way. Perhaps he's forgotten how to express that love?'

'Oh, he knows how to express love all right. He gives expensive watches and perfume. He takes his love out for elegant meals and stays in glamorous hotels. He's attentive, and caring, and romantic . . .'

'Well, that sounds great to me!' laughed Philip. 'What's wrong with that?'

'I'm never there, Philip. He's never, ever been like that towards me. I'm lucky if I get a Chinese meal in the town on my birthday. Beyond that, I can whistle.'

'He's having an affair?'

'Affairs, plural – one after another, year after year. The first one I knew about was when I was pregnant with Matthew. She actually came to see me. Thought I knew all about it, you see, because Richard had told her that we'd agreed he should leave me.'

'And you had no idea at all?'

'I had no more idea about her, than she had that I was pregnant. Funny really. We ended up becoming almost allies over that!'

'What was his reaction when you challenged him?'

'The same as it's always been ever since. I imagine things. Did you know that?' She looked at Philip, her face desolate and drawn. 'I imagined that woman's existence. He'd never even heard of her. I was off my head again.'

'Again?'

She flushed, and whatever it was she'd intended to say next, changed her mind.

He watched her for a while then squeezed her hand gently. 'You can trust me, Louise. I'm a good listener.'

Almost without thinking, she tilted her head until it rested against his. She covered his hand with her own, still saying nothing.

'Above all else, I'm your friend. And I think you need one. Talk to me. Please.'

She began so quietly he had to strain to hear her.

'I suppose, looking back, I was never the most confident of people. I grew up in a family of sisters who all seemed to be brighter, prettier, more outgoing than me. The only thing I really excelled in was music – and that suited me fine, because while they were hanging around with lads, and falling in and out of love, I lost myself in music. With my piano, I had all the company I needed. I didn't need to be brilliantly clever or attractive for that. I could just play to my heart's content, and lose myself in the world my music created. Romantic, elegant, beautiful – I was the centre of it all. Inspiring too. I found myself particularly drawn to religious music, especially when I got the chance to nip into our local church and play the organ there. I never played for services or anything like that. I'd never have thought myself good enough, but I really loved the glorious sound of the organ.'

She smiled then, looking affectionately at Philip. 'But I think you know that, don't you?'

'So, you went off to college,' he prompted. 'Did you enjoy that?'

'The music itself, I loved. The life of a college student was harder to adjust to. I've never been very good in a crowd, and you know what students can be like – noisy, gregarious. You're either in or definitely out . . .'

'Which were you?'

'Out, I'm afraid. The more confident and noisy everyone around me was, the more I retreated into my own world. And gradually, I began to realise it was a world in which I experienced great extremes of emotion – tremendous heights of exhilaration and inspiration, followed by hours, sometimes days, of deep, angst-ridden lows.'

'What set those lows off?'

'Usually something most people would think quite trivial – like not being able to play a certain piece, however hard I practised; overhearing some off-hand remark about how, when it came to dress-sense, I had absolutely no style at all; looking in the mirror and seeing a midriff bulge I'd not noticed before; the fact my hair was straight, or I had a spot on my chin, or my shoe had sprung a leak! The smallest comment or observation or feeling could set me off.'

'So what happened then? How did you get out of it?'

'Sometimes it just lifted, not for any particular reason, but because it did. Sometimes I was too depressed to care what anyone else thought of me. My world became no bigger than the four walls I hid myself in. I didn't eat. I couldn't sleep. I just wallowed in lethargy, as if I was incapable of any feeling. And then . . .'

She looked down at her hand, still cradled under his.

'. . . and then, it would go. I'd snap out of it. I'd just wake up one morning, and feel like eating. That was always the first sign. I'd have a bath, change my clothes, dig out my music and emerge from my room, like a butterfly from a chrysalis.'

'Didn't people miss you, though? What about friends? There must have been someone, at least, who'd notice you weren't there, and worry about you?'

'I knew people, other students, of course I did. But I never really got close to anyone.'

'Why not?'

'Confidence, I suppose. I suddenly came up against students who had such wonderful musical talent, I wanted to fade into the wallpaper in their presence. I began to realise the silly little pipe dream I'd had of being a performer myself was nothing more than that – a silly dream. Those bright young things were destined for the spotlight. I was a backroom person, an accompanist, a teacher. I was terrified of drawing attention to myself and my inadequacies. I just wanted to stand in the shadows, listen to their conversation rather than join it, watch the action rather than take part in it, to stand alone.'

'Sounds lonely.'

'It was – desperately – but it was easier than acknowledging my own inadequacies reflected in the pitying eyes of those more talented than me.'

'I wonder if they ever really gave you any thought at all? In my experience, very talented people are usually so involved in developing their own potential that they're far too busy to waste time on other people's failings.'

'Oh, I'm sure you're right. It was just me. I was the one who was too preoccupied with my own feelings to think about other people much at all.'

'And then you met Richard?'

'And then I met Richard, in a café, quite by chance. Perhaps because he wasn't a musician, perhaps because he had the bluest eyes I'd ever seen, perhaps because, even though he was young and uncertain in so many ways, he already preferred to do most of the talking – whatever it was, I just found myself falling for him. And you have to remember I'd never had any man look at me as if I was interesting before. It just swept me off my feet. And because I was so bowled over with the romance and excitement of it all, I didn't analyse my feelings, or his, in any great detail.'

'Well, he must have been bowled over too, if he asked you to marry him?'

'Perhaps. I think it had more to do with the fact that he was offered a management training position with his company. You know they've got quite a big office here in the town, although he's up at headquarters in London most of the time now.'

'Why get married because of a job?'

'I think he figured it would give him more status, that he'd seem more reliable and settled if he was a married man with responsibilities.'

'And you were fairly settled and happy, at least in those early days?'

'At first, yes – well, certainly. I was. But before long, he was spending more and more time at the office. Then, as he got promoted, he was often away from home for days on end, on business trips and courses.'

'How did you react to that?'

'Insecurity swept over me again. All the confidence I'd built up through what I believed was his love and commitment to me, dissolved away. I found myself slipping back into times of black depression again.'

'Did Richard realise?'

'He was totally perplexed by it. He didn't understand that I couldn't help myself. Just kept telling me to pull myself together, grow up.'

His face full of sympathy, Philip began absent-mindedly to stroke her hand as she spoke.

'But didn't you realise that almost certainly it was no one's fault, certainly not yours, but an illness that medical care could probably help?'

'It took me ages to take myself along to the doctor – and, believe it or not, it was Dr Bevan I saw on that first occasion nearly twenty years ago. I've been seeing him regularly on and off ever since.'

'What made you finally decide you needed to see a doctor?'

'Well, actually, I didn't go along about my depression at all. I went to see Dr Bevan because I was pregnant with Matthew. I was probably about six months then. I'd been popping along to the surgery for ante-natal visits every four weeks or so, but on that particular occasion, Dr Bevan realised that I was coping with a lot more than just pregnancy.'

Philip eyed her quizzically.

'I'd just had that visit from Richard's mistress. I'd behaved wonderfully well while she was there – swapping stories about my husband, hearing about the time they spent together and his plans to leave me! Really, you'd have been proud of me. I acted with such dignity and control . . .'

'Until she left?'

'. . . then I collapsed, and not just in a physical sense. All my insecurities came flooding over me again. Of course I'd never be enough for a wonderful man like him. I was inadequate. I was plain. I was boring and conventional and uninspiring. And I was pregnant – fat, bloated and frightened about the responsibility of becoming a mother. No wonder I couldn't keep his love. Of course I'd never be good enough for him!'

'Oh, Louise.' Philip's voice was barely a whisper.

'And, do you know,' she continued, eyes now bright with tears, 'it took me days to tell him about her visit? I just couldn't face asking him. I felt it was my fault. If I'd been worth more, he wouldn't have had to look elsewhere, would he?'

'You know that's no excuse . . .'

'But, you see, I *didn't* know! I just felt I'd had my share of luck in marrying him, and predictably that luck had run out. I couldn't see beyond the thought that it was all my fault . . .'

'And when you tackled him?'

'He denied it. Said he didn't know her. That I was imagining things. He talked down to me as if I was a small, stupid child – and because I thought I *was* stupid, I agreed with him!'

'Oh, Louise, that was never true.'

'Dr Bevan realised there was something seriously wrong the moment I walked into the surgery. I know I looked awful, with dark circles round my eyes, and I'd completely lost my appetite. And being the wonderful man he is, he took the time to try and get to the bottom of what was troubling me. I didn't tell him about Richard, of course – how could I? We'd only been married a year and a half. I was hurt and ashamed and full of guilt. I simply couldn't talk to anyone about that. But he did manage to persuade me to tell him about the bouts of depression that had dogged me for so long. To my surprise, he didn't just write me off as a complete inadequate. He explained to me that I had a *physical* rather than a *mental* condition – and of course, that was what I'd always worried about. I thought I was going mad!'

Seeing her distress, Philip eased himself closer to her, putting a supportive arm around her shoulder as she spoke.

'Because I was pregnant, at first Dr Bevan said it wasn't safe for me to have medication right away, in case it harmed the baby. So during those months, although I was really pleased that I was going to have Matthew, there were times when I got so low, cared so little about myself, that I began to think being dead would be preferable to being alive.'

'You thought about suicide?'

'Often. It was never far from my mind. And it was worse when I'd had the baby. I was exhausted and constantly on the go, as all new mums are. I found the medication almost as bad as the depression itself so I just stopped taking it – and, of course, that made life even more unbearable. I was always tired, always short-tempered, and things between Richard and me reached rock bottom. Of course, Eileen was living just a couple of doors down from us then, and she was such an interfering old biddy . . .'

She stopped, suddenly appalled at herself. 'I'm sorry, that was an awful thing to say.'

'But true?'

Louise smiled faintly. 'Oh, yes, I'm afraid it was definitely true. She stuck her oar in at every conceivable opportunity. Criticised and undermined me whenever she could, and then took great delight in telling tales about how dreadful a mother and wife I was.'

'And what about Richard? How wonderful was he as a husband, when you so badly needed his support?'

'He was away most of the time. And if he was home, his mind was still on his work.'

'And the mistress? Was she still around?'

'Not that one, at least, I don't think so. But it wasn't long before I started getting phone calls on evenings when he was due home, and whoever it was simply put the phone down if it was me who answered. I began to recognise the signs. Mostly, it was perfume on his clothes that gave him away. And sometimes, when I got particularly desperate, I would go through his diary while he was in the bath or the garage, somewhere out of the way. And I'd search his pockets and his briefcase, his letters and bills. I was demented with jealousy.'

'And when you found evidence that he'd been with another woman, what did you do?'

'Usually, nothing. Just knowing was enough. I accepted he looked elsewhere because I was so inadequate. I felt I had no right to criticise.'

'Louise, how could you think that? Of course you had rights. And so did Matthew. He had a right to a father who was committed to him, and his mother.'

'Oh, I think Richard was always totally committed to his son. Matthew was his pride and joy. He boasted about him to anyone who'd listen – which was strange, really, because there were many times when he wouldn't see Matthew from one end of the week to the other.'

'But didn't he notice, didn't he *care*, that his own wife was suffering so badly?'

'Honestly, Philip, he wasn't interested. He was a hungry young businessman, destined for high places. A neurotic, moody wife was the last thing he needed. So he just ignored me. He ignored the problem, and plainly hoped I'd "pull myself together", as he said I should.'

'How did you react to that?'

Louise didn't answer immediately. She looked hard at Philip for some seconds, as if considering exactly how to answer. In the end, she didn't speak at all. She took her hand from his, and pushing her jersey sleeve up to her elbow, turned it over so that it was palm up. Across her wrist was a series of long, thin scars. With shock registering on his face, Philip gently turned over her other hand, to find similar ugly marks.

Without thinking, his hand went up to cover his mouth, as if he were choking from the sudden emotion that welled up in his throat and clouded his eyes.

'Louise, my poor dear . . .'

'It was Eileen who found me. Too soon, I'm sorry to say. Matthew was at nursery. I knew he was all right.' She looked desperately into Philip's eyes. 'You mustn't think for one minute I didn't love him. I loved him more than you can imagine. But because my husband didn't love me, I couldn't love myself.'

'Thank God Eileen found you. Where were you? What state were you in?'

'Upstairs in the bathroom, unconscious. When I came to, I was in hospital. I opened my eyes and looked directly at Richard standing there, and in those first few seconds, before anyone else could see, there was such disgust in his eyes. He thought I was weak. He thought I was worthless and unreliable. He despised me, I knew he did. And I knew without a shadow of doubt in that moment I could never hope to have his love again.'

'But then, a couple of years later, Lizzie came along. Had you patched things up a bit with him by then?'

'Oh, I was expected to do my duty as a wife. Sex never stopped between us. Every weekend, if he was home, he'd claim his conjugal rights. But even then, I couldn't mistake what he was doing. He was claiming me, demanding obedience, because I was his wife, and he was allowed to. There was no love in it.'

'And what about your depressions? Did they continue? Did Dr Bevan help you to cope with them?'

'He helped me to control them, but I went through some real downers before I got that far.'

'And when Lizzie came along? With two young children to care for, you must have been very vulnerable?'

Louise nodded, and Philip became aware that her hands were shaking as she spoke.

'One night, it was about ten o'clock . . . Lizzie and Matthew were both in bed. Richard had been at home quite a lot that day, working from the office upstairs. He said he was going away that evening because he had a series of sales meetings over the following couple of days at the London office. He was busy on the phone nearly all the time, and angry because he was late when he left. He rushed out, hardly even said goodbye, except to the children, of course. It wasn't until about an hour later I came upon a piece of paper that he'd obviously dropped in his panic to get out. It was a map and directions to a hotel in Oxford, and their confirmation that Mr and Mrs Kenton were booked in for a double room that night.'

Philip realised her whole body was shivering as she spoke.

'I put the letter down on the hall stand and simply walked out the door. I walked and walked. I didn't know where I was going. I didn't care. But when I finally got to thinking about where I was, I realised I was near the river – you know, over near Letts Bridge?'

He nodded.

Tears began to drench her face now, silently coursing down her cheeks as she picked incessantly at the side of her thumb.

'I nearly did it. I was sitting on the side of the bank, with my feet already in the water. I was just going to slide in and disappear. I was so nearly there when he stopped me . . .'

'He?'

'I don't know who he was. He was only young. A runner, I think. He just put his hand on my shoulder and hung on to me. When he asked me if I was all right, I just said "yes" – but he knew I wasn't. He realised what I'd been meaning to do. He didn't say anything more. He just helped me to my feet and back up on to the bridge. He had a car there. He asked for my address and drove me home. He sat in the car until he saw me put the key in the door and go inside. Then he drove away. I never saw him again.'

'But there was no one there for you. Did you ring Dr Bevan?'

'Not then. Funnily enough, the need was not so urgent after that. I went up to the bedroom and looked at Matthew and Lizzie, still sound asleep, just as I'd left them, and knew I was glad to be alive. That was enough of a turning point to get me through.'

Anger flared in Philip's voice. 'And Richard? He never knew about this! Did you ever tell him?'

'Yes, I told him. He was furious with me. I'd put the children at risk. He considered me nothing more than a risk myself.'

'But he should have been made to take responsibility for you, to care for you as you need to be cared for.'

'What was the point, Philip? I wasn't worth it, not in his eyes. Not in my own. I was plain, ignorant and round the bend. What could he possibly see of any worth in me?'

'There is so much that's wonderful about you! Where you've

got the idea you're anything less than lovely just beats me. You're beautiful, Louise. A beautiful, misunderstood, unhappy woman, who's suffered from illness, not failure.'

She shook her head violently, pulling away from him.

'You don't understand, Philip. I was a hopeless child, a hopeless wife, a hopeless mother . . .'

'You *are* a wonderful mother, and one of the most caring people I've ever known. You're an incredibly gifted musician, and with a depth of ability I envy with all my heart. You're intelligent and sensitive and intuitive. Believe me, Louise you must never doubt your worth.'

'You don't know me. Everything about me, all the things I can't do, all the times I've been a complete failure, all those moments when I've been such a coward, I just wanted to stop living! How could anyone feel anything but contempt for me after all that? There's nothing to admire in me, nothing to love. Who could ever love me?'

'Me. I could. I do . . .'

His words hung in the air between them as she turned her surprised, tearstained face towards him. And the last thing she was aware of, as his face drew closer and his lips reached hers, was the burning intensity within her, reflected in the blazing heat of his eyes.

Chapter Eight

Any normal person walking past Steven's room would have been so bowled over by the volume of music coming from behind the closed door, they would consider it impossible for any reasonable conversation to be going on in the bedroom. But Jamie and Steven weren't normal people. They were teenagers, and so managed to chat quite comfortably, apparently oblivious to the deafening rhythm around them.

'All I'm doing, Steve, is passing on a message. Sarah definitely told Phil the other day she likes you. You wouldn't have to do much to get off with her.'

When Steven didn't answer, Jamie tried another tack.

'Look, everyone fancies Sarah. It'd be quite something if you ended up going out with her, 'specially when Phil's been after her himself for months.'

Steven appeared to be concentrating solely on the music.

'Steve? What do you reckon? About Sarah?

Steven looked at him absent-mindedly. 'Oh, yeah. Maybe.'

Jamie wheeled his stool across the room until he was right beside the bed where Steven lay stretched out.

'Maybe what? Maybe you'll give her a ring? Maybe you think she's ugly? Maybe you're not listening to a word I say?'

'I'm listening.'

'Well?'

'Yeah, she's OK.'

'OK? She's gorgeous!'

'Why don't you ask her out then?

'Because it's *you* she says she fancies! You know, the one with big boobs and legs up to her ears! *She* fancies *you*!'

'Yeah, well, I'll think about it.'

Jamie was speechless with exasperation. He rolled his stool back to the other side of the room, and pulling a box out of his back pocket, counted the few cigarettes left inside before lighting one up.

'OK, what is it? What's wrong with you?'

'Nothing.'

'It's not that Liz girl, is it?'

Once again, Steven didn't bother to answer.

'You're just friends with her, right?'

'Right.'

'You're not involved with her or anything?'

Silence.

'Steven? You're not getting involved with her, are you? After all you said about her at that party.'

'Yeah, well, I know her better now.'

Jamie stared at him in amazement.

'But she's dumpy, and she plays the cello!'

'So?'

'You don't like dumpy girls. You've always said so.'

'Well, I like this one.'

'How much?'

'I just like her, all right? Now shut up, will you?'

Jamie took a drag on his cigarette and eyed his friend thoughtfully.

'And because of Liz, you're going to miss out on a chance with Sarah? Even though everyone else would give their back teeth to go out with her?'

'Look, I'm not interested in her. It's got nothing to do with

Liz. I'm just not that fussed about Sarah. Let Phil have her, if he fancies her so much.'

The CD ended. Jamie got up and selected another one before coming over to sit on the end of Steven's bed.

'So, are you two an item?'

'Oh, belt up, Jamie. It's not like that.'

'Why not, if you like her so much?'

'Probably *because* I like her so much!'

'Wow! This sounds serious. You like her so much, you haven't tried to get off with her? I don't believe I'm hearing this.'

'Look, we're friends. She's great, she really is. I just like her, that's all.'

'But could you fancy her?'

Steven considered for a while before answering. 'Yeah, I probably could, but it wouldn't be like it's been with other girls. I mean, Liz is my friend. It would seem a bit, well, you know . . .'

'But at the party, you were snogging and all. What about that? Doesn't she think it's a bit off that you keep your distance now?'

'I don't know. We don't talk about it.'

'Why not?'

'I don't know. We just don't.'

'*You* don't, you mean.'

Steven shrugged but ventured no opinion. Jamie, on the other hand, was in full flow. 'It can only be because you feel a lot more for this girl than just "liking". You're not falling for her, are you? You can't be!'

'If I am, it's none of your business.'

''Course it is. I'm your best mate. And mates have to look out for each other.'

'Look, Jamie, I don't know what I feel, if I feel anything. That night at the party, I didn't want to get landed with her and wasn't interested in finding out what she was really like at all. But since then, well, it's changed . . .'

'Yeah?' prompted Jamie enthusiastically.

'She's good fun. She beats me on the computer and never rubs it in. She likes the same TV programmes as me. There's no pressure from her to spend time together, and because of that, I find myself ringing her more and more. We're not going out. We're not a couple or anything like that. I just like her.'

'A bit like one of the boys, right?'

Steven smiled. 'Yeah, I suppose she is, except that I don't think she'd like it if she saw what I'm really like when I'm with you lot!'

'The disapproving type, eh?'

'No, not at all. It's just the time I spend with her is different. Can't see the two mixing really.'

'And when you two are together, there's no kissing or anything?'

'No.'

'And she's happy with that.'

'Seems to be.'

'And you don't think she wants more?'

'I don't know. If I made a move and she didn't want it, I'd feel such a fool. I wouldn't want to lose her as a friend, so I'm not going to risk it.'

'Hmm,' said Jamie with a knowing smile. 'Seems to me you don't know a lot about girls.'

'And you do?'

'More than you, I reckon. Of course she wants you to make a move. All girls do!'

Steven shrugged without comment.

'And you? How do you feel? Don't you want more?'

'Sometimes, yes. Sometimes I think that's what I'd like most of all. And then, I don't want to change anything. It's OK as it is.'

'You're not falling in love or anything stupid like that, are you?' asked Jamie, with an expression of sheer disbelief.

'Me? Never. Don't be a prat!'

But when Jamie went over to turn up the volume on the CD player, Steven's thoughts were plainly not on the music.

In the room next door, Ruth grimaced as she felt the floor vibrate with the bass notes. She banged on the wall. 'Turn that down, Steven, or you'll have to turn it off. Mark and Rachel are asleep!'

There was no reply, but seconds later the volume was fractionally lowered. Ruth turned back to what she was doing. She was on her knees with the contents of her chest of drawers on the floor around her.

This is ridiculous, she thought to herself. We've been married for twenty odd years – and here I am, searching for sexy underwear!

Without enthusiasm, she picked up one of the more respectable bras, and the most recently purchased knickers, already slightly frayed round the edges. It was no good. She simply wasn't the sexy type. Knowing Philip, he'd laugh hysterically at her efforts to try and be something she wasn't. He knew her too well – and loved her anyway.

She sat back on her knees and gazed towards the bed. It was true, though, there'd been very little activity in this room in recent months. She couldn't remember the last time they'd made love. Christmas Eve, wasn't it, after they'd put the children's stockings out?

She smiled to herself. Well, she hadn't needed stockings and suspender belt then to get him interested, and she didn't need them now. They loved each other. They had years of loving each other to draw on. They had both allowed their lovemaking to slip away and now it was time they changed that. And when he finally did come home this evening, she would make herself absolutely clear on the matter.

And with that warming thought in mind, she bundled up her undies and began squashing them back into the open drawers.

★

At exactly the same moment, Philip was looking at his watch. Twenty-five past nine. Time he went home.

But he didn't switch on the engine and move off as he should. He continued to sit quietly in the dark, in the out-of-the-way spot where he'd pulled off the road half an hour before.

Never in all his life had he been in such turmoil. The events of that evening replayed in his mind – the story of Louise's life; the deep ugly scars across her wrists; the anger that rose in him when he thought of the years of neglect and insult Richard had dished out to her; her hands shaking uncontrollably as she talked of trying to take her own life; her sad, desolate eyes – and her face, with that expression of such disbelief and wonder when he'd kissed her.

He had kissed her. *He* had kissed her. He'd kissed her, and there was nothing in the world he'd wanted more. He wanted to kiss and hold and possess her. To comfort and console her, to cradle and protect her, to caress and make love to her. He wanted all of that – but after the shattering impact of that one kiss, they'd pulled back from each other in stunned amazement. They had not spoken. Neither knew what to say. No words were necessary when the longing that flared between them was tangible in the air.

He'd left her then. She showed no surprise. She didn't try to stop him, clearly as shocked and moved by the unexpected emotion between them as he was.

. . . *as long as you don't find someone you'd like to have.* Minnie's words came back to him.

Well, he couldn't have Louise. There was no question of this going any further than it already had. She would know, as he did, before anything even started, that this was the end. He was a minister. He loved Ruth. God, he loved Ruth!

And as his wife's face swam into his muddled thoughts, he leant forward over the steering wheel to blot out the image. How could he ever face Ruth, with his mind full of thoughts like these? She knew him so well. Would she suspect? Did she already? She'd made her reservations about Louise very clear in recent weeks.

And the children? Their children. *His* children. How could he look them in the eye again?

And God?

> *Almighty God,*
> *to whom all hearts are open,*
> *all desires known,*
> *and from whom no secrets are hidden . . .*

All desires known? From whom no secrets are hidden?

Oh, God! The words of the Holy Communion Service came back to haunt him. Every Sunday he said those words. He knew them to be true. And if they were true, how could he ever again say them in front of God and the congregation, knowing that Louise was just yards away from him? That would be impossible.

Perhaps she should leave? Perhaps they should find someone else to play the organ?

But how could her sudden departure be explained? And why *should* she leave the church through which she had so recently, and joyfully, come to faith?

Then he should go.

Away from the church to which he so clearly belonged? With the centre opening coming up? What possible reason could he give to the Bishop? To Ruth? To their children? To the congregation? That he was deeply and dangerously drawn to a woman who was filling his mind with wonder and his body with physical longing?

No, to go was impossible. But to stay was impossible too.

And God would know. He already knew the innermost secrets of his heart.

Was this a test? The kind of temptation Jesus faced in the wilderness? Jesus was strong. He didn't give way.

But then, Jesus was Jesus, Saviour and Lord. And I'm nothing more than just me, thought Philip miserably, as he bent his head to pray.

Our Father who art in heaven, lead us not into temptation, forgive us our trespasses . . . cleanse the thoughts of our hearts by the inspiration of your Holy Spirit, that we may perfectly love you, and worthily magnify your holy name.

Dear Lord, what am I doing? What's happening to me? Father, please help me! Help me, please . . .

It was with some relief, a couple of hours later, that Ruth heard Philip's key in the door. She'd stayed up waiting for him for quite a while, planning to be ready with a welcoming cup of tea and perhaps an offer to rub his shoulders, just as she used to when they were first married. By eleven o'clock, her lids were dropping. It had been a long day. Where he was at this hour of the night, she had no idea. She just found her intention to pamper and seduce him on his return faded considerably when it became mixed with a deep irritation that he hadn't thought to ring her. There were people in this house who loved him dearly. It was about time he remembered that, and took their feelings into account once in a while. So, at last, it was with very mixed emotions that she climbed defiantly into her comfiest old nightie, only to lie awake in the darkness listening for the sound of his car.

When he did arrive, he didn't come upstairs immediately. She strained to hear movement and guess what he was doing. Surely he hadn't gone into the office to do more work at this hour of night? She sat up in bed, trying to make out what he was doing. Finally, at the sound of his footstep on the stairs, she lay down quickly. He opened their door with utmost care, obviously thinking she was asleep. She stretched over immediately to snap on the bedside lamp.

'Oh, you are awake.'

'I was worried. Where have you been?'

Why did I ask that? she thought. I wasn't going to rise to it. Why did I have to ask?

He sat down heavily on his side of the bed, back turned to her. 'Oh, nothing much. Just meetings. So many of them at the moment . . .'

'Was Louise with you?'

I just can't leave it, can I? Why can't I just leave it?

His back stiffened. 'Earlier on she was, yes.'

'Where were you? At her house?'

Still he didn't turn.

'Darling, can we talk about this in the morning? I'm bushed, really I am.'

'Did you see your messages, down on the hall stand? Did you see that the Archdeacon rang? He said he's been trying to get hold of you for two days.'

'I'll ring him. I'll do it tomorrow.'

'Don't forget. It sounded important.'

He turned round to her then and she was shocked by the tired, blank look in his eyes. Her voice softened.

'Philip, you're doing too much. You're exhausted. Could you have a lie-in in the morning? Is it another early start?'

He drew his hand across his forehead and rubbed his eyes. 'I don't know. I'm not sure.'

'Then I'll decide for you. We'll let you sleep until you wake up. No arguments. Come on, love, get into bed.'

Like a child, he allowed her to undress him. Gently she lifted his feet and tucked the covers round him. He lay still, saying nothing, as she walked back round the bed and climbed in at the other side. Once the light was switched off, and her eyes accustomed to the darkness, she looked at the shape of him, lying with his back towards her. Gently, she reached out to stroke his shoulder, then brought herself in closer to snuggle up against him.

'Philip,' she said softly, 'do you think a cuddle might help?'

But there was silence. He was asleep. At least, she thought so. But then, with his face turned away from her, she couldn't see that although his breathing was even, his eyes were wide open and welling with sad, despairing tears.

At the end of school the next day, Mark caught Rachel as she walked through the gate on the way home.

'Tell Mum I'll be late this evening, will you?'

'Why? What are you doing?'

'Oh, nothing much.' His face was carefully casual. 'Ben and I are going somewhere with Robbie.'

Rachel was instantly suspicious. 'Robbie? Robbie Palmer? You don't go round with him, do you?'

'Sometimes.'

She looked at her younger brother closely. 'Are you sure, Mark? That family has a reputation for getting into all sorts of scrapes. Don't you think you ought to ask Mum yourself, before you just take off?'

'No, I'm going now. It's all arranged. If you don't approve, don't tell her where I've gone. Just say I'll be home in an hour or so.'

Rachel still looked doubtful.

'Please, Rachel.' Mark was pleading now.

After a moment's thought, she turned to walk away. 'OK, but don't blame me if you get into trouble. I tried to warn you.'

It was some minutes later when Mark finally spotted Ben coming towards him. And, wonder of wonders, Robbie Palmer was with him. It must be true, then. He really was going to have a look at the bike. Brill!

Robbie didn't waste time on niceties as he and Ben reached Mark. 'Now look, you've got to understand Trev's very protective about this bike. It's real special to him. Don't get cocky, and don't get too nosy, or you're out. Got it?'

'Oh, yes,' nodded Mark earnestly.

With the briefest of glances towards Ben, Robbie led the way, with Mark trying to contain his excitement as he galloped along behind them.

'Well?' demanded Barbara, when Brian arrived back from the church centre that afternoon. 'Did you talk to him?'

'No, not really,' answered her husband uncomfortably.

'Brian, you promised!'

'I said I'd do my best, and I did. That's not the same thing as promising.'

'Brian, did you or did you not agree that something must be done to help Philip see what to the rest of us is perfectly clear? That woman is making too many demands on him. And he's falling for it!'

'Well, I'm not sure I entirely agree with all of that – but yes, I do think a word in his ear might be a good idea . . .'

'And did you agree,' Barbara carried out relentlessly, 'that you would find an opportunity at the soonest possible moment – the *soonest* possible moment – to broach the matter with him?'

'Well, I said I'd try my best . . .'

'And have you done it?'

'Sort of. I've sort of mentioned it to him. He wasn't very . . .'

'Have you done it?'

'Well, not exactly, but I will. It's important to get the right moment . . .'

'Then I will!'

At that point Barbara turned on her heel and marched out of the kitchen, slamming the door behind her. She walked to the study, and closing the door, picked up the receiver. She waited for a while as the number connected, then spoke with a beaming smile when the phone was answered at the other end.

'Margot! How lovely to find you at home. How *are* you? It's Barbara here.'

She listened intently as Margot obviously told her, at some

length, exactly how she was. Plainly all was not entirely well as Barbara's response was a series of sympathetic clucks and sighs.

'It seems, Margot, you could do with a little cheering up. How about tea at Crispin's sometime next week? Oh, this week would be better? Well, how about Thursday then? I can't get away until after school has finished, of course, but would about four-thirty suit you? Wonderful. See you there.'

With that, she replaced the phone with a flourish. Yes, tea with the Bishop's wife would be very nice indeed.

Mark stood awkwardly to one side of the group as the discussion went on.

'Aw, come on, Trev,' wheedled Robbie. 'He's harmless. Just let him take one look. He won't tell no one.'

'Robbie, you could cause me a lot of trouble here. This isn't a blessed peep show.'

'Trev, look at him! He's just a scrappy kid. He can't do nothing.'

'And I think I've found a buyer for it. The bloke might come round this evening.'

'Trev, we won't even take it out of the garage. We'll just have a quick look, promise!'

Trev eyed his younger brother suspiciously. 'I know you. You'd only have to look at it to wreck it.'

'No, I won't.'

'*They* might,' Trev retorted, starting pointedly at Ben and Mark.

'Trev, come on, please.'

Trev glared at Robbie with irritation for a moment before giving in. 'Go on then. But be quick about it. I want you back here in twenty minutes. And don't let anyone see you!'

'Why not? Mark whispered to Ben. 'Why can't anyone see it?'

Ben looked pityingly at him as he followed Robbie towards a lock-up garage at the back of the Barton Road Estate.

'Is it because it's so valuable?' asked Mark, hurrying to keep up.

'Something like that. Now shut up or clear off!'

Glancing swiftly around him before turning the key in the padlock, Robbie heaved up the garage door and signalled to the two younger boys to slip inside. A flick of the light switch revealed a scene that took Mark's breath away.

The garage was full of bikes – racers, mountain bikes, ladies' bikes with baby seats, even kiddie bikes with baskets and water bottles attached. Some were obviously new. Others looked less pristine, but nonetheless in good condition.

'Wow!' breathed Mark, eyes bright with excitement. 'Your Trev really does know his bikes, if he collects them like this. This lot must be worth a fortune.'

'Yeah, well, keep your mouth shut, OK?' snapped Robbie.

'Oh, yeah, sure,' agreed Mark. 'You don't want too many people to know about this place or you'll have them nicked.'

'They *are* nicked, you idiot!' hissed Robbie. 'Where do you think Trev would get money to buy stuff like this?'

The smile dropped from Mark's face. 'You're kidding?'

Robbie walked off, and with a shrug of his shoulders, Ben followed.

'But where from? demanded Mark. 'Where'd he nick them from?'

'Oh, here and there,' replied Robbie vaguely.

'And then what does he do with them?'

'Look,' said Robbie, peering down at him impatiently, 'do you want to see this Muddy Fox or not?'

Mark swallowed. A difficult decision, this. He knew he should leave. Every fibre of his body said he should leave right now. But to see a Muddy Fox? How he'd love to see one, perhaps be able to touch it, even sit astride the saddle . . .

'Are you coming then?'

Mark turned towards a plastic cover that had been thrown casually over an interesting-looking shape in the corner. With one quick movement Robbie removed the cover to reveal the most beautiful bike Mark had ever seen.

'Wow!' was all he could say. 'Wow!'

'Come and have a proper butcher's then. Don't just stand there!'

Slowly, reverently, Mark ran his hands over the gleaming chrome and paintwork, touching the gears, the lights, the brakes, the seat.

'Wow!' It's. . . it's. . .' For once in his life, Mark was speechless.

'Can he ride it? asked Ben.

Mark shrank back. 'Oh, I couldn't do that. Suppose I came off or something? It's quite big for me . . .'

'Are you chicken 'cos it's nicked?'

Mark didn't answer. He didn't need to.

'Please yourself,' said Robbie abruptly, starting to lay the cover back over the bike.

'But didn't Trev say we couldn't take it out of the garage?'

'Well, that depends, doesn't it?' retorted Robbie. 'We're only talking about you taking it round the block. Can't see the harm in that, so long as you don't get noticed by anyone – like if you're daft enough to cycle into something and attract attention.'

Whatever reservations Mark might have had inside, his face was a picture of sheer excitement.

'Have you got a helmet?'

'Why? You're not going to come off it, are you?'

'Oh, no! I've taken my Cycling Proficiency.'

With one more patronising look in his direction, Robbie began to wheel the bike towards the garage door.

'Right. Get going. And be back in five minutes. No longer. Right?'

Once outside, Mark clambered on to the bike, shaking with

anticipation. Ben and Robbie watched him as he nervously wobbled the first few yards down the road, before getting into his stride and disappearing round the corner.

'God, he's wet behind the ears! Why do you bother with him?'

'Dunno really. I probably won't, not after this.'

'And then, if we get through to the second round, we have to perform on the stage of the Town Hall!' enthused Lizzie at the tea table. 'Graham says he thinks we're in with a real chance.'

'Oh?' said her mother, her mind only half following Lizzie's enthusiastic gabble.

'And he says – although I'm not sure if I believe him or not, 'cos he does get things wrong sometimes – that the judge at the Final will be Julian Lloyd-Webber. I've always wanted to meet him.'

'Mmm,' agreed Louise, stretching over to pour the tea.

'So we've got to work really hard – you know, put in hours of practice – and, who knows? Perhaps I'll end up playing the cello in front of a celebrity! That would be so cool!'

'Are you going to Steven's tonight?' Louise cut in sharply.

Surprised by the change of subject, Lizzie had to think before answering. 'Not to his house, no. We're meeting up at the Wimpy at quarter to five. Heck! That's only ten minutes away. If he rings, I've left, OK?'

On her way to the door, she suddenly stopped to peer at her mother closely.

'Are you all right? You seem half asleep. You're not going down with something, are you?'

Not just going down, Louise thought. I'm plummeting at breakneck speed, unable to check my fall, or prevent the inevitable . . .

'Mum?'

'I don't like raspberry jam!' announced Eileen from the other side of the table at just that moment. 'I've never liked raspberry jam. It's all those pips. They get under my dentures.'

'That's not raspberry jam, Eileen. It's strawberry,' replied Louise.

'Well, I don't like it. It's got pips in.'

'Oh, for heaven's sake, Eileen, there *are* no pips in that strawberry jam! Just stop moaning about everything, and start eating.'

Lizzie looked at her mum in astonishment, just as Eileen's face registered tearful indignation. Louise sat back in her chair, looking suspiciously close to tears herself.

Soothingly, Lizzie turned to her grandmother. 'Come on, Gran,' she said. How about Marmite on that bit of bread? Marmite's your favourite.'

'Marmite's my favourite,' repeated Eileen, sobbing theatrically as she spoke. 'But I don't like raspberry jam. It's got pips in.' And, bending down, she took the slippers off her feet and gathered them up to her in a comforting cuddle.

Louise stood, pushing back her seat abruptly. She picked up several plates from the table and walked wordlessly into the kitchen.

She placed one hand on each side of the sink then leant forward, staring down into the dishes and soapy water.

Stupid, stupid, stupid! Why snap at Eileen like that?

She sighed. She'd snapped because she was in such a state of dazed confusion she didn't know what she was thinking, feeling or doing.

She turned round then, leaning back against the sink, folding her arms tightly round her waist as if she had stomach cramp.

Stupid, to let one little kiss affect her like this. Stupid, to find her thoughts constantly filled by him: what he said, how he looked, what he did. And so very stupid to harbour even the smallest hope that the most wonderful man she had ever met in the whole of her life, could really feel something for a foolish, insignificant nobody like her.

But when she closed her eyes – remembering how his lips felt, picturing the longing in his eyes – for a moment, just a single moment, she allowed herself the luxury of daring to hope.

★

Mark had never experienced anything like it. This bike went like a dream, smooth and stylish. Swift too. With one easy flick of the gears, he was up the slope on Nightingale Hill without even catching his breath. The best bit, though, would be when he came down the other side, back towards Barton Road, and the safety of the garage.

He stopped at the brow of the hill to relish the slope beneath him. He should be able to get up a cracking speed before he needed to slow down for the left-hand turn into Barton Road. How he wished his big brother could see him now! Mark Barnes, champion biker, known throughout the world for his skill and speed – on his amazing customised Muddy Fox! Almost without realising it, he began the countdown out loud. Five! Four! Three! Two! One! Lift off!!!

And he was away, soaring like an eagle down the hill, wind in his face, hair streaming behind him. Such power! Such exhilaration! Such . . .

'Oy!'

Mark caught sight of the policeman stepping off the pavement before he noticed the panda car parked to one side of the road.

Does he mean me? thought Mark, glancing around to see who else he could be talking to.

'You! On the bike! Come over here. Where's your helmet when you're pelting down hill at speed like that?'

In all his life, Mark had never been challenged by a policeman before. It may have been the knocking of his knees that nearly had him catapulting off as he struggled to stop the bike, but in seconds the officer was with him, holding the bike steady as the boy climbed off to stand beside him.

'Now just suppose, young man, there'd been an elderly lady crossing the road at the bottom here. You'd have sent her flying, wouldn't you? I reckon I ought to charge you with riding without due care and attention – don't you?

Mark nodded dumbly, feeling the blood drain from his face as the policeman bent down to look more closely at the bike.

'A Muddy Fox, eh? Rather nice piece of gear that. Cost a pretty penny, didn't it?'

Mark was dumbstruck with terror.

'What's your name?'

'Mark Barnes,' he managed to whisper.

'And where do you live, Mark?'

'The Vicarage, St John's Road.'

'The Vicarage? You're not Philip's boy, are you?' The policeman peered at him closely.

'Everything all right here?' his colleague asked, as he climbed out of the police car to join them.

'Well,' replied his partner, 'what we've got here is Philip Barnes's lad. You know, the vicar over at St John's? He's a long way from home and riding this rather nice bike.'

The second policeman stooped down to examine it more closely. 'Wouldn't mind one of these myself! Could never afford it, though. Had it long, have you?'

'It's not mine,' mumbled Mark.

'Not yours, eh? Whose is it then?'

'My friend's.'

'Oh, yes, and which friend is that?'

'He lives in Barton Road,' gabbled Mark, 'the yellow house on the corner.'

The second policeman looked up curiously. 'Not the Palmer household, by any chance?'

Mark nodded.

'And exactly who does this bike belong to? Who's your friend?

'Robbie. Well, he's not exactly my friend, but my other friend knows him really well and *he* said I could have a look at the bike if Trev didn't mind . . .'

'Oh, so it's Trevor Palmer's bike, is it?' asked the first policeman, who seemed to Mark to be looking down on him from a very great height.

The two men exchanged glances. 'Well,' said the first, kneeling down to find the serial number on the bike frame just beneath the seat,'we'll do a check on this shall we? Just to be sure . . .'

'No!' interrupted Mark, in a voice that was much louder than he'd intended it to be.

'Why's that? Why shouldn't we check? Know something about it, do you?'

Mark's mouth went dry. He tried to speak but suddenly had no idea what to say.

Keeping his eyes firmly fixed on Mark's pale face, the policemen spoke into the radio on his shoulder strap.

'Gulf Victor from 1160. Can you run a property check for me, please, on a Muddy Fox mountain bike. Serial Number 471753? I'll hold.' Still his eyes didn't leave Mark's face.

It was probably only a minute, but seemed like an age before the voice came through again on the other end of the line. The policeman put his ear to the receiver but Mark didn't need to hear the words to know what the reply would be. This bike was stolen, and he'd been caught riding it. What's more, it looked as if he'd dropped Robbie and Trev in it too.

Cold dread slithered down his backbone. If he wasn't in enough trouble with the police, and then with his dad, he'd certainly be in fear of his life if Trev's friends ever got hold of him. To his horror, hot tears began to slide down his cheeks as he looked miserably up at the policeman.

'You're in a lot of trouble, young man.' The constable turned to his colleague. 'I'll take this one back to the station.

Can you radio for Malcolm to come over with a van to collect you and the bike, then I suggest the two of you pay a call on Mr Trevor Palmer on your way back to the nick.'

He turned to Mark. 'I want you to understand that I am arresting you. I believe this bike is stolen and that you *know* it's stolen. Because of that, I'm arresting you for handling stolen goods. You don't have to say anything but it may harm your defence if you don't mention when questioned something which you later rely on in court. Anything you do say may be given in evidence. Do you understand that?'

Although the only word Mark heard from the whole speech was 'arrest,' he nodded in dumb agreement, tears still streaming down his face. He felt the policeman take him by the arm and lead him to the panda car, where he was helped into the back seat. And even as the car drove away, he was unable to take in that this was really happening to him.

'Rachel, have you seen Mark?'

Ruth was setting the table, unsure exactly how many mouths she was feeding this evening. Sometimes Steven turned up for tea, sometimes he didn't. Often Rachel had music or drama rehearsal, and arrived late. Most of the time these days, Philip didn't manage to join them at all. But usually, the one person you could rely on being first at the table for any meal was Mark.

Rachel's hand shot to her mouth. 'I forgot to tell you. He asked me to say he'd be late.'

'Why? Where's he gone? He didn't tell me he was going anywhere.'

'To a friend's, I think.'

'Which friend?'

'I'm not sure.'

Ruth eyed her with curiosity. 'Really? That's unlike him. He knows he's not allowed anywhere unless I know in advance. He's only twelve years old, for heaven's sake!'

Although Rachel carried on helping to set the table, there was something about the casual way in which she was avoiding the conversation that made Ruth suspect she knew more than she was giving away.

'Come on, out with it! Where is he?'

'Honestly, mum, I don't know.'

'Rachel!' Ruth's reply was sharp. 'Where is he?'

'I'm not sure, really I'm not, but I think he was going somewhere with Ben.'

Ruth started to move towards the telephone. 'So he may be at Ben's house?'

'Not necessarily.'

'Where then?'

'Mum, I'm really not sure.'

Checking Ben's number on the list pinned beside the phone, Ruth rang immediately.

'Oh, hello, Pat. It's Ruth here. Is Mark with you, by any chance? He's not? Well, has Ben come home? Do you think they're together then? And you've no idea where they might have gone? No, neither have I, but Mark's due to be grounded for a week when he finally does put in an appearance! Yes, certainly, and I'll ring if I hear anything before you do. 'Bye.'

She frowned. 'He's not there, and neither is Ben. Pat has no idea what their plans were.' She went over to the stove, to take the lid off the *bolognese* sauce that was bubbling there. 'Well, I hope he's back soon, because his tea's ready.' She stirred thoughtfully for a while, but her mind was obviously not on cooking. 'I wonder where on earth he could be?'

She jumped as the phone rang again. Taking the dripping spoon with her, she rushed across the kitchen to pick it up.

'Hello?'

'Sorry, wrong number,' mumbled an indefinable voice, before the line was abruptly cut off.

Ruth started at the phone curiously. Could that have been

Mark? Was that him? Perhaps he'd try to ring again? She waited a few moments, staring at the phone – and when it didn't ring, picked up the receiver and rang 1471.

Louise was shaking as she slammed down the receiver. Stupid! Stupid to think he might be there! Stupid not to realise, of course, it was more likely to be his wife who would answer the phone at this time of night. She walked back through to the lounge, picking at her thumb nail as she went.

The agony of not knowing what he was thinking, how he was feeling after yesterday was driving her insane. Didn't he want to talk to her too?

Clasping her thumb nail between her teeth, she walked back into the kitchen to glare at the phone.

Ring me please, Philip. Please, Philip, ring. Damn you, phone, RING!

The panda car drove round the back of the police station and into the yard. Mark had managed to stop crying for a while in the car, but felt tears weren't far away as the policeman helped him out of the back seat and held his arm to lead him through the glass door at the rear of the building. He was taken to a small room where another uniformed policeman was sitting behind a large desk.

'Sit down there, Mark,' said the officer who'd brought him in, pointing towards a long wooden bench with its legs screwed to the floor. 'I'm PC John Coleman and this is Sergeant Gries. He's our Custody Officer this evening. I have to tell him why you're here. This is Mark Barnes, Sergeant. I spotted him riding a mountain bike in a very dangerous and irresponsible way. When I stopped and spoke to him, it became clear the bike was not his, and that there was some question about who in fact owned it. I did a property check and discovered that this particular bike was stolen from a residential garage in Pelham Avenue ten days ago.'

The sergeant's eyebrows rose slightly. Otherwise he showed no reaction at all. 'And do you believe this young man is responsible for the theft?'

'Not necessarily, Sarge. It seems he borrowed it from a friend of his – Trevor Palmer!'

The sergeant nodded in understanding.

'I do believe, though,' continued the constable, 'that Mark was aware that the bike had been stolen and I, therefore, arrested him at 4.52 this afternoon for handling stolen goods.'

'Have his parents been informed?'

'Not yet. He's Philip Barnes's boy. You know, *Reverend* Barnes. He'll be well chuffed to hear about this, won't he!'

'What's your phone number, Mark?' The sergeant looked at him more kindly. The boy was obviously distressed. 'Shall we ring your parents and get them here to keep you company?'

Mark reeled off the number without expression, as the sergeant wrote it down. 'Right, take him down to the Detention Room for me, would you, John? When his parents arrive, we'll interview him properly.'

'Fine. Come on then.' PC Coleman ushered Mark out ahead of him before stopping to turn back with a grin to the sergeant. 'And I thought it was only vicars' daughters that got into trouble, Sarge!'

Chuckling as he walked, the PC took Mark along the corridor where he opened the first door they came to. It was a small, sparsely furnished room. Along one side a low shelf was covered by a thin plastic mattress, and there was a loo in the corner. Nothing else. No seats. No table. This might be called a 'detention room', but to Mark it was simply a cell.

'Make yourself at home. I expect your mum and dad will be along soon.'

The door closed behind him with a metallic clunk. Mark moved slowly towards the bed where he squatted down into a ball drawing his knees up tight to his body, as he thrust his thumb into his mouth in an attempt to stop shaking.

Upstairs, Sergeant Gries tried the number Mark had given him. It was engaged.

Louise! It was Louise who'd rung, then put the phone down!

Hang on a minute, thought Ruth, her mind racing. Could it have been Lizzie ringing for Steven? No, of course not. They were already together. Steven had come home, and left again some time ago, saying he was going to meet her at the Wimpy. They'd be there now.

No, that was Louise's voice. And she had put the phone down because she wanted to speak to no one but Philip.

At that moment, Ruth wasn't sure who she was more angry with: Louise for being obvious and conniving or Philip for being so gullible about the trap he was being drawn into.

And she was mad at Mark too. Where had he got to? He knew the rules about always letting her know where he planned to be. He was going to be in very big trouble when she finally found him.

But where should she start to look? Brian. Perhaps he'd gone there to do some work on the train set. Of course! That was it! With relief, she began to dial Brian's number.

And so, when Sergeant Gries tried the number of the Vicarage again, it was still engaged.

'Margot, my dear. How very nice to see you.'

Barbara squeezed her way through the tightly packed tables to where her friend had already expansively installed herself. She'd obviously called into a few shops on the way to Crispin's and was surrounded by an array of rather classy carrier bags. But then, Margot *was* classy, with a private income thanks to the generosity of her doting, elderly parents who, rumour had it, owned a large chunk of Shropshire. Probably now in her fifties, she was acutely aware of her position in the upper eche-lons of county life, and dressed, entertained and shopped accordingly. Well, being the Bishop's wife was undoubtedly a very serious responsibility. She had to look the part. People would expect nothing less.

Exactly how their acquaintance had begun, neither Barbara nor Margot could quite remember, but certainly long before David became a Bishop, in the days when he was a humble, but obviously ambitious, parish priest in the neighbouring town. Perhaps it was when Margot became a governor of the board of the school at which Barbara was Deputy Head? Perhaps it was through the WI? But however they met, the two women recog-nised qualities in each other they prized in themselves - education, style, common sense, and a great gift for organising others, particularly their husbands, who both needed a strong guiding hand on the tiller.

Having decided on Earl Grey and a selection of the exquisite tiny sandwiches for which Crispin's was famous, they got down to the serious business of conversation. Subjects ranged from Barbara's new conservatory and Margot's Christmas holiday with their daughter in the Far East, to a few harmless indis-cretions about well-known members of the Anglican circle.

'And tell me,' asked Margot at last, 'how are things at St John's?'

'Well!' began Barbara, settling herself comfortably into her seat. 'There are one of two things going on I'd really like your advice on . . .'

'Louise?'

Her relief at hearing from him at last was overwhelming.

'Philip! Where are you? *How* are you?'

'Listen, I've not got much time on this phone. My money's running out. I'm at the hospital, and wondered if you could manage to come over to the chapel here for a while? There'll be no one else using it this evening and I really think we need to talk, don't you?'

'Yes, yes, of course. I'll ask my neighbour, Mrs Betts, to come in and mind Eileen. As soon as she arrives, I'll leave . . .'

'You know where the chapel is? Don't go in the main entrance. It'll be quieter if you come by the west door, turn right, and it's at the end of the corridor. It'll be locked, but knock and I'll know it's you.'

'Right, I'll be there in about twenty minutes. Philip, it's so good to . . .'

The pips cut in. He was gone.

'Mrs Barnes?'

'Yes.' Ruth didn't recognise the voice at the other end of the phone.

'Mrs Barnes, Sergeant Gries here, the custody officer from Walsworth Road police station.'

'What?' Her blood ran cold. 'What's happened?'

'Your son Mark is here at the moment. He's got himself into a spot of trouble.'

'What sort of trouble? Is he hurt?'

'No, Mrs Barnes, he's fine – but we do need to talk to you and your husband. Could you both come down straight away?'

'Of course! We'll be right there!' And she slammed the phone down, not realising she hadn't said goodbye.

Mark was in trouble. What trouble? Had there been an accident? Philip. . .Where was Philip? She had to find him!

She knew he wasn't at the church, so rang the parish office. She rang the church centre. She rang the parishioner she knew he'd planned to visit some time that day. The nearest she got to finding him was when she rang the hospital, to be told they were almost certain he'd left the building about ten minutes before.

Ruth replaced the phone thankfully. He must be on his way home then.

Five minutes later there was still no sign of him. She couldn't wait any longer, but knew she couldn't go to the police station on her own either. She picked up the phone again. What a relief to hear Brian's voice! Quickly she explained about the call from the police, and how she couldn't find Philip.

'Stay put,' said Brian without hesitation. 'I'll be round to pick you up in two minutes.'

Grabbing her coat, Ruth ran up to Rachel's room.

'I knew it!' said Rachel. 'I knew as soon as he told me he was going to see Robbie Palmer they'd be up to no good!'

Ruth stared at her. 'Robbie Palmer? Rachel, why on earth didn't you tell me that earlier?'

'Mum, just go! And if Dad comes in, I'll get him to join you there.'

But Ruth was already halfway down the stairs before Rachel had finished the sentence.

'Of course,' continued Barbara confidentially, 'we might be completely wrong. But several of us have noticed, and people are starting to talk . . .'

'And Philip? What does he say?'

'He's very prickly about the whole subject. Refuses to talk about it. When Brian tried to have a tactful word, Philip almost snapped his head off.'

'But you're convinced there's something going on?'

Into Barbara's mind shot the memory of Philip and Louise locked in embrace that day in the church. Should she tell? No, of course not. She wasn't one to spread rumours.

'I really can't say, Margot. All I do know is that Louise Kenton is a very predatory woman where Philip is concerned. I'm not saying we're not grateful to her for stepping in at the last minute when Bill was taken ill . . .'

'Oh, of course not!' agreed Margot, relishing every gossipy word.

'But it seems to me that she's after a very personal service from our vicar.'

'And Ruth? She's such a sensible girl. Surely she's the best person to nip this in the bud?'

'Well, it's difficult to know if she's even aware of it.'

'I see. Well. . .' Margot drummed her well-manicured nails thoughtfully on the chintz tablecloth. 'Do you think it would help if I had a quiet word with David? Very discreetly, of course.'

'Oh, of course,' agreed Barbara, delighted at the suggestion.

'Philip and he are such old friends. David knows only too well how much priests appreciate pastoral support at times like these.'

'Absolutely.'

'A quiet chat, that's what's needed. And if necessary, I suppose I could have a word in the ear of Mrs Kenton myself.'

'Most sensible. A wonderful idea.'

'Leave it to me, my dear.' As she leant over to give Barbara's arm a comforting pat, Margot caught a glimpse of her watch.

'Heavens! It's half-past five. I must dash. There's that wretched cocktail party we simply *have* to go to tonight!'

With a flurry of scarf, parcels and Christian Dior perfume, Margot made a hasty exit. And with mission accomplished, at a much more leisurely pace, Barbara followed her towards the door.

Mark leapt to his feet as he heard the key turn in the lock as a cheery-looking officer popped his head around the door. 'Visitors!'

But before the word was finished Mark had covered the distance between the bunk and his mum. Ruth enveloped him in her arms and the two of them sobbed with relief at seeing each other.

Brian came in next, followed by PC Coleman. Waiting discreetly until both mother and son were more composed, the constable eventually suggested they all go next door to one of the interview rooms so that Mark could make a proper statement. With one arm round his shoulders, Ruth reached out to grab Brian's hand as they turned into the corridor and the door of the interview room shut noisily behind them.

Louise felt like a thief as she hurried to the chapel, waiting breathlessly outside until her quiet knock was answered by Philip. He opened the door just wide enough to let her slip in, locking it again once she was safely inside.

The awkwardness between them was unbearable. Both started to speak at once, and then neither could think of anything to say. They sat in the corner of the chapel, where they felt safe and private, but that same need for privacy added an unnaturalness to their meeting that had never been there before.

'Is this going to be a Dear John speech?' asked Louise at last.

Without thinking, Philip reached out to clasp her hand. 'No, nothing like that.' He ran his other hand through his hair, something he often did when he needed time to choose his words carefully. 'It's just that I should never have behaved as I did last night.'

'Philip, don't say that. Please don't!'

'It was unforgivable of me. I'm your priest. You have a right to turn to me in safety, knowing I'll care for you in a professional and compassionate way. I took advantage of you when you were distressed and vulnerable. I don't know what came over me. I . . .'

'I love you,' she said simply, looking directly into his eyes. 'I love you as I have never loved anyone before. I love you more than life itself.'

'Louise, you mustn't say that . . .'

'Why not? It's true.'

'Then I don't deserve it.'

'Look, Philip, you mustn't worry. I understand. I understand your commitment to your family, and to God. I expect nothing, because I never expect anything else. What happened last night, what you said – well, I can't begin to explain what it means to me. But you mustn't worry that I'll rock the boat. I understand. Because I love you, I could never hurt you.'

'Oh, Louise,' he said simply.

She looked down at her hand, clasped in his.

'It's an odd thing. If it weren't for my search for God, I wouldn't have found you. I can't help feeling that his hand is in this somewhere. If we truly believe that God has a plan for us all, don't we have to accept that he wanted this to happen?'

'But then he gives us choice. We have to choose the right path.'

She smiled sadly. 'Isn't it a tragedy, then, that something which feels so right should be so very wrong?'

He touched her cheek tenderly. 'Yes, my love, it is.'

Slowly, so slowly, she leant forward, gently meeting his lips with hers. He didn't pull away, but he didn't immediately respond either. She sat back from him, her eyes bright with despair and longing. This time it was Philip who drew them closer. As he pulled her into the circle of his arms, he closed his eyes and mind to everything except the feel of her against him, the smell of her, the soft shape of her, the essence of her that was seeping into every fibre of his being.

'Thank you, Mark,' said PC Coleman. 'That's it for now. This statement will be handed on to the Inspector for consideration, so a decision can be made about how we proceed from here. In the meantime, you'll be allowed home on bail, on the understanding that you and your parents report back here next Friday at four o'clock. Is that understood?'

'But Mark was obviously the innocent in the whole thing,' exclaimed Ruth. 'That will be taken into account, won't it? And he's never been involved in anything like this before. It's plainly a misunderstanding.'

The constable looked at her steadily. 'I have no doubt at all, Mrs Barnes, that your son knew the bike was stolen when he took it out to ride it. Handling stolen property is a serious offence.'

'But he didn't steal it!'

'No, he didn't, and Trevor Palmer had quite an interesting collection of stolen property in his lock-up when we took a look. Mr Palmer is being charged, of course, but that doesn't detract from Mark's part in all this. It's clear to me that your son knew exactly what he was doing. He took the risk and got caught.'

'Can I take them home now?' asked Brian, who was sitting quietly to one side. 'They both look all in.'

'Of course, sir, just as soon as we've taken Mark's photo and fingerprints.' Ruth turned to look at Mark, whose face was paler than ever now.

'And I'd like a word with your husband, Mrs Barnes,' continued the sergeant, 'when he's not so busy. Could you ask him to contact me? Here's the number.'

'Of course,' she said, taking the card. 'I'd like a word with him too. He should be here! He should *be* here!'

She watched as Mark's fingerprints were taken, one after another, and then her son was led to a separate room to have his photo taken. He emerged drained and wordless.

'Come on, son,' said Brian gently, laying Mark's anorak across his shoulders. 'Let's go home.' And cradling the boy's head against him, Brian led them all out to his car.

★

'Where were you?'

'At the hospital.'

'They said you'd left.'

'They were wrong. I was in the chapel.'

'Why didn't you ring me? Why didn't you ring even once during the day, to let me know what you were doing? To find out how *we* were? Why didn't you think of that?'

With the familiar gesture of running his fingers through his hair, Philip didn't answer. They were standing a few feet apart, at opposite ends of the kitchen work surface. This is dreadful, thought Philip. How did this ever happen? How could there be such a distance between Ruth and me?

He moved towards her then, hoping to take her in his arms. She walked away to stand beside the table.

'What's going on, Philip? Is there something I should know about?'

'Like what?'

'You tell me. We've always prided ourselves on being completely honest with each other. Well, I'm being honest. I think there is something going on, and I think you should tell me about it.'

'Ruth, I don't know what you're talking . . .'

'And I think it has to do with Louise Kenton. I'd like to know why she rings here, then puts the phone down when I answer. I'd like to know why you're spending so much time with her. I want to know why none of her studies can take place here, in our home, where anyone else's lesson would happen. I want to know why you're so preoccupied all the time. And I want to know why we've not made love for months – since Christmas Eve, in fact – the day Louise Kenton came into our lives.'

Philip stared at her wordlessly. He made no attempt to answer. In the heavy silence between them, she glared at him accusingly.

'Perhaps you've lost interest in me? Perhaps it's my fault that you've become a lousy husband? But have you lost interest in the children too? Where were you when Mark needed you? How come he had so little guidance from his father, he got into a mess like this in the first place? And how can you hope to be much of a priest if you haven't even got time for your own family?'

The sudden pain in Philip's eyes took Ruth by surprise. He looked exhausted, defeated. Still he said nothing, and in spite of her anger, she found herself moved by his expression of bleak resignation. She turned then, stretching her arms out as she walked towards him. Thankfully, they sank into each other, clinging tightly.

Philip buried his head in her shoulder, breathing in the dear familiar scent of her. Ruth. His Ruth.

His voice was muffled as he spoke. 'I love you. You must never doubt that for a moment. I always have loved you, and always will. And of course I love the kids. They're all I live for. I'm as upset as you about what happened with Mark. I should have been there, I know I should . . .'

She held him tighter then, stroking his hair, making small soothing noises in his ear as if he were a child.

'And about Louise. . .' His voice faltered, as if he were unsure what to say. 'I don't know about Louise. I didn't realise you felt that way. I'll do something about it, I promise . . .'

She didn't answer. She couldn't. She knew he loved her, and that was all she needed to know. At least for now.

Steven walked to school with Mark that morning. It was just as well he did. His parents realised the boy was shaken by the experiences of the night before. What they didn't appreciate was just how scared Mark was of facing Ben, and most of all Robbie. He still didn't know exactly what had happened after he was taken to the police station. He thought he'd heard that Trev had been arrested and was going to be charged. Whatever the police might decide to do to Mark was nothing compared to what would happen if Trev ever got hold of him! And he didn't even need to do it himself. Trev had many friends, tough, unforgiving friends, who would turn Mark into pulp before he even knew what hit him.

It wasn't until Assembly that he spotted Robbie. He was on the other side of the hall, not far from the window. As Mark turned in his direction, he caught sight of the other boy's face, with its expression of cold fury. Slowly, very deliberately, looking directly into Mark's eyes, Robbie drew his finger across his throat. Mark looked away quickly, palms sweating, his face flushed. He kept his head down, looking at no one, a hard lump of fear lodged painfully in the pit of his stomach.

It was much later that afternoon when Mark saw him again – except that Robbie saw him first. Mark turned a corner, late as usual for Maths, and Robbie was there, blocking his path with the help of two other, much bigger lads who between them managed to span the whole corridor.

Robbie walked slowly, oh, so slowly towards Mark, until the younger boy was forced to the side, pinned against the hooks, coats and bags that lined the wall. Robbie flattened the length of his forearm across Mark's throat, until he could hardly breathe. Mark squeezed his eyes shut, waiting for the first blow – but it didn't come. Instead, Robbie looked hard at him, jabbing a finger towards his face.

'You, Mark Barnes, are DEAD MEAT!!!'

And then he let go. He stepped back, and turned away, walking off with his cronies without a backward glance. Shuddering with fear, Mark was unable to move. Shocked and shaking, he crouched where he had fallen, terrified that if he tried to get further along the corridor, Robbie would be waiting for him.

'Mark! Are you all right?'

He was not in a state to respond, or register the dread he felt that Ben should be there at just that moment. Had he known Robbie was out to get him? Was Ben part of the gang who planned to make him 'dead meat'?

'It's OK, Mark. They've gone.' Ben was coming closer, trying to help him to his feet. Mark pulled away with all his might, tangling himself in bags and coats as he shot crab-like along the wall. Ben stood back, hands in the air.

'Look,' he said very deliberately, 'I swear I didn't *know* that bike was nicked.'

'Liar! That's why you took me there. That's why you suggested I take a ride.'

'Only because I knew you really wanted to. Look, I didn't know it was stolen. I just thought it might be, 'cos I know Trev's into that sort of thing.'

'They're considering whether to charge me. They might send me to a detention centre.'

'Mark, I'm really sorry. I didn't think this would happen.'

'I might get put away for a year.' His voice shook as he spoke. 'I've got a criminal record. They took my photograph and my fingerprints. I'm on bail. My parents are disgusted with me, and furious with each other. Trev's mates are going to turn me into dead meat. And you're *sorry*?'

'Yeah, I am,' said Ben miserably. 'Look, we're both late for Maths, but I need to talk to you properly. Lunchtime? Meet me in the Art Room cupboard. No one will see us there.'

With a half-hearted nod of agreement, Mark slowly gathered together the books that had tumbled out of his bag and followed Ben in the direction of the Maths Room.

Philip sat in his office at home, with his third attempt at the letter in front of him.

★

Dear Louise,

I would prefer to be with you, to tell you what I need to say, but under the circumstances I feel it would be better for both of us if I simply wrote.

And then he stopped. This was the point at which he always stopped. How could he say they'd never meet again? How could he write that it was all a mistake, and that for her sake above all else, whatever had begun between them must stop? How could he say all that, knowing in his head there was simply no alternative, when his heart was telling him otherwise? How could he bear the pain such a letter would cause her, and not want to hold her, to take the hurt away? How could he know her distress and sadness, then add to it?

And how could he sit in this house, his home, surrounded by all the echoes of love and family life within its walls, and still feel such overwhelming desire for another woman?

He grabbed the sheet of paper in front of him and tore it into pieces before tossing it in the bin. He couldn't write this. He must see her. He must explain in person. He had to sugar this bitter pill with love and compassion. He must help her find a way to manage without him – and hope she could give him the strength to do the same.

The phone rang.

'Philip, found you at last! David here.'

In fact no introduction was needed for Philip to recognise the Bishop's voice. The two men were colleagues rather than friends. Philip always found David aloof and difficult to make small talk with, someone who seemed to be embarrassed by emotion, even when it related to spiritual matters. He had to be in the mood for David. Now was not the moment.

'David, nice to hear from you,' he managed to reply,

wondering exactly what had prompted the call. 'How was the holiday? Far East, wasn't it?'

David was on safe territory here. The next few minutes were filled with a blow by blow account of their itinerary.

He's probably rung up about the centre opening, thought Philip. He'll want some suggestions for his speech. I did pencil some thoughts about that a few days back. I wonder where I put the piece of paper . . .

'. . . so I thought I'd ring just to make sure there's nothing bothering you?'

Philip realised he'd missed something important in the conversation. What did David mean? Bothering him?

'About the centre opening, do you mean?'

''Well, that of course. But more generally. Everything OK your end?'

'Fine,' replied Philip carefully. There was something on David's mind. What was it?

'Only I heard a little rumour, gossip really, that you're receiving rather too much attention from one particular lady parishioner.'

He froze.

'Philip? Are you still there?'

'Yes. I'm just trying to think what on earth you mean?'

'Well, I'm not sure really. I was rather hoping you could enlighten me. And I wanted you to know, of course, my door is always open if you'd like to chat. I know how difficult these situations can sometimes be.'

I doubt it, thought Philip. How could you begin to understand?

'Gossip, you say? Perhaps if you tell me what you heard, and where you heard it, I could work out how all this got dreamed up.'

David hesitated. 'Well, it was from a fairly reliable source. Something about your organist . . .'

Philip gripped the phone to his ear until his knuckles shone white.

'What nonsense! Our Mrs Kenton is a very respectable woman, extremely talented and generous with her time. We couldn't possibly have managed without her after Bill was taken ill.'

'Yes, of course, I understand,' agreed the Bishop quickly.

'Sounds like a bit of malicious tittle-tattle to me, David. A spot of jealousy, perhaps? You know how these things happen. I'd like to know where it came from, though, so I can nip it in the bud this end. Rumours like this can be extremely damaging and hurtful, as you know.'

'Yes. Oh, yes,' replied David uncomfortably. 'So, nothing to worry about then? Everything's under control?'

'Absolutely!' Even Philip was surprised by his glibness when it came to telling lies. White lies.

'And everything's on course for the opening?'

'Three weeks today, Good Friday. We're just hoping the toilets will be finished in time.'

David laughed, glad of the change of subject. 'And the guest list? Need any more help with that? Just ask Jenny if you do. She may be my secretary, but she's there for you too.'

'I appreciate that. Thank you, David.'

'Well, see you on the day then. And don't forget to let me have any notes about the centre you think I should incorporate into my speech. That would be most helpful.'

'Consider it done. Nice to talk to you, David. 'Bye.'

Philip put down the phone, only to find minutes later his hand was still gripping the receiver.

Chapter Nine

March blew in with a blanket of snow and howling winds that made it hard to believe Easter was less than three weeks away.

'That's the trouble with years like this one, when Easter is so early,' moaned Margie, as she handed out coffees from their makeshift kitchen at the back of the church after the service that Sunday morning. 'Just when you start thinking about Easter eggs, and how you'll be putting your thermal vests away in a few weeks' time – whoosh! Down comes another load of snow! Piles of slush everywhere. I'm fed up with it.'

'Hope it cheers up for the centre opening,' said her husband Bert, with his hands deep in suds as he washed a huge pile of coffee cups in the old washing up bowl that served as a sink. 'Don't think anyone will bother to come if the weather's like this.'

'Of course we will, Bert,' chipped in Sue, as she collected another plate of biscuits to hand round to members of the congregation who'd stayed behind for coffee after the service that morning. 'We wouldn't miss it for the world, not after all the work we've put in!'

Bert grinned, displaying an even row of gleaming white dentures. 'Suppose you're right,' he agreed, popping yet another soapy cup down to drain.

'Bert!' snapped Margie, who had to have eyes in the back of the head to see him from where she was standing, 'I've told you before! Rinse them!'

He grimaced goodnaturedly in Sue's direction as she headed off into the crowd, chatting as she went. But when she spotted Ruth standing on her own for a moment, she was by her side in a trice, guiding her friend to a quiet corner.

'How are things? Any more news about Mark? What happened when you went to the station on Friday?'

'Well, they decided to let him off with a caution, because it's his first offence. It was awful, though. We all had to be present as he was formally cautioned by Inspector Hallam. It had to be him, didn't it? I mean, Philip and I are always bumping into Ian Hallam at civic get-togethers. We're quite good friends, really. It was so embarrassing to be hauled over the carpet by him. Do you know, he even stood up and put on his hat to tell us off!'

'But it was only Mark he was talking to, wasn't it?'

'Somehow it didn't feel like it. We all looked at our shoes and took it as if he were the headmaster at school. It was so humiliating.'

'It could have been worse, though,' said Sue, putting her arm round Ruth's shoulders. 'They could have taken the offence much more seriously. He's really got off lightly. Hang on to that.'

'Oh, Sue, Mark looked so lost and hurt. I'm really worried about him. It's as if he's had all the life knocked out of him. He looks dreadful, he's not eating, and I know he's waking up a lot in the night. This whole thing has hit him hard.'

'Well, that may be no bad thing. He's not going to risk getting into any more trouble after this, is he?'

'No, I suppose not. I know I should be angry with him that it happened at all, I just feel sorry for him. I think what he did was stupid, not criminal. Funnily enough, if I'm angry with anyone, it's Philip. I can't get over the fact he should have been there, and wasn't.'

'How is he? How are *you*? Did you need those sexy undies?'

'Do you know, Sue, I think if I was dressed in rubber and hang-gliding from the chandelier, he wouldn't notice! He's so preoccupied all the time. I know there's something on his mind, something he's really worrying about, but although I've tried every way I can to prise it out of him, he just dodges all the time.'

'Louise?'

'Honestly, I don't know. I was watching them both really closely during the service this morning, and I didn't see him talk to her once. He could be avoiding her – or perhaps I've got this whole thing wrong?'

'I don't think so,' said Sue, as a sudden memory of the embrace Barbara had seen between Philip and Louise came to mind. 'I think you're right to be cautious.'

'I wondered . . .' started Ruth. 'Do you think he might be ill? Perhaps there's something physically wrong that he's scared to talk about? Perhaps this has nothing to do with Louise at all?'

'You've got to get him to talk to you.'

'Easier said than done. He just wants cuddles nowadays, lots of cuddles.'

Sue gave her arm a squeeze. 'Well, that's a pretty good start. It'll be all right, Ruth. This is obviously just a bad patch.'

As Ruth smiled at her gratefully, across the way something caught her eye. In a far corner, Louise was standing with her back to everyone else, talking discreetly to Philip. His face was turned away too, so it was impossible to see him clearly, but the discussion was obviously intense. Even though only her back was visible, it was plain from the slump of her shoulders that Louise was distressed. In a reassuring gesture, Philip stretched out to touch her arm – and it was in that moment, Ruth saw it. The infinite tenderness, the deep emotion in his expression as he looked at Louise.

He loves her!

A cold chill drained through Ruth as she stared, unable to take her eyes off his face. Then, as if suddenly aware of being watched, Philip looked up, straight across at her. His expression, the pain and regret she glimpsed there, rooted Ruth to the spot. And then he was gone, turning quickly to leave the room.

And beside her Sue, who'd seen it all, exchanged a knowing glance with Barbara. They all watched in fascination as Philip went out, banging the door behind him. And when curiosity turned their attention back to Louise, it was no surprise to find she had quickly and quietly vanished from sight.

Outside the door, Philip was unsure where to turn. His heart thumped, his palms were clammy, his breathing uneven, as if he'd been running hard. Where could he go to be safe? The church was full of people – friends, parishioners, family – and Ruth. He closed his eyes at the unbearable memory of her face as she watched him with Louise. She knew. Of course she knew. And that tore him apart – that, and the knowledge that his reactions were too complex, too intense, too confused for him to know what to do now. He was overwhelmed by a sense of inevitability, of helpless impotence.

How ironic for someone who glibly pontificated from the pulpit about the need for will-power to overcome the temptation of sin! *Forgive us our trespasses* . . . and yet, what was the good of asking God to forgive hypocrisy and desire that was simply unforgivable?

Mark began to take a different route home every night. Sometimes he would walk a mile or two out of his way, just so he could vary the streets he walked along and the time he arrived. One evening he even hid in a corner of the library for more than an hour, just to be sure Robbie was well away before he began his journey home.

That week had been a nightmare for him. Robbie hadn't come so close to him again, but the meaningful looks, the evil stares, the hatred in his eyes, made his intention clear. He meant to get Mark, and Mark was petrified at the thought.

From a distance, Steven was trying to keep an eye on him. It didn't take a genius to realise that crossing the Palmer family was a dangerous pastime – especially not after the conversation he'd had with Lizzie about a week after it all happened.

It was the exquisite Debbie who had enlightened Liz – except that Steven soon realised Debbie lost much of her charm once you took into account the company she kept.

'Trev and Debbie have been an on-off item for a couple of years now,' explained Lizzie. 'What she sees in him, heaven knows, but she keeps going back to him, even though they seem to be forever arguing and breaking up. He's like a magnet. She just can't keep away.'

'Mum said he's in prison. Is that right?'

'On remand, yes. He already had a six-month suspended sentence, you see, for a burglary he got caught for last year – and he's been done plenty of times before that, for everything from shoplifting to breaking into cars. The trouble is he's eighteen now, so for the first time he's being treated as an adult. That means they've put him on remand until his trial. Debbie reckons he'll go down for at least six months this time, and that's only if he pleads guilty.'

'Well, he can hardly plead anything else, with his lock-up full to the brim with stolen bikes!'

'I wouldn't put anything past him. He's not the brightest of fellas.'

'So he must be pretty mad about being found out?'

'Furious. And because he needs someone to blame, your Mark is in the firing line.'

'But he was just a patsy in all this! He didn't really know what he was getting into.'

'I'm not sure that matters.'

'Poor kid. I'm going to have to keep an eye on him as much as I can. I've noticed he's a bit of a Houdini at going home time, presumably to avoid coming across any of Trev's pals on the way. He's always hated me walking home with him in the past

– you know, little boy being escorted home by big brother – but I'm going to insist from now on.'

'But what can you do if the pair of you meet up with a crowd of Trev's mates? They don't muck around, you know.'

With some surprise, Steven looked down to see real fear in Liz's face.

'It'll be all right, Liz. I'm not worried about them. Bullies who pick on small boys usually back down if they're challenged. Basically cowards, you see . . .'

She grabbed the sleeve of his anorak, pulling him round to face her. 'Steve, you must listen. Don't get involved in this. Tell your mum and dad. Get them to talk to the police. Keep Mark at home for a week or two! Send him away! But *please*, don't get involved yourself. Please!'

'Lizzie, you're crying . . .' Steven reached towards her to wipe away a tear that was running down the side of her face. This was a Liz he'd never seen before. She was usually so cool – carefully, casually friendly. But there was real worry in her voice as she spoke, and he realised with a jolt that he was glad she cared. What a very comforting thought that was.

She was rubbing the back of her hand roughly across her cheek now, as if embarrassed by her outburst. She hadn't meant to reveal her feelings so clumsily. What a fool she was! Emotion embarrassed him, she knew that. He'd dismiss her as a blubbing, melodramatic idiot.

'I'm sorry,' she mumbled, keeping her head low so he couldn't see her face. 'What a nut I am!' She made an attempt at a light-hearted laugh.

But he didn't laugh. She knew he was gazing at her, but still she didn't dare look up as, very slowly, his hand began to stroke her cheek, moving in a soft caress down towards her chin. With a tenderness that took her breath away, he tilted her chin so that her eyes met his, their faces almost touching. He lifted both hands to cup the sides of her face, brushing her cheeks with his thumbs to soothe away the tears.

'You,' he said quietly, 'are lovely – just lovely.'

Lizzie closed her eyes as his face moved closer, savouring the feel of his lips as, at last, they met hers, gently at first, and then with small sweet feathery kisses that melted through her body. And when their mouths finally parted, neither of them pulled back but stayed close, fingers intertwined.

The promise in his eyes was unmistakable. The response in hers was just as clear. He tipped his head forward, until their foreheads were touching.

'So lovely. Very lovely indeed . . .'

Louise reached into the bathroom cabinet to grab her bottle of Amitryptiline. These were the most recent pills Dr Bevan had prescribed for her. Over the years, there had been many others. Sometimes she took them. Sometimes she poured them down the toilet. She hated being reliant on pills – but she needed them now.

'Take two daily after meals' said the label. Louise upended the bottle, tipped out four tablets and stuffed them into her mouth, washing them down with a mouthful of water from the glass by the sink.

Her head dropped, her shoulders sagged. To have found the most wonderful man – to win his love – but have to deny it! Not that she was surprised by the hopelessness of it all. Hope was something she'd abandoned years ago. She expected nothing. What she couldn't cope with was the hard knot of twisting pain lodged in her gut, taking over her every sense and thought.

Staring in the mirror, she began mechanically to brush her hair. They'd had so little chance to talk since their meeting in the chapel. And when they snatched a conversation after the service on Sunday, their timing was all wrong. Under the eagle eye of everyone else having coffee around them, what could they say that mattered? Well, they'd have a chance to talk properly today. He'd rung quickly that morning, suggesting they meet later out of town, in the car park of a country park where there were lots of quiet walks to lose themselves in.

She glanced at her watch. Two hours to go. Everything was organised. By the time she had to leave, Lizzie would be back from school to keep an eye on Eileen. She would tell her daughter she was going to the church to practise the organ. Lizzie understood about practising. She'd probably do the same herself on her cello while her mum was gone. Philip had said he'd be at the hospital all afternoon, and wouldn't be able to get away until after the small Eucharist Service he held in the chapel. *Their* chapel, she thought with a smile, as she remembered the time they'd spent together there. And she closed her eyes to taste again the touch of his lips on hers.

'Mark! Wait!' Steven ran to catch up with his brother as he hurried towards the back door of the school.

Mark didn't answer although he did stop, shrinking into an alcove as Steven joined him.

'Look, I'll just get my bag and we'll walk home together. OK?'

'There's no need.'

'Well, there might be . . .'

'If they're going to get me, I just wish they'd get on with it, so it's over. I can't stand this much longer!'

'I know, mate. But they're not going to get near you if I have anything to do with it. Look, just stay put. I'll go and get my stuff and meet you back here in two minutes.'

Mark nodded without comment, watching his brother's reassuring grin as his lanky frame disappeared round the corner.

'Barnes!'

Steven looked ahead, to see the forbidding figure of Mr Morrison, his Physics teacher, looming into sight.

'Sir?'

'Your folder! You left it in the Physics Lab. I'd like to know exactly how you plan to do your homework tonight if your folder isn't in your possession?'

'Sir,' agreed Steven, without enthusiasm.

'Well, you'd better go and pick it up. The lab might be locked by now. If it is, find the caretaker and ask him for the key.'

Steven thought of Mark waiting for him by the back door, and started running in the direction of the lab.

'And don't forget to take the key back afterwards!'

The lab was locked. Of course it would be! Now, where to find the caretaker? At this time in the evening, he could be anywhere. Steven turned on his heel, and began running in the direction of the main hall. Most likely he was there.

Ever since their conversation, Brian had been seething with cold anger towards Barbara. Even she was surprised by the depth of his reaction. She knew him to be a placid, easygoing man. His fury when she had told him about her chat with Margot was quite unexpected.

'You mean, you told that woman – that busybody – this stupid tittle-tattle about Philip? Knowing how much damage it could do – knowing that it's little more than malicious gossip – you *told* her?'

'Well, of course there's gossip, with Philip behaving as foolishly as he plainly is! What else could he expect? Obviously, we must try to limit the damage. We have a duty to get him pastoral support, if that's what's needed.'

'Nothing was needed! Certainly not interference by you that can cause nothing but trouble.'

'Brian, may I remind you that you are a church warden? We are both on the Parish Council. We have responsibilities . . .'

'We have responsibilities towards Philip and Ruth as our *friends*! They need our support, perhaps a spot of advice if it's asked for. But to go spreading this rubbish to someone as manipulative as Margot is sheer madness. And you know that family have a lot on their minds at the moment, with everything Mark's been through. Have you lost your senses?'

'Well, perhaps if Philip started behaving more like a responsible father and husband, and less like a lovesick teenager, his son wouldn't get into scrapes like that!' And with anger blazing in her eyes, Barbara spun on her heel and headed for the hall, yanking open the door of the cupboard under the stairs to pull out her coat and briefcase.

'When you've calmed down, I'll talk to you further about this. In the meantime, I resent your reaction. Something had to be done. You promised to talk to Philip, but you didn't. I've learned over years of living with you, Brian, that if I want a thing done, it's safer to get on with it myself. And that's exactly what I did!'

He opened his mouth to answer just as she slammed the front door shut behind her.

That conversation had Brian so riled, he seethed with fury throughout the day, eventually taking himself off to the centre in the afternoon to see how the finishing touches were going. With the opening now just ten days away, there were still so many loose ends – problems with the electrics, the cooker hadn't arrived, the central heating only worked when it felt like it, the skylight in the backroom was already smashed, and the unplumbed toilets were lying in a neat row down the middle of the main hall.

Ken the builder gave him a grin and a thumbs up sign from the top of his ladder. Brian just wished he could share Ken's confidence that everything would be ready in time. Well, there was nothing for it but to roll up his sleeves and give them a hand. And in his present mood, Brian could think of nothing he'd enjoy more right now than a bit of pummeling to get this centre into shape.

★

Where was that darn caretaker? Always around when you didn't need him, and never when you did. Steven pelted out of the hall, desperately thinking, where to try next. He could be down in his room at the back of the PE changing area. Yes, that's probably where he was.

Steven considered whether to swoop round to where Mark was waiting first, just to let him know what was happening. No, quicker to get on with it. His brother wouldn't be daft enough to go home without him.

The clock in the main entrance of the hospital said three-forty-five as Philip walked by. He'd been held up on a couple of wards that afternoon, and was cutting it fine for popping in to see Minnie before the chapel service.

He couldn't miss her, though. He had some exciting news. Jill, the Ward Sister, had heard from Social Services they'd found a place for her when she was discharged, which with luck would be at the start of the following week. It was a small nursing home that specialised in elderly patients. Having visited parishioners there in the past, Philip was familiar enough with the place to know that they would make Minnie very comfortable. He knew she'd probably be reluctant at first, but without a doubt it was a sensible move for her. It was very good news indeed.

He ran up the stairs two at a time, turning right at the top in the direction of Bunyan Ward. With a wave across the hallway to Jill, who was busy with another patient, Philip made his way over to Minnie with a smile. To his surprise she was sitting up in a highbacked chair beside the bed – not that she looked very happy about it.

'They won't listen! I told them I want to go back to bed, and they just keep ignoring me.'

Philip grinned at her, reaching out for her hand. 'Well, perhaps they know more than you do. It must be good idea for you to move around a bit, give that hip of yours a chance to get more mobile.'

'Unnecessary and uncalled for! I just want to be left alone.'

'No can do, Minnie, and we've all been very busy on your behalf. Guess what? There's a lovely nursing home called Shrublands just round the corner from here, and they say you can stay there for a few weeks while you get better.'

She stared at him then shook her head sadly. 'You don't listen either, do you? I'm not going anywhere.'

'You must, Minnie. They've plenty of other patients waiting for operations who need this bed. You would be much more comfortable in a nursing home. You'd have plenty of company there, and I would . . .'

'I won't need it. I won't be here!'

He smiled at her indulgently. 'Well, they're talking about Monday, Tuesday at the latest, for you to be discharged. Seeing how much better you look now, I think it's quite likely you'll still be very much with us by then. And just in case you are, we need to make plans. Shrublands is really nice, Minnie, believe me.'

'Why should I? You didn't believe me.'

Philip fell silent then, realising this was going to be more of an uphill struggle than he had imagined.

'Give it a chance, Minnie,' he said at last. 'I'll come and collect you, and travel with you in the ambulance. Shrublands is a lovely place, very homely. Don't you think it would be nice to relax and let other people do the worrying for a while? You could just concentrate on getting well.'

'I'm not *going* to get well. I told you. I'll be leaving this place in a box.'

'Minnie, life is a precious gift, and one that God wants us to value. Don't wish yours away. There'll be time enough to join him. But from everything Sister tells me, you've a good few years ahead of you yet, I'm delighted to say.'

He watched sadly as her eyes misted with tears of frustration. 'You of all people should understand. I don't want to stay here. I have nothing, absolutely nothing, to live for. I want to move on to the next world, to that eternal life he promises us. I know it exists now, and I want to be there.'

'It'll happen, Minnie. It will. But in the meantime, please let us help you to make a better life for yourself here. You never know, you might even enjoy it.'

'You see, Philip,' she went on, as if he hadn't spoken, 'none of this matters. What lies ahead means so much more. There's peace there. No pain. No being old. No petty rules and regulations. Just peace, and God's eternal love.'

'Amen to that, Minnie. Can we pray together now? Please?'

'You've got it all so wrong. We mustn't be fettered by the ties of this life. It's what lies ahead that's really important. We mustn't be afraid of it. It's where we belong. Where you belong. You must believe me!'

'Shhh,' soothed Philip. 'Come on, pray with me now – then I'll ask someone about getting you back into bed.'

Her shoulders slumped. 'You don't need to talk to me as if I'm a child. I'm not an idiot. I'm not losing my marbles. And, Philip, for a man who thinks he knows God, you have a great deal to learn.'

'I admit that, Minnie, and I pray I'll never stop learning. Forgive me, I didn't mean to upset you. I am worried about you, though. Promise me you'll give it some thought over the weekend? I'll come in again on Monday morning, and if you're still dead set against the idea, we'll think again.'

'There's nothing to think about. It's all in hand. God has it in hand.' And with that, she bowed her head.

' "Our Father," ' she began, ' "Who art in heaven . . ." '

Philip joined in, watching her fondly as he did, marvelling

at her determination and spirit. She might be difficult and un-co-operative – but there was something about this frail woman that touched him more than he could say.

It was a good quarter of an hour before Steven found the care-taker, dashed back to the lab to collect his folder, returned the key to the caretaker again, and finally headed back to the spot where he'd arranged to meet Mark.

He wasn't there. Steven wandered around a bit, opening likely doors, scouring the dressing rooms and grounds just outside the back exit of the school. But there was no doubt about it, Mark had gone.

Brian stood up stiffly from fixing the leaking radiator. He was too old for this lark. He ought to stick to Accountancy. It was kinder on the knees.

He looked at his watch. Five past four. Barbara would be back from school in an hour or so, but he felt no inclination to be at home waiting for her. Let her stew for a bit, wondering where he'd got to. It would be much nicer to call into the paper shop for his *Train* magazine, then wander round to the Vicarage to see if young Mark was home. Perhaps he could be persuaded out for a while. They had talked about nipping into town to take a look at a new bird book they'd heard about. The boy might enjoy that – and if anyone needed a bit of enjoyment, Mark certainly did.

Steven tried hard to think calmly as he ran. There was no need to panic. His brother had walked home on his own several times lately and come to no harm. He'd be fine. He was probably at the Vicarage right now, lying in front of the telly with his thumb in his mouth!

Which way was he likely to walk home? Steven knew he'd been varying the route quite a bit recently.

He came to the crossroads, looking at the two options. Did Mark turn right or go straight across? Steven hesitated for a few moments then stepped out confidently. Straight on! Even though to turn right was the obvious way to go, he had a feeling that on this occasion, Mark probably took the long way home.

★

But he hadn't. Mark had waited for more than ten minutes before deciding Steven must have found better things to do than walk his little brother home.

The school corridors were almost empty by then. If Robbie and his gang were waiting for him tonight, they'd probably reckon they'd missed him.

He set out quickly down the school path, turning right outside the gate. There were still a few youngsters hanging around the school, waiting for buses or for parents to collect them. Mark slipped past them as unobtrusively as he could, and headed off down the short stretch of road to the crossroads.

He scanned each direction, trying to decide which would be safest. Straight on probably. That was the way he should go. But suddenly, on a whim he couldn't quite explain, he decided he'd had enough of playing cat and mouse. The shortest way home was to the right – and that's the way he went.

He needn't have worried. The coast was quite clear. Apart from the odd group of youngsters and mothers clutching toddlers, there seemed to be surprisingly few people about. He turned into Ashbourne Avenue, relaxing a bit now that home was probably no more than half a mile away. He walked on, past the paper shop, past Mrs Evan's house, past the playground, and on towards the bus shelter.

And it was then, when he had gone too far to turn back, that he saw them – about six of them, stepping out of the shadow of the shelter directly into his path. The smallest of them was

Robbie but he was undoubtedly the ringleader, standing in their midst with an expression of cold hatred on his face.

'Here he comes, the vicar's little boy!' he hissed. 'Such a goody-goody, he drops other people in it! Well, vicar's boy, you picked the wrong one this time – and we're going to drop you!'

The last coherent thought Mark had as they moved towards him was that he was probably about to die.

As soon as Philip pulled into the country park he saw her car, parked away from most of the others in the farthest corner of the clearing. Peering cautiously into the other cars as he drove past them, he checked quickly to see if anyone he knew had seen him arrive. No. All the cars seemed empty. In seconds he had pulled his car alongside hers and opened the door to climb in beside her.

At first neither of them spoke. They just looked at each other, hands tightly locked together. Louise peered at him in the gathering dusk.

'You look tired.'

He shrugged, with a wry attempt at a smile. 'I'm not sleeping much.'

'Nor me,' she replied quickly.

'Is Richard home?'

'No.'

'Back at the weekend?'

'Probably. He usually is. He has rung, but I don't ask him anything about himself now. If he doesn't volunteer information, I don't question him. I don't care what he's doing.'

'Louise, you mustn't say that.'

'Why not? I feel it. Should I lie?'

'I don't think you're capable of lying to me.'

'I have no reason to, yet I think I've been living a lie for most of my life – right up to the moment you said you loved me.'

'Louise . . .'

'Hold me, please?'

'Louise, this is impossible. I can't do this. I mustn't do this. I'm a priest. I am forbidden to do this.'

Her hands began to shake.

'That's what I came to tell you,' he continued. 'We're both married. We both have children. I know you have little feeling for Richard, and after the way he's behaved over the years, I can't blame you for that – but I do love Ruth. I've always loved her. We are a couple. I'm her husband. I want to stay her husband, knowing I can look her in the eye with honesty, and tell her I've always been faithful to her.'

He became aware that the trembling in Louise's hands was beginning to spread throughout her body. Still she said nothing, simply looking into his face as he spoke.

'I can't explain my feelings for you. There's just something about your sadness, the pain you've been through, your strength in the face of it all, that touches the very heart of me.'

Still clasping her hand, he looked down to stroke her fingers. And then, with her voice hesitant, and so low he could hardly hear her, she began to speak.

'I've never allowed myself to get close to people, which is why what's happened between us is such a miracle to me. I realise now that one of the most wonderful experiences we can have in life is to be allowed to know someone else well – really know them, know them intimately and I don't mean just in a physical sense!

'Once you're married, once you've taken that vow "to forsake all others", that kind of intimate knowledge of any other person except the one you're married to is strictly forbidden. And I think that's a pity, because we're told we're made in God's image. Getting to know you, sharing my journey of faith with you. I've come to know God. Learning to love God, I've come to love you.

'I've never felt such love before, Philip. I'm sorry if it embarrasses you. I'm sorry if it compromises your position with your family or with the church. But I'm not sorry it's happened. I have never been so happy in my whole life. You make me happy. Being with you makes me happier than I have words to express. And a life in which I am not able to share my love with you would be no life at all.'

'Oh, Louise,' he said sadly, cupping her face with his hand, 'whatever am I going to do with you? Whatever can we do?'

The first fist caught Mark squarely on the nose, knocking him to the ground as he clasped his face, trying to stem the flow of blood. And then the kicking began. Dimly he was aware of feet around him, thumping his back, his legs, his stomach. And last of all, he looked straight up into a face contorted by hatred as Robbie's boot slammed into his chin – and everything went black.

Standing at the ironing board in the kitchen, Ruth glanced at the clock. Mark was late. But of course it was Wednesday when he had two periods of sport last thing in the afternoon. He was often late on a Wednesday.

Her brow creased as she ironed. On top of everything else, her youngest child was a real worry to her at the moment. He was so quiet, barely speaking, staying in his room for hours on end. Something was worrying him, she knew, but however hard she tried to get him talking, he wouldn't be drawn on it.

She sighed wearily as she came to the end of yet another shirt. That was the trouble with sharing a house with three men. Life was just an endless succession of shirts to iron.

She reached into the basket to draw out one of Philip's black clerical shirts. Pressing a button on top of the iron, a cloud of steam engulfed the shirt as she spread it out on the board. Mechanically, she began to glide the iron over the creases, while picturing Philip wearing this shirt – Philip in the church, talking to members of the congregation, with his arm around a bereaved wife, or laughing with a couple about to be married. Philip in their kitchen, Philip in the car, Philip standing beside her as they looked down at a sleeping Mark on Christmas Eve.

Whether it was the steam or the mist in her eyes that blurred her vision she wasn't sure. With a bang, she stood the iron on its end and sat down heavily on the stool behind her, burying her face in her hands.

If only he'd talk to her. If only she could see that familiar smile in his eyes to reassure her that everything was all right. If only they could laugh about this, as they'd always laughed their way through problems in the past.

If only Louise Kenton did not exist! If only she were dead!

Shocked at herself, Ruth sat bolt upright. She looked for the umpteenth time at the kitchen clock. Mark was late. Why waste a moment's thought on Philip, who didn't deserve it, when it was their son who needed her? Mark, who for days had been acting as if the life had been knocked out of him.

Brian couldn't resist flicking through the pages of his *Train* magazine as he walked away from the paper shop in the direction of the Vicarage. He was so engrossed that at first he didn't recognise what he saw. It looked like a black plastic bag sprawled across the pavement. He almost crossed the road to avoid it when something stopped him in his tracks. He peered at the black shape ahead of him. It wasn't a black bag, it was a black anorak, just like the one Mark wore to school. And as he cautiously drew nearer, dread flooded through him. It *was* Mark – battered, bleeding and lifeless.

Footsteps running towards him roused Brian from the shock of what he was seeing.

'Uncle Brian! Tell me that's not Mark? It's not him, is it?'

Steven came running up breathlessly, clasping his hand to his mouth in horror to see the huddled, bloody shape of his brother on the ground.

Brian recovered enough to snap into action. 'Run back to the paper shop as quick as you can. Ring for an ambulance! Go on! GO!'

He bent down to cradle his godson's head carefully in his arms. 'Hold on, son,' he said, emotion choking his voice. 'Help's coming, Mark. Just you hold on!'

Ruth sat on one side of the hospital bed, Philip on the other, inches apart, a gulf between them.

Beside them Mark was restless. Even in sleep, he was obviously in pain. The side of his head where the jaw had been broken was out of shape in a way that made his small face look hideously deformed. And although the doctors had said his nose wasn't broken, to Ruth it looked as if it was. It was split and swollen beneath the two purple rings that circled his eyes.

So far he'd not managed to speak, even to the policeman who had arrived in the hope of taking a statement. Steven had talked to him instead, telling him Mark's fears about Trev and Robbie. The policeman nodded in understanding.

'It just so happens,' said PC Coleman, 'that I was the one who arrested Mark the other night. That Trev Palmer's a nasty piece of work, and the rest of his family aren't much better.' He looked towards the still figure in the bed. 'None of us thought he'd be this vindictive, though. Poor lad! Cost him a lot, didn't it, that couple of minutes on a bike?'

He moved over to the nurses' station to find out from the Sister on duty that there was little hope of Mark's being able to say anything sensible before morning.

'Well, perhaps I'll have some good news by then, like we've nailed the yobs who did this to him. I'll be back about eleven, OK?'

Philip and Ruth continued to sit in silence, each with their own thoughts as they looked down at their sleeping son. At last, Philip got stiffly to his feet.

'I need a cup of coffee. How about you? You haven't eaten anything at all. Let me get you some tea and a sandwich?'

Ruth shook her head without looking at him. Philip was overwhelmed with compassion as he looked at her, so dear, familiar, wretched – and so very distant.

'Ruthie, come on, you need to . . .'

'Don't!'

She stiffened as he came towards her.

'Darling, this won't help. Mark is our son. We're his parents. He needs us both. He needs us to work together for him . . .'

'How come that means something to you now, Philip, when it meant so little before?'

'Ruth, I . . . we . . .'

But she had turned away from him, her gaze firmly fixed on Mark. 'Go away, Philip. Isn't there somewhere else you'd rather be?'

Chapter Ten

It was three days before Mark was well enough to be discharged from hospital. By that time, apart from very dramatic bruising and the injury to his jaw which would obviously take some time to mend, he was in fairly good spirits. Visits from his headmaster, from Ben and from PC Coleman, had all combined to reassure him the episode was now over. Fortunately, his school was one that took a firm stand on bullying and it seemed likely that, after being charged with the attack, Robbie would not be returning after the Easter holiday. In the meantime, all Mark had to do was get well, and put the whole unpleasant business behind him.

One of the nicest things to happen was Ben's reaction to everything that had happened. Seeing his friend so badly beaten had been a stark lesson, knocking the cockiness out of him. Perhaps it was guilt that had the youngster clamouring to spend time with Mark each evening, but Ruth was glad to see her son regain some of his old spirit in Ben's company.

If only all relationships could be repaired as easily! The atmosphere between her and Philip was strained and unnatural. He was trying hard to bridge the gap between them, but she found herself unable to respond. There were moments when she chastised herself for her brittle indifference to him, but she couldn't help but blame him. It wasn't just that he hadn't been

there physically when she needed him. She now knew that his
heart wasn't there either, and that was much harder to forgive,
or to bear.

Philip found himself on a rollercoaster of emotion: overwhelming sadness and regret for the distance between himself
and Ruth; worry about Mark; concern for the centre opening
which was looming in less that a week's time; and above all his
wildly fluctuating feelings about Louise.

He'd seen her only once since Mark went into hospital, and
that was for a few snatched minutes in the vestry when she'd
popped into the church during the week. The loving care in her
expression as she looked at him unhinged the emotion he'd kept
dammed inside himself all week. As she cradled his head in her
arms, rocking him gently, he allowed the tears to come. He cried
for Mark, he cried for Ruth, he cried for Louise – and most of
all he cried for himself. In all his life, he'd never cried that way
– but then, never before had so many crises hit him, one after
another.

At last, his shuddering sobs subsided, and he sat back beside
her, spent and exhausted.

'We can't do this any more.'

'I know.' Her eyes were enormous pools of sadness as she
replied.

'I do love you, but we can't do this. I can't do this – because
of Mark, because of Ruth, because of my faith – and most of all
because of you. This is wrong for you. You need and deserve
someone better than me.'

'Philip, they don't come any better than you.'

'Louise . . .'

She placed her finger against his lips, eyes brimming with
tears to match his own.

'Shhh. I know.' She drew her finger longingly around the
outline of his lips.

'I shall never stop loving you, Philip. But I do understand.
God bless you always.'

She got to her feet, leant over to kiss the top of his head, and with deliberate steps left the church.

'I just don't know what's wrong with her. There's definitely something on her mind, but whatever it is, she won't talk to me.'

It was a glorious if chilly spring afternoon, at last after all the wintry weather so far that month. Lizzie and Steven had needed no encouragement to escape into the privacy of the woods, to walk, to chat, to be alone together. As they meandered along, he'd taken her cold hand, and held it inside his roomy coat pocket as he replied, 'But would your mum usually talk to you about personal things? Would you want to talk to her like that?'

'Well, we've always been quite close. But then, I think girls and mums often are. I do know she has a hard time with Gran, and Dad doesn't help a lot.'

'Does he have to be away so much?'

'I suppose he has no choice. But even when he's home, he's very distant and preoccupied.'

'Just with her or with you too?'

'Not so much with me.'

'Do you think they're happily married then, your mum and dad?'

'I suppose . . .' Lizzie chewed her lip thoughtfully. 'I suppose she must feel neglected quite a bit of the time. He doesn't bother much about her. Even I can see that.'

'So is that what she's worried about, now do you think?'

'Honestly, I don't know. There are times when I catch her smiling to herself, others when she looks as if she's about to burst into tears. Either way, she's not herself at the moment.'

'Bit like my mum right now . . .'

'Really? I've always thought your mum and dad were the happiest couple I've ever seen.'

'Yeah, well, normally they are, but lately things are pretty dire between them.'

'Why? What do you mean?'

'I'm not sure what it's all about. Dad's out a lot, what with the church centre and everything. But it's more than that. As if his head's in the clouds all the time. He's just not with it, you know? Even I've noticed it, and I can see it drives Mum mad.'

'Gosh, I can't imagine your mum mad at anyone.'

'Funnily enough, neither can I. She's angry with him most of the time, and I'm sure there's more to it than him just being late every now and then.'

'Perhaps she doesn't trust him?'

Steven looked at her in surprise. 'Don't be daft, he's a vicar!'

'Well, I know my mum doesn't trust my dad. I thought all couples were the same?'

Steven laughed. 'Not mine. That's one of the really infuriating things about my dad. Totally predictable, always does the right thing. He'd probably be a lot more interesting if he were less trustworthy!'

Lizzie didn't laugh with him. 'Not interesting, Steven. It's frightening. It's frightened me for as long as I can remember – the thought that my dad will finally go off with someone else and break up the family.'

'Has he got someone else, then?'

'I don't know for sure, but I reckon so. Things I've heard him say on the phone, the way he dresses himself up sometimes. I've noticed, and I know Mum has too.'

'Your poor mum. It must be dreadful to know the person you're married to is having an affair.'

'Yes, it's been really hard on her.'

'Well, thank goodness that's never likely to happen to my parents!' replied Steven. 'Dad's far too old to think about things like that now, of course, but even if he did have the inclination, his choice is fairly limited. Sue Golding perhaps? No, she's too noisy – she'd drive him crackers. Barbara Gilpin – too bossy!

He'd be terrified. What about your mum? She could do with a bit of cheering up!'

Lizzie giggled. 'Mum would never do a thing like that – far too respectable! But I know she thinks the world of your dad, after all he's done for her. I reckon if she ever threw her hat at anybody, it would be him.'

Steven drew his hand out of his pocket to slide his arm round her shoulders.

'A bit of a liability really, aren't they, parents? Tell you what, you worry about your mum and I'll worry about you.'

She nestled into him, speechless with contentment. He bent his head towards her, drawing her to him as the kiss deepened. Then, taking her hand, he led her away from the path, through the bracken, towards a dense patch of trees. And there, hidden from prying eyes, he pulled her down on the ground beside him, until every part of their bodies touched. She reached out to bring him even closer to her as she felt his hand slip inside her coat to find the warm softness of her breast.

Is this love? Is this how it feels? she thought in wonder as she moulded her body against his. But there was no need for words as she gave herself up to the delicious overwhelming closeness of him, the desire in his eyes, and the passion of his searching, caressing hands.

Louise never really worked out exactly what happened. It was Monday morning and she'd been upstairs, making the beds, knowing Eileen was safely installed in front of the television. Monday was the one day when the day care centre couldn't offer her mother-in-law a place, the day of the week when Louise knew she had to be based at home.

The king-sized bed she shared with Richard allowed them both the distance they wanted during the night, but it was the devil's own job for one person to change the cover on a duvet that size. Finally, as she fastened the last popper along the base of the cover, Louise sat down on the bed with a sigh of relief. Immediately, her thoughts went to Philip – nothing unusual, because she could think of little else these days.

She had seen him the morning before, during the church service. He'd kept his distance, and she'd hardly dared look at him for fear of her emotions being clear for all to see. She was already aware of Barbara Gilpin's interest in everything she did. Barbara was a woman to be wary of – a practical and efficient ally, but not someone to cross.

Louise lay back against the pillows, closing her eyes to be private with her thoughts. How she missed him! How she missed their long conversations and intense spirit-filled debates about the complexities of the Bible. She missed the smile in his eyes as he looked at her. Missed his support and encouragement. Missed his love. Dear God, how she missed him!

Suddenly a deafening, inhuman scream filled the house. She sat bolt upright, unable to make sense of what she was hearing. It was coming from downstairs. Eileen was downstairs . . .

Taking the steps two at a time, she raced below, following the sound that came from the kitchen. Bursting into the doorway, an appalling sight met her eyes.

Eileen was doubled up next to the cooker, where one gas ring was alight. She was wailing in fear and pain, clutching her arm to her. Even from a few feet away, Louise felt nausea rise in her throat as she realised the nylon of her mother-in-law's dressing gown had melted into the raw, blistering skin of her forearm where a flame was still smouldering.

Philip kept his promise to Minnie to pop in and see her on Monday morning, although he wondered what sort of reception he'd get. Jill had told him at the Palm Sunday Service the day before that she hoped the old lady would be released that morning. But would she go to Shrublands? He'd soon find out.

He mounted the stairs, turning right at the top towards

Bunyan Ward, but stopped abruptly when he reached Minnie's bed. It was empty. She's up, he thought. That's good. They've got her out of bed, and ready for the off this morning.

Grinning to himself, he turned to look for Jill, spotting her immediately as she walked towards him from the nurses' station.

'You're too late, I'm afraid . . .'

'She's not gone to Shrublands without me, has she?' he asked with a smile. 'Trust her to have the last word.'

Jill touched his arm gently. 'She's gone, Philip. She died this morning.'

'What?'

'She just slipped away in her sleep, so peacefully we didn't really notice for a while. She looked really contented lying there.'

Philip sat down heavily on the bed. It took him some moments to speak.

'I think she probably *was* content at long last. Well, I never! She said she'd never leave this place alive, and she meant it.'

'I'm sorry, Philip. I know you'd grown quite fond of her.'

'Yes,' he agreed, still dazed from the news. 'I can't believe it.'

'She left you a note. She must have written it during the night. I haven't read it.' Jill fished into her pocket to draw out a single sheet from a notebook, roughly folded in two.

Philip's hand was shaking as he reached out for it.

Dear Philip,

I told you this would happen, although I know you didn't believe me. But just in case you're feeling sorry for me – don't! You and I both know I've gone to a better place. I'm tired. There's too much pain here. I want to be with God, so I can stop hurting.

You know, you have a lot of knowledge, but no instinct at all when it comes to faith. You have bound yourself up in man-made rules. You imagine you know the will of God – but how can you possibly guess the infinite workings of his mind? How can you begin to understand his purpose? We're simply not clever enough to presume anything. We're too blind, too afraid to draw back the curtain between this world and the next.

Some things just happen because God wills them that way. Nothing we do, nothing we decide, can change the inevitable. Sometimes we must simply accept what God brings us, because we can't change it. His purpose, not our own – that is what we must strive to find.

Don't be afraid of what lies ahead, Philip. Once we're there, the purpose and challenges of this life will be made clear to us. The peace of eternal life. I long for that peace, as perhaps one day you may long for it too.

Pray for me, as I will for you.

I have enjoyed knowing you,

Minnie

And there on her bed, in the middle of the ward, Philip bowed his head to pray, only to find he was crying instead.

The queue in Accident and Emergency was thankfully thin when Louise screeched to a halt outside the main entrance. Ignoring the double yellow lines she parked on, she ran into A&E, yelling for someone to come and help get Eileen out of the car.

They brought a wheelchair so that they could swiftly and gently transfer the moaning, distressed woman into a small cubicle where space was so limited the nurse suggested Louise should wait outside. It was some time, and two cups of machine tea later, before the nurse reappeared, asking her to come and talk to the doctor.

They'd moved Eileen to a side room where she lay in a bed that seemed too high and enormous for her. Louise's heart lurched with pity as she saw the confusion and pain in her mother-in-law's eyes. 'Richard,' she wailed softly. 'He's a naughty boy. Richard . . . where's Richard?'

'We'll be keeping her in, of course, Mrs Kenton,' said the ridiculously young doctor who'd been looking after Eileen. 'I'm afraid your mother's got a first-degree burn on her arm. The hot nylon of her dressing gown attached itself to her skin, and kept on doing damage even after she'd taken her arm away from the heat. Nor surprisingly, she's suffering quite severely from the effects of shock too.'

Louise leant over to stroke her mother-in-law's hot forehead. Eileen seemed unaware she was there, her eyes wild and glassy, her mind a jumble of disconnected thoughts.

'Is she in pain?'

'Inevitable, I'm afraid. We'll keep her sedated, of course, but yes, with a burn like that, she probably is feeling a certain amount of discomfort at present.'

Louise's eyes filled with tears. 'I don't know what happened. I don't know why she turned the ring on. I just don't know what she thought she was doing . . .'

'Well,' said the doctor gently, 'she probably didn't know either. Injuries like this are quite common when patients have such advanced dementia.'

'I should have been watching her more closely. I was making the beds, you see . . .'

'You mustn't blame yourself, Mrs Kenton. These things happen. It was just an accident.'

'My husband won't see it like that.'

'Look,' said the doctor, noticing how her hands were trembling, 'this has plainly been quite a shock for you too. Let me give you something to calm your nerves a bit. Are you on any medication at the moment?'

She nodded blankly.

'Do you have a GP locally?'

'Dr Bevan, Queens Road Surgery. He's Eileen's doctor too.'

'I know him. I think you should call in and see him yourself as soon as possible, just to let him know what's happened. I'll give you a letter to take, bring him up to date on your mother and let him know I've given you this prescription for some tranquillisers. You can get the pills at the pharmacy here.'

Louise couldn't control the tremor in her hand as she stretched out to take the prescription.

'We'll be taking your mother up to the ward any minute. Would you like to go with her, just to help settle her in?'

In fact, it was about a quarter of an hour before a porter arrived to transfer Eileen to the ward two floors above. Long before that though, the sedation had taken effect and she was in a deep sleep. Having settled her into bed, the nurse told Louise that it was unlikely Eileen would wake for some hours.

She was unsure what to do. It seemed pointless to stay, and yet there was nowhere for her to go. She remembered the prescription in her bag. That's what she could do, go to the pharmacy. It was down towards the main entrance, so she could call there on her way out.

Predictably, the queue was long and slow-moving. Louise could feel the tension rising in her as she stood and waited. The shock is getting to me, she thought. That doctor's right, I do need something to calm me down.

At long last, exhausted and wretched, she stumbled out of the pharmacy and, head down, made for the exit.

'Louise?'

His voice stopped her in her tracks.

'How come you're here? Is everything all right?'

Just seeing him there, his dear face, the caring in his eyes, the pressure of his hand on her arm, was more than she could bear. She felt her knees buckle as she leant against him.

'No, I don't think I am . . .'

'What's wrong? Are you ill?'

'Not me. Eileen.'

Philip became aware that eyes were turning in their direction. 'Come on,' he whispered urgently, 'let's get you out of here. Where's your car?'

'Just outside – it's probably plastered with tickets by now.'

'Give me your keys. I'll drive you home.'

Relief coursed through her as he took charge. Philip was here. She relaxed against him as he guided her out of the door and into the passenger seat of her car. Quickly he turned the key in the ignition, then squeezed her hand before driving off. She sank back against the seat and closed her eyes until she felt the car draw up outside her house.

Philip supported her arm as she walked up the path into the unnaturally silent house. The kitchen was exactly as she'd left it. Charred remains of Eileen's housecoat littered the hob and the floor. The stool lay on its side knocked over in the panic. Louise bent over wearily to pick it up then she sensed rather than felt Philip take firm hold of her, guiding her towards the settee in the living room.

He sat beside her for a while, looking at her closely, brushing stray strands of hair out of her eyes. Suddenly, she stiffened.

'Richard! I haven't told him about Eileen yet. I thought I'd wait until I knew exactly how bad it is. I must ring him . . .'

'Would you like me to do it? You're too upset.'

'No! He'd hate that. No, I'll ring him right now.'

'I'll be in the kitchen putting the kettle on. Call me if you need me.'

It was hard for Philip to concentrate on making the tea and clearing up the mess in the kitchen while overhearing snippets of her conversation with Richard. Louise's voice was sometimes low and apologetic, then raised and defensive. At last, when he could stand her distress no longer, he marched in to stand beside her.

She was crying, tears of shock, frustration and despair rolling down her face. It was clear her husband was giving her a hard time. Anger welled up in Philip, as he snatched the phone from her. Cutting across Richard's tirade on the other end of the line, Philip's voice was low and firm.

'Mr Kenton, it's the Reverend Philip Barnes here. Your wife has had a very distressing morning and really can't continue this conversation with you at the moment.'

'Put Louise back on the phone at once!' ordered Richard.

'Your mother is quite safe and resting comfortably at the hospital.'

'I want to know how this happened! How could it happen?'

'I'm sure, Mr Kenton, there will be plenty of time when your mother's better to decide how such an accident might best be avoided in future, but . . .'

'I can't turn my back for a moment without something like this happening. Last time, she was allowed to wander the streets in her nightdress! I simply can't trust Louise with anything!'

'This was not her fault.'

'You don't know my wife very well, Reverend Barnes, or you'd realise that a great deal is Louise's fault. Put her back on the phone immediately.'

'I'm sorry, I won't do that. The last thing she needs at the moment is insults from you!'

'I beg your pardon? You dare say that to me? You who've filled her head with all this God nonsense! You who've encouraged her to abandon her duty to my mother, because she's conveniently useful to the church at the moment. Get out of my house – and get out of our lives before I knock you out!'

Philip was too shocked to answer. He didn't need to because Richard wasn't finished yet.

'And that goes for your whole bloody family. Tell that snivelling son of yours to stay away too! He's always sniffing around my daughter, keeping her from her studies. Just clear off, the lot of you!'

Philip heard no more. Speechless with fury, he slammed down the phone.

Wordlessly, he sank down beside Louise, enveloping her in his arms, rocking her, soothing, stroking, comforting her. And kissing – urgent, hungry kisses to take away her pain, to warm and reassure her. And then more, as she responded with a passion to match his own, her body lifting and arching to be closer to him. Closing his eyes, he let himself flow with the feeling, the longing within him to make her feel whole and worthy and real again. He thought he heard her call his name. He remembered seeing her face, alight with want and passion. He felt her hands moving over him, searching, finding, caressing. And then all thought was gone. Just the feeling. And the deepest purest love.

'How's Mark?'

Ruth smiled to hear Sue's voice on the phone.

'Quite an easy patient really. Keep him supplied with videos and he's happy. Steven has even rigged up the Megadrive in his room, and allowed him unlimited access to his precious games. Mark can't believe his luck!'

'And Philip?'

Ruth didn't answer.

'Things still bad, eh?'

'We're hardly speaking.'

'Who's not speaking? You or him?'

'Me. I can't. I'm so angry with him.'

'Look, Ruth, he's obviously going through a bad patch at the moment. If he doesn't feel welcome at home, is it surprising that he looks for comfort elsewhere?'

'So it's my fault, is it?'

'I didn't say that. And you know that's not what I meant. It's just that you and Philip have always been so good together. Don't let this silence get too entrenched.'

Sue heard Ruth sigh at the other end of the phone. 'You're right, of course. I think I've avoided talking about it because I'm scared of what I'll hear. I love him so much, Sue. He's my rock. He's just the whole world to me. If I ever lost him . . .'

'You won't lose him. He knows where he belongs. For heaven's sake, give him a hug and welcome him back into the fold again. That's where he wants to be, I'm sure of it.'

'Are you?'

'Absolutely.'

'Whatever would I do without you, Sue? You really are a very special friend.'

'Well, I won't be very popular if I don't get a move on. I'm still at the salon, and I'm due at the college to take a keep fit class at one. Keep your chin up. I'll give you a ring later.'

Ruth replaced the phone then picked up the tray she'd prepared for Mark. He was sitting up in bed, deeply engrossed in the TV screen as he pummelled the Megadrive hand control with rapt concentration.

'Brill, Mum. Thanks.' He spoke without taking his eyes off the screen.

Ruth smiled at him. His face was still badly misshapen, and all the colours of the rainbow, but without a doubt he was on the mend. She tousled his hair affectionately before bending down to pick up socks, pens and the odd coin that littered the floor of his room.

'Is Dad coming home?' he asked, without pausing in his button-pushing.

'Maybe. I'm not sure.'

'I miss him. I've not seen much of him lately.'

'None of us has. He's really busy, with the centre opening and everything.'

'He's not mad at me, is he? About all this trouble?' For a moment, Mark's fingers were still as he peered anxiously at her.

'Dad could never be angry with you for long. He's just glad you're safe and feeling better.'

He turned back to the screen and started playing again.

'He's all right really. As dads go, he's OK. I think so, anyway.'

And Ruth found herself smiling as she pulled the door to behind her.

Mellow and euphoric, Louise watched as Philip abruptly moved away from her. He said nothing as he quickly picked up his discarded clothes, averting his gaze from her as he dressed. She watched fondly as he stooped to tie up his shoes then slide his arms into his jacket. He was almost at the door before she realised he was leaving.

'Philip?'

As he turned back, the remorse and self-loathing in his expression shocked her.

'Philip, this had to happen. We knew it would.'

He pulled away from her, gripping the door as he spoke.

'Louise, this is wrong. Unbelievably wrong. I'm sorry. It will never happen again. Never.'

He was halfway through the front door before he heard her call his name. She ran after him, clutching her coat around her nakedness, her face pale and distraught.

'Philip, don't go like this! Please, don't go!'

She was standing in the doorway now, clutching at his sleeve to stop him leaving. He looked around in panic.

'Someone will see, Louise! Let go. Just let go of me, please.'

The quiet insistence of his voice shocked her into silence. Gently, he withdrew his arm from her grasp, and pushing her inside, shut the door behind her.

And because he walked quickly away with his head down, he didn't see the little white car that was driving past. En route from the salon to the keep fit class, Sue had slowed down to watch the whole episode in fascinated disbelief.

★

Philip went straight home. He found Ruth in the kitchen. Without a word, he scooped her into his arms, clinging tightly to her as if his life depended on it.

'Philip? Whatever's the matter?'

With his head buried in her shoulder, his voice was muffled and breaking with emotion.

'I love you, Ruthie. I love you.'

Baffled and curious, she was unsure what to say.

'Hold me close. Just hold me . . . I love you so much . . .'

And to Ruth's surprise, she realised his whole body was shaking in her arms.

'Honestly, Barbara. I wouldn't have believed it if I hadn't seen it with my own eyes. She was practically naked!'

'And he was leaving?'

'He was trying to. She was hanging on to his arm, to stop him going.'

'And do you think they'd . . .?'

'It certainly looked that way.'

Both of them fell silent, the awful implications of what Sue had seen filling their thoughts. It was Barbara who spoke first.

'This is absolutely unforgivable. He's not fit to be a minister. A disgrace to his calling.'

Sue eyed the hardness in her expression nervously.

'Look, there's probably a good explanation for all this. Perhaps we should just have a quiet word with Philip, get him to explain . . .'

'Oh, I most certainly *will* be having words with him! And more than a few.'

'Perhaps I should do it? After all, I saw . . .'

'I'm on the Parish Council. My husband is church warden. *I* will speak to him.'

'It's probably not his fault. There was never any problem

before Louise came along. Perhaps it's her we should be speaking to?'

'Indeed, yes. I'll be having words with that madam too!'

Sue was beginning to regret calling in to see Barbara. What she'd seen had been burning a hole in her all afternoon. She'd been bursting to tell someone. And who better than Barbara, who was just as concerned as she was about the rumours surrounding their vicar? But seeing her now, so righteous and determined, frightened Sue. If she breathed a word of this to anyone, it could be blown out of all proportion. And if Ruth ever heard . . . Well, that thought was just too dreadful to contemplate.

Philip clung to Ruth in bed that night. He just wanted her arms around him, like a child afraid of the dark. He wouldn't talk. All her questions were ignored or brushed aside. There'll be time for answers later, thought Ruth. He's safe. He's home. He's with me. All's well.

Richard arrived back the next day. He didn't even bother to go home before visiting Eileen in hospital. If he was surprised to see Louise sitting by the side of his mother's bed, he made no comment. He didn't acknowledge his wife at all, and Louise found she was beyond caring whether he noticed her or not.

Nothing mattered to her any more. Philip was gone. He had loved her – and left. There had been no word from him since. Nothing mattered any more. Nothing at all.

For Brian, the last few days before the opening of the centre were manic. They'd managed to get the toilets in, except the water hadn't been connected up yet to make them work. And they were beginning to understand why the central heating boiler one of their parishioners had managed to get hold of on their behalf, had come so cheaply. It had only cost half the usual price, and it only worked half the time.

Ken and his team were painting furiously. Just the kitchen flooring to go down now and they could start cleaning up. Brian worked as hard as anyone to get things done, and because he was still pretty angry with Barbara, he was quite happy to be out of the house. Apart from regular visits to Mark, these days he seemed to live, eat and sleep at the centre. He couldn't have been happier.

It was on Wednesday evening that Barbara finally pinned him down. Philip was in the parish office, catching up on some paperwork, when she strode in, shut the door behind her and leant against the desk where he was working.

'You, Philip Barnes, are a disgrace! A hypocrite and a cheat!'

He stared at her uncomprehendingly.

'You haven't even had the decency to hide your shameful affair. You are the lowest of the low!'

Her words felt like a physical blow. He sank back in his chair, ashen-faced.

'You were seen . . . that woman with no clothes on, hanging on to your arm as you left her. A married woman! A mother! Not that that means anything to a hussy like her.'

'Don't you dare insult her! You know nothing about her.'

'But you do, don't you? You know all about her. You know her very well indeed. *Intimately*!'

'You don't understand . . .'

'*What* don't I understand? That you're married to the sweetest wife, who deserves better than an adulterer like you? That you have children you're never there for? That being a priest means nothing more to you than spouting commands to everyone else, while you do whatever you like? You're a disgrace! Scum, that's what you are! And when Bishop David comes on Friday, I'm going to tell him so!'

Richard had been stonily silent ever since he'd come home. It was obvious that not being at the office in London was a great inconvenience to him, and he made his displeasure starkly clear.

Although he said nothing to her, Louise understood from phone conversations she overheard that he was making arrangements for Eileen to be moved into residential care. Good, thought Louise. She'll be much better off there. Not that Louise cared much. She seemed incapable of caring about anything.

And when that night without a word, Richard climbed on top of her, she lay flat and immobile, closing her eyes tightly to block out what was happening. He was claiming her. She belonged to him. His property. And when it was over, she turned away from him, curling up in a small ball, her legs tightly together, her fists clenched.

Philip. Oh, Philip . . .

But he was gone. Richard owned her. And life was not worth living.

When Philip got back from the parish office, Ruth realised immediately that something had happened. He was completely changed. Withdrawn. Distant.

He wouldn't eat with them, didn't even go up to talk to Mark. She saw him take his Bible down from the shelf in his office then shut the door. Shut her out. And as desperate as she was to comfort him, she knew it would be a mistake to intrude on him when he so plainly wanted to be left alone.

It was Maundy Thursday. There was a special service in the church that morning. To Philip's relief, Louise came. He'd wondered if she would choose not to, but hadn't had the courage to ring and ask her. He knew he couldn't speak to her. He couldn't speak to her because he wanted to so much.

He hadn't slept a wink since the conversation with Barbara. He'd been able to think of nothing except her accusations, and the consequences if she carried out her threat to speak on Friday to Bishop David. That would be the end. The end of his career. The end of his vocation. The end of his marriage. The end of him.

He knew he had to warn Louise. That was the very least he could do. His heart filled with pity when he saw her making her way down the aisle towards the organ. She looked pale, not even responding to congregation members who smiled in her direction. She looked terrible, distraught and hurting. And he had caused the hurt. He was to blame.

He began the service without really thinking about the words he was saying. All he could think of was Barbara – her hard accusing eyes glaring at him from the front pew. She meant to go through with it, he had no doubt about that.

And then there was Ruth, dear Ruth, standing alongside Rachel in the choir. Ruth whose face lit up when he glanced in her direction.

How could she ever forgive him? How could he forgive himself?

What was it Minnie wrote? *Nothing we do, nothing we decide, can change the inevitable . . .*

Was Louise right? Had God brought them together? Was there an inevitability about this he was powerless to fight? Or was that just an excuse? A way to explain what was really no more than his own selfish greed?

Forgive us our trespasses . . .

And as he lifted his eyes, and the communion cup, to heaven, Philip knew there were some sins that God alone might be able to forgive – but he himself never could.

★

He caught her as she brushed past him on her way to the door.

'We need to talk.'

'Oh yes!' Louise's eyes were dark pools in her pale face.

'Barbara knows. She's threatening to tell the Bishop tomorrow.'

Louise's hand shot to her mouth.

'When can we meet?' whispered Philip urgently. 'Tonight?'

She nodded.

'Here in the church? About nine?'

Again she nodded, before dropping her head, and walking away. And every step she took was watched by three pairs of eyes – Sue's curious, Barbara's narrow and knowing, and Ruth's filled with unbearable sadness.

Philip was already in the church that night when she arrived. The building was practically dark except for the small amount of light that spilt through from the vestry door.

He'd meant to keep his distance, but all that was forgotten after one look at her gaunt face, the despair in her eyes, her shaking hands. Without thought, Louise walked into his arms. She belonged there.

Philip was out again. Ruth could only guess where. The pain of it stabbed like a physical wound. But however much she hurt, she would not beg. She had her pride, and she'd made a decision. If Philip continued to betray their marriage, and the loving trust that had grown between them over all their years together, she would leave him. And if she went, the kids went with her. No argument. No discussion. A simple ultimatum. The decision was his.

That's what she'd tell him – but not now, not tonight. She sagged under the weight of pain-filled weariness that engulfed her. Her head ached. Her throat felt raw. She was too tired to think clearly.

As she reached up to the bathroom cabinet to take a dose of that cold remedy that always knocked her out for the night, she caught a glimpse of her reflection in the mirror. She looked old. Ugly and bitter. Battered and hurt. And tired, so very tired. She put her hands up to her eyes, pulling back the skin so that the creases round them momentarily disappeared. Letting go suddenly, both her face and her shoulders sagged forlornly. Who could blame Philip for looking elsewhere?

The bottle wouldn't open – how she hated these child locks that were adultproof! Tears of frustration pricked her eyes. She fumbled until at last the lid was off and she took two huge gulps, gagging on the second one. Without replacing the lid, she thumped the bottle down on the sink and stumbled off to bed. And in the two minutes before she fell into a deep sleep, her pillow was soaked with hot, hurt tears.

Good Friday dawned bright and cold. A perfect day for the opening, thought Brian, as he walked down the path towards the church to get things ready for the service. It was due to start at ten-thirty, but with the Bishop due for coffee half an hour before that, they were all anxious that everything was well and truly prepared.

He turned the key in the lock and opened the door. Someone had left the light on in the vestry. Wasteful! That was the sort of thing that made their electricity bill so high.

He strode up the aisle towards the vestry. And as he drew near the front of the church, what he saw ahead of him stopped him in his tracks.

Two candles had been taken down and placed below the altar, where they'd been lit until they'd burnt out. Beside them, spread out neatly, was the altar cloth. And beneath the cloth, arms wrapped around each other, lay Louise Kenton and Philip Barnes. Louise was obviously dead. And if Philip was alive, it was only just.

as we forgive those . . .

Chapter Eleven

First, it was voices. Far off, unfamiliar voices, up close and loud, then fading, fading away. No words, only sounds – and dazzling light that flashed red hot in the darkness.

Hands – pulling, touching, restraining.

Rough fabric on his skin – damp, cold, clammy skin – and searing heat that burned through his head, sapping strength and movement.

Another voice, nearer now, a voice he knew. Ruth? Was that Ruth?

Movement. A shadow in the half light, a figure moving slowly, tantalisingly out of reach. Ruth?

She turned then, scorching his soul with eyes that were pools of deep, drowning sadness.

'Louise!' he cried out, heart breaking at the sight of her. But his cry was silent. She couldn't hear him. Couldn't see his outstretched hand.

And then she was gone.

She stood to one side of the door, where she could peer through the glass without being seen. She could just glimpse the bed, neat, clinical and anonymous, the plastic water jug, the blue curtains, the chart with its spidery graph and figures. She could sense the quiet bustle of hospital life around her, the faintly sickening smell of antiseptic.

Alien. Unfamiliar. A place of fear and death.

She could make out the shape of him, rigid and still beneath the covers, his hands on the sheet, his face on the pillow.

This man she knew so well – and didn't know at all.

'Go in,' said the voice behind her. 'He needs to hear your voice. Help him back.'

For seconds she didn't respond. Then, slowly, Ruth turned, and walked away.

They rang as many of the congregation as they could that morning to tell them the service was cancelled. Yes, and the centre opening too. That's right, only postponed. Oh, of course, the whole event would be rearranged once things were more settled. Would they kindly pass the message round that St Faith's up on Western Road would be glad to welcome anyone from St John's to their Good Friday service?

They didn't explain in any detail why the church was closed. Better not, the police said.

But the gaggle of newspaper men who gathered outside St John's soon set the grapevine buzzing. Their cameras clicked and flashed as, one by one, shocked members of the church community placed forlorn bunches of garden flowers on the porch step.

There were flowers too outside the door of the Vicarage. But only journalists rang the door bell. The locals knew better. This was a family they loved, a family who knew they were surrounded by quiet, compassionate support – but for now, needed to grieve in private.

Brian put down the phone after what he hoped was his last call about the cancelled service, then sat back wearily in the ancient comfy chair by Philip's desk. Ever since that awful moment when he'd found them, he'd been too busy to think, fully occupied with the ambulance, the police, the congregation, the Bishop's office, the press – and the family.

He reached up to take off his glasses, wiping a hand over his eyes. In all his life, he'd never faced such a dreadful task. He couldn't forget Ruth's face, at first shocked, then fearful, until finally something less definable crept into her expression – a hardness edged with anger.

It was Ruth who told the children. She'd insisted on it, and had chosen her words carefully. They were full of questions, but she was sparing with her answers. They didn't know exactly what had happened yet, and certainly didn't know why. In the meantime, they all had to be brave and strong, just as Dad would want them to be.

'What do you mean, Louise Kenton was with him? Why was she with him?' demanded Steven.

Ruth looked at him steadily. 'Steven, I don't know.'

'Are you all right, Mum?' asked Rachel, gazing at her with enormous troubled eyes.

'I don't know that either, love,' replied Ruth, squeezing her daughter's hand. 'But if we stick together, we'll get through this.'

'Is Dad going to die?' It was Mark who spoke, voice unnaturally shrill.

'They say he'll probably be fine when he wakes up. They'll need to keep him in for a few days, but he should be OK.'

The phone rang, disturbing Brian, lost in his thoughts. It was another journalist, another national newspaper.

'Look,' he said firmly, 'the family need their privacy at the moment. Thank you for ringing, but we'd be grateful if you didn't call again.'

He replaced the receiver firmly, and then, on second thoughts, took it off the hook and laid it on the table. Let them think it was engaged for a while. He could do with a moment's peace, a chance to get his own thoughts in order. A bit of space to work out why, *why*, Philip could possibly have done it? And why, as close as he was, hadn't Brian himself realised his dear friend was in such despair? Why hadn't he known? Why hadn't he seen? And if he had, what in heaven's name could he possibly have done?

He pulled a starched white hankie out of his pocket, and began absentmindedly cleaning his glasses.

And why *now*? With all the excitement, and the personal triumph of the church centre opening, why on earth had Philip reached such a crisis now? What had happened? What was he afraid of? What had pushed him over the edge?

Pushing his glasses back on to his nose, Brian sighed as he ran a hand over his neat, thinning hair. He had a feeling the tragic news of this morning was only the beginning. The questions to be asked, and the answers they might come up with, could implicate and devastate them all. Nothing would ever be the same again.

Slowly, he replaced the receiver. It rang again immediately. And as he reached to pick it up, he realised with some surprise that in spite of his clean glasses, he couldn't see clearly for the mist in his eyes.

'How is he?'

Jill came into her fellow Ward Sister's room and closed the door. Years before, the two women had studied together as young nurses. Knowing Jill was a friend of Philip's, Maureen had been half expecting her all morning.

'He's stable. Not conscious yet, but I think he soon will be.'

'Have you seen the crowd outside the main entrance?'

'You could hardly miss them. They've even got a couple of television cameras there!'

'Who's dealing with all that? Is anyone talking to them? Perhaps they'd go away if someone gave them a statement or something?'

'Well, *he* seems to be in charge.' Maureen nodded through

the glass towards a uniformed officer deep in conversation with a constable in the corridor. 'Ian Hallam. Do you know him? Inspector Hallam from Walworth Road police station.'

Jill's eyes widened. 'The police are involved? Why?'

'Well, she died, didn't she? And who knows how that came about? Or why?'

'So they'll need a statement from Philip when he comes round?'

'More than that, I think. I mean, we've no idea, have we? He might have killed her . . .'

Jill's hand shot up to her mouth. She shook her head fiercely. 'No! I've known Philip Barnes for years. He'd never hurt anyone. He's probably the most compassionate and caring man I've ever met. He couldn't have had a hand in her death – never!'

'Then how did she die? If it was suicide, whose idea was it? And how come he didn't die too?'

Jill's eyes clouded with concern. 'Poor Philip,' she said softly. 'Poor, poor man.'

'It's his wife you should really be sorry for. He may not be dead, but her marriage certainly is! And one of the porters was telling me earlier that the Vicarage is besieged by press people too. I really feel for her. Fancy being married to a man like that. Such a hypocrite! Do you think she knew? How on earth must she be feeling now?'

When Steven tried Liz's number for the third time, and it was still engaged, he realised he wasn't going to be able to get through to her on the phone. Their house was probably like the Vicarage, with the family barricaded inside while the press camped on the doorstep. He slumped back into the chair beside the hall stand, and buried his head in his hands.

He hadn't cried. He hadn't felt like that at all. What he felt was cold, cold anger. Anger for himself. Anger for his family. And most of all for Liz – the girl who was not only facing the body blow of losing her mother, but who, like him, had to come to terms with what had obviously been going on between her mum and his dad. Obvious, that's what it was. Now they knew.

So why hadn't he worked it out before, knowing both families as he did? Why hadn't he realised what was going on, and perhaps tried to stop it? He might have prevented this – if only he'd known!

His clenched fist thudded against his knee – once, twice, and then again – but the agony of anger still gnawed at his insides until he ached with the pain of it. He thought of the scene in the kitchen, his mum's face drawn, every movement and expression tightly controlled. He thought of Mark, face ashen beneath the yellowing bruise where his jaw had been broken. He thought of Rachel, sobbing on her bed upstairs.

Then he thought of Liz, and wished he could be with her, to share the pain, to search for answers.

And his father? He had only one thought about his father. He should have died too. That would have been easier for everyone.

Even for a rugby player, Matthew had never seen a scrum like it. When he grabbed a taxi from the station to take him home, he simply hadn't expected the scene that greeted him: the jostling crowd that swarmed around the car, jabbing cameras and microphones towards his face. On top of the news that had already brought him hurrying home from university, this physical onslaught left him emotionally battered. With shock, he realised tears were pricking his eyes. He never cried. Never. And he wouldn't cry in front of them now.

It was Lizzie who stood behind the front door, opening it just wide enough to allow him to slip through. One look at her gaunt face did it. Wordlessly, the two of them reached out for each other, clinging together in grief as they did when they were children. For minutes they stood there, swaying, holding, letting tears come. They didn't speak. Nothing to say. Too much to ask.

Matthew lifted his head as he caught the sound of his father's voice in the living room. He looked down at his sister, gently wiping away the tears from her cheeks and pushing her fringe back from her face. With one arm around her shoulders, he led her into the room where his father was speaking on the phone.

'Well, thank you, Maurice, I would really appreciate that.' Matthew recognised immediately it was the family solicitor on the other end of the line.

'I just want to ensure,' continued Richard, 'that the police act properly over this. That man killed my wife. He seduced her, used her, then discarded her by killing her. I want justice.'

There was silence while Richard nodded in agreement with whatever Maurice was saying.

'Yes, I think a statement would be an excellent idea. And that might get the pack of vultures off our doorstep too. Can you come round right away? Fine. 'Bye.'

There was the hint of a smile on his face as he firmly replaced the receiver. Then he turned, reaching out to shake Matthew's hand.

'Hello, son. Good journey?'

Matthew shrugged in reply. What had he expected? A hug from his dad? Dad didn't hug.

'Look, don't worry about a thing. I'm going to sort this. I'm going to sort out that man for good. He's going down for a very long time. He killed your mother, and he'll pay for it.'

Matthew sat down heavily, eyes closed as he leaned his head back against the settee.

'You look all in,' said Lizzie quietly, moving over to touch his shoulder. 'I'll put the tea on. Just get your breath back for a bit.'

'I want to know what happened.'

'He killed her – in the church, of all places.' There was a

bitter edge to Richard's voice. 'He drugged her, and she was dead when they found them this morning.'

Matthew nodded. 'Did she suffer, do you think?'

'I don't know – but *he* will!'

'How is he?'

'Still alive. He'll soon wish he wasn't!'

'But *why*? What led up to this?'

'You know he's been making a nuisance of himself for weeks, since Christmas? You remember all that fuss about her playing for services at the church, the disruption that caused? Well, he didn't give up. He started coming round here at all hours of the day – only when I wasn't here, of course – to brainwash her, presumably for his own purposes . . .'

'That's not true, Dad.' Lizzie's voice was dangerously low.

'Of course it's true. Your mother was always very naïve. Sometimes downright stupid, let's be honest. She got caught up in all his rubbish, and now look what's happened. Obviously it was more than her soul he was after!'

'You can't possibly know that!'

'Lizzie, you are even more naïve than she was. You wouldn't understand about these things.'

'I understood Mum! I know she was happier during these past weeks than I've seen her for a long time . . .'

'Well, that's brainwashing for you!' snapped Richard. 'You don't know what you're talking about, Lizzie. Your mum was emotionally unstable for years. Unpredictable and unreliable.'

'I won't listen to this . . .'

'That's just what she used to say! She wouldn't listen either. Twice she tried to take her own life. Now someone else has done it for her.'

The blood drained from Lizzie's face. 'What do you mean – take her own life?'

'When Matthew was born, and again when you were small. I couldn't take my eyes off your mother for a moment, without wondering if she was going to top herself!'

If Richard saw the pallor of his daughter's ashen face, he took no notice.

'You must have known about all this? You must have realised that at times your mother behaved hardly better than a child herself? She was so gullible, believed everything anyone told her, except me. And that man, that vicar, took advantage of her.'

'He's not like that! You don't know him!'

'But he's going to know me. He's going to regret the day he ever crossed paths with me and my family.'

'Dad, please . . .'

The phone rang. Richard picked it up, listening for a few seconds to whoever was speaking.

'Yes, we will be issuing a statement. Our family solicitor, Mr Maurice Lambourne, will be arriving shortly. We will speak to you then. That's all. Goodbye.'

And as he replaced the receiver, preoccupied with his own thoughts, he barely noticed Lizzie get up and leave. Silently, she made her way up to her room, locking the door behind her. From the dressing table, she picked up a silver-framed photo. It was of her, Matthew and their mum, bronzed and smiling, a snapshot taken years before on a family holiday. Louise's hair was shorter then, her expression carefree and untroubled.

Was it true? Had she tried to take her own life before now? Was she really that unhappy? How could she be? Why?

Mum, oh, Mum! Lizzie took off her glasses and tumbled sobbing on to her bed, curling up around the photo, rocking backwards and forwards. And much later, drained and spent, it was Steven's name she whispered into her pillow.

'Philip! Can you hear me? Philip, open your eyes if you can.'

A voice he didn't recognise.

'Philip, can you open your eyes?'

A voice calling to him from the darkness. Where was it coming from? Who was it?

'Well, he's not quite with us yet, but I don't think it will be long.'

Fingers on his face. A bright searing light scorching into his eye. Who are you? Where is this?

'Keep an eye on him, Sister. I'll pop back in an hour or so, when I've done the rounds.'

Don't go, I'm here. Wait for me. I'm here.

But the words wouldn't come. The words he shouted in his head never reached his lips. And there was silence again.

'Oh, Barbara, Margot here. My dear, I am so *sorry* to hear the news. How *are* you?'

'Margot, how kind! Fine, I'm fine. Dreadfully shocked, of course. We all are.'

'Well, naturally. Tragic, absolutely tragic.'

'So unexpected. I never dreamed . . .'

'Well, of course not, my dear, how could any of us have guessed?'

'I can't help blaming myself. I should have done something earlier.'

'Oh, but you did, my dear. You told me, and I told David, and he did ring Philip, you know. It's just that none of us ever suspected how involved it all was. Tragic, so tragic.'

'Unbelievable!'

'Such a dear man, and a brilliant career cut short this way. To be taken in and trapped like that! We always thought he'd make Archdeacon one day . . .'

'Margot, I don't honestly think he stood a chance with that woman. She made a beeline for him the moment she met him. She schemed and manipulated and beguiled him. I really don't blame him one bit. None of us does!'

'Naturally.' There was a slight pause from Margot's end of

the phone. 'Nevertheless, his future is very uncertain now. David is in discussion with Timothy Fulford about it, even as we speak.'

'Well, they'd have to make plans, of course. The congregation of St John's is completely bereft. They need firm action. Guidance. Thank goodness David is our Bishop. We can rely on him to do the right thing.'

'And Ruth? How is she?'

'Brian's there. Our families have always been extremely close, as you know, so he would be with them at a time like this. I've not heard directly from him yet, but I do know the news people are still camped outside their door.'

'Oh, I know. We've had them on the phone to us too, asking about the church's reaction to what's happened. We've said nothing, of course. Nothing can be decided until we hear all the facts from Philip himself. He hasn't come round yet, I understand?'

'Hasn't he? I've heard nothing.'

'Really? Well, perhaps I'm more up to date than you are. Apparently he's still unconscious but they expect him to come round quite soon. This afternoon, possibly. And the moment we hear he's well enough, Timothy will be waiting to talk to him.'

'Poor Philip.'

'Dear man. And dear Ruth. Please pass on our deepest sympathy to her, won't you? She must be feeling wretched at the thought of what her husband was up to. All that gossip and everything . . .'

'Dreadful!'

'We must protect her from all that. People can be so cruel.'

'She'll need a great deal of support and friendship. She will appreciate knowing that your thoughts are with her, Margot.'

'Well, my dear, do ring me if there's anything you think I should know. Anything David or I can do. Don't hesitate!'

'That's so kind, Margot. I'll keep in touch. That will be such a comfort. Goodbye.'

And as Barbara replaced the receiver, she smiled to think how fortunate she was to have the friendship of someone as caring and influential as the Bishop's wife. So in the know, and such a tower of strength at a time like this.

'Ruth?' Brian tapped quietly on her bedroom door. 'Ruth, I've got a cup of tea here. Can I come in?'

He wasn't sure if he heard a reply. Tentatively, he pushed open the door. The curtains had been drawn against the cold, early-afternoon sunshine, so the room was almost dark. At first he couldn't see her. The bed covers were smooth and neat. It was only as his eyes grew accustomed to the half light that he glimpsed her, huddled in a corner beside the bed, a box of papers strewn on the carpet around her. Without a word, he walked around to sit on the bed, holding out the cup to her.

'Come on, you've not had anything all day. You need this.'

Without expression, she took it. After one sip, she placed it carefully on the floor beside her.

'What are you doing?'

'Looking for Philip's birth certificate.'

'Why?'

'I thought I might need it.'

'Why?'

'I just thought I might.'

Brian wasn't sure what to say.

'I found our wedding photos.'

'Oh?'

'April twenty-seventh. Nineteen years ago. It's our anniversary soon.'

'He'll be home by then.'

She looked at him steadily for a while, then gazed down again at the box, picking up a brown photograph folder.

'This was taken when we were first engaged. He looked so young then. It was the sixties fashion, I suppose. I thought he was very sophisticated.'

'He's always been a good looking man. Not much dress sense, though,' agreed Brian, peering at the fading photo. 'Where was this?'

'At some dance or another. I remember it was a lovely sunny evening, and we were all dancing outside.'

He handed it back to her with a smile. 'Nice memory.'

'Yes,' she said, and lapsed again into silence.

'I rang the hospital. Philip's showing signs of stirring. They think he should wake up pretty soon. I wondered if you'd like me to take you to see him?'

'No.'

'Ruth . . .'

'No.'

'It would mean so much to him, to see you there.'

'No.'

'Well, leave it then, for now anyway. I'd like to go over, though, perhaps later tonight. Do you mind if I do?'

'No.'

'Any message?'

'None at all.'

He sighed. 'Is there anyone you'd like here with you? Barbara, perhaps?'

She shook her head.

'Your sister? I could call her. Perhaps you'd like me to call her anyway, just to let her know . . .'

'No. Thanks, Brian, but I don't want anyone.'

He looked at her helplessly. Finally, he got to his feet. 'Well, I'll be off home then. I'm going to leave my mobile phone with you because I think you should keep the house phone off the hook for a while. I'll ring you later to let you know how he is.'

She made no comment until he was almost at the door.

'How are the kids? Are they all right?'

'No, not really. Mark keeps asking a lot of questions, but the less he knows the better, for the time being at least. Sue's down there with them. She's organising lunch, although they probably don't feel like eating at the moment.'

A spark of interest flashed across Ruth's face. 'Sue's here?'

Brian smiled. 'She didn't disturb you because we thought you might be sleeping. Shall I send her up?'

Ruth nodded slowly. 'Yes,' she said, 'Yes, I think I'd like that.'

'Doctor, Reverend Barnes is coming round. You wanted me to let you know.' Maureen replaced the phone and left her office to head towards the small side ward in which Philip was lying.

Poor man, she thought to herself as she walked. If he knew what he was waking up to, he'd probably prefer to stay asleep.

'Hello, Philip. Welcome back. How are you feeling?'

It took a while for him to focus his eyes so that he could see clearly. He didn't recognise the face before him. His brow furrowed with concentration as he tried to remember. So many jumbled thoughts. What was real? How much was just a dream? A nightmare?

He tried to turn his head, although it thumped mercilessly. Quickly he closed his eyes again, to stop the room spinning around him.

Where was he? This wasn't his bed. So where was this? And where was Ruth? She would know what was happening.

The room smelt funny. The kind of smell he remembered from his school days. Disinfectant.

Why was he in a room that smelt of disinfectant?

A hospital! But why? Had there been an accident? Did he hurt anywhere?

Suddenly, his eyes shot open again. He remembered.

And the first thing he saw was the policeman sitting at the end of his bed.

'Jamie! It's me. I need your help!'

He had clearly not expected a phone call from Steven.

'Steve, are you all right? What's happening over there?'

'Not a lot really. It's like being under house arrest, with all these people camped outside.'

'You're a celebrity, mate!'

'Believe me, Jamie, I don't want to be. It's just unbelievable. None of us can really take it in.'

'What happened? Was something going on between your dad and that woman?'

'Liz's mum. Maybe. We don't really know yet.'

'I heard she died . . .'

'Yes – and that's why I need your help. I've been trying to get through to Liz all morning but their line is constantly engaged, like ours. I wondered if you could get a note over to her?'

Jamie sounded doubtful.

'Look, Steve, is that a good idea? Your family's hardly flavour of the month with them at the moment.'

'I don't care what they think. I just need to speak to her . . .'

'I can tell you what they think. Her dad's all over the news bulletins! Didn't you watch? Put your telly on, see for yourself.'

'Yeah, I will. But if I write a note to Liz, would you go over and put it through her letterbox this afternoon? Please?'

'Sure. I'll be over in ten minutes.'

Steven raced up to his room, taking the stairs two at a time. He had no idea exactly what he'd write. What could he say? He just hoped the words wouldn't matter to her so much as the knowledge she was in his thoughts.

But after all that had happened, why should she care?

★

'Reverend Barnes, how are you feeling?'

This voice belonged to a face Philip did recognise. Ian. Inspector Ian Hallam. A chill of foreboding slithered through his body.

'I feel,' began Philip hesitantly, 'as if I've been run over by a steamroller.'

'Do you know why you're here?'

'I'm not even sure where *here* is. Where am I?'

'A place you should recognise very well, Philip. You are Chaplain at this hospital. You visit every week.'

'Hospital?' he repeated blankly. 'Louise . . . Where's Louise? Is she here too?'

'Louise Kenton is dead. She was found in the church with you early this morning.' Ian stopped, seeing the crushed expression that transformed Philip's face, an expression that was more than just sadness or shock. It was desolation – bleak and agonising.

'No – oh, no! Dear God, don't let that be true!'

'It is true,' continued Ian Hallam quietly. 'And I would like you to tell me all you can about the circumstances of her death.'

'Dead? Louise! Oh God, she's dead . . .' Philip's voice descended to little more than a moan. His face was pale and distraught, hands clutching desperately at the sheet that covered him.

'That's enough for now.' Philip became dimly aware of the doctor who'd been keeping his distance at the corner of the room. 'Inspector, in my opinion Reverend Barnes really isn't well enough for this discussion yet. Give him a couple more hours, please. You can talk to him then.'

Inspector Hallam rose slowly, eyes fixed on Philip's face. 'Right,' he said. 'I will be back, and I look forward to speaking to you in detail then.' And with a slight nod to the doctor, he left the room.

Not that Philip noticed. As his body shook with racking sobs, he was too distraught to notice anything.

Sue walked into the bedroom and without a word wrapped her arms around her friend's shaking body. At last Ruth cried. She cried and cried. And when she could cry no more, they sat together in the darkening room, hands clasped, saying nothing.

'I'm tired,' said Ruth finally, 'so tired.'

'I'm not surprised,' replied Sue. 'You've been through an emotional mangle. You must be exhausted.'

'And it's not over yet.'

'No,' agreed Sue. 'Have you been to see Philip? What does he say?'

'I've been. I couldn't stay.'

'No. Perhaps not.'

'I couldn't. He's a stranger to me. I don't know the man lying in that bed.'

'You do, Ruth. He's still the same Philip, whatever he's done. He must be very frightened and alone right now.'

'So am I.'

Sue nodded in silent agreement.

'So I was right. They were having an affair . . .'

'Is that certain? Are you sure?'

'Why else would they try and kill themselves? Why else would they have felt such despair? Because they loved each other. Because they could do nothing about that love. Because it was hopeless . . .'

'Ruth . . .' murmured Sue, putting an arm around her, to steady her shivering body.

'He loved her, Sue, and I knew it! I knew it, and could do nothing to stop it. I just had no idea he was so near the edge . . .'

'That's the strangest thing about all this. I'd never have thought of Philip as a man who'd even consider taking his own life.'

'He's not. He wasn't. She changed him. What happened between them changed him. *She* did this to him. She killed our marriage. She nearly killed him. *She* did this.'

'And lost her own life doing it,' said Sue softly. 'But he's alive. She's gone, but Philip is still here. He's alive, Ruth, and I believe he needs you more than ever now.'

'No.'

'But you love him. You've always loved him. You must talk to him, at least. See him, please.'

'No.'

'Not yet – or not ever?'

Ruth's bleak expression matched the gloomy darkness. 'I don't know, Sue, I just don't know.' Her body slumped as she leant her head wearily against her friend's shoulder, voice barely more than a whisper. 'I don't know anything any more.'

Darling Liz,

What can I say? What is there to say? My dad. Your mum. I just never thought. None of us did.

I don't know what you think of me now, knowing I'm my dad's son. I would understand if you hated me. I just know I can't stop thinking about you. How I wish I could hold you, take some of your hurt away.

Can we meet? Please say we can. I'll wait in 'our' place in the woods from eleven o'clock tomorrow morning. Please come. Please. And ring Jamie if you need to get a message to me.

Steven

Lizzie refolded the letter and pushed it carefully back into the envelope. Then she lay back on her bed, hugging the envelope to her. Steven was thinking about her. And somehow, amid all the pain and anger, that was the only comforting thought.

*

True to his word, Inspector Hallam returned in precisely two hours. He found Philip lying peacefully, apparently asleep. In fact, although his eyes were closed, sleep was impossible for Philip now. Images danced before his eyes, memories jostled for attention. He wondered if he'd ever sleep again.

'Now, Philip,' the Inspector began without preamble, 'can you tell me exactly what happened?'

For a few seconds he opened his eyes. Then he closed them again, sighed and began to speak in a low, expressionless voice.

'I met Louise Kenton on Christmas Eve. She stood in as our church organist when our regular musician was taken ill. But she soon got involved in the life of the church, playing for all our services and our pantomime too.'

'And this brought the two of you into close contact?'

'Yes – not so much because of the music, but because she embarked on a spiritual search of her own and asked for my help with that. I saw her regularly after she first came to us at Christmas. Almost every day, in fact. We had very detailed discussions about the Bible and her Christian faith. She was a remarkable woman. Intelligent. Full of questions.

'So was the relationship between you purely professional, that of a minister for his parishioner?'

'It was then.'

'But it changed?'

'Slowly, yes, it did. She had a lot of problems.'

'Such as?'

'With her mother-in-law. She suffers from dementia.'

'I saw that the police were called out to her on one occasion not long ago.'

'Yes. In many ways, that was the start of it all.'

'The start of all what?'

'Us becoming real friends. Getting close.'

'Were you lovers?'

'Not then.'

'But soon after?'

'It wasn't that simple. It wasn't something either of us intended to happen. Louise was so unhappy . . .'

'About her mother-in-law?'

'Yes, but mostly within her marriage. She didn't get on with her husband.'

'Why?'

'Because he is the most insensitive, unfeeling man I've ever come across! He's had a series of affairs virtually throughout the whole of their marriage. He's a bully. He belittles her. He makes her life hell.'

Philip paused for a moment. '*Made* her life hell.'

'So she turned to you?'

'Yes, but as her minister I asked her to. She was so desperate, lost and demoralized, and yet the courage and commitment she showed to her growing faith was nothing short of inspirational.'

'But she inspired you in more than just a spiritual sense. You were attracted to her in other ways?'

'Not at first. At least I don't think so. I liked and admired her. I thought she was misunderstood and brave. I admired her spirit. And I felt so helpless when I saw her distress over her husband.'

'So you helped her by getting closely involved with her. Physically involved?'

'With reluctance, yes, I did.'

'Reluctance?'

'I hated myself for the way I was drawn to her. Whatever you may think of me now, Inspector, I am not an insincere man. Before this, I'd never even thought of being unfaithful to my wife or my principles . . .'

'Until Louise Kenton?'

'Until Louise,' agreed Philip wearily.

'How did it happen?'

'It was unplanned, impulsive at first, but we pulled back, shocked and frightened by what we felt.'

'You tried to break it off?'

'We both did. We were married. And Christians.'

'But in the end, that didn't stop the inevitable?'

'No – her mother-in-law burned her arm very badly, and was brought to hospital as an emergency. I met Louise here quite by accident. She was so upset, and terrified about what her husband would say . . .'

'Why?'

'He was away all the time, but very dogmatic about how things should be run at home. He considered Louise incompetent and unreliable, neither of which was true. But she was very scared of his reaction.'

'How did he react?'

'He was completely unreasonable. Even when I spoke to him that day, he was abusive and insulting. I've never heard a tirade like it! And Louise had to put up with that for years and years . . .'

'And?'

'And, before we knew it, I was no longer just comforting her, but making love to her. I loved her. That's all I knew.'

'Then?'

'And then I left.'

'Did she mind you leaving?'

'She was very upset, but I couldn't stay. I couldn't believe what I'd done. I'd betrayed everything I hold dear to me – my wife, my family, my parishioners, and worst of all, my faith. I was appalled and destroyed by what I'd done. I could never forgive myself.'

'So that was the end of the affair?'

'It should have been. We meant it to be. We agreed it had to stop, that we couldn't go on.'

'Harder said than done?'

'The hardest thing I've ever done in my life – but we meant it. And perhaps it would have been OK, if it hadn't been for . . .'

'Yes? For what?'

'For the church centre opening on Good Friday. Good Lord, that's today, isn't it?'

'It was cancelled.'

Philip nodded bleakly.

'Well, the Bishop was coming. It was a very important occasion for us, a triumph for St John's, the culmination of so much effort and work by the whole community.'

'But how did that affect your relationship with Mrs Kenton?'

'Because we'd been seen. Someone – I'd rather not say who – knew about us. We'd been seen, and she threatened to tell the Bishop during the Good Friday ceremony. I couldn't let that happen! It would have destroyed the occasion for so many people. It would have shattered the trust of dear friends I loved and owed so much. I didn't know what to do – and so I asked Louise to meet me.'

'Last night?'

'Yes, in the church. I knew it would be quiet there, a chance for us to talk.'

'But you did more than talk?'

Philip turned his head to look steadily into the Inspector's eyes. 'Yes. We cried. We held each other, and we cried some more. We talked and talked, and were still in despair. We had no future. No future together. No future apart. And no future amongst those we loved and cared for, if our love for one another became public.'

The Inspector fell silent, waiting for him to continue.

'And as we had no future on earth that we could face, we started talking about the only future left to us – a future with God. Because we believe in a forgiving God, we felt that perhaps he would understand what others would find incomprehensible. More than our love for each other, Louise and I shared our love of God and a belief in his love for us.' He broke off, running his fingers through his hair in a familiar gesture of agitation. 'I don't know. I can imagine how that sounds to you – but in our despair, in the deep, drowning emotion of the situation, it began to make perfect sense to us.'

'Who first had the idea to take pills? Where did they come from?'

'Louise had a full bottle of tablets in her bag. She'd been prescribed them by the hospital, when she was so upset and shocked about her mother-in-law's accident.'

'How did you take them?'

'We made a sort of ceremony of it. We were praying all the time. Praying for guidance. Praying others would understand what we were doing, praying that God would support them through the hurt this would bring them, that we were doing the right thing.'

'And do you really think you were?'

Philip's eyes filled as he answered. 'Perhaps it would have been if I were dead now too. That's what we wanted. And we failed. I failed.'

'So, you were both praying?'

'And we drank communion wine. We sang together. We held each other, and cried. Then she gave me the pills, and we took them together. We looked at each other and took them, washing them down with wine. It was beautiful. Maybe you can't imagine it – but it was perfect. Pure, loving and immensely beautiful.'

'Did you feel ill?'

'No, not really. We felt tired – but then I think we were both exhausted with all the emotion and despair. We got cold and so we wrapped the altar cloth around us. Then we just lay there, in each other's arms, talking, touching, praying – and, I suppose, at last sleeping. I don't really remember.'

'Can you explain why Mrs Kenton had a much higher chemical content in her blood than you? Were you aware that she was taking more pills than you?'

Philip looked surprised. 'No, she divided the tablets more or less equally.'

'Well, Reverend Barnes, in fact she did take a much greater

quantity than you. Unless she'd been found immediately, there was never any real chance her life could have been saved.'

Philip nodded dumbly.

'Whereas you . . .'

'I took the same amount, I know I did.'

'Whereas you, having a larger physical frame, and taking a great deal less than Mrs Kenton, would only have been in real danger of losing your life if several more hours had elapsed before you were found.'

'I don't understand. How can that be? We took the same pills. She gave them to me. She measured them out in front of me.'

'No, Reverend Barnes, I don't understand it either.'

'What are you saying?'

'Nothing at all. I'm hoping you can explain the discrepancy. Because, sir, as it stands at the moment, we have to keep a very open mind about Mrs Kenton's death.'

'What do you mean?'

'Well, you are a priest, a respected member of the community, a married man. In your own words, today was to be the culmination of a major project of yours, when the church centre was officially opened. Mrs Kenton had declared her devotion to you. You've said yourself she was a vulnerable, distressed woman, unhappy with her life for a number of reasons. A bit of a loose cannon, perhaps? Someone who could ruin your career and family life? With her out of the way, perhaps you could rebuild your life and start again. But she can't, can she?'

Philip stared at him in amazement.

'You think I killed her? That I wanted her to die?'

'I'm not saying anything, sir, merely thinking aloud. And if you have more to tell me that may help me settle this enquiry one way or another, I would be very pleased to hear from you. You can rest assured we will be making a thorough investigation into the circumstances surrounding Mrs Kenton's death.

In the meantime, one of my officers will be on duty outside your room.'

The knock on her bedroom door was so timid, Ruth almost missed it. When no one came in, she got up, opening the door to find Mark leaning against the wall, his head down, face stained with dried tears. Without a word she hugged him to her. Putting an arm round his shoulders, she led him in to sit on her bed, *their* bed, the bed she used to share with Philip.

'I don't understand, Mum. What happened to Dad? Why was he in the church? And what was Mrs Kenton doing there?'

'We don't really know yet, Mark.'

'What did Dad say when you talked to him?'

'Nothing.'

'But you went to see him this morning! What did he say?'

'He was still asleep, Mark.'

'So when are you going again? Can I come with you?'

She tenderly brushed the hair from his forehead. 'No, darling, better not – not yet.'

'But I want to see Dad! I want to know he's all right. He is going to be OK, isn't he?'

'I expect so.'

'Why are all those people outside the house? Why can't I go out?'

'They're waiting to find out what really happened, just as we are . . .'

'Mr Kenton was on the telly. He said Dad was responsible for her death. What does he mean, Mum?'

'He's talking rubbish, Mark. Don't listen to gossip. I promise you, I'll tell you everything you need to know when I'm sure I've got my facts right. In the meantime, we've just got to stick together and be patient.'

Mark's bruised face crumpled with exasperation. 'I want

Dad. I want to talk to him. I want to know what happened. I want to go and see him – now!'

'Mark,' Ruth said firmly, 'the best way to help Dad is for us all to . . .'

But he was up and out of the room. 'Stop treating me like a baby, Mum! You always do that. Why won't anyone *tell* me what's going on?'

Philip was lying with his face away from the door when Brian went in, so it was difficult to make out whether he was awake or asleep. Brian crept round to the other side to find Philip's eyes were wide open, but unseeing.

'Phil?'

When there was no response, Brian reached over to draw up a chair beside the bed.

'It's me, Brian. How are you? How are you feeling?'

Philip shook his head, a wry smile briefly playing on his lips.

'I'm OK, I suppose. Still alive.'

'Well, thank God for that!'

'I'd have thanked God more if he'd let me die.'

'Don't say that.'

Philip turned his head to stare steadily at his old friend. 'I meant to die, Brian. That would have been better for everyone.'

'Don't say that! If only you knew how much love there is out there for you . . .'

'Yes, from people I love too, people I've hurt beyond belief. How can I ever face them again?'

'If they can then so should you. You owe them that at least.'

Philip slumped back. 'Brian, they'd be better off without me. They deserve better.'

Alarmed by his agitation, Brian fell silent. Finally, he reached down into the holdall he'd brought with him.

'I've brought you some bits from home – pyjamas, clean clothes, your shaving gear.'

No reply.

'A carton of fruit juice, and some of those mints you like.'

Philip eyes were shut tightly, as if squeezing painful images from his mind.

'The police think I killed her.'

'What? How could they think that?'

'Apparently she had a good deal more of the tranquilliser in her blood than I had in mine. They think that means I wanted her out of the way.'

'Oh, that's ridiculous. They don't know you at all . . .'

'Do you? Do you recognise the man you're talking to now?' He sighed heavily. 'I don't even recognise myself.'

'Philip, you've been under a lot of pressure – the church centre opening, the trouble with Mark. People react to stress in different ways. We all understand, of course we do.'

'You can't. No one can, least of all me.'

'The only thing I can't figure out,' Brian persisted, 'is why now? With the big ceremony planned for this morning and all the work you'd put in. However bad you thought things were, why choose the worst possible moment for all of us? Were you worried about today, was that it?'

'Louise and I had been seen.' Philip hesitated for a moment, eyeing Brian thoughtfully. 'And the person who knew about us threatened to tell the Bishop this morning. I couldn't let that happen. I was too much of a coward to face all that.'

'Who?' demanded Brian. 'Who was going to tell the Bishop?'

Philip was silent for a while, before deciding to go on.

'Barbara. She paid me a visit at home the other night and told me in no uncertain terms what she thought of me, and what she intended to do about it.'

Brian's face was ashen.

'I'm sorry if it hurts you to hear that, Brian – but you mustn't blame her. She was right and I was so very, very wrong. That was why I . . . well, that's why we did what we did. It seemed to be best for everyone.'

Brian didn't answer. Then, to fill the uncomfortable silence, he began to busy himself arranging Philip's belongings in the locker beside the bed.

'How's Ruth?' asked Philip at last.

'Ruth's – well, she's shocked, not sure what to think really. But she's managing. You know her.'

'And the kids?'

'Confused, a bit frightened, especially with all the press outside the door . . .'

Philip's eyes widened. 'The Press?'

'You're big news, Philip. We're under siege.'

'I never thought of that. I never dreamed . . .'

'And they're camped outside the Kentons' house too. Richard Kenton has been on television.'

'That man! I can imagine his reaction. Full of compassion and understanding? Hardly!'

'He's angry, righteous – and out for your blood.'

'Well, I can hardly blame him, can I? But he should take his share of blame too. If he'd treated Louise with more care and love over the years, she'd still be alive now.'

'Look, Phil, the sister told me I wasn't to tire you. You need rest, so I'll be off now. But is there anything I can get you? Messages for anyone?'

'Ruth . . .'

'Yes? You'd like to see her?'

'Would she come?'

Brian looked uncomfortable. 'I'm honestly not sure.'

'I do love her, you know. I've always loved her.'

'Yes. Well, you get some rest. I'll pop in again in the morning.' For a moment, Brian stood awkwardly by the bed before grabbing the holdall and quietly leaving the room.

*

Much later that night, Philip woke with a start. Someone was in the room. Someone touched him.

He strained to peer through the darkness, until gradually his eyes focused in the gloom on a figure standing at the end of the bed.

'Ruth?'

She didn't answer. She simply stood, looking down at him, her face bereft with sadness. Not anger. Not revenge. Just heart-stopping sadness.

'Ruth! Oh, Ruth, I am so sorry, so very, very sorry . . .'

And still she said nothing. Silently, she stepped back into the shelter of the shadows and when he pulled the covers back to reach for her she was gone. Gone, as if she'd never been.

Perhaps it was only a dream.

Chapter Twelve

'Whatever were you thinking of? How could you possibly have imagined a threat like that would bring anything but trouble?'

'I thought it was for the best. I didn't expect him to react so drastically.'

'You didn't think at all! You stuck your nose in and took the high moral ground. And look what happened – Louise Kenton is dead!'

'And I'm responsible?' Barbara's flushed face contorted in defensive indignation. 'Are you saying I'm to blame for the actions of that irresponsible, unstable woman? Are you?'

'Philip is a decent man. You *know* that. He'd got himself into a mess, and needed support and friendship, not threats and recrimination. He might have turned to us, asked for our help because he thought we were his closest friends. But how could he turn anywhere with your threat hanging over him?'

'He knew I didn't mean it! I wouldn't really have done it. He knew that . . .'

'No, he didn't, Barbara. That's why he's in hospital, with his life in shreds. That's why Ruth and the children are left with their family destroyed. And that's why Louise is dead.'

'I refuse to listen to this,' snapped Barbara, turning swiftly to leave the room.

'But that's the problem, isn't it? You're too fond of your own voice ever to listen to anyone else.'

She spun round abruptly, eyes blazing in fury.

'How dare you? How dare you say that to me?'

'I dare — because I've been married to you for more than thirty years, and I've watched you change from a dear, caring soul into a know-all who expects to dominate everyone and everything around her. And unless you change, unless you realise what you've become and how difficult it is even to *like* you nowadays, I don't think you and I will be seeing any more years together.'

Barbara stared in stunned astonishment at the fury in his face. She had never seen her husband as anything but easygoing and mild-tempered. She didn't recognise the cold angry man before her now. And it frightened her.

'Where are you off to?'

Lizzie jumped guiltily at the sound of Matthew's voice.

Her face was carefully casual. 'I need to get out the house for a bit.'

He walked over to join her by the banister at the top of the stairs. 'Is that a good idea? There may still be a few of those press people hanging about.'

'I'll risk it. I'll go mad if I stay here any longer. I'm sick of all that pack of vultures outside, the police and all their questions. I just need to get out.'

Matthew watched her closely as she spoke. She was nervous and on edge.

'Where's Dad? he asked.

'Don't know. Downstairs on the phone, I think.'

'Good. I want to talk to you. In here, quick.' And he ushered her inside his room, closing the door firmly behind them.

'Where are you going, Lizzie?'

'Nowhere special.'

'I'll come with you then, shall I?'

'No!' There was panic in her face. 'No, I need a bit of space, time to think – you know.'

'Have you heard from Steven Barnes?'

'What makes you ask?'

'That letter you took such pains to hide last night. I saw who brought it. That was Steven's mate Jamie, wasn't it?'

Lizzie didn't answer. She didn't need to.

Matthew pulled her down gently to sit beside him on the bed, taking her hand in his.

'Look, Liz, you're a big girl and your life's your own. I'd be the last one to criticise . . .'

'But?'

'But, under the circumstances, contact between our two families is probably not a good idea right now.'

'Look, Matthew, Steven isn't responsible for his father's actions, any more than you and I are for Mum's. It wasn't our fault, and it isn't his either.'

'The fact is, Lizzie, if Mum had never met that family, she'd be here with us now.'

'And the fact is, Matthew, meeting Steven was the best thing that ever happened to me. He's my friend, my closest friend. And when things are awful, just the way they are at the moment, it's your best friend you need most of all.'

'But not him, Liz, you must see that? What on earth will Dad say if he finds out?' And he's right. On this occasion, he really is.'

'How would he know? He's not interested in how I feel, he never has been. And he never cared about Mum's feelings either. Why else would this whole thing have happened?'

'That's not fair . . .'

'How would you know what's fair? You don't live here any more. How could you know about how unhappy she was? About the way Eileen needed her attention every minute of the day and night? Were you around long enough to see how much pleasure it brought her to get involved with Philip and the church? Of course not. You and Dad – you're never here. But I was, Matthew, and I saw how she blossomed over the past few weeks. Did you have any idea how badly Dad treated her or how desperately lonely she was? Well, I watched it all – and I think the blame lies in our house, not the Vicarage. I'm not angry with Philip Barnes, I'm sorry for him. And I'm sorry for Steven and me too, because we don't deserve this!'

Matthew sat back in astonishment at her outburst, but when Liz finally dared to look at his face she was surprised to find him smiling.

'Like that, eh? How serious is it between you two?'

Lizzie's face reddened.

'Do you know what you're doing? He does realise, I hope, that you are the most precious girl in the whole world, and if he hurts you – if he *ever* hurts you, even one little bit – your big brutal rugby-playing brother will come and sort him out. He knows that, does he?'

She grinned. 'Not yet, but I'll tell him.'

'And Liz, be careful. Dad will never approve of this friendship. Take care. Promise me?'

'Yes, I will.'

He hugged her then, and she sank into the huge familiar comfortableness of him.

'Is he worth it, Lizzie?'

'Oh, yes,' she replied softly. 'Yes, he certainly is.'

The doctor finished his check and stood back from the bed to speak.

'Well, Reverend Barnes, you are a very lucky man. In spite of what you pumped down yourself, you seem to have got away without too much damage. I'd like to monitor you for another day, just to make sure, but I see no reason why you shouldn't go home tomorrow.'

Can't you? thought Philip. Of course I can't go home tomorrow. I can never go home again. I have no home. I have no life at all beyond this room.

Ruth felt better that morning. It might have been the doctor's prescription that knocked her out. It might have been that the cold she'd been fighting for several days seemed finally to be coming to an end. Perhaps it was just that the first dreadful shock of it all was now behind her. Whatever the reason, she felt she'd moved on. Still no nearer any decision that mattered, but she felt stronger, human again, more like herself at last.

The first visitor of the morning was Inspector Hallam. She squirmed at the memory of the last time they'd met, when he'd given Mark that dressing down about the bike. Seeing him again under such circumstances came very near to dampening her early morning confidence. She perched herself on the edge of their comfy old settee, watching him closely as he sifted through notes in the book he produced from his pocket.

At last he looked up. 'Were you aware of the relationship between your husband and Mrs Kenton?'

'Partly. I'm not sure I know everything even now – but yes, I had been aware for some weeks that a – um – friendship had developed between them that was less professional than I would have expected it to be.'

'Less professional? In what way?'

'I thought she was making unnecessary demands on his time.'

'Unnecessary? Why? She was a parishioner and organist at your church. She was also, so I'm told, making a commitment to faith. Wouldn't you expect him to spend a good deal of time with her under those circumstances?'

'Yes.'

'But you felt uncomfortable about their meetings. Why?'

'Because I know my husband. Because I know how professional he usually is, especially when women parishioners become too attached to their minister. It's a fairly common situation.'

'Did he consider her attachment an embarrassment? A burden?'

'I don't think so. I think, in her case, he enjoyed it.'

'How did you react to that?'

Ruth looked at him coldly. 'How would you expect me to react, Inspector? I have been married to Philip for nearly twenty years. We have a home, three children we both adore. I have never had any doubts about his fidelity before. And then, Louise came along. How do you think I felt?'

'Did you know they planned to meet that evening?'

'No. I didn't know where he was, but thought they might be together.'

'When he didn't return home, why didn't you raise the alarm?'

'Because I had a heavy cold and took some night-time medication to help me sleep. I don't remember a thing once my head hit the pillow. The first I knew was Brian banging on the door the next morning.'

'Does it surprise you to learn that your husband tried to take his own life?'

'Yes, I do find that unbelievable. The Philip I know would never consider such a thing.'

'Then why do you think he did it?'

'Because, with her, he became someone I don't know at all. She must have planted the idea in his head. He could never have thought of it himself.'

'Is he in the habit of taking medication?'

'No, never. I can't even get him to take aspirin when he's ill.'

'He has no medication in the house?'

'None.'

'What about the rest of the family? Are there pills stored in a medicine cabinet somewhere?'

Ruth's eyes widened. 'A few. Not many, because I hate having half-empty bottles of pills lying around. Why?'

'Is your husband in the habit of drinking?' Ruth almost laughed. 'Look, Inspector, what are you getting at? Are you trying to get me to say that Philip was a drunkard and pill-popper? Well, I can't, because he wasn't. He'd rather have a cup of tea than a glass of whisky any day. And when he's ill he's a terrible patient because he'll never let me give him anything to help.'

'Would you mind letting me have a look at your medical supplies?'

'Help yourself. You'll probably only find a packet of plasters, some ear drops and an old bottle of cough medicine. What exactly are you looking for?'

'When they were discovered, Mrs Kenton had significantly more chemical substances in her blood than your husband. In fact, with the amount she'd taken, it was very unlikely she could have survived, even if she'd been found much earlier.'

'And you think Philip did that? You think he deliberately killed her, but not himself?'

'I'd prefer to know what *you* think.'

'I'll tell you what I think, Inspector. I think Philip was in despair. His feelings were out of control, and he simply didn't know what to do. He felt compromised at the deepest possible level, fighting his conscience. I think he was a frightened, desperate man. But no, I don't think he deliberately killed her and spared himself. He's simply not capable of it. And I pray God will forgive me for saying this, but I now know without a shadow of doubt that I could do what he never could. If that woman were alive today, for all the misery she's brought upon us all, I could quite happily kill her myself.'

As soon as she turned the corner towards the familiar clump of trees, she saw him. He was sitting on the uprooted log that had always been a favourite place of theirs, out of the way, sheltered, private.

An unexpected shyness engulfed her as he came towards her but at once he was beside her, enveloping her in strong comforting arms. 'Lizzie, oh, Lizzie,' he whispered. 'I am so sorry, so very sorry.'

For some minutes they clung together, salt tears mingling with sweet kisses. No words. None needed. Time for words later. She was trembling, emotion shuddering through her body. At last, encircling her in his arms, he led her gently over to the log. And there they sat, fingers linked, heads touching, drawing strength from their closeness.

Philip was sitting on the side of his bed when Inspector Hallam came in. If the Inspector was surprised by the gaunt bleakness of his expression, he made no comment.

'Well, Reverend Barnes, I have news for you. We've made extensive enquiries into the circumstances surrounding Mrs Kenton's death, and after consultation with my Detective Superintendent, we have decided that no further action should be taken.'

Philip's shoulders visibly lowered. 'Thank God,' he whispered. Then he turned back to the Inspector. 'But what about the level of chemicals in Louise's body? How did they get there?'

'It seems Mrs Kenton was under supervision from her doctor for some years. She had a history of mental instability. Were you aware of that?'

'Yes, she told me. I knew she'd tried to take her own life when the children were small.'

'And apparently she suffered from severe bouts of depression periodically ever since. Her doctor had recently given her a new prescription, Amitryptiline. Four days before her death, she collected fifty tablets from the local pharmacy. In the bathroom cabinet at her house, that bottle was found with less than a dozen pills in it. She must have been taking them like sweets.'

'Poor Louise,' sighed Philip. 'I really didn't know. There was so much I didn't know.'

'Anyway, this means you can now put the whole unhappy episode behind you.' The Inspector hesitated. 'And that's not going to be easy, Philip, I know that. Have you any idea what you'll do, where you'll go?'

He shrugged his shoulders. 'I tried to take my own life because I couldn't face living with the mess I'd made of everything. And my punishment for that act of cowardice is I couldn't even get that right! I've ruined everything. I've hurt everyone I love. And Louise – dear tragic Louise, who so richly deserved love – is dead because of me. I've nothing left here. My family haven't been near me, and who can blame them? I've lost everything. I've nowhere to go. No one to go with. And no one but myself to blame.'

'When are they discharging you?'

'Tomorrow, so the doctor says.'

'Well, just in case there are any press hanging around still, if you need help getting out of the hospital, let me know. Give me a ring, Philip, if there's anything I can do – not just as a police officer, but as a friend.'

He almost smiled. 'Thanks, Ian.'

And as Ian Hallam got up to leave the room, Philip buried his face in his hands while his body rocked with sorrow.

'I'm sorry, Liz, but I just can't forgive him. I can't believe what he's done to Mum. How could he betray her like that? I thought he really loved her. He always acted as if he did. And the way he's betrayed us – Rachel, Mark and me! He was always telling us what we should do, how we should behave, and look at him! He's a hypocrite and a failure as far as I'm concerned.

And, most of all, how can any of us forgive him for what happened to your mum?'

'That may not have been all his fault. Mum was a very complex person, and although I don't know everything, she certainly had times before this when she was really down. I can remember lots of days when I was growing up when she just didn't get out of bed. Sometimes she'd be like a zombie, not hearing what you said to her or noticing what was going on around her.'

'Was she getting help for that? What about your dad?'

'He never had much patience with her. I think she'd been very unhappy for a long time.'

'But that's doesn't excuse what my Dad did!'

'What did he do? He listened to her. he encouraged her to think more deeply about what she really believed in. He became a very dear friend to her, I know that.'

Steven looked down, his face thoughtful. 'I think they were lovers, don't you?'

'I'm not sure. That would be so unlike Mum . . .'

'And before this, I'd have said unlike Dad too. But something drove him to the depths of such despair, he tried to take his own life. What else could account for that? What could possibly fill him with such guilt and remorse he couldn't face life any longer?'

Liz nodded sadly. 'I suppose you're right. Perhaps we'll never know for sure.'

'I keep thinking about them,' continued Steven, 'imagining them together. And the thought makes me feel physically sick.' He caught sight of her expression.

'I'm sorry, Lizzie, if that upsets you – but I'm just sickened by the whole thing. They're our parents – and after all the rules and regulations they hand down to us, it turned out he'd got no morals or feelings for anyone else at all! I'm disgusted by him!'

'Have you been to see him?'

'No, and I don't intend to.'

'How is he?'

'He may be discharged soon – tomorrow maybe.'

'And then what?'

Steven sighed, squeezing her hand. 'I don't know, Liz. He can't just come back home, can he, as if nothing's happened?'

'What does your mum say?'

'Nothing. Nothing at all. I don't know what she's thinking really. She just looks shattered, as if the life's been knocked out of her.'

Liz was silent. After a while, Steven tipped her face up towards him, so the tears that filled her eyes rolled down on to his hand.

'Oh, Lizzie, I'm sorry. That was insensitive of me.'

'It's not your fault, Steven. I don't blame anyone. It's just that I miss her so much . . .'

And he drew her close to him, rocking her in his arms as if she were a child.

Brian wasn't sure what to make of Barbara's behaviour. After his outburst first thing that morning, he'd expected more of a reaction from her. An explosion of angry denial perhaps? Accusations, blame flung in his direction? At the very least, a dressing down to dismiss argument and quell rebellion. Silence was unlike her. It wasn't just worrying, it almost frightened him.

She'd left the house almost immediately – curious on Easter Saturday morning, which wasn't even a school day. Where could she have gone? Instead of her usual minute-by-minute catalogue of exactly what the day had in store for her, she'd left without a word. She'd had breakfast alone too. True, his own breakfast setting was left neatly laid for him, but without comment or explanation. She no longer seemed angry as she had before. She was expressionless and self-contained, avoiding his eyes and his company.

As Brian sat down heavily on the hall chair to do up his shoelaces, he tried to work out how he felt about her silence. Did it upset him? Was he angry with her? Did he miss her conversation and presence, however abrupt they sometimes were?

Too much on my mind to worry about her right now, he decided, smoothing back his thinning hair and straightening his glasses. My priority at the moment is the Barnes family. Barbara may not need me. They do.

When Timothy Fulford arrived at the hospital, Philip was stretched out on the bed, his eyes closed, apparently asleep. Timothy wondered whether to leave, but glancing at his watch and remembering his tight schedule that day, he knocked firmly on the panel of the glass door. Philip's eyes opened, staring hopefully towards the door although his expression clouded with apprehension as he recognised his visitor as the Archdeacon.

'I thought you'd come. I almost expected you before now.'

'Well, Bishop David – and all of us, of course – have been most concerned about your well-being. It was important for you to be on the mend, feeling stronger, before any proper discussion about – well, things.'

Philip smiled to himself. Timothy was a tall, gangling man, relatively new to his job as the Bishop's Archdeacon, and his nervousness showed at times of tricky encounter or delicate discussion. No wonder he'd taken a while to come. He must have been dreading this.

Timothy spent a while awkwardly pulling a chair towards Philip's bed, then folding one lanky leg over the over. He settled finally, drawing a sheaf of papers from his briefcase and clearing his throat.

'Well, Philip how *are* you?'

'I've felt better.'

'I hear you may be discharged tomorrow.'

'Apparently.'

'And what are your plans?'

'I have no plans, Timothy. How can I possibly have plans?'

'Are you ready to talk about what happened?'

Philip sighed. 'You can work most of it out for yourself, can't you? I got too close to a woman parishioner, so involved that in the end I couldn't see any way out. I have no one to blame but myself. I will live with the eternal shame of what I've done, and the results of my selfish, unforgivable behaviour, for the rest of my life.'

'Philip, I've been a parish priest too. We all know how complicated and difficult it can be when someone in need comes to rely on you too much . . .'

Philip's head turned sharply in his direction. 'I am – *I was* – a professional. I was trained to deal with situations like that. I should have known better. I should have backed away earlier, for Louise's sake as well as my own. I should have been a better Christian, not just pontificating on principles but keeping them myself. And I should have remembered my marriage vows. I was a married man . . .'

'You still are.'

'Am I?' Philip's expression was bleak. 'I don't think so.'

'Philip, all marriages today are under constant pressure, and clergy marriages are no exception to that. But for them, it's not just the love but the Christian commitment of the couple involved that can keep them together and strong. What they have is not just a partnership with each other but a triangular relationship that includes God. You and Ruth have always seemed so well suited. You share your faith. You share the responsibilities of family and parish. You've been through so much together. Don't give up on it now, not when you need each other more than ever.'

'Why would she need me, Timothy? I've hurt and betrayed her. And I compounded my cowardice by trying to take my own life.'

'Do you love her?'

Philip stared at him. 'Always. More than ever. I long for her.'

'And what has she said?'

'Nothing. She's not been here.' He hesitated. 'At least, I don't think she has. The shock of all this must have been so painful and humiliating for her. She's had enough. I understand that. I've lost her.'

'So, you can't go home tomorrow?'

'Timothy, I can never go back to that house. How could I? We both know you've come today to tell me I must leave the parish. Of course I must. I have no illusions about that.'

'Well, perhaps a spell away from the area, time to reflect on where you feel your future lies . . .'

'You're not saying that you honestly believe there can be a future for me now within the church?'

Timothy nodded uncomfortably. 'No. We don't think so, Philip.'

'No,' he agreed quietly. 'So that's it. I can't see a future. I have no plans. The answer to any question you could possibly ask me now is that I just don't know.'

'We have the retreat house at the Cathedral, you know. It's empty at the moment, although I believe a small group will be arriving for a few days in the middle of the week. Would you like to go there tomorrow? Just to tide you over?'

Philip shook his head. 'Thanks, Timothy, but I don't think I'm ready to face Bishop David, and all those patronising expressions of gracious judgement from the hierarchy at the Cathedral. I am deeply ashamed of what I've done. I know what other people must think of me, and I deserve every damning word. I just can't face them yet.'

Timothy shifted in his chair, horrified at the embarrassing thought Philip was about to cry.

'So,' he began hesitantly, 'what will you do?'

Philip looked at him bleakly. 'Well, I suppose I might just catch the first train I find, and see where it takes me.'

'You'll let us know where you end up? You'll keep in touch?'

'Perhaps. But first I think I'll just lick my wounds for a bit, until I feel stronger.'

'Of course,' agreed Timothy. He took off the lid of his ball point pen then carefully replaced it. 'But you do understand the future of St John's needs to be considered immediately . . .'

Philip nodded. 'I hear the centre opening had to be cancelled and I'm so sorry about that. After all the work that's gone into it . . .'

'Well, the general feeling seems to be that the community should simply start using the centre as planned, even if the opening ceremony has to be postponed, or possibly abandoned altogether. We can cover the services at St John's for the next few weeks, but then we'll have to think about putting someone else in the post.'

'I understand.'

'Now, there will be no pressure on Ruth and the family to move out of the Vicarage before they're ready, of course, but . . .'

'. . . but the new minister will need the house. I understand that.'

'Yes, well.' Timothy shuffled to his feet. 'I'll leave you to rest then.'

Philip seemed too engrossed in his own thoughts to answer. Timothy got as far as the door before he turned back.

'You know where I am, Philip, if you need any pastoral help. I'm not sure how you feel at the moment about your priesthood, or how all this has affected your faith?'

'That makes two of us.'

'Would it help to talk?'

'Probably, but not yet. Perhaps when my thoughts are less muddled.'

Timothy beamed with relief, back on firm ground. With a

cheery wave of his hand, he closed the door behind him. Philip sank back wearily against his pillows. Without a shadow of doubt, Timothy Fulford was the last person he could ever speak to about his faith, or lack of it. In fact, he wasn't sure he would ever be able to speak of his feelings about God coherently again. Philip could hardly remember a time when God was not at the heart of his very being. And yet now, when he needed him most, why was it that his prayers were simply disappearing into the ether? Going nowhere. Just like him.

'Mum, why not? I want to talk to him!'

Ruth ran distracted fingers through her unruly curls. Her hair needed washing. Another thing she hadn't done.

'Mark, I'm not being awkward. I just don't think Dad's up to visitors yet.'

'Why not? Is he really ill? Won't he get better?'

'Of course he'll get better, darling, but he needs rest at the moment.'

'And then he'll come home? When's he coming home?'

Brian, who had been on his way through to the kitchen during their conversation, caught the look of uncertainty on Ruth's face.

'Oh, Mark, there you are. Just the man I need. Can I borrow him for an hour or two, Ruth? I could do with his help.'

She nodded gratefully. Pink with exasperation, Mark dragged his gaze away from his mother. 'Why won't anyone round here tell me *anything*? I'm not a baby, you know. I love him too.'

'Come on, son,' said Brian kindly. 'Get your coat. We've got a train to catch.'

Rachel pulled her chair closer to her mother as the two of them watched Brian and Mark leave. Rachel felt adult enough to understand the dilemma of loyalty and betrayal her mother was facing. Heavens, at fourteen she was nearly a woman!

So why, she wondered sadly, did she long for her mum's arms around her, so she could block out all the confusion and misery by sobbing her eyes out like a small, lost child?

As there were still a couple of reporters by the front of the house, Lizzie skimmed round the block, letting herself into the back garden though the gap in the fence Matthew and she had used since they were children. A few yards up the path she stopped. The daffodils were out. Her mum's daffodils, the clump below the kitchen window she'd watched and waited for each year. Lizzie's eyes misted as she stooped to pick one single stem, its flower still in bud. Then carefully clutching it to her, she let herself into the house.

She reached into the cupboard for the long, elegant vase that had been a wedding present to her parents. Louise had always cherished it. Standing in the vase, the bud looked awkward and lonely.

It will be out soon, thought Lizzie. Mum would like that.

Carrying it almost reverently into the study, she sighed as she felt the comforting, gentle presence of her mother soothe and calm her. This was where Lizzie remembered her most, at the piano with her pupils, encouraging and patient. And then, when they'd gone, this room had become Louise's private world, where she could lose herself in the pathos and anger of her music. As a child, Lizzie had often listened, crouched beside the open door, shocked and fired by the emotion in her mother's playing. And at last, she would notice Lizzie there and hold out her arms to welcome her daughter into the warmth and safety of her love.

Tears flowing freely now, Lizzie placed the vase tenderly on top of the piano.

The flower will be out soon, she thought again. Mum would really like that.

She became aware of her father's voice in the lounge. He

was on the phone, obviously assuming he had the house to himself. The light intimate tone of his conversation stopped her in her tracks. It wasn't that she hadn't overheard him speaking in this flirtatious, familiar way before. Over the years, she'd been aware of many such phone calls. What shocked and appalled her was that he should be doing this now, a matter of hours after his wife's death.

'Honestly, Amy, I don't see why not. There's nothing to keep us here now. Providing I can find suitable care for my mother, anywhere in West London would suit me nicely.'

He listened for a while as Amy plainly added a suggestion of her own.

'A good residential home near you in Barnes, is there? Well, yes, I agree it's certainly worth looking into . . . Can you get the phone number for me and I'll pop in for a look at the end of the week, perhaps on Friday? No, Thursday's out . . . Really, an afternoon off? Tempting, darling, but I think I'd be missed if I didn't turn up at the funeral, don't you . . .' He looked up suddenly as a white-faced Lizzie abruptly opened the door.

'Amy, I've got to go. Call you later.' He replaced the receiver, keeping his eyes fixed on Lizzie as he asked casually, 'Where've you been?'

'Who were you talking to?'

'Just my secretary. I asked you a question, Lizzie – where have you been?'

'Since when did you call Mrs Carter *darling*? And her name's not Amy!'

'Mrs Carter's on holiday. I've got a temp in. And don't change the subject! Where have you been?'

'What was all that about London?'

'That was about work, Lizzie – and it's very rude to eavesdrop on other people's private conversations . . .'

'How could it be work if you were talking about Nan and putting her in a home up in London somewhere? Are you thinking about moving?'

Richard settled himself comfortably on the sofa. 'Well, it would certainly work better for me. I spend so much time travelling to and from London. Now your mum's gone I obviously need to be with you much more. It seems a sensible suggestion really . . .'

'And when exactly were you planning to talk to me about this? After you'd booked Nan into a home, and sorted out where *Amy* would find it most convenient to visit you?' Lizzie's eyes were blazing with fury.

'Oh, for heaven's sake, Lizzie, stop being such a baby. What's the point of our staying now? How could you possibly want to be here, knowing everyone will be nudging each other and gossiping about what your mum did?'

'I have friends here. *Good* friends!'

'Forgive me, my darling, but I can't say I'm very impressed with your taste in friends. Something you inherited from your mother, I suppose. If you think non-entities like the Barnes family are worthy to be your friends, I'm sorry for you. You have a great deal to learn.'

Lizzie's hand lashed out viciously across his face, taking him completely by surprise. Shock and pain mingled with his disbelief but she didn't stay to register his reaction. Turning on her heel, she marched from the room, slamming the door behind her.

Normally, Mark needed little encouragement to climb into the centre of the loft and lose himself in the joys of running the complex railway system. Today he was preoccupied, restless and unable to settle. Brian's heart went out to the boy, with his bruised jawline and furrowed brow. He'd been through so much, poor lad, and yet Brian was unsure how to comfort him. Mark was too big for cuddles. That would embarrass him beyond belief. But how much should he be told about what had happened between his father and Louise? He was so young.

Did he have to face the harsh realities just yet? What would be best?

Finally, Mark stopped pretending to be interested in realigning the points and stepped back from the layout. 'Don't fancy this at the moment, Uncle Brian. Do you mind if we stop?'

'I was just thinking I fancied a bag of crisps and a can of something. How about you?'

Mark clambered gratefully over to the side of the loft, where the two of them sat back against the wall and opened their cans in companionable silence.

'Have you seen my dad?' Mark asked suddenly.

'Umm, yes, I saw him last night.'

Mark turned bright eyes to look at him directly. 'How is he, Uncle Brian? No one will tell me how he is. Is he going to be OK?'

'He's going to be fine. He's very tired at the moment, which is why the doctor has suggested visitors should be kept to a minimum, but . . .'

'I'm not a visitor. He's my dad. He'll want to see me.'

'You bet, of course he does! But he's a bit low right now, and it may not be best for you to see him just yet.'

'When then? Will you take me this afternoon? Can we go now?'

Brian eyed him thoughtfully. 'I'm not sure, Mark. I'll ask your mum, see what she thinks.'

'Mum will say no. She says no to everything at the moment. Why's she like that? She's not the one in hospital. She's OK. It's him that's ill.'

'Well, the whole thing's been a bit of a shock for her. She's trying to sort out what she feels about it all.'

'Why? That's Dad in there. Mum loves him. They're always cuddling. Dad will want to see her, I know he will.'

'Yes, well, in view of what happened to Mrs Kenton, Mum wants to do a bit of thinking . . .'

'Why? Dad must have tried to save Mrs Kenton, and that's how he ended up ill too.'

'No one quite knows what happened yet, Mark. Your mum's just waiting for everything to become clearer.'

'Well, why doesn't she ask Dad? He'll explain everything.'

'He may not be able to, son. She's rather hurt at the moment.'

'Why?' Mark's face clouded over. 'She can't think that Dad was interested in Mrs Kenton or anything daft like that. That would be stupid! He's our dad!'

'Grown ups can't always see things that easily, Mark. Their emotions get muddled and confused, like your mum's at the moment.'

'But she knows Dad. She knows he loves us, and would never do anything to hurt us. This is all a great big mistake, that's obvious. Do you think I should tell her?'

'It's more complicated than that. You see, she feels that your dad was rather disloyal to be with Louise Kenton at all.'

'Why? Because he used to talk to her a lot? Dad was always doing that, with everybody.'

'Well, he may have been doing more than just talking to Louise . . .'

Mark stared at Brian as he digested this information.

'What?' he asked finally. 'Do you mean they *liked* each other?'

'Yes, Mark, I rather think they did.'

'Oh.'

Mark fell silent, absentmindedly working his way through a packet of crisps.

'So, I suppose he's just got to wait for Mum to come round, then. She will in the end. She always does. Mum's good like that. If I do something she doesn't like, she gets all upset for a while – and then she just forgets about it. That's what will happen with this.'

'I hope so,' agreed Brian quietly.

'It'll be all right, Uncle Brian, believe me. If it was anyone but Mum, I might be worried. But she'll soon get things back to normal.'

'Well, there will have to be a bit of sorting out all round. Your dad may not want to stay at St John's . . .'

'Whyever not? We live here! This is our home!'

'Yes, well, your parents will have to talk about it, but you do know they like to move people around from church to church every now and then. It may be time for your dad to try somewhere different . . .'

'But what about the centre? That was all his idea. He'd never want to leave that!'

'It may not be his choice in the end. The Bishop might have other plans for him.'

'My dad will fight that. Anyway, I don't want to leave my school and all my friends. No, we can't move. Dad won't let that happen.'

Brian nodded without comment as Mark looked at him earnestly. 'And I wouldn't want to leave you. How would you ever manage all this train stuff without me?'

'Never! I'd make an absolute mess of everything,' laughed Brian.

'Well, that's that then.'

Mark took a noisy gulp from his can of Coke.

'Tell you what, though, Uncle Brian. Mum doesn't seem to realise I'm grown up now. She's always trying to keep things from me, as if I'm still a kid. Can we have a pact? If she won't tell me what's going on, I won't worry about it. I'll just come and talk to you instead, man to man.'

Brian felt his eyes prick with tears as an unexpected surge of love for his bright-faced, plucky godson overwhelmed him. He got up suddenly, brushing down his trousers to hide his embarrassment.

'Come on, you! Call yourself a worker? You have far too many tea breaks for my liking!'

And stretching out a hand to help Mark to his feet, the two of them grinned at each other as they got back to work on the train set.

Steven called into Jamie's house on his way back from seeing Lizzie. The atmosphere at home was claustrophobic and depressing. He needed a break, and Jamie was always glad of his company. As it happened, he arrived right on lunch time, and before he knew it Jamie's parents had invited him to take a seat at the table and help himself. Try as they all did to keep everything light and conversational, it was inevitable that the events at St John's finally crept into the conversation. The friendship between Ruth and Jamie's mum, Hilary, dated back to the days when they'd both been pupils at the local girls' high school. Hilary had known Philip since those days too, when he and his friends from the corresponding boys' school used to hang around on the green in the middle of the town, hoping to delay some of the girls on their walk home.

'How's your mum, Steven? I've been wondering about ringing her, but I didn't want to intrude.'

'Better not to call at the moment. Things are still a bit chaotic, you know . . .'

'And your dad? How is he?'

'Don't know. I haven't seen him.'

'Is he getting better?'

'I suppose so.'

Sensing Steven's reticence, Hilary changed the subject.

'How are your studies going? "A" Levels coming up a bit fast, aren't they?'

'A couple of months.'

'Do you think you'll pass?'

Steven's face hardened. 'I don't want just to pass. I want to do really well, so I can get away from all this.'

Hilary and her husband, John, exchanged glances. 'Get away?'

'I got a letter this morning, from that university I had the interview with up in London. They've offered me a place, providing I get two Bs and a C. I should manage that.'

'Your mum must be pleased!'

'She doesn't know. She probably wouldn't care much at the moment.'

Hilary nodded, recognising she was delving into a sensitive subject as far as Steven was concerned. For a few minutes they continued their meal without further conversation.

'Pudding, anyone?'

'Not for me, thanks,' replied Steven.

'Nor me, Mum. Mind if we go upstairs for a bit?'

Without waiting for an answer, the two boys scraped back their chairs, and escaped to the privacy of Jamie's room.

'Poor lad,' breathed John, as he watched them climb the stairs two at a time. 'This is pretty tough on him – on all the kids, really.'

'Umm,' agreed Hilary, getting up to switch the kettle on. 'I will give Ruth a ring later on tonight. She can always tell me to push off. She knows I'll understand. I just want her to know we're here for her. If there's anything at all she needs – *they* need – we're here for them.'

The evening was drawing in as Brian turned the car into the Vicarage driveway. If any reporters were hanging around, he couldn't see them. Probably too cold. Certainly too wet.

Mark climbed out of the passenger seat and together they made their way to the front door, opening it with the spare key Brian always kept. The spicy aroma of cooking greeted them.

Following his nose, Mark arrived in the kitchen to find Ruth stirring chicken pieces into a sweetly pungent sauce on the hob.

'Brill, Mum! My favourite!'

She smiled at him. 'That's why I made it. We all like this, and I reckoned we could do with a bit of cheering up. It'll be ready in ten minutes. Go up and wash your hands, would you, and tell everyone I want them down here pronto.'

Standing in the doorway, Brian watched her as she bustled about the kitchen. When he was sure Mark was out of sight, he crossed the room towards her, clasping her above the elbows, searching her face.

'Don't, Brian. I'm OK, really I am. We just need to get back to normal, that's all. I know we've been through the mangle, and nothing can ever be quite the same again, but a bit of usual routine is what we could do with right now.'

He smiled down at her. 'You're right. Absolutely right. I'm proud of you. And Philip will be proud too.'

A shadow crossed Ruth's face as she turned away towards the stove.

'He's been asking about you, Ruth. He wants so much to see you.'

She didn't answer.

'Give him a chance, please. He's so desperate, hardly recognisable as the man we know. He needs to talk to you.'

'The dinner's nearly ready,' she said, apparently deep in concentration as she busily tossed chicken pieces and vegetables in the pan. 'I wonder where those kids are?'

'I'm about to go to the hospital now. Please can I tell him you'll be coming in later?'

Still she didn't reply.

'He's being discharged tomorrow. He's got nowhere to go, Ruth. He doesn't know where to turn.'

She spun round to face him then.

'Neither do I, Brian. Neither do I.'

★

Philip was sick of the four walls of his room. He wasn't coura-geous enough to venture far beyond them, aware of every pair of eyes staring at him whenever he even took a trip to the bath-room. Still, he was sick of this room. It felt like a cage. And yet it wasn't the walls that kept him in. Through his own actions he had imprisoned himself. He tried watching television, but the programmes were banal and pointless. He tried reading his Bible, and the words swam before his eyes. He tried praying, but knew in his heart that even God wouldn't want to hear prayers from someone as low as him. He closed his eyes, and might have nodded off to sleep – until a vision of Louise's sorrowful face filled his mind and he woke with a start. Since then he had simply lain on his bed, staring at the ceiling, feeling empty, worthless and painfully alone.

Steven made his way downstairs to the kitchen to find his mother had prepared a proper meal. Not just something and chips, but proper chicken and rice the way they liked it. He considered telling her he'd had a big lunch at Jamie's earlier that day, but one glance at her set, brittle expression made him think better of that idea. He sat down between Rachel and Mark without comment, and began to spoon rice on to his plate.

The phone rang immediately. Ruth ignored it, but Mark was up and grabbing the receiver immediately.

'OK, I'll get him. Steve, it's for you! Some girl.'

Aware of Ruth watching him. Steven got up, and walked casually over to the phone.

'Steven, it's me. Lizzie. I know you can't talk now – I've got the same problem this end – but I *must* see you!'

He glanced towards his mum, worried she might suspect who was on the line.

'Yeah, fine. When?'

'Tomorrow afternoon? About three? Usual place?'

'Great.' He hesitated, turning his face away from the curious observation of his family. 'Things OK with you?'

'No, not really. That's what I need to talk to you about.'

'Yeah, well, take care of yourself.'

'And you. Steven, I miss you. I need to talk to you so much.' He could hear she was dangerously near to tears.

'Just hold on, OK. Ring me if you need to. But I'll see you tomorrow. Right?'

'Bye,' was the whispered reply, and she was gone.

And when Steven turned round to return to the table, he could tell from one look at his mother's face that she knew exactly who'd been calling. To his great relief, though, she made no comment as she stretched out towards Rachel to dish chicken on to her plate.

It was just after seven o'clock when Brian put his head around Philip's door. Philip made a brave attempt at a smile but was defeated by the pallor of his face and blankness in his eyes. Remembering the handsome, confident man who, just a matter of weeks ago, had led the Christmas service at St John's, and brought the house down as an Ugly Sister, Brian realised the friend he knew had gone forever. The shadow in front of him now was someone he didn't know, someone who had to rebuild his life into whatever he could make of it. For one brief moment, Brian was tempted to put his arms round Philip, hoping to take the bleak shroud of despair from his expression. He didn't. Men don't do that sort of thing.

'I heard from Timothy Fulford this afternoon. He called in at the Vicarage earlier to talk to Ruth. He'd already been here, I think.'

'You know then? I am to leave the area, and our home will be needed by the next incumbent of St John's.'

'Well, not immediately. There's no rush.'

Philip looked at him steadily. 'Maybe not. But the church needs to move on, and the sooner this embarrassing episode is behind them, the better.' He hesitated. 'What about Ruth? What was her reaction to all that?'

'She's not saying much about anything at the moment.'

'Is she all right? Is she being looked after? Supported?'

'Of course, Philip. You know how much everyone loves her. Sue's been there quite a bit, and I've been at the Vicarage more than I've been at home this weekend.'

'Barbara won't like that.'

'She has no right to mind, after her part in all this!' The bitterness in Brian's usually mild voice took Philip by surprise.

'You mustn't blame her. The blame is totally mine. She was right to come and see me. And it was right for her to accuse me as she did.'

'She says now she didn't mean what she said, that she would never really have told the Bishop.'

Philip looked at him thoughtfully. 'Oh, I think she would. And I think she was absolutely right. I'm a disgrace. Don't let her blame herself. And don't you blame her either.'

When Brian didn't reply, Philip sighed, running his fingers wearily through his hair. 'Brian, I've lost my wife through all this. I deserve nothing less, and will regret that for the rest of my life. Just make sure, my dear friend, you don't lose yours too.'

'Right at the moment, Philip, I don't think I care very much.'

'Well, you should do. You and Barbara go back such a long way together. You've a daughter and grandchildren. Don't do anything to put all that at risk, Brian. You don't realise how precious your family is, until you've lost them.'

Hoping to change the mood and the subject, Brian rummaged in his holdall to bring out some fruit and a bag of the dry roasted peanuts he knew Philip usually enjoyed.

'Timothy didn't come up with any constructive ideas about where you might go tomorrow, then?'

Philip shook his head. 'Only the retreat house at the Cathedral, and that's a bit like being stuck on a stool with a dunce's hat on my head.'

'Then I've a suggestion. You know Barbara and I have had that little flat on the North Devon coast for some years? We don't manage to get down there often nowadays, and it could do with an airing. It's nothing special, of course, quite tiny and basic – but would you like to base yourself there for the time being? Just till the dust settles a bit, and you can think clearer about the future?'

The look of grateful relief on Philip's face was all the answer he needed.

'Right, that's settled then. As soon as you get the all-clear from the doctor in the morning, I'll pop over and pick you up. And don't worry about things you need from home. I'll go to the Vicarage on the way, and pick up all the bits I think might be useful.'

Philip was plainly moved by the offer. 'Thanks, Brian,' he mumbled. 'Thank you.'

This time, Brian did hug him. They clung together for some seconds, averting their eyes as they pulled apart, so as not to let the other see how much it meant.

'Must go,' bustled Brian, gathering up his bag and heading for the door.

'Brian, did you speak to Ruth? How is she?'

'She's coping, as we all knew she would. She's desperately hurt and confused, and refusing to talk about anything that matters.'

'Did you tell her how much I'd like to see her, especially if I'm leaving town tomorrow?'

'I did.'

'And . . .?'

'And she's thinking about it. Give her time, Philip. This has been tough for her.'

'I know, I know! I just want to try and explain – ask her forgiveness – let her know I never stopped loving her . . .'

'Yes, well, perhaps I'll see her later on. I'll have another word with her.'

Philip sat down heavily on the bed. 'It's all right, Brian. I know what you're saying. I do understand. I can't really expect anything else, can I?'

And because Brian could think of no way to disagree with him, he closed the door quietly as he left.

Apart from coming downstairs to make the brief phone call to Steven, Lizzie had remained locked in her room for most of the day. When later that evening she heard voices downstairs, she realised with relief that Matthew was back. She knew he would come up to see her. There had always been a strong bond between them.

She heard his quiet knock at the door, and quickly let him in.

'Phew!' he said, peering at her. 'What have you done to Dad? He's in a foul mood.'

'Because I rumbled him. He's got some woman called Amy he's on the phone to all the time, and I heard him talking to her about looking for a house for us up near where she lives – in West London somewhere. He's planning to go and see a residential home that may be able to take Nan, and then he's dragging us both up there.'

'Well, he won't be dragging me. I'm up in London during termtime anyway, don't forget.'

'Exactly! So why has he been so secretive about this? Why didn't he just tell me what he's thinking?'

'Perhaps he hasn't got very far with it at the moment, and didn't want to worry you?'

'The worst thing was the way he was talking about Mum. He thought it was really inconvenient he'd have to go to her funeral on Thursday, when he'd rather be up in London with that woman. How *could* he be so unfeeling? I don't believe he ever really loved Mum! No wonder she felt desperate enough to take her own life.'

'Lizzie, I'm sure that's not true . . .'

'Yes, it is! *He* drove her to this.'

'Lizzie, be careful what you say. You're very upset – we all are – and it's easy to say things you'll regret later.'

'I'll never regret it. It had to be said. And I don't regret what I did either.'

'What you did?'

Lizzie grinned sheepishly. 'I whacked him! I was so mad, I just clocked him one right across the face. It felt wonderful.'

But Matthew wasn't laughing. 'Take care, little sis. You're not old enough to strike out on your own yet, and Dad and I are all you've got now. Wherever we end up living, I'll be away most of the time, so you and he have just got to get on.'

She sighed. 'I know. But never again will I be the compliant, dutiful daughter. I'll finish my studies then I'll be off. And from now on, every time he looks at me, he'll be aware that I *know*. I know how he treated Mum. I know about all his girlfriends and nights away. I know if it weren't for his treatment of her, she'd be here now. Perhaps he hasn't got a conscience – but I will never let him forget. And I will never, *never* forgive him.'

At half-past eight the wards were clearing of visitors as Philip made his speedy, discreet way back from the bathroom. Conversation and interested stares were the last things he needed. He slid in through the door to his room – and then he saw her. She was on the chair beside the bed, perched at the very front of it, as if ready for a quick getaway.

'Ruth!'

She made no move towards him, and her expression revealed nothing of her feelings. Torn between wanting to scoop her into his arms, and knowing that if she pushed him away it would break his heart, he was uncertain what to do. Finally, he sat on the opposite end of the bed facing her – inches apart, a chasm between them.

'Ruth, there's so much to say. I don't know where to start . . .'

'Don't say anything, Philip. There are some things I don't need to know, not now. I couldn't cope with any more. I just want you to answer some questions.'

'OK,' he agreed, dreading what was coming.

'Did you love her?'

'Yes, but not in the same way I love you.'

'Were you lovers?'

'Once. Only once.'

'Why not again? You must have wanted the affair to continue . . .'

'No, Ruth, I wanted it to stop. I tried to stop it. We both did.'

'But not hard enough. Why else did you keep on meeting?'

'We hadn't planned to but we were seen. Someone knew about us, and that someone threatened to tell the Bishop during the opening ceremony.'

'So you met that night to plan what you'd do?'

'We had to. We'd made the decision to part, but knew if the relationship between us was made public, so many people would be hurt. Her family, mine . . .'

'Oh, so you thought of us? We did cross your mind at some point in all this.'

'Ruth, you and the children never left my mind. I love you! I love you all! I can't imagine how this madness happened, or what came over me. It just happened – and if that sounds pathetic and unforgivable, I agree with you. I can't explain it, and I'm deeply deeply ashamed of myself. And when I thought you'd find out, that everyone would find out, I just fell to pieces. So did Louise.'

Ruth kept her distance although her eyes brimmed with hot tears as she spoke. 'But, Philip, to try and take your own life . . . I've known you forever, and yet I don't know you at all. I could never have believed you'd do such a thing and yet . . .'

'And yet, that night, it made perfect sense. It was the ultimate way out. I had compromised and betrayed everything and everyone I hold dear. You . . .' he stretched out towards her, but she didn't respond ' . . .the children . . . all our friends and parishioners at St John's . . . the church – and most of all, God. I seemed to be plummeting down into chaos, out of control, frightened and hurting – and then, Louise started talking about eternal life, about God being able to forgive what no one else could. Minnie said almost the same thing just before she died, and suddenly I knew what she meant. Peace in eternity, in place of the turmoil I was in.' He buried his head in his hands as he went on. 'Ruth, I don't expect you to understand. Why should you? But I need you to know that I never, ever meant any of this to happen. I didn't mean to hurt you. It just happened – and I am so desperately, desperately sorry!'

Ruth said nothing, although her tearful face was pale and she was steadying her hands by clasping them tightly together.

'Why her, Philip? Why was she so attractive?'

'It wasn't that sort of attraction, not physical in the sense you probably mean. She was sad and hurt. She'd been bullied all her married life, so in the end she didn't feel she was worth anything to anyone. I wanted to comfort her, reassure and encourage her . . .'

'Making love to her probably did the trick!'

'No, it didn't, Ruth. In the end it destroyed her. I destroyed her. And the knowledge of that has destroyed me.'

As if she could bear no more, Ruth got abruptly to her feet.

In a second he was up too, grabbing her arm to stop her leaving.

'Ruth. I can't ask anything of you. I wouldn't dare ask for your forgiveness. What I've done is unforgivable. But because you've known me so well for so long, I hope you might find it in your heart to try and understand – not all of it, but enough not to despise me. Without you and the children I am nothing. You are my life. I know that now. Too late.'

Slowly, she turned round to look at him, studying his face really closely as if seeing him for the very first time.

'I love you, Ruth,' he whispered.

Perhaps she didn't hear him. Perhaps she didn't want to hear. She simply stepped back, away from his grasp, away from the room.

At first when Brian put the key in the door, he thought the house was empty. With the exception of the kitchen light, everywhere was in darkness. On the table, though, were signs that Barbara had been home – a half-empty cup, a plate, a neatly folded teatowel. For someone as meticulously tidy as her, discarded crockery was unusual to say the least.

He walked back into the hall to hang up his coat in the understairs cupboard when he became aware of a flickering light barely visible through the half-open lounge door. Curious, he walked over to push the door a little further ajar. To his surprise, Barbara was there, sitting quietly in front of the flickering electric fire, apparently deep in thought. As a silent Barbara was almost as unusual as an untidy one, he moved towards her with a hollow sense of foreboding.

'Barbara?' he called, gently putting a hand on her shoulder. 'Barbara, are you all right?'

Instead of looking towards him, her head and body seemed to curl in on themselves, so that she became a cowering, shivering ball. 'No,' she whispered, 'no, I don't think I'm all right at all.'

Brian's heart lurched at the sight of his wife, confident, domineering Barbara, quaking like a trapped, defeated animal. Gently cradling her shoulders, he moved round to crouch in front of her, holding her hands and stroking her hair, until the shaking subsided and her body relaxed.

'You're a good man, Brian Gilpin,' she sighed at last, 'a very good man.'

'Well, you're not bad yourself,' he grinned, trying to lighten the atmosphere.

'Oh, I am,' she countered wearily. 'I've been a dreadful person, someone I really don't like at all. Dreadful about everything, dreadful to everyone, most of all to you . . .'

'Come on, I'm used to it! I know your bark is worse than your bite. I'm probably pretty dreadful to live with at times too.'

'I'm a perfectionist, I know. I hate mess and disorder. I like things to be nice and orderly. I expect people to do the right thing.'

'Who's to say what the right thing is though, eh, love? You can't always see the whole picture in other people's lives. Nobody can.'

'I know that now. I just learned the lesson too late. Too late for poor Louise . . .'

'Barbara,' said Brian softly, stroking her hand as he spoke, 'everything we've learned about her since this awful affair began suggests that she was a very damaged, unstable person. She had an air of need and sadness about her, that drew others to her. We all felt it. She was fragile and grateful and unsure of herself, and we all flocked to help her. But Louise Kenton's story was a tragedy that would have happened anyway, whether we'd been there or not. And the real tragedy is that Philip, dear, caring, well-meaning Philip, was drawn in until there was no way out.'

'But I made it happen. If I hadn't poked my nose in, if I hadn't threatened to expose them . . .'

'I believe, my love, that something else would have happened. Louise's story was never destined to end happily.'

She looked at him then with a softness in her eyes that Brian hadn't glimpsed in her for many years.

'How come I know so little about you?' she asked. 'Why didn't I know what a wise, lovely man you are?'

For a moment, he was lost for words.

'I know I need to change,' she went on, 'and I know I can't do that without your help. I must learn to be more tolerant, to live and let live, and that will be hard for me. And I've been thinking – it will be hard to make difficult changes like that if my everyday situation remains the same. So . . .'

She looked directly at him as she spoke. 'What do you think of the idea of me retiring? Leaving the school a couple of years early?'

'Leave school? But you love it. You can't wait to get to that job every morning.'

'But that's the trouble, isn't it? I rule the roost there. As Deputy Head, when I speak, everyone jumps. The trouble is I never stop being a teacher, do I? I even treat you like a pupil.'

'You mustn't worry. Most of it goes over my head.'

'Does it? Does it really? I wonder. You've always been such a clever man. You set up that accountancy firm of yours, and made it successful. You have so many qualities to be admired, and over the years I've stopped seeing any of them. I've stopped seeing you.'

Brian shrugged. 'Isn't that marriage? Isn't it inevitable that our partners become so commonplace and familiar, we never see them as others do?'

'Perhaps – but I don't want to live like that any more.'

'Well, amen to that,' agreed Brian. 'What exactly have you got in mind?'

'I'd like to retire, and learn to *enjoy* life a bit more. You can help me with that. You spend all your days doing exactly what you enjoy most – organising the centre, your train set, even getting up in the middle of the night to go bird watching. Well, I want to learn to do that too.'

'What? Bird watching?' asked Brian doubtfully.

'No, that's not for me, and I'd drive you mad if I tried to tag along with whatever you did. But, there are lots of things I do fancy having a go at. I like walking. I've always wanted to try brass rubbing. And, do you know, I never learned to swim? Well, that's something else I'd like to get under my belt.'

Brian almost laughed with delight as he looked at her, seeing not the staid, middle-aged lady she'd become, but the young, enthusiastic, compelling woman she once was, in those heady romantic days when they'd first met.

'Do you know, Barbara?' His expression was serious in the dappled light of the fire. 'I love you.'

'Thank God for that,' she replied, her face almost touching his. 'And I love you too.'

Chapter Thirteen

Ever since Ruth could remember, Easter Sunday had begun with eggs and cards, and the children hunting for tiny brightly covered chocolate treats hidden around the house and garden. Not this Easter Sunday though. No one was in the mood.

They all sat at the breakfast table: Ruth, Steven, Mark and Rachel. They didn't talk much. Apart from Mark, no one was in the mood for that either.

Steven caught his mum's eye, and smiled. They had sat up till the small hours, talking into the night. And by the time they fell into their beds, their relationship had changed forever. Still mother and son, but now woman and young man. Two individuals linked by love, each with their own life to lead.

Ruth glanced at the clock and looked around the table. 'Right. Are we ready for this?'

They all nodded in agreement.

Her smile was full of love and pride as she got to her feet. 'OK then, let's go!'

The doctor made his rounds early that morning. It took little more than a couple of minutes for him to confirm that Philip was recovering well. He could leave whenever he wanted to. He was discharged.

And so he found himself alone again, packing his few possessions into a carrier bag. Then he sat and waited. He was scared. Scared and lonely.

He reached over to switch on the television. A church service was being transmitted. Easter Sunday! He'd almost forgotten in the muddle of the last few days. How could he have forgotten Easter Sunday, which had for him always been the most important day of the year? The heart of his faith, the Day of the Resurrection? Because of this day, Christians everywhere had reassurance of God's love and faithfulness, hope for the future.

Philip thought of his future, without love, without God. And he knew there could be no loneliness like it.

Someone else was playing the organ at St John's. The Archdeacon had organised that. He'd also organised for Christopher Spencer, a much-loved but elderly local clergyman, to come out of retirement for a few weeks, to hold the fort at the troubled church until a more permanent replacement could be found.

The congregation arrived in twos and threes, conversation hushed and tense as they tried to imagine the scene that must have taken place in front of their altar on Maundy Thursday evening. The sense of shock and uncertainty was almost tangible. But they were here. This was their church, their community. Together they'd come through.

The choir were lined up in the vestry, ready to begin the procession through the church towards their seats, when a sudden hush fell over them all. One by one they turned towards the back of the building. There, framed in the doorway, stood Ruth and her children. Deliberately, as if unsure not just of their own feelings but of others' too, they began to make their way slowly towards the front pew in which the family always sat. Step by step, hand in hand, they looked forward, aware that all eyes were on them.

'We love you, Ruth!'

Someone, somewhere in the congregation, cried out. Ruth never knew who. But as the sound of applause grew around them, and loving hands reached out to greet them, she knew she'd come home.

Lizzie's father made no reference to their argument the day before, for which she was grateful. In fact, he tried to win her round, bringing up a mug of tea and a plate of toast to her room, something she remembered her mum doing often.

Her heart sank, though, when he sat on her bed, obviously wanting to talk. 'Lizzie, I'm sorry,' he began. 'I know you're upset, and I know I've not been around for you much. I'll make it up to you, I promise.'

She didn't reply. There was nothing to say.

'About London – I'm only thinking about it at the moment, but is it such a bad idea? We have so many unhappy memories here. Wouldn't it be better to move on, put all this behind us?'

'My memories are happy. Mum was here. I feel her everywhere, in everything I do, everywhere I go. I don't want to leave.'

'I'm just asking you to keep an open mind about all the possibilities for our future. Whether it's best to stay here, or whether a new start might help us, you and me, to start again? I simply ask you to give us a chance. Give me a chance. Please Lizzie?

She nodded dumbly. Really, there was nothing to say. Nothing at all.

★

It was shortly after half-past twelve when Brian arrived at the hospital. To Philip's surprise he wasn't alone. He shrank back when he saw Barbara. He wasn't ready to face her yet, perhaps never would be.

But this was a Barbara he didn't recognise. There was no bitterness in her face as there had been last time he'd seen her. She was smiling, her expression soft and affectionate as she looked first at Brian and then at Philip himself.

'I've come to apologise,' she said simply. 'I behaved very badly, and my actions caused a lot of harm. I really am very, very sorry.'

The unexpectedness of this statement took Philip's breath away.

'I just want you to know that I don't think you deserve what's happened to you. At heart you're a good man. What's happened is tragic, absolutely tragic.'

Philip sat down in amazement. 'Barbara, I don't know what to say. I blame no one but myself. But the fact you've come here today means more to me than I can tell you.'

'Well, Brian and I just want you to know that you can rely on our love and friendship, not just now but always.'

Seeing that Philip was near to breaking down, Brian interrupted. 'I've brought a couple of bags for you from the Vicarage. I'm hopeless at packing for myself so I don't expect I've done very well for you. Still, you'll have the basics.'

'And I've made up a box of rations to keep you going for a week or so,' added Barbara. 'The flat's quite comfy. You'll have plenty of peace and quiet there. Stay as long as you like. It's yours if you need it.'

Lost for words, Philip got to his feet, to envelope her in an emotional embrace.

And her pupils in the fifth form would have been amazed to see that the formidable Mrs Gilpin was crying and laughing at once, relieved and released, her face covered with hot, shiny tears.

★

Ruth was packing too. She'd arranged everything, tied up all the loose ends. People had been so thoughtful. She'd been over-whelmed by their kindness.

But it was time to leave. And as she loaded bags into the back of the battered old family car, she knew she'd made the right decision. She had to go.

Philip opened the car window as the sea came into sight. It was a bright, windy day, the front deserted as waves crashed against the sea wall.

This will do, he thought. I can hide here.

Brian turned the car off the promenade into the maze of back streets that tumbled away towards the small town centre. Finally he drew up in front of what had obviously once been a large family house, now divided into two flats.

'Ours is on the top floor. Better view!' said Barbara, leading the way upstairs. She opened the door on to a narrow hallway which led through to a small, light living room. Philip moved through to look at the view. From one side of the window you could almost see the sea. Almost, but not quite.

They brought in the bags while Barbara put the kettle on and bustled about in the kitchen, turning on the fridge and sorting out the central heating. They perched around the small lounge table, eating luncheon meat sandwiches and talking about the weather. Then, reluctantly, Brian looked at his watch, knowing it was time to go.

They got to their feet, unsure how to take their leave. Awkwardly, they all hugged one another.

'Ring us!' ordered Barbara. 'Ring us if there's anything at all you need. We won't bother you – but keep in touch, please?'

'I will,' promised Philip, standing at the top of the stairs until their car disappeared from view.

He shut the door, locking himself in with the musty unused smell of the place. Then he sat. He pulled up a chair to the table, put his head in his hands, and just sat.

This time they walked. They didn't care who saw them. As Steven said, they had no reason to hide. They'd done nothing wrong. And they loved one another, of that there was no doubt.

'So, it's all been arranged,' he was saying. 'Mum sorted the whole thing out this morning. She's been brill!'

'Yes,' agreed Lizzie sadly. 'Mums usually are.'

'I've just got to work really hard now, to make sure I get my grades. That university is pretty good. I think I'd enjoy it there. And, of course, I'd be away from home then – for good.'

Steven stopped to turn her towards him. 'But, Lizzie, the best thing is we'll both probably end up in London! If your dad goes ahead with his plan, and I reckon he will, we can still see each other.'

'Do you think so?'

'We've got to, Lizzie. We've got to make it happen. We've been through so much together, and I don't want to lose you! I know it might be difficult at first, if we have to meet up secretly, but if we care enough about each other, we'll make it work. I want that so much. How about you?'

With a small sigh, she laid her head against his shoulder. 'Oh, yes, Steven. Yes, please.'

Philip stood at the window, watching the light fade as it shrouded the unfamiliar rooftops in dingy darkness. He wondered if he was hungry. Probably not. Perhaps there would be something to watch on television? No, probably not that either.

He thought he heard knocking on a door. Not for him, of course. Probably someone visiting downstairs.

Then he heard it again, louder this time. Curious to know where it was coming from, he went out into the hall. There it was again. Someone at *his* door.

Half scared of who he'd find there, he only opened the door a fraction. And there she was. Ruth. His own dear Ruth!

She looked as if she was about to speak, almost as if she had been practising what she'd say at this moment. And then the moment was gone as he held out his arms and pulled her towards him. Speechless with surprise and relief, he buried his face in her soft curls, whispering her name over and over again. They clung together, afraid to let go, tasting the dear, familiar rightness of each other. For minutes they stood there, holding and touching, laughing and crying.

'I can't believe you've come. I can't believe this,' he whispered, his voice choked and overwhelmed. 'I don't deserve this. I don't deserve you. Ruth, I love you so much.'

It was later, much later, drained and exhausted, they sat curled up together on the lumpy old sofa, fingers entwined, heads touching.

'What changed your mind?' he asked at last.

'You. You've been an idiot. You made a mistake. Human beings do that. You hurt a lot of people, including me. But making a mistake doesn't change what you really are, what I've always known you to be – a good man with a foolish oversized heart.'

'But will you ever be able to trust me again?'

'Can you trust yourself?'

'After all I've been through? Without any shadow of doubt!'

'Then I trust you.'

'But I've hurt you so much.'

'And I can't forget that. I'm wary of you now. It will take me for the wounds to heal, for me to be sure of my feelings. I promise nothing, but I'm willing to try.'

'And I'll spend the rest of my life making it up to you.'

She stopped him by putting a finger to his lips. 'I don' want your guilt, Philip. I don't want you feeling you're foreve in my debt. There is no way forward for us if you are alway looking back, paying for past sins. It's not that I don't recog nise the burden of guilt you feel – but if we're to have a chanc of rebuilding our marriage, we have to lay that burden to on side, or it will crush us. What is it we say? *"Forgive us our tres passes, as we forgive those who trespass against us"?* Don't just sa it. Mean it! Let's start with forgiveness, and see where tha takes us.'

He couldn't reply. Instead, he leant forward to plant th gentlest of kisses on her soft, willing lips. Finally, he asked, 'Wha about the kids? Will they ever be able to forgive me?'

'Mark and Rachel already have. You're their dad. They lov you. They need you. They'll be all right.'

'And Steven?'

'He's very bitter, Philip. You know he's grown fond o Lizzie. She's lost her mum, and to his way of thinking he's los his dad too. He didn't expect this of you. And he can't accep it.'

'What does that mean? Where is he?'

'He's been offered a place at that university he was inter viewed at in London, starting in September. He's got to ge good grades, of course, and we've had a talk about that. But h doesn't want to live at home any more . . .'

'You mean, he doesn't want to live with me?'

'Just at the moment, I'm afraid not. And because as a famil we probably can't stay anywhere near St John's, we had to work out how he could continue his studies at the sam school.'

'Poor Steven! What have I done to him? I've ruined every thing for him.'

'No, you haven't. I had a long talk with Hilary and John thi morning. They've offered to put him up until he's ready to go to university. Jamie and he have always got on so well. Hilary says Steven feels like another son to her anyway.'

'And he's happy with that?'

'He's over the moon about it. Steven has grown up a lot in the last few days. He's a good kid, Philip. He reminds me of you in so many ways, although I wouldn't dare tell him that right now.'

'But what about us? Where can we go? Have you thought about that?'

'Not really, but it seems to me we have a clean sheet ahead of us. We have a wonderful family, some terrific friends. We're healthy, we can work hard – and we love each other. That's not a bad start.'

'No,' agreed Philip, 'but how will we live? I can't be a priest any more.'

'Does that make you very sad?'

He thought for a while before answering. 'I always thought the only thing I wanted was to lead others in faith, but I realise now what a daunting responsibility that is. I think for the time being I'd prefer to find out what I really believe, get my own priorities right.'

'Do you doubt your faith then?'

'In the most basic way possible, no, I don't. I feel as if I've been tested to the very limit, brought face to face with my own humanity and frailty. I thought I knew all the answers. I thought I knew what was God's will. But we never do, not really. Minnie taught me that. Do you think she found the peace she longed for?'

'I think so.'

'And Louise?'

'She deserved to. She had so little peace in life.'

'And us? Will we find peace too?'

'We'll be OK, Philip. I know it.'

They fell silent then, each caught for a while in the web of their own thoughts. Ruth laid her head back against his shoulder, gazing towards the window.

'It's getting late. It's dark out there now.'

She got up to pull the curtains, and stayed to look out at the rooftops and the twinkling lights before her. Philip rose to join her.

'We went to church today,' she said. 'We all went, the children and I – and it was so moving. Everyone was wonderful to us.'

'Easter Sunday,' he said softly. 'Promise, hope, a new beginning.'

She turned slightly, stretching out her hand towards him. 'The Day of Resurrection . . .'

'For us too.' And clasping her hand in both of his, he drew her close.

At the house in Wycombe Avenue, light from the hall spilled through the half-open door on to Louise's piano. On top stood a tall, elegant vase holding one single daffodil. Bright, brave, brittle – and dead.

SARAH HARRISON

THAT WAS THEN

Newly single, safe and sorted . . .

Eve's separation from Ian is amicable, her daughter Mel is a high-flier, and her son Ben, the apple of her eye, is the local charmer. She has a congenial job, good friends, and all the time in the world to improve her tennis. But passion is no respecter of plans, and Eve's chaste tranquillity, like Ben's boyhood teddy, is about to go out of the window with a vengeance. Because when sons grow up, mothers must too . . .

'believable and touching . . . Harrison's writing is lively, crisp [and] full of humour'

The Times

'Written with Sarah Harrison's usual verve, this story offers new insights into the dangers of a mother's over-dependence and the absolute necessity of letting go.'

Good Housekeeping

Sarah Harrison lives with her family in Cambridgeshire and is a regular broadcaster on Radio 4. Her previous novels, LIFE AFTER LUNCH and FLOWERS WON'T FAX (Shortlisted for the 1997 RNA Award) are available from Hodder and Stoughton.

HODDER AND STOUGHTON PAPERBACKS

A selection of bestsellers from Hodder & Stoughton